OMEGA
GERMANY'S LAST HOPE.
OMEGA
THE ALLIES' GREATEST NIGHTMARE.
OMEGA
AN AWESOME SECRET—MISSING.
THE TERRIFYING RACE IS ON.
D1012718

MEN AND WOMEN, TRAPPED IN A COUNTDOWN TO TERROR . . .

ANDREW CHAPMAN—handsome, fearless, the only American on the team of commandos whose mission will decide world history

MARGARET BROWN—a British nurse whose passionate love for Chapman breaks all the rules

NICHOLAS FALZETTI—veteran New York cop, his investigation of a strange double murder leads to a frightening discovery that could crush the Allies

STREETMAN—A mysterious Long Island millionaire whose innocuous public facade masks a desperate soul burning for vengeance

SCHELLENBERG—Nazi mastermind gambling his very life on *OMEGA*'s triumph

JANICE PORTER—she and her lover find themselves fighting for their lives as they try to outwit a madman

THE OMEGA DECEPTION

Other Bantam Books by Charles Robertson
Ask your bookseller for the titles you have missed

THE CHILDREN
THE ELIJAH CONSPIRACY

The Omega Deception

Charles Robertson

BANTAM BOOKS
TORONTO · NEW YORK · LONDON · SYDNEY

THE OMEGA DECEPTION

A Bantam Book / January 1984

ISBN 0-553-23709-3

Published simultaneously in the United States and Canada

Bantam Books are published by Bantam Books, Inc. Its trademark, consisting of the words "Bantam Books" and the portrayal of a rooster, is Registered in U.S. Patent and Trademark Office and in other countries. Marca Registrada. Bantam Books, Inc., 666 Fifth Avenue, New York, New York, 10103.

PRINTED IN THE UNITED STATES OF AMERICA

H 0 9 8 7 6 5 4 3

The Omega Deception

Prologue

April 1945

His name was Ernst Luddeck, and he wore the uniform of an SS Standartenführer. He was one of the lucky ones. He was to be executed at dawn.

During the night he had heard the screams and garbled, choking coughs of some of the others in the Flossenbürg prison compound as the SS guards strangled them with piano wire. Rumors had passed among the prisoners that these agonized death throes were being filmed so that the Führer could have the pleasure of watching the torture of his enemies.

Luddeck did not believe that.

Fortunately he was not considered a traitor. His crime was simply failure. Therefore, he was to be shot rather than tortured.

He felt a strange sense of gratitude to his executioners. Quickly and without malice, they would transport him from this shattered nation and his shattered dreams.

He had prepared himself carefully, smoothing out the wrinkles in his rumpled SS uniform as well as he could. He had no belt, no boots, no hat, but such were the ignominies of failure. He had asked for and received permission to wear his Iron Cross First Class on his left breast pocket. He had also asked for but had been refused permission to wear the Leibstandarte Adolph Hitler monogram on his shoulder straps.

He had not expected permission. It would have been unthinkable to allow the execution of a man wearing the markings of the Adolph Hitler Life Guards—especially one who had once been part of the Führer's personal bodyguard. It was enough that they allowed him to wear his Iron Cross. At least then his executioners would know that he was not being shot for cowardice.

For the past fifteen minutes he had heard the rifle reports of the firing squad in the courtyard. Every two or three minutes the sound would shatter the silence of the morning. The two other wretched creatures who shared his cell shuddered and shook with each volley. Both were struggling desperately to maintain their composure.

Luddeck smiled a little. He had not expected to survive the war anyway.

His smile, if it could be called a smile, was grotesque. A Russian flame thrower near Budapest in November of 1944 had severely burned the left side of his face. His mouth on that side was curled in a perpetual snarl, and his left eyelid had been roasted away, leaving the eye miraculously unharmed but staring as if in horrified remembrance of that terrible moment.

He heard footsteps in the hallway and turned to face the door. His companions instinctively shrank back.

The heavy door opened, and a soldier stepped into the cell. "Luddeck," he said, looking at a list of names.

Luddeck stepped forward. "Standartenführer Luddeck," he reminded the sergeant.

The sergeant began a sarcastic smile, but Luddeck strode past him to the door, and the smile, stillborn, slipped from the sergeant's face.

At the door Luddeck looked back over his shoulder. "Coming, Sergeant?" he asked, his terrible grimace piercing the jailer's soul.

They walked down the corridor and out into the courtyard, Luddeck in the lead, two corporals with Schmeisser submachine guns on either side. The sergeant brought up the rear.

The cobblestone courtyard of Flossenbürg prison was a bustle of early morning activity. As Luddeck went up the flight of stairs that led from the underground cells he paused momentarily on the top step and looked at what was likely to be the last thing he would ever see.

The courtyard was square, bounded on all sides by the high, gray granite walls of the prison buildings. In the corner to his left stood a gallows—three ropes swaying innocently in some undetectable breeze. In the right corner stood a thick pole, two meters high. A large ring, like some great door knocker, was imbedded in the wood at the midway point. Behind the post, sandbags were piled against the wall to a height of almost ten feet, extending fifteen feet on either side.

Luddeck hoped this was not a comment on the marksmanship of the firing squad.

Between those two corners was an opening in the wall, large enough for a truck to pass through. At that moment the gates to it were open and the rear end of a truck projected into the courtyard. A soldier with a wheelbarrow was working his way toward the truck. The corpse in the wheelbarrow, that of a fat man, was not properly centered, and the soldier was having difficulty maintaining a straight course.

As Luddeck began his march across the courtyard he saw two men who had been standing beside the truck come to the assistance of the man with the wheelbarrow. They laughed, no doubt belittling his performance, and the man hung his head in a parody of shame.

Together, the three hoisted the body aboard the truck, one holding the arms and one the legs, the third pushing mightily from the middle. Two men on the truck bed then dragged the body forward to join a pile of corpses.

The soldier with the wheelbarrow appeared surprised to see Luddeck already halfway across the courtyard. Most prisoners did not appear so quickly or march so forcefully toward their appointment with the firing squad. The man had to pick up his pace so that he could leave the wheelbarrow near the post and withdraw before this one arrived.

Luddeck walked past his firing squad, six soldiers leaning on their rifles, as he made his way toward the thick post.

Several groups of officers were spaced around the right-hand corner. Some talked seriously while others laughed, their faces and gestures showing how enjoyable they found each other's stories. At first Luddeck thought they were like an audience waiting for a performance, but he quickly realized, as his hands were bound behind his back with a leather thong and then tied to the ring on the post, that none of these men would pay him the slightest attention. His final moments, his long awaited death scene, were not of even momentary interest to them. Death was too commonplace to merit a reflective pause.

For a moment his resolve withered, and he felt his knees buckle and his sphincters loosen. He willed himself to hold on.

"Sergeant," he said to the man who was walking toward the firing squad after having tied him to the post.

The sergeant turned.

"Are you to lead my firing squad?"

Puzzled, the young man nodded, anxious to finish with this one and escape his relentless tortured gaze.

"I would prefer an officer to do the honors, Sergeant."

"It is not required," the sergeant said simply and turned again toward the squad, who were already forming into a line.

Ignoring the sergeant's reply, Luddeck called, in the most authoritative voice he could muster toward the group of officers closest to him.

"You!" His voice cracked out like a pistol shot, reverberating around the courtyard. Conversation ceased immediately, and all eyes turned to him. "I would like an officer to lead my firing squad," he said, his voice firm and strong. His resolve had returned.

The faces of the men in the courtyard showed astonishment. One officer even dared to laugh. Luddeck's head snapped around in the man's direction, skewering him with his grotesque stare. The laugh choked back in the man's throat, and silence fell across the courtyard.

The sergeant attempted to begin the proceedings, but his voice had lost its snap. The men of the squad seemed to be waiting for instructions from someone else. Nervously, the sergeant realized that their eyes were on Luddeck. They were, somewhat uncertainly, waiting for instructions from the man they were to execute.

An SS major approached from across the courtyard. "Get on with it!" he said sharply to the sergeant.

"Yes, sir!" said the sergeant, barking at his men who quickly responded.

The officer turned to look at Luddeck, who stood erect, bootless heels together, head and shoulders straight. He saw Luddeck's shattered face, his Iron Cross, and above it the small red ribbon for the Winter Campaign in Russia. Instinctively his hand went to his own ribbon, and Luddeck nodded.

The major held up his hand, and the sergeant spluttered in mid-command. "I will conduct the squad," he said without explanation.

The sergeant stood aside, and the officer took his position beside the firing squad.

"Ready!"

The squad brought their rifles to their shoulders.

"Aim!"

Luddeck stared into the barrels of the Mausers. Against his will, he found himself wondering how it had happened that he stood here, now, at this time.

He could not know that men he had never met—men who, in most cases, had never met each other—had brought him to this final moment.

"Heil Hitler," he called out just as the officer screamed, "Fire!" and six 7.92 mm lead core bullets slammed home.

The force of the volley crashed Luddeck into the post; then he jackknifed forward from the waist, dangling from the leather strap.

The officer paused for a moment. Every eye in the courtyard had watched the drama unfold. His hand reached for the pistol at his side but withdrew, as if it were hot to the touch. He turned to the sergeant. "You finish him," he said, then added, "if it's necessary."

He walked back to rejoin his group as the sergeant took out his Luger and approached Luddeck.

September 1943

Nineteen forty-three was a disastrous year for Nazi Germany. After the easy victories of 1940 and 1941 the tide had turned against Hitler in 1942. By 1943, even though German military might was still as great or greater than any of the other major combatant countries, the combined might of the Russians, Americans, and British left the outcome of the conflict no longer in doubt.

Massive losses at Stalingrad and in North Africa coupled with Allied landings in Italy sent a shock wave of foreboding through the German High Command.

It was obvious that desperate measures were required if defeat was to be averted.

In September 1943 the British government received the news it had been dreading since April of 1940, when the Germans had invaded Denmark. The news, from several independent sources, was that the Germans had decided to place Dr. Niels Bohr, the Danish scientist and the preeminent nuclear physicist in the world, under house arrest and force him to collaborate with German scientists in an attempt to create a nuclear device that would rescue the Nazis from the certain defeat they now faced.

The British contacted Dr. Bohr through the Danish underground and informed him of the German plans. Dr. Bohr was also informed of an escape route, which had been mapped out well in advance, and given instructions to follow if he desired to use it to escape to England.

Dr. Bohr was not told that if he refused this opportunity of escape, the messenger had been ordered to kill him.

1

SS Hauptsturmführer Ernst Luddeck took the steps of the Reich Security Administration building on Berkaerstrasse, in Berlin, three at a time. He ignored the salute of the two SS guards at the door and burst into the building. Startled by the commotion, a third guard, on duty in the interior foyer, whirled and leveled his Schmeisser submachine gun at Luddeck before realizing who it was.

The guard jerked the barrel skyward and snapped into a heel-clicking salute.

"My apologies, Captain," he barked, but Luddeck was already past him and on his way to the staircase.

Luddeck dashed up the steps to the second floor and approached the outer office of Brigadeführer Walter Schellenberg, the director of the Sicherheitsdienst (SD), the intelligence arm of the SS.

Schellenberg's adjutant, Hans Griebl, who was the same rank as Luddeck, sat behind a desk, his eyes raised to take in the figure at the door. He stood up cautiously as Luddeck came toward him. Luddeck was obviously agitated about something.

"I must see him right away," said Luddeck.

Griebl nodded noncommittally and went to the door at the right of his desk and knocked quietly.

"Come," was the response, and Griebl slipped inside Schellenberg's office.

Schellenberg sat behind a huge mahogany desk, looking at some photographs. His office was sumptuously decorated with the treasures of a plundered continent. At thirty-three Walter Schellenberg was a rising star in the setting sun of the Third Reich. He was handsome, aristocratic in bearing, and considered himself a patron of the arts. He had been personally recruited for the SD by Reinhard Heydrich and had not joined the Nazi Party until long after Hitler had come to power. After Heydrich's assassination in Prague in 1942, Schellenberg, his protégé, took over the SD.

Schellenberg was athletic with sharp linear features, dark hair, and large, sympathetic eyes. He had several dueling scars on his chin, and his *Personal-Berichte* listed him as a "pure Nordic." To superiors and subordinates alike, he exuded a kind of boyish charm from his well-proportioned, five-foot-nine-inch frame, and his soft-spoken manner often misled some into believing that he was not as hard driving, ambitious, or totally ruthless as the whispered rumors claimed.

But as a man who had previously worked for the Gestapo convincing the General Staff that the political executions conducted by the SS were a military necessity, he was, in fact, all of these things.

He looked up when his adjutant gave a nervous cough. "What is it, Hans?" he asked.

"Captain Luddeck is outside, Brigadeführer. He is *demanding* to see you." He hoped his emphasis on the word "demanding" would place the matter in perspective. "He seems thoroughly agitated, and I wondered if you would prefer to have him disarmed before he enters your office."

Schellenberg laughed. "That won't be necessary, Hans. Thank you for your diligence. You may show the Hauptsturmführer in."

Schellenberg was certain that Luddeck would never shoot him. Take his job? Yes. Send him to the gallows? Yes. Command his firing squad? Yes. Shoot him? Unlikely.

Besides, concealed in Schellenberg's desk were two specially constructed machine guns. By depressing the foot pedal in front of his chair Schellenberg could rake the room with gunfire. One three-second burst would devastate the room and anyone in it. He smiled in the knowledge of his own security.

Luddeck impatiently brushed past the adjutant at the door. "He's gone," he said simply.

"Gone? Who's gone?"

Luddeck's shoulders sagged. "Bohr. Professor Bohr. He's gone."

The smile left Schellenberg's face. "How? he asked, his face growing hard. "How could he have known?"

"Best told me that he talked with our Danish resistance informer only a few hours ago."

"And?"

"The resistance found out about our decision to arrest Bohr."

Schellenberg's eyes narrowed. His face was gray, devoid of expression. "When?"

"Day before yesterday."

"That decision wasn't made until the day before yesterday."

Luddeck nodded, waiting for Schellenberg to say the obvious.

Finally he did. "Apparently the traitors in the Abwehr are still active."

"Get rid of them all," said Luddeck. "Canaris, too." When he said the name, his voice hissed.

Schellenberg shook his head sadly. "If only it were possible." He shrugged. "In peacetime—yes. But in the midst of a war it is impossible to emasculate an entire intelligence service."

"What good are they? They can't be trusted."

"We need definitive proof."

"Proof!" said Luddeck, the word exploding from his mouth in a shower of spittle. "We know that someone in the Abwehr informed the Dutch military attaché of the invasion of Denmark and Norway."

Schellenberg shrugged in agreement.

"And," Luddeck went on, "that someone in the Abwehr informed Belgian and Dutch representatives that we were about to place their countries under protective occupation."

The phrase "protective occupation" made Schellenberg smile. Luddeck, no doubt, had heard that one from Himmler himself, who had no doubt heard it from Goebbels. If nothing else, the propaganda minister had a wonderful way with a phrase.

Schellenberg watched as Luddeck continued to rant

against the traitorous machinations of the Abwehr. Luddeck was tall, handsome, blond, and blue-eyed—everything that the new Germany should be. No wonder Reichsführer Himmler himself was so impressed with the Hauptsturmführer's abilities.

Luddeck was a product of the Hitler Youth and a graduate of the first group from the Holstein National Political Training School (Napolas). As a top student at the Holstein Napolas he was selected to attend the Citadel of the Order of Blood (Blutordensburg) in Vogelsang Castle, where the future elite of the Nazi party were trained. From there he had moved on to the SS Junkerschule in Klagenfurt for his final training as an SS officer. So glowing were his fitness reports that he was inducted into the Leibstandarte Adolph Hitler Regiment at the beginning of the war and actually spent more than six months at Wolfsschanze in East Prussia as part of the Führer's personal detachment.

Schellenberg noted that he still wore on his sleeve the silver stripe with the Führer's name, denoting his personal service to Hitler.

In July of 1942, Luddeck had volunteered for service on the Russian front, where he had served ably with the 5th Waffen SS Division, winning the Iron Cross First Class at the Battle of Kursk in July of 1943, where he was severely wounded by Russian artillery fire.

While recuperating from his wounds at the Hohenlichen Hospital reserved for the SS, he received orders from Reichsführer Himmler to report for duty at his earliest convenience to Reich Security Headquarters in Berlin.

A genuine hero of the Reich, thought Schellenberg as he watched him warily. Luddeck was someone to be watched carefully.

Even his uniform called out for attention.

Although both men wore the same black SS uniform, Luddeck's bore the subtle decorations of the hero. In addition to his Leibstandarte AH insignia, he wore the Knight's Cross at his collar, the Iron Cross First Class at his breast pocket, and the red ribbon of the Winter Campaign in Russia. Schellenberg also wore the Iron Cross, but his was for an espionage operation early in the war during which he had kidnapped two British intelligence agents and smuggled them back to Germany from Holland. This operation, known as the Venlo incident, had brought Schellenberg a certain amount of notoriety, and the Führer himself had awarded Schellenberg his Iron Cross.

Schellenberg knew that his exploit paled in comparison with Luddeck's heroism on the Russian front.

The final decoration, and the one that Schellenberg envied more than any other, was in actuality not a decoration at all. On his right sleeve Luddeck wore a single chevron that indicated that the wearer had been a member of the Nazi party prior to 1933. Schellenberg was painfully aware that some of the old-line party members referred to him scornfully as *Marzveilchen* (March Violet) because he had not joined the Nazi party until after it had come to power in March 1933. It was only then, said the old-time party members, that the violets bloomed and the opportunists emerged from hiding.

As Luddeck continued his harangue against the intelligence service of the German General Staff, Schellenberg stood up, folding his arms in front of his chest.

"What are you going to do about this?" snapped Luddeck in a display of disrespect that angered Schellenberg.

He said nothing, letting his cold eyes hold Luddeck's in a stare. For a moment he was afraid that he had overestimated his own power, but finally Luddeck's eyes drifted from his.

"Excuse my impertinence, General," Luddeck said. "I did not mean to imply that you were in any way responsible for this disaster."

Schellenberg smiled soothingly. It never hurt to be pleasant to one of Himmler's fair-haired boys. He himself was regarded as a personal favorite of the Reichsführer's. "Of course not, Captain," he said. "I understand perfectly your distress at this situation."

His smile broadened, and he motioned Luddeck into a seat in front of his desk. "Rather than raving against the Abwehr, I think we should spare no effort to find

Bohr before it is too late. It is absolutely essential that this man not be allowed to elude us."

Luddeck seemed calmer, more rational now. "It may already be too late. He may have already crossed into Sweden."

Schellenberg nodded, his elbows on his desk, his fingers forming a pyramid upon which his chin rested. "We have people in Sweden," he said. "Make sure they are alerted to the possibility that British agents may try to get Bohr out."

Luddeck's head shook slowly. "If the British get their hands on him—"

"For the sake of our Führer," said Schellenberg, interrupting him, "and our nation, you had better hope that that is not the case."

2

October 7, 1943

The De Havilland Mosquito swept in low over the Skagerrak, threading a careful course between German-occupied Norway and Denmark, below the German radar.

"Ten minutes," called the navigator as he made his calculations on the Dalton computer strapped to his right thigh. "We should be picking up the lights from Lysekil any time now."

At the controls, Flying Officer Michael Reynolds struggled to keep the tension from his voice as he replied to his flight sergeant. "Okay, Bill. Keep a sharp lookout."

It wasn't the danger of flying over occupied territory that clutched at Reynolds' throat like a too-tight collar. He had flown over occupied territory at least twice each week for the past three months. It wasn't even the threat of German night fighters that made the sweat run inside his sheepskin flight jacket. His Mosquito, its Rolls-Royce Merlin engines pounding fiercely, could outrun any night fighter in the air.

What troubled Flying Officer Reynolds was that this was not one of his typical reconnaissance flights over enemy territory. Usually he would take off from Scotland in the dead of night, timed to arrive over his target at dawn. He would swoop in like a hawk over a hare, as low as he dared, while his navigator, Flight Sergeant Quinn, operated the high resolution cameras buried in the underside of the Mosquito's nose. The long shadows created by the rising sun helped the intelligence people back in Scotland determine the size and placement of the objects he had been sent to photograph. After no more than a few quick passes over the target, Reynolds would take the Mosquito up to altitude, which was higher than any German fighter could effectively pursue, and head back to base.

As exciting as all that seemed and as dangerous as he could make it sound to the girls at the Barrowland Dance Hall in Glasgow, the work was fairly routine. Usually, his only fear was that engine trouble might bring him down over enemy territory or—God forbid—the North Sea.

Tonight, however, things were considerably different. Tonight he was scheduled to fly over occupied territory and then make a landing and pickup in neutral Sweden. Visions of betrayal and ambush danced in his head. Although neutral, the Swedes lived with the constant fear that Hitler would occupy their country as he had occupied their neighbors'. This fear bred a cooperation between Sweden and Germany that many in England claimed went beyond the bounds of neutrality. Churchill, however, had put the situation into perspective. "If you were small, and weak, and frightened," he had told a group of his ministers who had complained about the one-sided Swedish neutrality, "and your neighbor was a madman with a vicious dog, you too might be inclined to some degree of cooperation."

Flying Officer Reynolds imagined a truckload of German soldiers waiting at the landing site. He could picture them laughing and joking as their officers impatiently scanned the night skies, awaiting his arrival.

Farfetched? He knew that, but still the image haunted him. Photo reconnaissance was quick and clean—in and out—that's what he liked. This was something else and he didn't like it at all.

Flight Sergeant Quinn spoke again. "Got it," he said. "Lights ahead will be Lysekil."

"Good job, Bill," said Reynolds, giving his navigator the thumbs-up sign, banking his aircraft to the left and beginning his climb to a higher altitude.

Navigation at low level is extremely difficult under the best of circumstances. At night, over enemy territory, and with no landscape features as reference points, it was almost impossible to fly nearly seven hundred miles and arrive exactly where you wanted to. But here they were. Quinn had done it again.

"Follow the fjord," said Quinn.

Reynolds turned to his navigator. "What's the ETA?" he asked.

Quinn looked at his watch. "O-Three-hundred hours," he said, then added, "in twelve minutes."

Their eyes met for just a moment and quickly disengaged. Both knew what the other was thinking. Both wished they were somewhere else tonight.

Beneath them the ground whisked past like a toy landscape in an elaborate train set. The fjord, glinting in the moonlight, curved north in a great scimitar, sweeping past farms and churches and small groups of buildings.

Then they were following a river, a shimmering beacon on the darkened landscape below, moving gently east.

"Fork ahead," said Quinn. "Follow the left fork."

Reynolds's hand moved gently, expertly, on the stick. As the Mosquito immediately responded, Reynolds smiled. She was a remarkable plane, he thought, admiring her as only a pilot could.

The Mosquito was indeed remarkable. With the speed

and maneuverability of a fighter and the range and payload of a light bomber, the versatile Mosquito could perform more tasks than any other plane in the wartime skies. But perhaps her most remarkable feature was that she was built of wood, causing her to be dubbed the "Wooden Wonder" by her admirers and "Termites Dream" by those less certain of a wooden plane's place in modern warfare.

"This could be it," said Quinn as they passed over a large, apparently flat area.

"Keep a look out for the signal," said Reynolds.

"There!"

Below them a flashlight flickered skyward, and as Reynolds circled the field, a row of flares, one by one, burst into life.

"See anything?" Reynolds asked as his plane banked steeply left to give both men a view of the ground.

Quinn shrugged. "No. Nothing." He knew what Reynolds was thinking. "If there are any uninvited guests down there," he added, "we couldn't see them anyway."

Reynolds nodded. "Gear down," he said, banking the Mosquito into an approach turn. The plane shuddered as the landing gear descended, and Reynolds struggled to hold his airspeed.

The row of flares below formed an upside-down L with the short end pointing to the left, indicating the perimeter of the landing area and the wind direction. Reynolds, aiming for the intersection of the two lines, began to bring his plane down as Sergeant Quinn called out his altitude.

"One hundred fifty...one hundred twenty-five...one hundred . . . seventy-five . . . fifty . . ."

They crossed a road and Reynolds had a sudden jarring thought. Power lines! He had been so damned preoccupied with other concerns that he had forgotten to look for the power lines that were a pilot's nemesis. He grimaced in expectation of the suddenness of his demise, but the plane flew on.

"Twenty-five . . . twenty . . . fifteen . . . looking good. . . ten . . ."

Reynolds took a quick glance at his airspeed indicator, preparing to throttle back if needed, but he and his machine were, as usual, perfectly synchronized.

The Mosquito bounced a little on touchdown, then quickly hugged the surface as it raced on to the end of the landing area, where Reynolds spun the plane around, faced in the opposite direction, prepared for immediate departure.

He throttled back to a high idle, the big, twelve-cylinder Merlins firing beautifully. "See anyone?"

"Not yet."

"I'm opening the bay doors now," said Reynolds. "Do you have the picture of our passenger?"

"Got it," said Quinn, removing his gloves and extracting a glossy three by five photograph from one of the snap pockets on his flight suit.

"Someone's coming now," said Reynolds, his voice hoarse.

Quinn looked in the direction of Reynold's gaze. "Two someones," he said, then took a quick look around the area.

All seemed quiet. Except for the two approaching figures the field appeared deserted.

Reynolds's fingers tightened around his Webley service revolver. "Look like our boy?"

"Could be," Quinn answered, peering into the darkness at the running figures. "I'm getting out now. Keep your eyes peeled."

"Righto," said Reynolds as he shut down the engines. "At the first sign of trouble get your arse back in here."

Climbing out of the cockpit, Quinn laughed "Don't worry. I'm not going far."

He dropped onto the field and stood near the tail section. The Mosquito's tail knifed into the sky from the gracefully tapered fuselage like a shark fin breaking the surface of a peaceful sea. "Hold it," Quinn called when the men had drawn as close as fifteen paces.

Both men stopped dead in their tracks, and Quinn snapped on his flashlight, directing it into the face of the first man.

"Not me," he said, shielding his eyes and pointing to his companion.

The first man was short and powerful looking. Perhaps thirty. Definitely dangerous.

Quinn redirected the flashlight to the second man, who squinted but did not cover his eyes.

"I believe that I am the man you are looking for," he said.

He was middle-aged and balding but stood erect, shoulders back, giving the impression of quiet dignity.

Must be a pretty important character, thought Quinn, to risk a plane and crew to get him back to Britain.

He appeared to be the man in the photograph.

"Greenfields?" asked Quinn.

The man looked puzzled, his face blank. He turned to his companion, who mumbled something to him, and then back to face Quinn. "The fields lie fallow until the spring," he said sheepishly, as if embarrassed to be playing this little game.

The dangerous one spat on the ground to show what he thought of this foolishness.

"Let's get a move on then, professor," said Quinn, motioning the man forward while giving a reassuring wave to Reynolds in the cockpit.

The younger man reassured the older, who seemed bewildered by all of this.

"Do you have baggage?" asked Quinn. "I was told you'd be carrying important documents."

The man he had called professor looked around as if expecting some miraculous assistance. "I have nothing," he said. "I left everything."

Quinn paused, about to comment, then shrugged as if all this were really none of his business. He crouched down beside the open bomb-bay doors, reached inside, and pulled out a canvas bag from which he removed an insulated flight suit, gloves, and boots. "Take these," he said to the man. "You'll need them."

As the professor slipped into the flight suit the other man stepped forward. "I have a message that I'd like you to pass on to your people in England."

"Do what I can," said Quinn.

"It is essential that Special Operations be told that the Hunter group in Copenhagen has been compromised. Anything of significance should be relayed to me personally and to no one else."

"And you are . . . ?"

The man fixed Quinn in a steely-eyed stare. "Tell them you talked to Hunter."

"I'll be sure to pass along your information, Mr. Hunter," said Quinn, extending his hand.

The man called Hunter squeezed Quinn's hand gently, just enough to let him feel the power in his grip. "Please, do that," he said simply. "It is of utmost importance."

Quinn helped his passenger clamber awkwardly inside the bomb bay and gave him a fur-lined cap with earflaps and an extra blanket. "Once we clear enemy airspace, we'll be flying at high altitude, and it's going to be very cold down here," he said. He pointed to an oxygen mask dangling from one of the racks above the man's head. "As soon as we get airborne, use this. Be home in less than three hours."

The professor nodded, his eyes wide open in the fashion of one who pretends to comprehend a bewildering array of instructions.

Quinn stepped back and gave a quick hand signal to Reynolds. The bay doors hissed, then swung upwards, sealing the passenger safely inside.

"Thanks, got to rush," said Quinn, waving to Hunter. He climbed back into his seat as the Mosquito's great engines coughed into life. In seconds they were rumbling in unison and the airplane was bouncing its way down the makeshift runway. The plane picked up speed, dark trees whistling past on either side. A blackness, darker than the dark sky, rushed toward them from the end of the runway.

"Long enough?" asked Quinn, a small measure of concern creeping into his voice.

"I should think so," said Reynolds calmly. Now that they were on their way, his fears had vanished.

The outlines of the trees that formed the blackness

were now plainly visible, growing in size as they raced ever closer.

Quinn cleared his throat quietly.

On the ground Hunter watched the Mosquito speed across the field. Painted black and without identification markings of any kind, it was already slipping from his view. Only the engine exhausts, bright and fiery, betrayed its presence below the line of trees that encircled the field.

Then finally, after an agonizingly long wait, the plane hurtled into the night sky. He watched the plane, visible now against the deep purple sky, circle the field, engines growling triumphantly.

"Everything okay?" Reynolds asked.

"Yes," said Quinn, eyes fixed on the line of flares below. Already Hunter was busy extinguishing his markers. "Everything's fine."

Something in Quinn's tone made Reynolds uneasy. "What is it?" he asked. "What's wrong?"

"He didn't have anything with him," said Quinn. "No bags, no parcels, no papers . . . not a thing." Quinn watched the river below. The moon was hidden behind a heavy cloud cover, and the river no longer sparkled. "The impression I had was that he was supposed to be carrying something vitally important."

Reynolds, happy to be airborne, waved away his doubts. "That's not our problem, Bill," said Reynolds. "We've done our bit. We'll just have to let the brass worry about what he's left behind."

"I suppose you're right," Quinn said, resignation in his voice. "I just get the feeling that the boys in jolly old England would be a lot happier to see our boy if he had brought his luggage."

Below, the dark shape of some kind of vessel was apparent on the glasslike waters of the fjord.

3

It was 6:11 A.M. London time when the phone rang at 10 Downing Street. Churchill's military aide, Colonel Withers, answered the phone on the first ring.

"Yes," he said tonelessly.

"This is Major General Hartwick," said the voice on the other end. "I must speak with the prime minister."

"I'm sorry, sir," said Withers, "the prime minister retired for the evening only a few hours ago with strict instructions not to be disturbed."

Hartwick was undaunted. "This is top priority, Colonel. The prime minister himself told me to call the minute I received this news."

Colonel Withers was apologetic. "I'm sure that's true, sir, but the prime minister was in conference until after four this morning." He was about to suggest an appropriate time when he sensed a figure on the stairs and turned to see Winston Churchill approaching.

The prime minister wore a battered, maroon robe over striped pajamas. His face was tired, eyes dull. His slippers could not conceal the swollen feet and ankles that burdened his every step. "Who is it?" he asked.

"A General Hartwick," said Withers, placing a hand over the mouthpiece of the phone. "Says he has some priority information that you personally requested." He started to explain how he had been about to suggest a later call, but Churchill was already taking the phone from his hand.

"Good morning, General," he said grumpily. "You have good news for me, I hope."

"I'm afraid not, sir."

Churchill's face sagged. "Couldn't you get him out?"

"Nothing like that, Mr. Prime Minister. Right now the good professor is recovering from his ordeal at the RAF hospital near Edinburgh. It seems that his oxygen mask pulled loose, and he was unconscious upon arrival." He paused, then added quickly, "But I'm assured by the RAF doctors that he will be just fine in a day or two."

"Then what's the problem?" asked Churchill, his face wrinkled in a frown. "That's what we wanted, isn't it? To make sure he didn't fall into German hands?"

"That's true, sir," said Hartwick, "but apparently he came without a stitch."

"I don't understand."

"No baggage—nothing!"

"Nothing?"

"Yes. He's left everything behind."

"I thought the instructions were to bring out the man and all of his scientific papers."

"That's correct, Mr. Prime Minister, but when the RAF people got there, the professor had nothing with him—not a blessed thing."

"Did he say what he did with his papers? I hope he had the good sense to destroy them."

Hartwick sighed. "I'm afraid, sir, he did not destroy them."

"What then?"

"It seems that when the resistance informed him he was about to be picked up, he gave all of his papers to a colleague, with instructions to get them out of the country."

"And?"

"Apparently the colleague was concerned that he too might be arrested. He got himself out of the country, but left the papers behind."

Churchill drew a sharp breath.

"You mean those papers are still in Denmark?"

"Yes, sir, I'm afraid so."

Churchill said nothing.

"I'm sorry, sir," said Hartwick. "The RAF boys didn't know what to do, so they just brought him out."

"They did the right thing, of course." Churchill

thought for a moment. "How soon can Professor Bohr be here in London?"

"In a few days, I think."

"Good. Get him here. I should think that some of our intelligence people might wish to talk with him. I'd like to talk with him myself."

"Very good, sir."

"I'll have to inform the president of this rather distressing turn of events," said Churchill to Hartwick. In actuality, he was speaking to himself. "If possible, we should call a meeting of the Combined Chiefs. Perhaps this news might dissuade the Americans from their insistence on the cross-channel invasion."

Hartwick stifled a sigh. It was common knowledge in military circles that the prime minister was against the frontal assault on the continent that the Americans believed was the only way to bring the war to a rapid conclusion. "Perhaps you're right, sir," said Hartwick.

"Yes, of course," mumbled Churchill, his mind already on his next move. "Thank you for calling, General," he said and hung up the phone.

4

Even though the British had been able to duplicate the machine that enciphered much of the German military and intelligence wireless traffic, and the Americans had broken the Japanese military codes, the prime minister had complete faith that his own secret communications with President Roosevelt on the transatlantic radio circuit were beyond detection.

Developed by the Bell Telephone Laboratories, the American device enabled the president and the prime minister to communicate by voice rather than printed message. It was faster, eliminating the need for coding, cabling, and translating, and therefore less troublesome than other methods. Most important, the system allowed the two great friends and leaders to communicate on a more personal level.

It was a modern engineering marvel. This foolproof system split the frequency band into smaller bands, then inverted and mangled the normal sound of the human voice into an unintelligible garble. In addition, the frequency was constantly switched in random patterns, so that in the unlikely event that anyone did happen to monitor the scrambled sounds of the transmission, the circuit would suddenly change—rendering useless any deciphering efforts.

President Roosevelt's scrambler phone was installed by the Army Signal Corps in September 1939 in a soundproof basement room in the White House. The prime minister's scrambler phone was in a similar basement room at Whitehall.

Free of the restrictions of red tape, both leaders had long and frequent discussions on the course and character of the war.

On the same day as his conversation with Major General Hartwick, Churchill talked with Roosevelt, mostly about events in Italy. Naples had fallen on October 1, and Churchill was hopeful that the new Italian government could be persuaded to declare war on Germany. "It would be little more than a psychological victory," he said. "The Italians are finished. They don't want to fight anyone. But the German people would be sorely vexed if their oldest and strongest partner turned on them at this juncture."

Roosevelt was more positive. "I think the Italians could prove a valuable asset," he said.

Churchill grumbled an excuse for a laugh. "Tell that to Mr. Hitler."

Their conversation drew to a close, but Roosevelt detected something in Churchill's voice. "What's troubling you?" he said, expecting to hear another plea for delay of the invasion.

Churchill paused, and the president could hear him

chomping on his cigar. "There is some bad news, Mr. President."

Roosevelt was instantly alert. Churchill only called him Mr. President when something particularly distressed him. "Go on," he said gently.

"We got Professor Bohr out of Denmark, but apparently all of his research material has been left behind."

At first Roosevelt did not react. "In Denmark?" he asked finally.

"Yes."

The president exhaled slowly. "Could this material fall into German hands?"

"At this time," said Churchill, "it is impossible to say, but the consequences could be catastrophic for our cause."

"Perhaps it is not as bad as we imagine."

Churchill shook his head sadly. "My advisers tell me that it is quite possible that the Germans are as much as a year ahead of us in nuclear research. Some speculate that they might have an operable bomb by this time next year. If they gain possession of Dr. Bohr's notes, that timetable could be cut by half."

"Then," said the president, "we must be certain that this material does not fall into their hands."

■

At the Deutsche Reichspost monitoring station in Eyndhoven on the coast of occupied Holland, an agent watched for the red light on the descrambling machine to signal that the transmission was completed and the transatlantic connection broken. He waited for just a few seconds to make sure that nothing else would come over the machine, and then switched the equipment to the standby position.

By that time the electric typewriter had already typed the transcript of the transmission, missing only a word or two where the frequencies had switched.

It had taken the Germans three months from America's

entry into the war to complete their monitoring station, which from that moment on descrambled and recorded every important conversation made on the transatlantic radio-telephone.

The agent carefully detached the message from the paper roll in the typewriter and handed it to the SS officer who had watched over his shoulder during the entire operation.

The officer smiled as he looked over the message. Then, as was his usual practice, he transferred the transcript to Berlin on a teletype machine equipped with its own scrambler.

In less than two hours a translated transcription of the conversation between President Roosevelt and Prime Minister Churchill lay on the desk of Reichsführer Heinrich Himmler at SS headquarters on 8 Prinz Albrecht Strasse, Berlin.

5

Luddeck seemed despondent when Schellenberg showed him the report that verified Bohr's presence in England. At first he closed his eyes as if to deny some awful truth, and Schellenberg knew that he was thinking the unthinkable—Germany was finished. Then he began shaking his head back and forth in mindless rhythm.

Schellenberg watched him for a few moments from across his office desk, unwilling at first to interrupt Luddeck's grief. As a veteran of the Russian front, Luddeck was well aware of the precariousness of Germany's present position. Schellenberg saw before him a man who had begun to hope for miracles. He knew that Luddeck had placed his hopes for Germany's salvation—unreasonable as they were—on finding Dr. Bohr before he could escape. This news had shattered those fragile dreams.

In a way Schellenberg felt sorry for him. True patriots like Luddeck always had their dreams destroyed—in defeat or victory—one way or another.

"So what did the scientists at Dahlem say?" Schellenberg finally broke the silence. Luddeck seemed not to have heard him, and Schellenberg was forced to speak again. "You did speak to Professor Vogler, didn't you?"

Luddeck looked up. "Yes, Brigadeführer," he said, his eyes misty with moisture. "I did as you instructed."

"And?"

Luddeck went back to shaking his head again, and Schellenberg was afraid the man would break down in his office. "It's hopeless," he said finally. "They couldn't even venture a guess as to when they might have this weapon."

"None at all?"

"Heisenberg and Vogler were both there. I asked them, 'One year? Two years? Three years?' They looked at each other as if I'd given them the riddle of the Sphinx."

Schellenberg sighed. The news was not unexpected.

"They tried to placate me," said Luddeck, "by listing the new vengeance weapons, V-1 and V-2, ready to rain down on England. They don't understand that it is too little and too late. We need the ultimate weapon—the final Vergeltungswaffe."

"The Omega weapon," said Schellenberg softly. He liked the sound of it.

Luddeck nodded, his face a mask of grief.

"Did you ask if Bohr's calculations would help?"

"Yes. Both were certain that Bohr would be of immense value. Both seemed excited by the prospect of working with him." Luddeck's eyes came alive for a second, mirroring the excitement of the two scientists, but then realization returned. "He's gone," he said with a sad shrug. "That's that."

"His papers are still here," said Schellenberg encouragingly.

"Bohr's laboratory and home were searched when he disappeared. There was nothing."

"True," said Schellenberg, allowing a slight smile to form on his lips.

Luddeck looked up, his eyes widening in surprise as he caught the expression on Schellenberg's face. "Do you know where they are?" he began, hope rising in his breast.

"No," said Schellenberg with a total lack of concern.

Luddeck's eyes narrowed—suspicion and puzzlement fought for control of his expression. "Then . . . ?"

Schellenberg shrugged. "I've been giving this matter some thought," he said carelessly, as if it were of minor importance, "and I've concluded that we'll just have to let the British tell us where they are."

He leaned back in his chair, hands locked behind his head, enjoying the bewildered expression on Luddeck's face.

6

Every morning Walter Schellenberg left his home near Kurfurstendam and was driven by limousine to the riding stables in the Tiergarten, the magnificent park in central Berlin. There, each day at 7 A.M. in what amounted to a perverse ritual, he greeted his old friend—and mortal enemy—Admiral Wilhelm Canaris of the Abwehr. Each morning the two men went riding together through the treelined bridle paths of the park, occasionally pausing to rest the horses and chat informally about the state of the art of intelligence work.

Schellenberg admired and at the same time despised Canaris.

The older man represented everything that the young man was not. In 1943 Admiral Canaris was fifty-five and had been head of German military intelligence, the Abwehr, since 1934. He was a legitimate hero of the Great War and as such held the respect of the German military establishment, which, of course, Schellenberg did not.

Canaris was kind, compassionate, and soft-spoken. His kindness was legendary and in some circles used as evidence against his fitness for his job. His affection for animals, particularly dogs, was well documented, and Abwehr agents understood that a love for animals was a prerequisite for advancement in the service.

Canaris's long, sad face was generally devoid of expression, but Schellenberg had noted that his eyes would grow misty whenever casualty reports from the Eastern Front were discussed. But if Schellenberg ever thought that this kindness and compassion was a sign of weakness, he had only to remind himself that in 1916, during the first war, Canaris had escaped from an Italian prison by murdering the prison priest and donning the man's robes.

Under Canaris the Abwehr had done as much to thwart Hitler's dream of empire as the Allies themselves had done. Canaris was a patriot and an anti-Nazi, whose politics were well known even before his appointment in 1934. That appointment, as head of the Abwehr, had startled and dumbfounded intelligence personnel everywhere. Why, they wondered, would Hitler place such an important post in the charge of a man who, if not a sworn enemy, was at the very least an unbeliever?

Although no one ever knew for certain, it was assumed by most that Hitler had given the post to Canaris to assuage the fears of many of the old-line military men who felt that Hitler, through his paramilitary party organizations, was out to destroy the traditional branches of the German military.

Canaris was well respected in the military establishment and his appointment did placate some, but the truth was that Hitler never considered the position to be that important. He considered himself a man of action, with no need for the distasteful subterfuge and deception of the intelligence service. "Let them worry about deception," he had said in 1939. "I will strike wherever and whenever I choose."

Hitler was unaware that Canaris and his deputy, Colonel Hans Oster, had leaked the news of Germany's impending march into Czechoslovakia in 1938, in the vain hope that France and England would force the Führer to cancel his plans. In 1939 the Abwehr had leaked advance news of Germany's invasion of Poland. Again to no avail.

It was the Polish campaign that turned Canaris irreversibly against Hitler, when Abwehr agents reported that special SS and Gestapo murder squads, called Einsatzgruppen, were engaged in a mass slaughter of Polish civilians.

Canaris had been instrumental in the formation of the anti-Hitler conspiracy that the SD had named the Schwarze Kapelle—the Black Orchestra. The men of the Black Orchestra believed that a defeat for Germany would be a disaster, but that a victory for Hitler would be a catastrophe, and had at every turn attempted to place obstacles in Hitler's path. Russia was warned of the impending invasion, but Stalin scoffed until the Wehrmacht was knocking at the gates of Moscow.

As they rode in silence Canaris kept a watchful eye on his young companion. Something was bothering Schellenberg today—of that the Admiral was certain. Canaris, as was typical of him, would say nothing until Schellenberg decided that it was time for conversation. The usual civilities between the two had been more strained than usual.

As he followed Schellenberg along the bridle path he wondered, as he often did on these mornings, why he should have had the great misfortune to be opposed by two such brilliantly amoral antagonists as Reinhard Heydrich and Walter Schellenberg.

Schellenberg was thirty-three and had been head of the SS intelligence service since 1942, having succeeded the assassinated Heydrich, the "Angel of Evil," whom Hitler had eulogized as the "man with the heart of iron." After Heydrich's death, Canaris had hoped that Hitler would fill his SD post with one of the Gestapo thugs who were always available for such duty. The

Führer, as usual, had been distressingly perverse, and to Canaris's dismay, had appointed Schellenberg.

To Canaris it was as if Heydrich had been reincarnated. All of the former SD leader's plans to supplant and replace Canaris had been reborn in Heydrich's protégé, Schellenberg. Canaris fully expected to someday fall from grace and himself face the feared Gestapo interrogators in the basement of the SS headquarters on Prinz Albrecht Strasse. When that day came, he was certain that the agent of his destruction would be Walter Schellenberg.

He was, as usual, quite right.

Schellenberg reined his horse to a stop in a small clearing in the trees. It was one of his favorite spots for informal conversation, although Canaris wondered if any conversation with Schellenberg could ever be regarded as informal.

"He got away," began Schellenberg, looking back over his shoulder as Canaris pulled alongside.

Canaris stopped beside him, struggling a little to hold his horse steady. He seemed uninterested. "Who got away?"

"Bohr."

Canaris raised an eyebrow. "Professor Bohr? The Danish physicist?"

"Yes."

"What do you mean, he got away? Where could he go?"

"England. The British took him out by plane."

Canaris almost smiled. "Quite daring of them—don't you think?"

Schellenberg ignored the admiral's apparent lack of concern. "Don't you find it rather strange that they would take him now?"

Canaris did not find it strange at all. It had been partly through his offices that the British had known of the Gestapo detention order for Professor Bohr. He looked earnestly into Schellenberg's face, his blue eyes devoid of the guilt that Schellenberg sought. "Strange?" he asked. "I'm not sure I understand you, Walter."

Impatient with the delay, Schellenberg's horse moved

forward a few paces, and Schellenberg yanked on the reins, pulling back the animal's head violently. Canaris winced and patted his mount reassuringly.

"What I mean," said Schellenberg, "is that we have occupied Denmark for almost four years. They could have taken Bohr out at any time, but as long as we did not disturb the professor they did nothing. They allowed the foremost nuclear physicist in the world to go on quietly about his business in a country occupied by their greatest enemy."

Canaris said nothing, allowing Schellenberg to make his own point.

"And then," Schellenberg continued, "when the decision is made to bring Bohr to Berlin and have him work with our scientists, he disappears and the next thing we know he is in England."

"How can we be sure that he is in England?" said Canaris innocently.

Schellenberg smiled. The tapped transatlantic radiotelephone was strictly an SS operation. Canaris could not be trusted with such vital information. "We have been informed," he said, his tone indicating that nothing more would be said.

"Do you think it's possible," said Canaris, "that the British found out about our plans for Professor Bohr?"

Schellenberg eyed Canaris, his eyes narrow slits. He wanted to scream at his riding companion. No, you bastard, I think that *you* found out! You or one of your traitorous assistants. You told the British that we were going to bring Bohr to Berlin, and they decided it was time to get him out.

Instead, he shrugged and spurred his horse forward, saying nothing. As he wended his way along the path, carefully avoiding the few low limbs, Schellenberg had the feeling that Canaris was laughing behind his back. He wanted to turn around quickly, but knew that if he did he would only be confronted with the dour, expressionless face of the admiral.

And so he rode on in silence.

Later over breakfast in the Tiergarten Plaza, an enclosed solarium on the edge of the park, Canaris broached the subject obliquely. "What does our Russian friend say about all this?"

Schellenberg chewed and swallowed his mouthful of egg before responding. "It's too soon. We won't get another report until next week."

On this subject, Schellenberg could speak freely. He knew that Canaris was already aware that one of Stalin's top aides was in reality a German agent who had already supplied the Germans with some of the most useful information of the war. With few exceptions, Hitler's spies in England had been totally ineffective, and German spies in America had been equally unsuccessful, but this one top man in the Kremlin—code-named Red Lady—was worth his weight in gold.

The Red Lady was a conduit of tremendous importance. Privy to a great deal of information about the Russian military, he was also, and more importantly, aware of much of the information sent to Stalin by the Allies. In addition to these communications, voluntarily given to Stalin by the British and Americans, the Red Lady also had available to him a plethora of information gathered by Russian spies and communist sympathizers in both countries. In effect, Stalin had it both ways. He received a great deal of information that the Allies were willing to transmit to him, while at the same time his spies and sympathizers provided him with material that, for one reason or another, they were not.

Thanks to the Red Lady, Hitler knew almost everything that Stalin knew.

"He has told us," said Schellenberg quietly, "that the British and Americans are continuing their research in atomistics." He sipped his coffee. "We even know what they call it—the Manhattan Project."

"How long," began Canaris cautiously, "before they have this so-called atomic bomb?"

Schellenberg shrugged. "According to the Red Lady, not for some time."

"I can't believe that the British would ever use such a weapon. The Americans perhaps—but not the British. It would be so out of character for them."

Schellenberg's face was contorted in a sneer. He was

sure that he had never hated Canaris as much as he did at this moment. The man was a known anglophile but this was beyond reason. "Character?" he snarled. "When did your fancy English ever exhibit character? It was the Führer who allowed them to withdraw their armies at Dunkirk in hopes that we could conclude a reasonable peace. And what was their response? The bombing of Berlin. Widening the war to include innocent civilians—women and children. The Führer would never have permitted the destruction of London if Churchill had not first bombed Berlin."

His face expressionless, Canaris wondered if Schellenberg actually believed most of the things he said. Or did he just make sure that he never placed himself in a dangerous situation? Just as Canaris was certain that he himself would not survive this war, he had abiding faith that Schellenberg, and a host of others like him, would be there at the end to pick up the pieces.

Now he merely said, "What you say is, of course, absolutely true, Walter. But this seems somehow different. If our scientists are to be believed, one of these bombs could devastate a city and everyone in it." He looked through the windows of the solarium to the leafless trees outside. "This would be warfare carried to its ultimate and most horrible extreme."

Schellenberg moved his eyes around the room. As was customary, the tables around the pair were left empty so that the two could talk privately. "Hitler would never use such a weapon. He is not interested in such instruments of destruction."

Canaris's eyes widened slightly in disbelief. For him it was an uncharacteristic demonstration of emotion.

Schellenberg leaned forward choosing his words carefully. "I talked with Speer in July. He told me that he had tried to impress upon the Führer the importance of our having this weapon."

"What did the Führer say?"

Schellenberg drew himself erect in his chair, as if sitting at attention. "According to Speer, the Führer had tears in his eyes when Speer explained the destructive potential of this atomic bomb."

This time Canaris did not allow his disbelief to show.

"The Führer was adamant," Schellenberg went on, "that Germany would never use such a weapon."

"But," Canaris said, "Speer was able to convince him otherwise."

Schellenberg shrugged. "Not exactly. Speer was able to convince the Führer that the only way to prevent the British and Americans from using this weapon on our people was if we too had the potential to devastate their cities."

Canaris nodded. Schellenberg's logic was impeccable.

"Two years ago," Schellenberg said, "we were content to let the might of our armed forces speak for us, but now"—he paused, his eyes drifting around the almost empty room as if he were searching for eavesdroppers before mentioning the unmentionable—"with our advances stalled in the east and the British and Americans preparing an invasion for this coming spring, the course of the war has changed dramatically."

Canaris was surprised. For Schellenberg, this was an uncharacteristically frank observation. Others had been arrested for making similar "defeatist" remarks. "On this we are somewhat in agreement," said Canaris softly.

"But even more important," Schellenberg continued, dabbing his napkin to his lips, "if we had this atomic bomb, the war would be over."

"Please tell me, Walter," Canaris said. "How does a weapon that will never be used end the war?"

Schellenberg smiled. "The proposed invasion would be, of course, unthinkable. Knowing that we had the potential to devastate any invading army, the Allies would not dare make the attempt. Their plans would have to be abandoned."

"And the Russians?"

"Retreat or be obliterated."

"And what if the Allies decided to test our resolve? What would we do then?"

"Then we would be forced into a more concrete

demonstration." Schellenberg's lips curled in a cruel smile. "The destruction of Moscow would be a marvelous object lesson and one that very few—not even the British and Americans—would cry over."

"So, the unusable weapon might be used after all," said Canaris, with no hint of censure.

"Only under the most extreme provocation. You must remember that the Russians are receiving much of the information about this weapon through their network of agents. What a catastrophe it would be if Stalin got his hands on such a thing!"

Canaris nodded in agreement. His hatred of Russia and bolshevism was as well known as his predilection for things English.

"If we had the bomb," said Schellenberg confidently, "even if we both had the bomb, the Allies would be forced into a negotiated peace."

Sipping his coffee, Canaris said, "A very interesting scenario, Walter. There would be concessions on either side, but the important thing is that the Thousand Year Reich would be firmly established as the dominant power in Europe. We would control the continent from the North Sea to the Urals." He could not keep his cup from trembling as he placed it on his saucer. "And our Führer would rule the continent unopposed."

"Exactly," said Schellenberg, noting that the admiral's color seemed a little more gray than usual.

"Let me ask you something, Walter. And I don't want you to misunderstand me. I do not in any way blame you personally for what happened."

Schellenberg's eyes narrowed. "Yes." He gulped nervously.

"Why did the SS wait so long to pick up Bohr? If he is everything that you tell me he is—the most knowledgeable man in the world in this rather mysterious science of atomistics—why did we not arrest him in 1940? Why did we not force him to divulge his secrets? Perhaps," said Canaris with a slick smile, "we could then be enjoying a vacation in the Bavarian Alps and this mess of a war would be over."

"Then, we had no need for such a weapon."

"But we were permitting our scientists to conduct research in this area?"

"Yes, of course. And our scientists—as is usual in such things—were far ahead of any other nation in the search for these atomic secrets. The German mind is far superior in such technical matters. We needed no help from anyone. We expelled the Jews, who only contaminated our research. We didn't need this Danish scientist to do our work for us."

"What happened?" interrupted Canaris. "Why do we need him now?" He knew what had happened but enjoyed playing the innocent to see how much Schellenberg knew.

"Somewhere along the line," Schellenberg began, "perhaps because technical expertise was needed elsewhere, or perhaps because of the Führer's indifference, the program was emasculated. Only a few researchers were left to do the immense work that is required in a project of this nature."

"And they have failed?"

"No!" shot back Schellenberg. "They did not fail." He struggled to regain his composure. Canaris was the only man who could upset him so. "This *small* research team, working beyond endurance, made some minor miscalculation that has led them astray. As in any mathematical calculation, even a small mistake in any area of computation can have immense consequences to the accuracy of the conclusion."

"Of course," said Canaris, hiding his smile behind his napkin.

"What remains now is simply to backtrack and discover where the computational error was made."

"Sounds simple enough."

Schellenberg's face registered his uncertainty. "Perhaps," he said, "but it will take time. Dr. Vogler at the Kaiser Wilhelm Institute has informed me that Bohr's participation could have appreciably shortened the time it will take to discover this error."

Canaris pushed his cup aside, signaling that the breakfast meeting was almost over. "Too bad, Walter," he said. "It seems that you have missed your chance to win the war all by yourself."

Inside Schellenberg was seething. He wanted to grab Canaris by the lapels of his double-breasted navy jacket and accuse him of complicity. He—or someone in his organization—had leaked word to the Allies that Bohr was about to be picked up. Schellenberg was sure of that. The Abwehr was teeming with traitors and defeatists. Since the early days of the war—no, he thought angrily, even before war—the organization that was supposedly dedicated to the security of the Reich had bungled and fumbled its way from one misadventure to another. Even though the Gestapo had uncovered the complicity of several Abwehr agents—at that moment Canaris's deputy, Colonel Hans Oster, was confined to house arrest in Dresden—the admiral himself had somehow managed to avoid falling into the Gestapo's net.

Schellenberg eyed him coldly, as Canaris gestured to the headwaiter. Soon, Schellenberg thought, your day will come. One hour in the basement of Gestapo headquarters and you will tell us everything we want to know.

Canaris turned his attention back to his breakfast companion. "Now that it is too late, Walter, what do—"

"I didn't say it was too late," snapped Schellenberg, his cool facade crumbling.

Canaris' eyes widened. "I thought you said—"

"That Bohr had escaped? Yes"—Schellenberg smiled, his face wolfish in anticipation of the admiral's distress—"but it seems that the good professor was in too much of a hurry to escape our hospitality."

"I don't understand."

"It seems that he has left behind all of his notes and papers."

Canaris was outwardly sanguine. "And we have this material in our possession?"

Schellenberg shrugged as if the outcome was certain. "Not yet, but it is merely a matter of time."

The admiral seemed stunned. He struggled to keep his expression calm, but Schellenberg noted the subtle change in his manner.

Canaris forced a smile. "I have every confidence that German science will prevail."

"Of that, my dear Admiral," said Schellenberg casually, "we can both be certain."

November 1943

In November of 1943 Niels Bohr and his son Aage arrived in New York and were immediately incorporated into the most secret project of the war. Bohr's immense contributions to the Manhattan Project were ultimately limited by his lack of commitment to the endeavor. The good professor found it difficult to believe that such an awesome force should ever be unleashed, even against an adversary as vile as Hitler.

Many of his colleagues found his manner and attitude unsettling—perhaps because he stirred secret doubts that they too felt—and as a result Bohr was not terribly popular with his fellow scientists.

Although he worked diligently, he proceeded at the same plodding pace that had been his characteristic in Denmark. Others picked his brains, were excited by his theories, and then moved on to complete the work without him.

Practically friendless and concerned for his wife, who had remained in Sweden, in late 1943 Bohr suffered through what was surely the worst winter of his life. His only friend other than his son was Dr. Adam Weissman, an Austrian Jew whom Bohr had known in Europe in the early thirties. Weissman had persisted in befriending Bohr when the others on the project, after failing to find any friendly response, had long since ceased to try.

Weissman had anticipated the outcome of Hitler's madness and escaped the continent in 1936. He had worked on the British atomic project until 1942 and then, along with many other prominent British scientists, had come to America to work on the Manhattan Project.

Weissman and Bohr spent several long wintry eve-

nings in New York playing chess and locked in philosophical discussion as to the morality of what they and the others on the project were doing.

Neither Bohr, the British, nor the Americans were aware that Weissman was a communist who passed along as much information as he could gather to the Soviet consul in New York City.

7

When Lieutenant Nicholas Falzetti, N.Y.P.D., arrived at the scene, the old man had already been out on the eighth floor window-ledge of the Hallmark Hotel for over twenty minutes. Falzetti watched him without comment for a few minutes, then turned to his partner and said simply, "He's gonna do it." The partner, Detective Second Grade Tim O'Connor, shrugged matter-of-factly, knowing that Falzetti's judgment in such matters was infallible. If Falzetti said the man would do it, it was just a matter of time before the man on the ledge went airborne.

They watched the man sway gently on the ledge like a tree rocking in the breeze while two uniformed policemen in the windows on either side talked to him in animated fashion. The man's eyes remained fixed on some distant shore. A voice in the crowd questioned, "Why don't they go out and get him?" and Falzetti looked at O'Connor, who shook his head in disgust. It was against department regulations for a policeman to go out on a ledge with a potential suicide, and this was one of the very few regulations that was faithfully observed. No cop in his right mind would risk his life for someone who might pull him down too.

The gathered crowd fell into hushed silence as if some primeval instinct in their collective being sensed disaster. Falzetti turned away. He lit a cigar and between puffs said to his partner, "Any time now." He too had sensed what the crowd felt.

There was a gasp as the man, eyes still focused on a scene that was far away from the one in which he was the principal player, stepped off the ledge. A woman screamed, but the predominant sound was a hiss as the crowd sucked in its breath and the man plummeted toward the sidewalk.

The sound, like a sack of rotten grapefruit thrown against a wall, was gut wrenching, stomach churning.

Falzetti took a deep breath and made his way through the crowd, which, after recoiling from the sound, had closed ranks around the point of impact. The lieutenant took a brief look to verify the obvious, then turned to one of the uniformed officers who was trying to push the crowd back. "Get some ID off of him. I'll be inside." He motioned to the hotel.

The officer grimaced at the thought, and Falzetti smiled, glad that he didn't have to do it.

The Hallmark Hotel had been built in the 1880s, when this part of lower Manhattan had been somewhat more fashionable than it was today, but in 1943 the hotel was a run-down remnant of what it had been sixty years before.

Passing through the heavy front doors Falzetti noted the worn carpeting, faded paint, and generally shabby appearance of the front lobby. As he walked across the lobby to the front desk an elevator opened to reveal a rather gaudily dressed young woman. She stepped into the lobby, adjusting the shoulder straps of a tight-fitting dress, then noticed Falzetti and made a face.

"Evening, Florence," he said politely. "How's business this evening?"

"Christ, Falzetti," she said, "didn't you retire yet?"

Falzetti ignored her and went over to the desk, where a potbellied, bald-headed man sporting a thin mustache across a large upper lip was reading the *Daily News*. He looked up as Falzetti approached and then with practiced disdain looked back to his paper.

"You the manager?" asked Falzetti.

"That's right."

"You the one who called the police?"

The man looked up. "Lotta' good that did."

"Could I have your name, please?"

The man studied Falzetti a moment as if he was deciding whether or not to accede to the request. "George Malone," he said finally and turned back to his paper.

Falzetti leaned forward, his elbows on the desk, but just as he was about to say something to the hotel manager the elevator door opened again and a young uniformed patrolman stepped into the lobby. "Lieutenant?" he said tensely. "I think you'd better come upstairs."

Falzetti turned to face the patrolman, and Malone, his interest suddenly piqued, stood up to get a better look.

"What is it?" asked the lieutenant.

"We found a body up on the eighth floor."

Falzetti pursed his lips and turned to Malone. "Nice place you run here, Mr. Malone—dead people all over the place."

Malone sat down and returned his attention to the sports page of the *News*.

"What's your name, son?" Falzetti asked the patrolman as they went up in the elevator.

"Powers, Lieutenant. Kevin Powers."

"Johnny Powers's kid up at the Twenty-first?"

Powers smiled. "That's my uncle. My dad's a sergeant at the Hundred Twenty-second on Staten Island."

Falzetti chuckled. "Runs in the family."

"I graduated from the academy with your son Frankie. How's he doin'?"

"He's with the Eighty-second Airborne. I had a letter from him two weeks ago. According to him he's having a great time chasing after English girls."

"I believe it," said Powers.

As they continued toward the eighth floor Falzetti fell into silence, his mind on that early summer day in 1942 when his son Frank had graduated from the Police Academy on the third floor of the 84th Precinct in Brooklyn. More than two hundred of the three hundred members of that class were now serving in the armed forces.

"How'd you beat the draft?" asked Falzetti absently.

Powers blushed. "Four kids."

"Jeez, you Irish are something."

The young man laughed. "My wife's Italian."

"That doesn't surprise me either."

They walked across the hall to the eighth floor room, where Falzetti found another young patrolman standing in the middle of the room as if afraid to touch anything.

"This is Dan Winston, said Powers. "He's my partner."

Falzetti nodded an acknowledgment and looked around. There was a double bed against one wall and a dresser and two large stuffed chairs badly in need of reupholstering. Directly across from the front door, a window was wide open, curtains flying in the draft. The bathroom door, to the left, was also wide open.

It was easy to see that the Hallmark had once been a much finer establishment than it was today. The room was large, with high ceilings and tall windows that would admit plenty of light and a good view of the city.

Falzetti went to the open window. "This the one he went out?"

"Yes, sir," said Winston. "He climbed out and went down the ledge five or six feet to the left."

Falzetti stuck his head out. The ledge below the window was less than a foot wide, and Falzetti shuddered at the thought of a man balancing on that precarious foothold. On the street below he saw the antlike remnants of the crowd that had gathered and the flashing lights of a police ambulance. Looking out across lower Broadway, he noted with some satisfaction that the city seemed brighter since the wartime dimout had been partially rescinded on November 1. Unmasked traffic lights, shrouded for almost two years, now seemed unnaturally radiant, but the dark mass to the north that was Washington Square Park showed that the city had not yet fully repealed the wartime restrictions.

He took a deep breath of the nighttime air and pulled his head back inside the room. "What about the other guy?" he asked Powers.

"In here," said Powers, leading him to a doorway on the right side of the room. "The door was closed when we got here, and we didn't realize there was another room. Thought it was a closet."

The room, although smaller than the outer room, was still fairly large. There was a double bed, a dresser, and a stuffed chair next to a window. On the chair, his tie loose, shirt open at the collar, sleeves rolled up, sat the dead man. His head, rolled to one side, rested on the back of the chair. His jacket lay neatly on the bed.

If not for the dark bloodstains on the head of the chair, he might have been sleeping.

Falzetti moved behind the man and bent forward to look closely at his head. Just behind the left ear he saw the small entry hole. Around the dark hole and congealed blood were the dull red marks of powder burns. "Small caliber. Close range," he said to no one in particular. He turned to the two officers. "You see the gun around here?"

Both officers shook their heads.

Falzetti looked beside and behind the chair. Nothing. "There a phone in here?" he asked.

"No," said Powers.

"Somebody—you, Winston—go downstairs. Tell the M.E. to get up here."

Winston nodded and left.

Falzetti turned to Powers. "What do you think happened here, Kevin?"

Powers looked around the room, hands on hips. He shrugged. "Double suicide? Murder-suicide?"

"Where's the gun?"

"Maybe the jumper had it on him."

"Good point. That would mean the jumper killed the guy in the bedroom and then went out the window."

Powers nodded and continued to watch Falzetti, who went around the room apparently taking in everything as he spoke.

"You talk to anybody on this floor who heard anything?"

Powers smiled. "This place cleared out like the Japs had landed at Battery Park, Lieutenant." He shook his head. "You know what kind of place we're in. When they heard police sirens, it was flushed like the sewer it is."

"You know Blond Florence?"

"The hooker?"

"Right. I saw her come down in the elevator a few minutes before you did."

"I'll talk to her," said Powers. "I know where she works. Maybe she heard something."

"Maybe. Talk to some of the other hookers on your beat too. Somebody might have heard something."

"Sure thing, Lieutenant," said Powers happily.

In New York City it was unusual for a patrolman to be asked to participate in anything more than street crime. The patrolman was expected to be first on the scene of any crime, make sure that no evidence was disturbed, and then, when the Detective Division arrived, go away quietly. Powers, however, knew of Falzetti's reputation. The older man was a good cop but also a teacher, who liked to work with and train young policemen.

Falzetti, in fact, had been a teacher at the Police Academy for five years in the late 1930s. He was now fifty-one years old, his thick, dark hair graying slightly at the temples. He kept himself reasonably in shape with regular workouts at the police gym, but no amount of exercise could prevent the thickening around the middle. He was of average height yet carried himself in such a way that he appeared taller than he was. As a young man he had been considered handsome, but now, after twenty-six years of police work that had given him an expression of perpetual cynicism, no one ever thought of him as being anything other than hard.

Powers watched him carefully as he went around the room. The patrolman hoped to trade in his white shield someday soon for the gold shield of a detective, and he knew that Falzetti could help him. He waited, saying nothing unless he was asked, observing the older man.

Falzetti turned to face the patrolman. "If this had happened in Queens or in Staten Island," he said, "we'd have people lining up to tell us what they saw or heard." He shrugged. "Manhattan . . . everybody disappears . . . nobody knows nothin'."

Followed by Powers, he went back into the other room and picked up an overcoat that lay across the bed. "Close that window, will you, Kevin? It's freezing in here," he said, holding the coat up by the collar, weighing it the way a butcher would weigh a chicken. He winked at the patrolman and patted the outside pocket of the coat. Taking a handkerchief, he reached inside the pocket of the coat and removed a revolver. "Smith & Wesson, twenty-two caliber," he said after a brief look. "Looks like this is the baby that did in our friend in the other room." He sniffed the barrel. "Been fired recently."

Falzetti dropped the revolver back into the coat pocket and draped the coat across the bed.

Just then patrolman Winston returned. "M.E.'s here," he said.

"Hello, Nick," said the new arrival.

Falzetti nodded. "Frank. Busy night."

Frank Downes sighed in response. Downes was the medical examiner and seemed ten years older than his actual fifty-five years. He was reed thin and had large bulbous eyes protruding from a sunken face. "I'm getting too old for this kinda work, Nick."

Falzetti pointed to the other room and Downes wearily made his way through the door. Falzetti stood in the doorway while Downes looked at the dead man.

"At least," said Downes, "this won't be as messy as the bag of strawberry preserves we just scraped off the sidewalk."

Detective O'Connor entered the outer room, holding up a large brown envelope. "I've got the jumper's ID and personals in here, Nick. I thought you might want to take a look at them."

Falzetti took the package from O'Connor. "You talk to anybody downstairs?" he asked.

O'Connor nodded. "Yeah. The janitor and some sad excuse they have for a bellboy. They don't know nothin'."

O'Connor was in his late fifties and had been a cop for well over thirty years. He had a round, red face and light-colored, thinning hair. Around his waist he carried over forty years worth of good beer. Although he had ten more years on the force than Falzetti, one escapade after another had kept him from rising above his rank of Second Grade Detective. There were some who whispered that if it hadn't been for the manpower shortages in the department caused by the war, he would already have been forced into retirement.

Reaching inside the envelope, Falzetti removed a bloodstained leather wallet. He opened the wallet and, seeing no money, looked at O'Connor, who shrugged innocently. "Was empty when the uniform gave it to me, Nick. Honest."

Falzetti returned his gaze to the wallet and read from a driver's license. "Dr. Adam Weissman, West One Hundred Thirteenth Street."

"That's up near Columbia," said O'Connor. "Maybe he's a professor or something up there."

Falzetti nodded, then removed a stiff, yellow card from the wallet and held it close to his face, squinting at the fine print. "U.S. Army," he said softly, handing the card to Kevin Powers, whose eyes bugged in amazement. "Ever see anything like that?" asked Falzetti.

Powers looked at the card, turning it over to read both sides. "Security-clearance card of some kind," he said and began to read aloud. "This card authorizes Dr. Adam Weissman to enter military restricted areas one through thirty-five."

"What do you think we should do now?" asked Falzetti.

O'Connor started to speak, but Falzetti silenced him with a look, and they waited for the patrolman to answer.

Kevin Powers looked at the card a few more times before he answered. He seemed nervous. "I think," he said, "that we should call the FBI."

Falzetti made a clicking sound with his cheek and gave Powers a wink. "Tim," he said, turning to O'Connor, "go downstairs and call the FBI office. Ask for Special-Agent in Charge Brownmiller. If he's not there, leave a message for him to get in touch with me back at the station."

As O'Connor left, Downes came out of the smaller

room. "Dead less than an hour," he said. "Close range, small bore, death instantaneous."

"I know that already, Frank."

Downes chuckled. "You're so hard to please, Nick." He shrugged. "Maybe I'll have more for you later."

Other plainclothes police had arrived, and the bright light of flash photography danced from the other room.

One of the men was applying black powder to the doorknob of the door to the smaller room. "Hey, Nick," he called. "Am I gonna find your prints on this door?"

Powers looked guiltily towards Falzetti.

Falzetti grinned. "It was either that, Sam, or go out on the ledge and come in through the window. I knew you'd be pissed, but I'm afraid of heights."

"I'm just wasting my time," sighed Sam as he kept dusting the knob.

"What's the difference? In seventeen years of dusting for prints, did anything you ever came up with lead to an arrest?"

"Keep it up, Nick. Just keep it up. My wife's cookin' a lasagna for Friday night. You think you're gonna taste any of it?"

"I'll be good, Sam. I promise."

"My daughter Kay is gonna be there. You better be good."

Falzetti forced a smile and turned away with a sigh. Sam Giovanni's daughter was twenty-eight years old, and on the last three occasions when he had been invited to the Giovanni's for dinner, the daughter had been there. Kay's husband had been killed in North Africa, and the burden of that loss showed in her face.

"Tell you what you can do, Sam," said Falzetti. "There's a revolver in that coat on the bed. Why don't you see if you can get anything from that."

Sam looked at him with a hint of mock disgust on his face. "That's probably got your prints on it too."

Falzetti shrugged.

Sam looked as if he was about to lecture his friend on the disadvantages of touching evidence before it had been dusted for prints. Instead he nodded and said, "Let's take a look at it."

As Falzetti watched Sam work he struggled with his impression that dinners at Giovanni's were not quite so casual as he had first imagined. Lately Kay was always there. She tried to be pleasant, but it was obvious that she was there only because her parents insisted. Kay was still slim and youthful, but her tragedy was like an open sore that oozed gloom.

Sam's wife, Julie, always insisted that Kay sit on the couch with Nick while Julie cleaned up after dinner. But usually after a few abortive attempts at conversation, Kay excused herself to go help her mother in the kitchen, leaving Sam and Nick to talk about the war and their favorite topic, police work.

Falzetti had been widowed in 1938 when a drunk driver hit his wife as she was returning from a movie with two friends. One of the other women was still in a wheelchair. The thought of his wife and the evening she had been killed still left his eyes brimming with tears six years later.

"Clean as a whistle," said Sam, snapping Falzetti from his reverie.

"Nothing?" said Falzetti, taking the weapon from Giovanni and inspecting it as though he might see something that the print-man had missed.

"Not a blessed thing. Must've wiped it clean before he put it in his pocket."

Falzetti pondered that for a moment and handed the weapon back to Giovanni. "I'm going downstairs," he said, "to talk with the manager."

At the door he was intercepted by Kevin Powers. "Was I right, Lieutenant?"

"About what?"

"About this being murder-suicide."

The lieutenant patted him lightly on the arm. "Yes, son, I think you were. Looks like the jumper shot the guy in the other room, put the gun in his coat pocket, and then went out the window." He added, "Good job."

Powers smiled as if he had known it all along.

As soon as Falzetti exited the elevator and stepped out into the lobby, Detective O'Connor approached and said quietly, "Nick, I've got an old man over here who claims he saw the whole thing from the street. I don't know if he saw anything important or if he just wants to talk with somebody, y'know?"

Falzetti looked over O'Connor's shoulder at the old man, who wore a rumpled wool overcoat and cradled a small white dog in his arms. The old man, in his seventies, round-faced and with a fringe of white hair around his balding pate, smiled encouragingly when he saw Falzetti looking in his direction.

"You want me to take his statement and get rid of him?" asked O'Connor. "Or do you want to talk with him?" When Falzetti hesitated, O'Connor added, "He seems pretty insistent."

Falzetti sighed. "Okay, I'll talk with him."

The two policemen walked over to where the man stood.

"Mr. Glassman," said O'Connor, "this is Lieutenant Falzetti."

Falzetti nodded. "Mr. Glassman."

"Glass*baum*," corrected the old man. "Nathan Glassbaum and this is Strudel." He held up his dog, and Falzetti, restraining a smile, motioned to a grouping of chairs off to one side of the lobby. Both men sat down.

"Now, Mr. Glassbaum, why don't you tell me what you saw."

"Well," began Glassbaum, his accent a thick mixture of New York and central Europe, "I was out taking Strudel for his evening walk. We usually go across Houston Street and down Broadway to Prince Street and then back up Lafayette Street, but tonight for some reason Strudel felt like going the other way. Sometimes he does that, you know." He stroked his dog. "You never know what he's going to decide. Keeps me guessing." He looked up at Falzetti, his face one huge smile. "Do you have a dog, Lieutenant?"

"No, I'm afraid not."

The old man shook his head. "You should get one. You'll never be lonely if you have a dog around the house."

Falzetti's eyes narrowed, and for one crazy moment he wondered if Glassbaum knew about his wife. He shook that thought aside. "Could we get back to your story?"

"Sure. I'm sorry. I do tend to get carried away. Anyway, we were walking up Broadway when Strudel stops and decides to lift his leg on a lamp post. So I just happened to look up." He leaned forward and whispered so the dog wouldn't hear. "He likes his privacy. Sometimes if I'm not thinking and I look at him, he won't go 'til I look away." He shrugged. "He's funny like that."

Falzetti, struggling to suppress a sigh, said nothing. He already regretted his detour.

"So—back to my story. I look up, and there he was out on the ledge, shuffling away from the open window. I think I must have been the first person to see him. I didn't see him climb out the window, but he must have just come out before I saw him."

"Why do you say that?"

Glassbaum thought for a moment, then said, "When I saw him he was still close to the open window. Then he moved away from it very quickly. I remember being afraid that he was going to fall right then. When he got maybe five or six feet from the window, he stopped. He never moved from that spot until he . . . fell." He smiled, stroking his dog, waiting for Falzetti to comment.

For a moment Falzetti did not speak. He ran his tongue across his teeth and started to get up. "Thank you for taking the time to talk with me, Mr. Glassbaum," he finally said.

The smile slipped from Glassbaum's face. "But I'm not finished yet. What I wanted to tell you was that I saw the other man."

"The other man?"

"The one who was in the room with him."

Falzetti's eyes narrowed in disbelief, but he sat back down. "You saw him?"

"Yes," said Glassbaum, his face alive with excitement, "and that's the reason I wanted to talk with you. I overheard the policemen on the street talking—" He made a face, then smiled. "I'm a Nosey Parker. Everybody in my building tells me I know everybody else's business." His face grew stern. "But I don't gossip—I don't meddle."

"I'm sure that's true, Mr. Glassbaum, but could you—"

"Okay. Sorry. I talk too much. Anyway I heard them say that the man on the ledge shot the man in the room and then went out on the ledge." He shook his head. "It couldn't happen that way."

"Why not?"

"Because I saw the man in the room after the other man was out on the ledge."

"How did you see him?"

"Simple," said Glassbaum, chuckling. "He stuck his head out the window right after the other one went out. At first I thought he was going to go out after him, but he just pointed at the man, then looked down at the street and went back inside."

"Pointed?"

"Yes, like this—" Glassbaum raised his right arm straight out and pointed at Falzetti. "The man on the ledge put his arms up across his face as if he couldn't bear to look at the other one."

"Did he have anything in his hand—the man who pointed?"

"I don't think so. I couldn't tell."

Falzetti leaned forward. "Are you sure you saw this man at that particular window? Maybe it was some other window. From street level to the eighth floor is a pretty good distance, Mr. Glassbaum."

"My eyes are good," said Glassbaum. "My feet—that's another story, but I got eyes like a hawk." He pronounced the last word as if he were clearing his throat. "I wear glasses to read but not for anything else. You could test me if you like. Go ahead."

"That's not necessary, Mr. Glassbaum. I'm sure that—"

"Go ahead, test me. I'll show you what good eyes can do."

With a sigh, Falzetti looked around the lobby. He spotted a sign between the two elevators. "How about that one," he said, pointing.

Glassbaum chuckled. "Says, 'No Pets Allowed in Rooms.'" He petted Strudel apologetically. "That's too close," he said. "I know blind men who could read that one."

Falzetti looked back toward the main desk. "How about that one above the desk?" he said.

Glassbaum squinted. "Oy," he said, "now you're talking." His lips moved as he read silently. "Says, 'Not responsible for articles left in rooms.'" He shrugged. "Then there's something underneath that I can't make out."

Falzetti couldn't make it out either. "That's very good," he said. "Your eyes are very good."

Glassbaum touched a finger to his right temple. "The brain is still pretty good too. Do you want I should describe this man to you?"

"If you could. It might be helpful."

"Well, he was very young." Glassbaum smiled. "Although to me anything under sixty is young."

"How young do you think he was?"

"No more than thirty—and a soldier."

Falzetti masked his surprise. "Are you sure?"

"He was wearing a uniform—an army uniform."

Doubt crept across Falzetti's face, and Glassbaum saw it instantly. "You want I should read another sign?"

"No, Mr. Glassbaum. Can you tell me anything else about this man?"

Now it was Glassbaum's turn to look puzzled. "You mean this isn't a good description of the dead man in the hotel room?"

"I'm afraid not."

Glassbaum smiled. "Interesting. Now we've got a third man."

Falzetti nodded. "Anything else you remember about him?"

"Well, I said he was young. His hair was light brown—blond maybe. He looked thin—y'know, slim—like he was in good condition."

"Would you recognize him if you saw him again?"

"I said my eyes were good—I didn't say superhuman." He laughed at his little joke. "Forgive me," he said. "I'm not sure. I mean I don't know if I could recognize features other than what I told you."

"Young, blond, slim?"

"Yes, and wearing a uniform."

Falzetti nodded. "Can you think of anything else? Did you hear a shot, for instance?"

Glassbaum shook his head. "I don't think so."

Both men got up from their seats.

"So tell me, Lieutenant—I was some help? I always want to be a help to the police."

"Yes, Mr. Glassbaum. You've been a great help, and I thank you." Falzetti took Mr. Glassbaum's address and told him that he might get back to him. He shook hands with the old man and even petted his dog before going to the main desk to talk with the manager.

"Mr. Malone," he said.

Malone turned, his face a mask of contempt, to the policeman. "How long are all these cops gonna be around? Can't you just drag that stiff outa here?"

Falzetti made his smile as pleasant as possible. "I realize, Mr. Malone, that your business is probably a little slow because of this incident, but we'll try to get out of your way as quickly as possible. I just have to ask you a few questions."

"Don't ask me any questions," said Malone. "I don't know nothin'."

Falzetti's eyes grew hard, and when he spoke again his voice was colder. "I have a feeling, Malone, that not much goes on in this hotel that you don't know about."

"I mind my own business. I don't know nothin'."

"Tell me about the third man."

"Third man?" Malone's voice was filled with disdain. "I don't know what you're talking about."

"The soldier, the man who was with the two older men."

Malone shrugged. "I told you. I don't know nothin'."

Falzetti leaned on the counter, moving closer to Malone. He spoke in a very soft voice. "We've got four options here, Mr. Malone. Four choices."

"Choices?"

"Yeah. The first one is—I can call the Fire Department and inform them that this hotel does not appear to have a fire extinguisher on each floor. That's a violation of the city fire safety ordinance."

Malone stood up, pointing. "I've got a fire inspection certificate right here on the wall, if you wanna look at it."

Falzetti shrugged. "For twenty-five dollars and the right inspector you can buy the certificate—I'm talking about a real inspection here. One where the inspector actually goes upstairs."

Malone was silent.

"The second option is even simpler. I can station a patrolman on the street right outside your door. That ought to cut into the little bits of extra money you've been picking up."

"Listen," said Malone savagely. "I pay what I'm supposed to pay—I'm talking about cops too. You know how it works. We're all in the same business." He saw Falzetti's eyes widen in anger. "So maybe you don't take money, Falzetti, but didn't you ever take a little graft. A free hamburger? A cup of coffee? An apple from the corner fruit stand? A free piece from the neighborhood hooker?"

"The third option," said Falzetti, ignoring Malone's remarks, "is the simplest of all. I come around behind your desk and break your jaw."

Malone sat down, his shoulders slumped. "What's the fourth option?"

Falzetti smiled. "Who was the third man?"

"I don't know—I'm serious."

"There were three men up in that room?"

"That's right."

"What do you know about them?"

"Nothin'."

Falzetti sighed.

"I'm serious, Falzetti. We get all kinds of people in here. This ain't the Waldorf—or hadn't you noticed? I don't ask for references. We get drunks, derelicts, hookers, and queers. As far as I'm concerned the two old guys was queers."

"What makes you say that?"

"C'mon, Lieutenant. Some guy with an accent that sounds like he just got off the boat from Transylvania, tells you his name is Mr. Smith and he is expecting a Mr. Brown, who turns out to look like another refugee. What would you think?"

"Had they ever been here before?"

Malone made a face. "Coupla times maybe."

Feeling as if he were extracting teeth, Falzetti asked, "When?"

"Last time was about a week ago. Another time maybe six months ago and maybe one another time—I'm not sure."

"Think about it."

"I think so," said Malone with a shrug. "About a year ago. Maybe."

"So they were here at six-month intervals and then twice within a week."

Malone shrugged. "Yeah, I guess so."

"What about the third guy—the soldier. Had he ever been here before?"

"Not that I can remember. The first guy—Smith—came in with him tonight at about six-thirty. They took the room and said that their friend would be along soon and that I should send him up." He smiled, displaying rows of yellowed, uneven teeth. "I figured the two old boys got tired of dorking each other and found a young stud to do it for them."

"Did they sign the register?"

"Register? I told you this ain't the Waldorf. They pay for the room in advance. I don't ask any questions about what they wanna do in it."

"Describe the soldier for me."

Malone grinned. "I didn't get much of a look at him. He kinda stayed out of the way—like he was embarrassed or something. He kept his face turned away from the desk."

"General description would be fine."

"Well, he was young, good build." He shrugged. "That's about it."

"What color was his hair?"

"Hard to say—he was wearing a cap. Blond maybe—light color anyway."

"Could you tell what outfit he was with?"

"I don't know anything about that stuff. He was an officer though. That much I know."

"Did you see him leave?"

Malone shook his head. "No. He could have gone out the back way, or when I went outside to look at the guy up on the ledge."

Falzetti thought for a minute. "If you think of anything else, call me," he said. "I may be back to talk to you again."

"I'm not going anywhere," said Malone without any discernable trace of enthusiasm.

8

After leaving the Hallmark Hotel, Lieutenant Nicholas Falzetti stopped for a quick dinner on Mulberry Street. After his conversation with George Malone he made sure to pay for his meal. Then he made his way back to Police Headquarters on Centre Street.

Erected between 1901 and 1909, the Police Headquarters building was a replica of the Old Bailey in London. With its massive granite pillars and domed cupola it was probably one of the most interesting pieces of architecture in New York. The five-story beaux-arts structure occupied the entire block between Grand and Broome streets, dominating the dividing line between Little Italy and Chinatown.

Grandiose as the building was on the outside, the interior was as mundane as the most ordinary structure in the city.

Falzetti mounted the stairs to the second-story detectives' squad room and entered the large, dingy space. The room was painted in sickly green and ghastly beige, but Falzetti had long since not bothered to notice. There were thirty-two desks grouped in pairs, back to back, and several desks standing alone. In deference to his rank and seniority, Falzetti occupied a solitary desk in a corner of the room. It wasn't an office, but it was as close to privacy that anyone below the rank of captain ever got.

The activity level bordered on the incredible. Detectives sat around the room in chairs, on desktops; eating sandwiches, drinking coffee; yelling at suspects, screaming at each other; wandering in, dashing out.

Falzetti had learned long ago to tune out all of it.

He had just sat down at his desk, lit a cigar, and started to hunt among the disorderly stack of papers in his file drawer for a form to make his report when one of the other detectives called out to him.

"Nick! M.E. is on the phone. Line three."

Falzetti nodded a thanks and picked up the phone. "Whattaya got, Frank?" he asked.

"Not much," said Frank Downes. "I haven't heard from ballistics, but I sent them the slug from the guy's brain. Looks like it came from the pistol you found in the other room."

"Anything else?"

"Guy's name was Theodore Marcovic. He was fifty-five years old and lived on Rutledge Street, which is in the Williamsburg section of—"

"I know where it is," said Falzetti, interrupting him. "You could have got that from his driver's license, Frank."

Downes laughed. "No, I got it from one of your detectives, who got it from his driver's license." He grew serious. "Like I said, there's not much."

"How about the jumper?"

"Here I might have something."

"Like what?"

"Well, I did a blood analysis to determine if he was drunk—"

"And?"

"I found heavy traces of some kind of drug in his blood."

"Like what?"

"Gimme a break, Nick. I'm only back in the lab a little over an hour. We're still running more tests."

Falzetti didn't bother with apologies. "Could it be some kind of medication?"

"Could be."

"But you don't think so."

"The guy is loaded with whatever it is."

Falzetti thought about that for a moment, moving his cigar from one side of his mouth to the other. "Get back to me, Frank, as soon as you have anything else."

"You talk with the FBI yet?"

"No. I just got back to headquarters a minute before you called. Why?"

"Two agents arrived right after you left. Followed me around like watchdogs."

As Downes talked Falzetti leafed through the messages on his desk. There at the top was a note to call the New York FBI office. "I guess I'll call them now, Frank. Thanks for getting back to me so soon."

He was dialing the phone when he spotted Tim O'Connor entering the room. When O'Connor waved and came in his direction, Falzetti hung up the phone. "Find anything?" he asked.

O'Connor shook his head. "Could be a robbery. Both stiffs had empty wallets."

Falzetti sighed. Most of the murder victims in New York City arrived at the morgue with empty wallets. Someone along the line, often the first officer on the scene, relieved the victim of any cash he might possess. It was doubly frustrating to Falzetti, not only for the implications about the integrity of the police force, but also because it often clouded the motive for the killing.

"Did you ever know anybody to jump out of an eight-story window because he got robbed?"

O'Connor laughed at his own foolishness. "Maybe the guy heard the gunshot in the other room and climbed out on the ledge to get away from the killer."

"So why didn't he come in when we arrived?"

A blank expression came over O'Connor's face, and Falzetti picked up the phone again. As he dialed he watched O'Connor wrestle with his last question.

It was O'Connor who had brought Falzetti the news of his wife's accident and had gone with him to the hospital to face that long terrible night. When the doctor finally appeared in the waiting room, it was O'Connor who had burst into tears when the doctor began with, "I'm sorry, Mr. Falzetti but . . ."

Nick Falzetti had never forgotten that.

The voice on the other end of the phone snapped him out of his memories.

"Federal Bureau of Investigation."

"Lieutenant Falzetti, N.Y.P.D. I'd like to speak with Special Agent Brownmiller please."

"I'll connect you."

Falzetti waited.

"Nick," boomed a voice in his ear, "how are you?"

"Fine, Tom. You?"

"Just great."

Falzetti massaged his temples. He was somewhat wary of such pleasantries from the FBI. It usually meant they wanted something. "I guess you got my message about the business at the Hallmark."

"Yes. Thanks for bringing us in so quickly on that, Nick."

"When I saw that security-clearance card, I figured—"

Brownmiller interrupted him. "This is a hot one, Nick. Some of the brass in D.C. are crapping in their pants over this."

"What's up?"

"This Weissman was working on a government research project and the people he worked for are really disturbed about his death."

"That's too bad."

"Nick, I want you to turn over to me everything you've got on this case—personal effects, the weapon, any documents, articles of clothing—everything."

"Everything?"

"Yes. The bureau will even take responsibility for the disposal of the bodies."

Falzetti was getting a slight headache. He pinched

the bridge of his nose between a thumb and forefinger. "I don't get it," he said.

Brownmiller was still being pleasant, but his tone was becoming more authoritative. "You can forget about this one. The bureau will take over. It's our ball game now."

"I've got two men dead in my precinct," said Falzetti. "One of them murdered, the other a suicide, and you tell me it's your ball game."

"This comes directly from Washington, Nick." The genial tone had all but disappeared. "If you like, I can give the police commissioner a call."

Falzetti was silent.

"I don't mean to lean on you, Nick—we've always had superior cooperation from you in the past—but this is our case now."

"You mean you don't want me to do another thing on this case—just forget it?"

"That's right. As far as you're concerned, it never happened. Don't let it bother you. It's a national security matter."

Falzetti shrugged in resignation. "That's good enough for me," he said. "I'll send over everything we've got."

"Thanks, Nick," said Brownmiller, the pleasant tone returning. "I appreciate it."

Forcing a laugh, Falzetti said, "Thank *you*. That's the easiest case I ever got out of my pending file."

After hanging up, Falzetti took the two wallets and placed them in a large brown envelope. He sealed it and wrote the address of the FBI office and Tom Brownmiller's name on the front.

"Tim?" he said and O'Connor looked up from his seat. "Get a uniform to run this over to the FBI office. Tell him to say that everything else will be with the medical examiner."

O'Connor nodded and took the envelope. "Sure thing, Nick."

Falzetti smiled as he watched O'Connor leave with the envelope. "One less problem to worry about," he muttered, but somewhere in his cop's mind he felt a distinct uneasiness.

He shook the feeling aside, relit his cigar, and plunged into the pile of paperwork on his desk.

9

Ernst Kaltenbrunner, chief of the German Security Services, sat behind his desk, sipping his brandy and staring intently as Walter Schellenberg, sitting in the chair in front of him, explained what he and his SD had been up to.

Kaltenbrunner was a giant, well over six feet tall, and with large hands that Admiral Canaris had once called "assassin's paws." His bull neck, prominent chin, and numerous scars gave him a fearsome visage. His tiny eyes, when not clouded by alcohol, could be quite piercing.

It was 11:15 A.M. and Kaltenbrunner was already well on his way to being drunk.

Kaltenbrunner didn't like Schellenberg. Didn't like his superior intellectual air that often implied that he, Kaltenbrunner, was not really in charge of the vast Reich security system under Heinrich Himmler.

Where was this Schellenberg, he thought, when we had to kick and claw our way in the streets to drag ourselves out of the muck that had been Germany in the twenties? Kaltenbrunner resented the fact that men like Schellenberg, who had played no real part in the struggle, now looked down their noses at the old guard. If it were not for men like me, Kaltenbrunner thought, weaklings like Schellenberg would still be begging for bread in the streets.

"That's fine, Walter," he said, interrupting Schellenberg's explanation. "I understand your zealousness in the matter of this Professor Bohr's scientific papers, but I still want you to inform this office when you take such actions. If it had not been for the inquiry sent to my office by Professor Heisenberg, I would not have known of your interest in this matter or of your requisitioning of what Heisenberg calls,"—he looked at the letter on his desk—"precious radioactive materials."

Schellenberg smiled through clenched teeth. He despised this monstrosity who sat before him like some powerful god. Kaltenbrunner was a dim-witted Austrian who had worked through the Austrian Nazi party for the union with Germany. In 1943 he was appointed by Hitler as second in command to Himmler in the party security machine.

If this is what we are fighting the war for, thought Schellenberg, God help us.

Kaltenbrunner crushed out a cigarette in the solid silver ashtray on his intricately carved desk and immediately lit another. Schellenberg could not help but notice the dark yellow-stained fingers that were an almost perfect match for the grotesquely rotten teeth. Kaltenbrunner consumed, on the average, five packs each day of the foul-smelling Russian cigarettes that were readily available in Germany. Most men in his position used their influence to procure French cigarettes, but Kaltenbrunner preferred the harsh, cutting bite of the Russian brand.

Kaltenbrunner's disgusting breath was legendary in the upper echelons of German society. A man in his position was always invited to private dinners, banquets, shooting weekends in the country, or any of the myriad diversions that upper-class Germans used to distract themselves from the awful dawning truth about the war. Kaltenbrunner's powerful position made it impossible not to invite him to many of these functions, and when he was in attendance, the scramble to avoid sitting next to him was well documented.

Foreign Minister Ribbentrop had once said that the mad avoidance of the seats around Kaltenbrunner was "like a scene from one of those insane American comedies of the 1920s." Himmler had said, "Men would die to stay out of range of Kaltenbrunner's breath," to which his angel, Heydrich, had replied, more in truth than in jest, "Many men have died who were unsuccessful in that endeavor."

But Kaltenbrunner wielded immense power, and few would dare confront him with the obvious. Even Reichsführer Himmler was unable to make Kaltenbrunner visit a dentist. The Führer, grateful for past services, tolerated the decomposing giant and would allow no mention of his distasteful habits on the *Personal-Berichte* that was forwarded to Hitler each year. It was whispered by those who were either very foolish or very brave that the reason for the Führer's tolerance was his own bouts with uncontrollable flatulence that often caused long embarrassed silences at dinner.

Schellenberg had the distasteful task of having to report to Kaltenbrunner's office each morning at eleven. He was forced to smile and pretend to enjoy Kaltenbrunner's brandy and watch the giant drink himself into oblivion. Usually, due to Kaltenbrunner's drunken condition, Schellenberg was able to make a perfunctory report and get on about his business.

But not today.

Schellenberg watched Kaltenbrunner brush away the ashes that had fallen onto the lapels of his jacket and wished that the man would do the same with the dandruff that accumulated around his shoulders. With all these unsavory distractions it was difficult to concentrate on what Kaltenbrunner was saying.

"What I want is a full report on any of these activities," Kaltenbrunner said. "Is that clear?"

Schellenberg nodded. "Absolutely. A full report will be on your desk tomorrow."

Kaltenbrunner smiled, flashing picket rows of yellowed teeth. He enjoyed putting Schellenberg in his place, but he knew there was only so far he could go before the dog bit back.

He also knew what was whispered around the corridors of the RSHA offices in Berlin: that he, Kaltenbrunner, was Schellenberg's boss in name only; that Schellenberg did exactly as he pleased whether Kaltenbrunner approved or not; that Schellenberg ran the Sicherheitsdienst as if it were an autonomous police force not under the general authority of Kaltenbrunner's Reich Security Administration. He also knew that Reichsführer Himmler considered Schellenberg his favorite—the reincarnation of the assassinated Heydrich, whom Himmler had loved as a son. Consequently Kaltenbrunner had to tread carefully in his dealings with Schellenberg, who could easily—and often did—go over his head to the Reichsführer. In Kaltenbrunner's estimation, Schellenberg was oozing with ersatz charm and filled with cunning ambition. Although Schellenberg's professed aim was to eliminate Canaris and bring the Abwehr under the wing of the RSHA, Kaltenbrunner was certain that the younger man was after his job too.

"So tell me again, Walter. What is the importance of this Bohr's papers?"

Explaining the significance of nuclear physics to a moron like Kaltenbrunner, thought Schellenberg, was like explaining Wagner to a Bavarian hare. "It is quite possible that the documents could provide clues to the manufacture of the most powerful weapon ever conceived."

Kaltenbrunner nodded.

"A weapon," went on Schellenberg, "that could destroy Moscow or London in a single blast."

"And these documents could provide such a weapon?"

Schellenberg shrugged. "Perhaps."

"But if the British have this Professor Bohr, won't they be able to build this weapon themselves?"

"I am sure it will take him some time to duplicate his research. Also, I am convinced that if our German scientists had this information at their disposal, they could deal with it much more effectively than the British."

"How do you propose to find these documents, Walter? Denmark may not be a large country, but it will still be immensely difficult to find lost or hidden documents."

"I propose to lead the British to believe that we already have the documents and furthermore that our own research in the area is very far advanced. That's why I needed the radioactive material from the institute at Dahlem."

Kaltenbrunner's eyes narrowed uncertainly. Much of this was beyond his powers of comprehension.

"Everyone knows the invasion is imminent," said Schellenberg. "We even know that it will be in the late spring. It cannot be delayed much beyond then. The Russians are desperate for the second front, and Churchill can't put it off much longer—if he does, Stalin might sue for peace and let the British take their lumps the way the Russians have. If the Allied powers think that we have this atomic bomb, they won't dare put an invasion force on the continent. Even if we can delay the invasion for a month or two, that would make it impractical for them to begin. It would be delayed until 1945. By that time we'd actually have the bomb."

Kaltenbrunner lit another cigarette. "Wouldn't they want more proof than that? Just saying that we had this weapon would hardly be enough."

"I think that we can give them enough clues to make them think that we actually have the bomb or are on the verge of its development."

Kaltenbrunner sat back in his chair, his eyes boring into Schellenberg. "I hope you are right, Walter. I wouldn't want to incur the Führer's wrath on this. After all—if you remember—last year I recommended that this Bohr fellow be placed in detention."

Schellenberg bit his lower lip. Up until a month ago, Kaltenbrunner had been unaware of the existence of the Danish physicist, but now, in typical fashion, he was ensuring that whatever blame was spread around would not fall in his direction.

"Precisely, Herr Direktor," said Schellenberg. "And I myself made the same recommendation to Gestapo Chief Müller, who I am sure relayed our concern to Werner Best in Copenhagen. Unfortunately, Herr Best did not see fit to act upon our recommendation."

Kaltenbrunner and Schellenberg, safely protected, smiled at each other. "Perhaps," said Kaltenbrunner, "our little game with the British will save Best's neck."

"Perhaps," responded Schellenberg, his cheeks beginning to ache from the strain of his forced smile.

10

Friday night dinners at Sam and Julie Giovanni's had become an embarrassing exercise in how not to bring two people together. Ever since Falzetti's wife had been killed, he had been a regular dinner guest at the Giovanni's on whichever Friday or Saturday night the two policemen were able to schedule together.

Lately, the Giovanni's daughter Kay had joined the family for these dinners, and Falzetti had found himself wondering why the young widow had never joined them before. The answer had finally become clear on his last visit when Julie Giovanni had said, "Nick, why don't you and Kay sit by the fire while Sam and I clean up in the kitchen." Sam and Julie had decided that their friend would make a good husband for their daughter.

On this night he looked across the table at Kay, who as usual ate little and said less. On her face was the perpetual look of sorrow, leading Falzetti to wonder if she ever smiled since the news of her husband's death. Or was it merely his presence and the knowledge of her parents' intentions that made her so sad and uncommunicative?

Falzetti remembered how she had looked at her wedding, bright and pretty and full of life. Her groom was a former prizefighter from Jersey City who had waited in line on December 8, 1941, to join the army. He was with the U.S. Army's 1st Division that challenged the Germans at Kasserine Pass in Tunisia. It was the U.S. Army's first real engagement with an experienced German panzer division led by Rommel. The Americans had been routed, and Sam Giovanni's son-in-law had been one of the unlucky ones who did not live to learn from the experience.

Falzetti watched Kay pick at her meal. She had long dark hair, large brown eyes, and a small bump in the middle of her nose. If she would only smile, thought Falzetti, she would be very attractive. Kay was taller than both her parents, and her figure was her strong suit—good breasts, wide hips, and long, well-tapered legs. Sometimes when he watched her walk, Falzetti began to entertain fantasies that maybe Sam and Julie's idea wasn't such a bad one. But then he looked at the sad eyes and came back to reality.

What would he, a fifty-one-year-old cop, gruff and grumpy and set in his ways, do with a very young wife who had two small children?

Falzetti had grown children of his own—two sons and a daughter. The eldest was Nick Jr., thirty, who was a foreman at the Republic factory on Long Island. His job and the fact that he had two kids kept him safe from the draft. Then there was his daughter Jeannie, twenty-eight, married and with two kids of her own. She looked more and more like her mother every day. She lived in Jersey with her husband, who worked at the Newark Ship Yards.

His youngest was Frank, who was twenty-four and a corporal with the 82nd Airborne Division. Both Nick and his son knew that the invasion was coming, and even though Frank never said anything about it in his letters, both knew that the 82nd would be in the thick of it when it came.

After dinner, when Julie was clearing the table and Sam got up to help, Falzetti turned to Kay. "Would you like to go for a walk?"

Kay's eyes widened in near panic, and Falzetti could see how she had dreaded this moment. She looked around helplessly for rescue, but her parents had, of course, disappeared. Finally, her head bobbing spasmodically, she said, "Okay, Nick. If you'd like to."

They got their coats, and Falzetti told Sam that they would be back soon. Sam's face lit up and he raced to the kitchen to tell his wife that Nick and Kay were going for a walk.

Julie came out of the kitchen beaming. "I'll save coffee for you," she said. "I've got cake too."

Without speaking, Falzetti and Kay went down the stairs from the Giovanni's apartment and out into the street.

"Which way?" asked Falzetti as they stood on the sidewalk, neither one looking at the other.

"Doesn't matter," she answered, and they went left toward Hudson Street.

They had walked for almost ten minutes without saying a word before Falzetti finally said, "You still working in that lawyer's office, Kay?"

"Yes, Nick."

Falzetti found himself unable to form the words that he wanted to say. The well organized and coherent speech that he had rehearsed since yesterday eluded him now. Instead he found himself saying, "I think I make you nervous in your mother's house."

"No, you don't, Nick," she lied. "You don't make me nervous."

"Has your mother said anything to you about me?"

She swallowed hard, and he could tell that he wasn't making any of this easier for her. He had planned a bright, cheerful chat that would leave them both smiling and relieved. What had happened? It had been a long time, he thought, since he had made small talk with a pretty girl.

"No, not really," she said finally.

"What I mean to say is that these little family dinners with me along are probably making you wonder what's going on."

She nodded a little.

"I want you to know that I had nothing to do with this," said Falzetti. "I just began to realize last week that your parents had something in mind."

Kay stopped walking and for the first time looked him straight in the eye. "My mother keeps telling me that I need a husband."

"And that I need a wife?"

She smiled a small smile tinged with embarrassment. "That too."

"How old are you, Kay?"

"Twenty-eight."

"I'm fifty-one."

"I know that, Nick."

"I've got a daughter your age."

She nodded without saying anything.

"Right now," Falzetti went on, "it seems like everybody is off fighting this damn war. There are plenty of young men around, but they always seem to be going somewhere."

She nodded again, beginning to understand where he was heading.

"This war is going to be over soon—maybe by this time next year. New York is going to be crawling with young men again, and I've got a feeling that half of them are going to be chasing after you."

She couldn't help the smile that raced across her features. "If you're trying to make me feel better," she said, "it's working."

"Now, me," he said, pointing a finger at his chest. "I need somebody old and fat to take care of me."

Kay actually laughed, and Falzetti could see how lovely she was. Her laughter reminded him of someone else, and Kay must have noticed the sadness in his eyes.

"How long has it been now, Nick, since . . ." Her voice trailed off.

"Six years," he said.

She shook her head. "Does it get any better? Does the pain ever go away?"

He shrugged. "Sure," he lied. "After a while. Time heals everything."

Kay put her arm through his. "Let's go back," she said.

He nodded, looking at her. "Yeah. Let's go back."

December 1943

In early December 1943, after meeting with Stalin and Churchill in what was called the Teheran Confer-

ence, President Roosevelt planned a stopover in Tunisia on his way back to the United States. The president called General Eisenhower at his headquarters in Italy and told the Allied Commander to meet him in Tunis.

When the president arrived, the general was waiting for him in a staff car, and as soon as the president was seated in the backseat of the automobile, he turned to the man at his side and said without preamble, "Well, Ike, you are going to command Overlord."

Ike was stunned. Not that he had not hoped for or expected the appointment, but the actual acquisition of such immense power was a thrill beyond comprehension. For the rest of the day he was able to converse casually with the president about the conduct of the war and even about the American political scene, but his mind was already on the coming campaign in France.

Although the naming of the new Supreme Commander was supposed to be a secret, word of the decision raced through every Allied command headquarters. The news of Eisenhower's appointment was greeted with equal amounts of pleasure, resignation, and shocked disbelief.

Most of the pleasure was on the American side; most of the resignation was on the British; the shocked disbelief came from those who felt that the British general Alan Brooke, chairman of the British chiefs of staff committee, should have been the logical choice to head the invasion forces rather than the relatively inexperienced Eisenhower.

The next day, when Ike returned to his command post in Italy, he found a congratulatory wire awaiting him from General Montgomery, commanding the British Eighth Army in Italy. Also awaiting Eisenhower were the reconnaissance photos that had been taken some days before of the French beaches. Since Rommel had been assigned to "inspect and improve" the coastal defenses on the Western Front in November of 1943, the Allies had noted an almost feverish intensity in the construction of defensive emplacements on the French coast.

Eisenhower turned to his chief of staff, General

Walter Bedell Smith. "Smitty," he said, "I'm going to send you off to England as my advance man. It will be at least a month before I can conclude matters here and begin the business of preparing the invasion. I've decided that Montgomery will also leave early to begin the overall ground forces preparation, but I need someone there whom I can trust to look out for our interests."

11

The periscope broke the surface of the water some five hundred yards off the French coast. Lieutenant Commander Thomas Leiningen of the Royal Navy in command of midget submarine X-132—which was affectionately known to her three-man crew as "Shorty" —placed his right eye against the viewing lens of the scope. Dead ahead the steep cliffs of the Normandy coast rose up out of the sandy beaches.

Squinting against the darkness, Leiningen turned the periscope to the left and then slowly scanned the beach as he brought the scope back to the right.

"Seems quiet," he said, his eye still pressed against the rubber lens cup. "Reduce speed to dead slow and bring her in another two hundred yards."

He watched for a moment or two as the small craft moved silently forward, then turned to the man sitting close by his elbow. "I'm afraid that's about as close as we can take you, Major Bishop. You'll have to do the last few hundred yards on your own."

Bishop looked from the lieutenant commander to the man with the glum expression who sat across from them. "No problem, right, Eric? It's a lovely night for a swim."

Eric—Lieutenant Eric Madsen—forced a grim smile.

Leiningen tried to be helpful. "Like Blackpool in August," he said.

It was in fact, France in December, and the water temperature was forty-seven degrees.

Although he did not relish the thought of a three-hundred-yard swim in freezing water, Madsen, a former officer with the 4th Infantry Regiment of the Sjaelland Division of the Danish army and now assigned to the special reconnaissance unit of Number 7 Commando, was anxious to leave the cramped confines of the midget submarine. He was over six feet tall, with light brown hair and blue eyes. He rarely smiled, and there was little to tempt him now.

Built for a crew of three, the sub held five tonight. The central compartment where the crew operated the craft was only eight feet long, five feet wide, and five feet high, and Madsen noted with displeasure that the sailors were short, selected no doubt to complement the cramped quarters of their tiny vessel.

He had found it almost impossible to move about without banging his head on some protruding valve or pipe; consequently he had spent the long hours of the voyage squatting in what he hoped was an out of the way position.

At the beginning of the journey the air in the vessel had had the aroma of grease and oil. As distasteful as that had been it was infinitely more preferrable to the stale, heavy odor of that air now.

Madsen was beginning to understand the meaning of claustrophobia and looked with pleasure upon whatever awaited him on the beach.

Bishop, on the other hand, seemed comfortable anywhere. He was only slightly shorter than Madsen, with dark, closely cropped hair and a small mustache. As usual, thought Madsen, the discomfort didn't seem to bother the major. Even in the dim light of the compartment, Bishop's eyes were twinkling.

"Let's get at 'em, Eric, my boy," he said, slipping out of the heavy parka that he wore over his black rubber frogman suit.

Madsen almost smiled when he heard himself referred to as "my boy." Englishmen, he thought, like to reduce everything to a diminutive. He had met uncounted numbers of Bobbys, Tommys, Willys, and Johnnys since his escape to England in 1942. As the name "Eric Madsen" seemed to defy conversion, Bishop, who was, at thirty, only two years older than Madsen, had settled for the occasional "Eric, my boy."

Bishop himself was, for reasons never adequately explained, called "Tidy" by those officers who knew him well.

Madsen preferred to call him simply, "Bishop."

They were a team. The Englishman, bright, alert, and open—the Dane moody, quiet, and distrustful.

"Shakespeare knew what he was bloody well talking about," Bishop had said on many occasions.

A crewman cracked the hatch, and the promise of fresh air had Madsen on his feet.

Bishop was going over their equipment when he caught Madsen's eye. He winked. "Let's not keep Gerry waiting," he said cheerfully.

Madsen sighed and began to remove his parka. One night, he thought morosely, Gerry *will* be waiting. This was their fifth visit to one of these French beaches this month. They all looked much the same to Madsen. At each one he and Bishop inspected the shore obstacles that Rommel had sprinkled all along the French coast, checked for mines, measured the incline of the beach, and, with the aid of an auger, took a sample of the sand composition.

Both Bishop and Madsen knew that they were providing information that would aid Allied Command in the selection of an invasion site. What they didn't know was that most of their nocturnal visits were useless. Some armchair soldier, who refused to leave any stone unturned before committing his men to battle, would question information gathered by one or another of the special reconnaissance groups. Bishop and Madsen, or others like them, would crawl under the German guns to bring back what, more often than not, merely confirmed previously gathered information.

But not tonight.

Lieutenant Commander Leiningen swung back the hatch and went up through the narrow conning tower.

He gulped in breaths of blessed fresh air before stepping out onto the narrow deck. Bishop and Madsen, their faces blackened with burnt cork, followed, and the three conversed in hushed tones for a few moments before all shook hands.

"We'll remain in this position until I see your signal," said Leiningen. "We can remain on station until one hour before dawn."

"Not to worry," said Bishop cheerfully. "What we have to do shouldn't take too long."

The crewmen below passed up the equipment, and the two commandos attached several items to the belts around their waists. Bishop pulled a cord on one square package, and with a soft whoosh of compressed air, a small raft—no more than three feet around—was inflated. While Madsen held the attached rope, Bishop placed the raft in the water and the rest of the equipment in the center before securing a canvas cover over the top.

"That's it," said Bishop, giving the thumbs-up, and both men slid silently into the frigid water.

"Good luck," whispered Leiningen, but the two were already stroking toward shore.

The naval officer watched them for just a moment before lowering himself back down into the submarine. He saw the question on the faces of his two crewmen. "How about a quick breath of fresh air before we take her down?" he asked.

"Bloody right, sir," said one as they moved toward the hatch.

Although they were not aware of it, Bishop and Madsen were swimming toward one of the beaches that always figured in Allied discussions of the invasion. Six months from that night it would be better known as "bloody Omaha," but tonight it lay still and serene under a moonless sky.

Three days earlier an American P-51 reconnaissance plane, while on a routine mission over the French coast, had provided Allied intelligence with some interesting photographs of German troops apparently in the act of burying something on the sandy beach.

Once developed, the photographs caused quite a commotion in England, and British intelligence was asked to investigate. The task was given to the special reconnaissance unit of Number 7 Commando.

Fifteen minutes after leaving the submarine, Bishop and Madsen came to the first group of beach obstacles, triangular steel and concrete formations intended to thwart any approaching landing craft. The tops of the posts barely protruded above the waves. Intelligence information was that these obstacles were not mined, but the two men did their best to avoid them anyway.

Finally their feet touched bottom, and the two men zigzagged their way between the spikes until, on all fours, they crawled up onto the shore.

They rested for a moment, scanning the beach for sentries before dragging their equipment up onto the sand. Bishop opened the canvas cover on the raft, removed and unwrapped his Enfield revolver. It was a fairly new weapon, replacing the standard issue Webley .455, and he was as yet uncertain if he preferred the new to the old. The Webley fired a larger bullet than the Enfield's .38, and although the ordinance people claimed that the smaller bullet had just as much stopping power as the larger, Bishop remained unconvinced. What had persuaded him to make the change, however, was that the Enfield operated effectively even after being dropped in salt water.

Madsen avoided the dilemma of a decision by continuing to use—against orders—a German Mauser machine pistol with a ten-round magazine. The weapon was in his possession when he arrived in England, and he had resisted all entreaties to use a more conventional British or American pistol. He had tried the American Colt .45 but did not care for its feel or balance and thought that it was ridiculously inaccurate.

Madsen stuck the Mauser in his holster and removed what appeared to be a backpack from the raft. He raised himself to his knees and slung the pack over his back, putting his arms through the attached straps and attaching the dangling clasps across his chest. Bishop unfolded a telescoping metal pole and extended it from its closed length of two feet to its full length of almost six feet. The metal pole had a flat disc at one end and at the other, two lengths of heavy shielded cable, which he attached to the pack on Madsen's back.

Madsen put on a headset and nodded to Bishop that he was ready. He was carrying, with some minor modification, the mine detecting device issued as standard equipment to British advanced field units.

Bishop affixed a steel spike into the sand at the waterline, attached the raft and a cord to it, and the two men advanced directly inshore, with Madsen leading and Bishop playing out the cord behind them.

Photo reconnaissance had determined the distance from the waterline at midnight to the area where the Germans had been spotted digging in the sand.

When he reached the end of the cord, Bishop tapped Madsen on the shoulder. They stopped and looked up and down the beach.

Madsen fumbled with his headset. "All quiet," he whispered.

Bishop nodded and pointed down the beach to the left. "Okay, let's go to the left. Stay parallel to the waterline."

Madsen nodded, replaced his headset, and the two men, crouching as low as possible, started down the beach with Madsen sweeping the detector ahead of him.

■

While the two commandos were making their way across the deserted beach, a phone rang in the home of the former mayor of St. Germain de Varreville. It was answered on the first ring by a German corporal, who, after listening for a few seconds, replaced the phone and went quickly up the stairs to the second floor.

Pausing for a few seconds to straighten his uniform, he knocked on one of the doors and entered.

"Pardon me, Captain," he said, using the army rank designation rather than the more appropriate one of the Waffen SS. The officer was already pulling on his boots. "That was Lieutenant Bremmer on the phone. He says there is some activity on the beach, near sector K."

The officer nodded as he proceeded with his dressing. As soon as he had heard the telephone he had known what it was. He slipped on his jacket, and as he began to button it, turned to the corporal who still stood in the doorway. "Get my car ready, Corporal," said Ernst Luddeck, "we're going to the beach."

■

Madsen stopped sweeping the detector back and forth and made a hand signal toward the sand. "Got something here," he said. "Maybe two feet down."

Both men dropped to their knees and began carefully sweeping back layers of sand. After removing each layer Bishop probed the sand with his bayonet and then they swept back another layer. Finally Bishop's bayonet touched something metallic.

"About six inches down," he said, looking at the bayonet in the sand. "Get the blanket."

Madsen opened a sack and removed a blanket and a long flashlight. Facing the sea, with the hole in front of him, he sat cross-legged, wrapped the blanket around his shoulders to shield the area from the view of anyone behind him, and then held the flashlight down in the hole before turning it on.

Bishop scraped away the remaining layer of sand until he had partially exposed the top of a curved metal object.

"A mine of some kind?" asked Madsen, trying to keep the edge out of his voice.

"Not like any I've ever seen," replied Bishop, scraping around the edges. "It's big—looks like a metal drum."

He continued digging, trying to get to the edges of the object. "It appears to be about three feet long," he said finally. "Looks like an ordinary fifty-gallon drum."

"Is it empty?"

Bishop tapped the container tentatively with his bayonet. "I don't think so."

"There's writing on it," said Madsen, tilting his head to read the German Gothic script. Even after scooping away more of the sand, he could only read the first few letters of each of four painted lines. "No good," he said. "Most of the words are underneath."

"Remember the letters that you can see. Maybe it will mean something to somebody," said Bishop, while digging at one end. At what was apparently the top of the container he uncovered a round metal stopper about three inches in diameter. He grasped it firmly but it wouldn't budge. "I think this is threaded," he said. "Hand me the adjustable wrench."

"You're sure it's not a mine? It looks as if it could be one of those navy depth charges or something."

Bishop fitted the wrench around the stopper. "I don't think so. There's no contact or pressure fuse. You could dance on this bugger and nothing would happen."

Madsen thought about that for a second. "Be careful anyway," he said.

Bishop chuckled silently, and Madsen saw his white teeth flashing. "Don't be nervous, Eric my boy," he said. "Nothing to worry about." He strained on the wrench and just as the stopper began to give Madsen snapped off the flashlight.

Startled by the sudden darkness, Bishop's hand slipped from the wrench and thumped against the drum. "What the—" he began, but Madsen silenced him with a swift motion of his hand.

"Someone's coming up the beach."

Bishop looked, his eyes straining in the darkness. "Where? I don't see anything."

"I saw the top of his head as he went up over one of those dunes."

"You sure?"

"Positive."

Bishop did not question Madsen again. Two men who did what they did survived only by implicitly trusting each other's judgment and senses. If Madsen said he had seen something, then Bishop did not doubt that he had.

They lay perfectly still. Listening. Watching.

Again Madsen saw movement before Bishop did.

"There," he whispered, pointing down the beach. "Two of them."

Bishop's heart was pounding, his mouth as dry as the sand around him. He saw them. Two figures coming in their direction.

"Soldiers?" asked Bishop.

"Yes," said Madsen without hesitation.

It was a foolish question and both knew it. All the beaches in northwestern France were restricted. A civilian would be shot for venturing here.

"Bayonets," said Bishop. A gunshot would have a thousand men on the beach in no time.

"Got it," said Madsen calmly. His earlier nervousness was gone. He drew his bayonet from the sheath strapped to his leg and waited for Bishop to decide.

"I'm going up the beach about twenty yards," Bishop said, pointing to his left. "If they discover you first, I'll circle in behind them. Wait 'til I strike the first one—then you take the other."

"Got it."

"If they stumble over me first, you—"

"Got it," said Madsen quickly. "Maybe we'll get lucky and they'll walk right past us."

Bishop shrugged noncommittally as if to say, don't count on it, but both knew that it had happened before. Last year, on a beach in Calais, a German sentry had walked between the two of them as they lay flat in the sand not twenty yards from each other.

Without another word, Bishop crawled up the beach

to a distance he felt he could retrace quickly and quietly if the soldiers discovered Madsen.

He waited.

Neither man gave any thought to surrendering if discovered. They were both aware of Hitler's order of October 18, 1942, directed against commandos, in which the Führer had ordered that the members of any raiding party be "slaughtered to the last man" when captured. Both of them knew that even seriously wounded men had been propped up beside their comrades and gunned down. There was no question of surrendering.

Bishop could see the silhouettes of two Germans clearly now. Both wore the standard greatcoat, and the Mauser 98k rifles slung over their shoulders were clearly visible as dark slashes against a gray background.

The two German soldiers advanced across the beach, their boots kicking up billows of sand as they went. Bishop estimated that at their present pace and direction they would stumble across Madsen in less than two minutes. He took several deep breaths and willed his heart to stop pounding.

One of the soldiers laughed, the sound racing past the two men waiting in the sand.

Good, thought Madsen, they've been drinking. That should make this much easier.

Just then a voice rang out from somewhere behind the two advancing soldiers, and Bishop could make out the shape of a third man running down the beach to join the first two.

"Christ," he whispered to himself, "another one." It was difficult for two men to eliminate two others without raising an alarm, but it was almost impossible to do so if there were three. His teeth clenched, he drove the bayonet into the sand beside him and took out his Enfield, confident that at that moment Madsen was doing the same. They would have to shoot the three and make a dash for the submarine before reinforcements arrived.

At the call of the third man the first two had stopped and waited for him to reach them. The third man seemed angry about something, and although he spoke in a subdued tone, he was obviously venting his anger on the other two. His voice carried down the beach, and Bishop, whose German was excellent, could make out an occasional word or phrase.

Bishop heard, "Restricted area... off limits... drunken fools... officer in charge... reprimand..." He could hear the other two trying to offer some inadequate response.

Finally the confrontation was over, and the third man marched back in the direction from which he had come, with the two interlopers, heads down in apparent shame at their misconduct, following a few paces behind.

Bishop waited until they had disappeared and then crawled back to Madsen, who was just returning his pistol to his holster. "Bit sticky there for a minute," he whispered.

Madsen nodded, his nervousness returning. "Let's get on with it," he said. Again he blocked the area with the blanket and snapped on the light while Bishop fitted the wrench over the stopper.

With one hard tug on the wrench, the stopper came loose, and Bishop was able to easily unthread it by hand. When he removed the plug, a liquid spilled from the opening.

Bishop put the stopper in a pocket in his belt. "Give me the light," he said and then held it close to the opening so that he could peer inside. "Seems to be filled with liquid."

"Must be something else in there with it. Could it be a lubricant for what's inside?"

Bishop probed inside the drum with his bayonet. "I need something longer," he said.

"How about the detector?"

"Okay—disconnect it from the pack and I'll give it a try."

In seconds Madsen had disconnected the telescoping tube from the backpack and handed it over to Bishop, who carefully inserted the tube into the opening, feeling for anything solid. He pushed the tube horizontally all the way to the back of the container and then let its tip sink slowly to the bottom.

"Nothing," he said, moving it from side to side. "There's nothing inside but the liquid."

"That's it then?"

Bishop thought for a second. "Too bad we don't have some kind of container. We could bring back a sample."

Madsen fumbled in his pouch and produced a waterproof wrap for the weapons. "Try this."

Carefully Bishop removed the detector tube from the drum. He was able to pour a small amount of the liquid that had been trapped inside the hollow tube into the waterproof bag.

"It's not much," he said, examining it.

"It'll do," said Madsen. "Let's cover this up and get out of here."

They replaced the stopper and pushed the sand back in the hole, smoothing it over as much as possible, then made their way back to the dinghy, which had been tethered to the spike. While Bishop pulled the spike out of the sand Madsen signaled with the flashlight. There would be no response, but they knew that the sub would be waiting.

They waded back out to sea, the freezing water taking their breath away. At waist depth they dropped silently into the water and began to swim, towing the raft behind them.

■

As the two commandos made steady progress away from the beach, Ernst Luddeck watched them through one of the infrared enhanced binoculars that were mounted at observation posts on the French coast. Finally, when he could no longer see them, he turned to Lieutenant Bremmer, who stood beside him. "Well," he said, smiling, "that went rather well, I think."

"Yes, Captain," said Bremmer, "I think so."

Luddeck's face darkened, and the smile slipped away as easily as it had appeared. "It could have been a disaster."

Bremmer swallowed the lump in his throat. "You can be sure, Captain, that I will deal severely with those two fools who wandered onto the beach."

"Yes," said Luddeck, but his eyes were back on the binoculars and his mind already far away.

12

"Radioactive!" said the American general.

The man in the dark three-piece suit who sat in the chair in front of General Walter B. Smith was Milton Collingwood, a senior aide to General Sir Collin Gubbins, the chief of Britain's Special Operations Executive. He had come to General Smith's London headquarters to personally report the disturbing news.

"Yes, I'm afraid so," said Collingwood. "The actual phrasing on the report said 'highly radioactive.'"

General Smith looked again at the reconnaissance photos that Collingwood had brought with him. They showed German soldiers burying what looked like canisters on the beach. One of the photographs revealed a small pyramid of similar containers stacked nearby. As he leafed through the photographs Smith puffed furiously on what Collingwood found to be a horrible cigar.

"Although the photographs show only one of these canisters being buried," Collingwood said, "you will note the other canisters and the areas of darkened sand at fairly regular distances from the burial site."

Smith studied the picture and nodded without comment.

"Our photo intelligence division," Collingwood went on, "estimates that the Germans are burying these containers every hundred feet or so along the beach."

"And you think it's some kind of anti-invasion weapon?"

Collingwood scratched the tip of his nose. "We can't be sure . . . but what else?"

Smith chewed his cigar. "Ike is not going to like this." He got up from his desk and went to the window, where he looked out at a gray, misty sky.

"Now let me get this straight," said Smith as he turned and perched on the windowsill. "The Germans are planting some kind of radioactive bomb or mine on the beaches?"

"As far as we can tell, it isn't a bomb."

Smith's eyes narrowed. "What then?"

"It's rather difficult to say, but some of our boys came up with a few ideas about the capabilities of such a weapon."

"Such as?"

"If, as seems evident, the Germans have laced their beaches with these containers—let's say one every few hundred feet—in expectation of the invasion, they will simply sit back and wait for our boys to come ashore."

Smith came back to his desk. "Then what?"

"Well, the object, as we see it, would be to hold as many men on the beaches as possible—not permit any sort of breakout. Crowd us onto the beaches, hoping that the whole invading force would be on the beach at the same time."

"That's not possible," said General Smith. "Our support groups and reserves won't hit the beaches until the advance forces have moved off and established perimeter lines in the interior."

"True," said Collingwood, "but the Germans don't know that."

Smith stared hard at the Englishman. "Any soldier worth his salt knows that, Mr. Collingwood. Field Marshal Rommel knows exactly what we have to do."

Collingwood accepted the rebuke gracefully. Before the war he had run the family import-export business. Excellent contacts on the continent had made him suitable for his present position. He knew little of military strategy. "Very well," he said, nodding agreeably. "But that still doesn't change the situation. The beaches will be crowded with men and equipment early in the invasion. At some point, during those first hours, the Germans will use some kind of radio-controlled device to detonate an explosive either inside or beneath the canisters." He raised his hands in the air to indicate the explosion and then let them flutter slowly back into his lap. "The men on the beaches would be showered with radioactive water."

Smith removed his cigar from his mouth. "That's it," he said. "The men on the beaches would be showered with water?" He almost laughed, but he saw Collingwood's jaw harden. Smith's eyes narrowed. "Then what?"

"Before the war," said Collingwood, "British scientists had done extensive research in nuclear physics and on the subject of radioactivity." Without moving his lips he gave Smith an approximation of a smile.

Smith was a soldier; he knew nothing about this new and mysterious science that suddenly was spoken of in hushed tones by almost everyone. As usual, when lost for words, he substituted bluster. "So?"

"Within twenty-four hours, anyone contaminated with this material would become sick—nausea, dizzyness. Within forty-eight hours their condition would deteriorate—diarrhea, vomiting, a total lack of energy."

General Smith's eyes closed. He was imagining a million men on sick call.

"We can't be certain," Collingwood continued, "but it seems highly likely that within two weeks of contamination, fifty or sixty percent of these men would die."

Smith's jaw dropped. "Two *weeks*?"

Collingwood shrugged. "What difference would it make? Within twenty-four hours of landing, these men would be totally ineffective as a fighting force. They would be unable even to defend themselves. The Germans could pick them off effortlessly." His eyes bored into Smith's. "The invasion would be a disaster."

Smith massaged his temples with the thumb and middle finger of his left hand. "If this is true," he said deliberately, seemingly reluctant to express what he was thinking, "the invasion will have to be called off."

Collingwood nodded. "Permanently," he said flatly.

Alone in his office, Smith sat in his chair chomping on his, by now, extinguished cigar and looked at the photographs that Collingwood had left with him to pass along to Eisenhower.

Smith, who had been with Eisenhower in North Africa and Italy and was now assigned to SHAEF headquarters in England, knew that his boss's fabled sunny disposition and unflappable demeanor were merely a mask that the general used to cajole and persuade his colleagues—particularly the British. Behind the pleasant smile, secreted from public view, was an iron will and an explosive temper.

Smith knew that the first thing Ike would say was, "Goddamned Montgomery. If it hadn't been for that SOB we'd be across the Rhine already, instead of sitting here with our thumbs up our asses."

It was a well known but equally well disguised fact that the British had no stomach for the war anymore. Even at this late date, after giving his grudging approval for the cross-channel invasion at the Teheran Conference in December, Churchill was still a reluctant participant. Stalin was screaming for a second front to take the pressure off his armies and had even hinted—although no one took him seriously—of a separate peace with Hitler. Still, Churchill and Montgomery held firm in their belief that they and their American allies were not ready for a full-scale assault on Fortress Europe.

Churchill used the debacle at Dieppe, where a Canadian landing force on the French coast had been wiped out, to justify his hesitation, but Smith and the other American generals were well aware of the real reason—the British army was physically and emotionally spent. Courage and determination were one thing, but the British no longer had the capacity to withstand the immense casualties that an invasion would entail.

Churchill hoped that the Germans and the Russians would bring each other to their knees, after which the British and the Americans could parade through Europe to a tumultuous welcome by the liberated populations. But Marshall, Eisenhower, and the rest of the American military were eager to test their immense and growing might against the battered yet still powerful forces of Germany.

General Smith took one last look at the reconnaissance photographs before dropping them into his briefcase. He chomped on his cigar and spoke aloud through clenched teeth. "Ike is not going to like this."

13

Walter Schellenberg looked up in surprise as the door to his office burst open. He was already on his feet, reaching for his pistol when he realized that the man who had forced his way into his office was Reichsführer Heinrich Himmler himself.

"Herr Reichsführer," he stammered, struggling to overcome his shock, "this is indeed a surprise."

Heinrich Himmler, interior minister, Reichsführer of the SS, was the man who presided over the totalitarian apparatus of the secret state within the German state. He was responsible for the secret police, the concentration camps, the SS military units, the collecting and use of slave labor and, of course, the implementation of the "final solution." After Hitler, Himmler was the most powerful man in Germany.

He was a small man, crew cut, puffy, and bespectacled. Schellenberg often thought it ironic that this man, architect of the system of Aryan supremacy, should resemble nothing more than a bank teller or a grocery clerk.

The Reichsführer fixed Schellenberg in a squinty stare through his steel-framed spectacles that further enhanced his impotent appearance. His lips were pursed as if ready to blow a balloon or receive a kiss and his normally pallid complexion was red with anger. "Explain yourself," he said and sat down by the fireplace, his back to Schellenberg.

Schellenberg, dumbfounded, stole a quick glance at the door where his adjutant waited apologetically in the doorway. Behind him stood two of Himmler's bodyguards. "Explain myself, Reichsführer?"

Himmler looked back over his shoulder at Schellenberg. His eyes were cold, his face expressionless. Instead of his typical black SS uniform, he wore a simple double-breasted tweed jacket and a white shirt with a dark tie. He might have been an insurance salesman rather than the most feared man in the Reich. "I just talked with Kaltenbrunner," he said, "and he informs me that you have embarked on a most ingenious scheme to single-handedly prevent the invasion."

Damn that Kaltenbrunner! "Not quite, Herr Reichminister. I act only under your instructions. It was never my intention to pursue this matter by myself."

"Don't contradict me, Walter," said Himmler sharply. "I am disturbed that you did not come to me with this scheme. It seems beyond the scope of your authority to proceed with something like this."

Schellenberg shrugged apologetically. "The plan is only under consideration, Herr Reichminister. It was never my intention to continue without your authority." He smiled, recovering a little from his earlier discomfort. "As a matter of fact, my adjutant is at this very moment preparing a *Vertrauliche-Berichte* for your office in which I detail the situation and solicit your advice and approval."

Himmler's eyes narrowed imperceptibly. "I would like to see that report."

"Hans," Schellenberg called through the open door, "please bring that report you were preparing for the Reichsführer."

Under the watchful eye of the two guards who had accompanied Himmler, Hans Griebl, Schellenberg's adjutant, went to his desk in the outer office. He opened the top drawer and removed a slim leather folder that was bound with a wide leather strap and brass buckle. Embossed on the folder in gold was the emblem of the RSHA, an eagle above an encircled swastika. Below the emblem was embossed, also in gold, the word *Geheim*—secret.

Griebl smiled to himself, marveling at Schellenberg's foresight. Each operation mounted by him, either approved by his superiors or not, was written up as if prepared for Himmler's eyes and then left in his adjutant's desk as if it were in the process of preparation. At first, Griebl had been somewhat mystified by the procedure, but he had come to accept it as one of his boss's idiosyncrasies. Now he knew that it was no mere idle task, but another of the many contrivances that made Schellenberg a survivor.

"Thank you, Captain," said Schellenberg, as Griebl placed the folder on his desk. He began to unbuckle the clasp.

"I'll take that," said Himmler testily and snatched the folder away from Schellenberg. He opened the pouch and withdrew several typed sheets.

Across each page, in large red letters, was printed "SSD"—very, very urgent—and then, just below, in smaller print, "Plan Omega."

"I really can't tell you how disappointed I am in you, Walter," said Himmler, looking up before reading the first page. "You know that I have expressly forbidden you to undertake such ambitious endeavors on your own."

He began to read.

Both knew that "endeavors" referred to Schellenberg's almost disastrous attempts in late 1943 to contact the Allies and enter into a discussion of a separate peace between Germany and Great Britain and the United States. This "peace" would have allowed Germany to devote all her might to the campaign against Russia.

Himmler and Schellenberg had discussed the idea and the overzealous Schellenberg, assuming Himmler's approval, had initiated discussions in Stockholm with members of the small contingent of Americans still conducting business in the embassy.

Word of Schellenberg's overture had traveled quickly to Allied diplomats in London, and as a price for continuing the discussions, the Allies had demanded Hitler's head. Schellenberg, quite suddenly and much to his surprise, was thrust into the position of a conspirator—a turn of events he had never imagined.

Somehow, the Führer learned that someone in his

party apparatus had made contact with the Americans, and he vowed that heads would roll. It was all that Himmler could do to cover their tracks and conceal that two of the highest ranking officials in the Reich were involved. The danger had since past, but Himmler had not forgotten the gut-wrenching fear he had felt when he had thought he might be exposed to his Führer's rage.

Schellenberg thought of that fearful time while Himmler scrutinized the pages of the report.

When Himmler had finished, he closed the folder and looked up at Schellenberg, who waited, confident of Himmler's reaction.

"Very good, Walter," he said, a small smile appearing on his lips for the first time. "Your plan has definite possibilities."

Inwardly relieved, Schellenberg smiled. "I would then like, Herr Reichsführer, to put phase two into effect."

"Which is?" asked Himmler, looking back at the pages.

"To let the Abwehr know that we have Bohr's papers in our possession."

Himmler's eyebrows went up. "The Abwehr?"

"Yes," said Schellenberg, his excitement growing. "I'm convinced that the military intelligence of the High Command is riddled with traitors. I cannot prove that Admiral Canaris is one of them, but I am sure that he is surrounded by weaklings who do not believe in the Thousand Year Reich. If the Abwehr had this information, I am sure that the Allied powers would hear about it immediately."

Himmler nodded noncommittally. "And then?"

"Then I would like to inform our agents in England to avoid major population centers—especially London—after May fifteenth."

Himmler seemed puzzled.

"We know," said Schellenberg, "that several of these agents have been turned. Their reports are unreliable and filled with confusing information that is supplied by the British."

Himmler nodded. This fact was common knowledge in the German intelligence systems. "What happens when May fifteenth arrives and nothing happens?"

"We inform our agents that the Führer has decided not to use the weapon until and unless the Allies invade France."

Himmler stood up and went to the cabinet where Schellenberg kept a water pitcher and several glasses. Selecting a clean glass, he wiped it with his handkerchief just to be sure, then poured himself a glass of water. Then he turned to face his subordinate. "And with this deception you hope to prevent the invasion?"

Schellenberg nodded. "With this and a few of the other ideas I have outlined in the report."

"If only it were so simple. The American buildup of men and materiel in England is awesome. I spoke with the Führer's adjutant, General Schmundt, only yesterday, and he told me that the Americans have brought enough equipment into England in the last six months to outfit thirty new divisions. Of course, the Führer has not been told this. He only wants to hear another of Ribbentrop's reports on how the Americans are getting tired of the Jews telling them how to run the war."

Himmler raised his glass in mock salute. "We are running out of time, Walter. If we had this secret weapon you talk about, instead of"—he waved a hand over the leather folder—"just pretending we had it . . ." His voice trailed off as he contemplated such a paradise. Then he slammed his glass down on Schellenberg's desk, the water splashing onto stacks of documents.

Schellenberg ignored his chief's display of anger. He had learned when to be silent.

Himmler went on. "We should have arrested this Bohr in 1940," he said, his voice rising to a shrill squeal. "We should have forced him to work for us. I tell you, Walter, no other nation on earth would have treated this man the way Germany did. The kindness of the German nation was extended to this man, and look what happened. He turned on us. Men like that understand only one thing—strength. They perceive kindness as weakness." He was shaking his head. "I tell you,

Walter, don't ever be kind to anyone. It doesn't pay. If we had demonstrated strength, we would already have this weapon our enemies are prepared to threaten us with."

Schellenberg spoke. "Perhaps it is not too late. Perhaps we can still get this weapon."

Himmler almost laughed. "I talked with Heisenberg last week. He said that if we put *all* of our resources into the research, they *might* have the weapon in a year." He wiped a palm across his forehead. "If we put all our resources into anything other than our own defense none of us will be here in a year. We'll be dangling at the end of a British noose—or worse." He went back to his seat by the fire.

"Perhaps Bohr can still help us," said Schellenberg.

"Don't talk nonsense, Walter. How can we get him to help us?"

"His research. His notes. He left everything behind."

"Yes," sniffed Himmler derisively. "And I understand the Gestapo has turned Denmark upside down looking for them."

"If my plan works, perhaps the Allies will tell us where to look," said Schellenberg, smiling confidently.

Himmler's face was still, his mouth a straight line, his eyes steady behind his spectacles. "Explain yourself," he said simply.

Schellenberg sat down on a chair next to the Reichsführer and began. He would tell Himmler what he never would dream of confiding to Kaltenbrunner.

"The Allies believe that Bohr is the key to the development of the atomic bomb—otherwise, why did they go to the trouble of getting him out of Denmark?"

Himmler was stonily silent.

"I propose, Reichsführer, through leaks and rumors and misdirection, to let the Allies think that we have perhaps discovered Bohr's documents and are well on our way to using this discovery to build the bomb."

Still, Himmler said nothing.

"If I implement my—our plan, what is the worst thing that could happen?"

Himmler thought for only a second. "That they will ignore the deception."

Schellenberg smiled. "Exactly. But what is the best that can happen?"

"They will indefinitely postpone the invasion."

"Yes, but it seems unrealistic to expect the cancellation of such an immense undertaking without conclusive evidence of what we claim."

Himmler nodded. "True. So the best we can hope for is a temporary delay."

"Suppose that delay was long enough that the invasion had to be put off until 1945?"

"Helpful—but again unrealistic."

Schellenberg nodded. "In 1940, when we were prepared to invade England, there were rumors circulating of a British weapon that would set the Channel ablaze if we attempted invasion."

"Yes," shrugged Himmler, "but I don't think we paid any attention to such a preposterous story."

"But only after we had sent in a team to inspect this rumored wonder weapon."

"The delay," said Himmler, "was only a few days. The Führer himself decided to postpone the invasion."

"Wouldn't the Allies do the same thing? Wouldn't they be forced to find out if we really had found Bohr's documents?"

Himmler's eyes brightened, and a smile formed on his pursed lips as he began to see where Schellenberg was leading. "They might. They would probably make inquiries through the resistance movement."

Schellenberg's smile widened. "Which we have infiltrated."

Himmler's smile grew. "They might even send someone in the resistance to verify that the documents are still in their hiding place."

"In which case it will be ours."

"But," said Himmler, his face growing troubled, "what if they decide not to do any of those things? What if they decide to send in their own people to recover the documents and take them back to England?"

Schellenberg had the answer. "They couldn't do that

without the cooperation of the resistance. As soon as they arrived we'd know. We'd be waiting for them. We'd follow them to the hiding place and then the documents would be ours."

Himmler couldn't stop the smile that radiated across his chubby face. "If we can accomplish that, Walter, the Führer will be eternally grateful."

Schellenberg's eyes were twinkling at the thought.

Himmler stood up, straightening his jacket. His face was once again serious. "You'd better get busy," he said. He started to walk toward the door, then turned. "I'd like Captain Luddeck to work with you on this one, Walter."

Forcing a smile, Schellenberg said, "As you wish, Reichsführer."

As Himmler left his office Schellenberg knew that he would have to be very careful with this Luddeck. It seemed that the Reichsführer was courting a new favorite.

January 1944

On January 14, after a two-week visit to Washington, during which he met with the War Department, as well as with President Roosevelt, who was confined to bed with a severe case of the flu, General Eisenhower returned to Europe to assume command of the Supreme Headquarters, Allied Expeditionary Force (SHAEF).

It was the last time that Roosevelt and Eisenhower would ever see each other.

That evening, the fourteenth, Eisenhower took his private railroad car, Bayonet, *from the airfield in Scotland to London, arriving on the fifteenth in a heavy fog that made visibility almost impossible. The general and his staff got lost in the heavy fog and were unable to find the headquarters of the European Theater of Operations, U.S. Army, (ETOUSA) in Grosvenor Square. Finally the commander was taken to his private quarters in Hayes Lodge, Mayfair.*

From these quarters he spoke by telephone with General Montgomery who, as ground commander of the invading forces, had returned to England on January 2 and begun the initial preparations in Eisenhower's absence.

Eisenhower, expressing to Montgomery his dismay at what he referred to as "rumors of new German wonder weapons," called for a meeting the next day of all senior ground, air, and naval personnel.

14

"Goddamned Montgomery," said a grim-faced Eisenhower as he hung up the phone. "We could be over there kicking the shit out of those Nazis already if it weren't for his foot-dragging."

General Smith gave a short embarrassed cough and looked to Ike's naval aide, Commander Butcher, who merely grinned at his colleague's discomfort. General Bradley, who stood near the fireplace, merely turned away as if to disassociate himself from his commander's remark. Smith noted that Ike never included Prime Minister Churchill in these tirades, only Monty or other British generals. It would have been impolite for the Supreme Commander to blast the British leader in front of his staff, even though all were aware that Churchill was more responsible for the delay than any of his generals.

Ike's orderly served drinks, and the small group sat around the fire that had been prepared for their arrival.

Eisenhower loosened his field jacket. "Let me see those pictures again," he said, and when Smith produced them, the general sat for a long time studying them as if he could see something that the intelligence people had missed. He stubbed out one cigarette and lit another. He turned the photographs so that he could view them from all angles. Throughout this time he was silent, and the other three men in the room knew enough not to say a word.

Finally he spoke, slapping the photographs down on the low table in front of his chair for emphasis. "How do we know this isn't a trick?" No one said anything. "How do we know this isn't some grand deception." He looked around the room, his jaw set, his eyes glaring at each man as if he were somehow responsible. "Maybe this is exactly what the Germans want us to think." He stood up and put his glass on the mantel over the fireplace. "Can you imagine how history will regard us if we put off the invasion because of some outrageous fabrication?"

Smith hesitated before turning Eisenhower's question around, and Bradley beat him to it. "What if it isn't a fabrication?"

A silence fell across the room as each man imagined the consequences.

"Then," said Eisenhower, "we've got a stalemate on our hands."

He looked around the room. No one could meet his eye. "I want to know everything about this secret weapon." He looked to Smith. "Smitty, send copies of everything here to Donovan at OSS headquarters in London. I don't trust the British to be objective on this. Then I want you to talk to someone about this radiation business. I want to know if this stuff is as lethal as the British seem to think it is." His jaw hardened again. "I don't want them to come up with any more excuses for delaying the invasion."

"Yes, sir," said Smith. "I'll get on it right away."

Ike finally smiled. "And see if you can get somebody to talk to that Danish professor the British brought out last year." His brow furrowed. "What's his name?"

"Bohr," volunteered Smith.

"That's it. Bohr. Talk to him. He's supposed to know everything there is to know about this atomic stuff."

"He was sent to New York last month," said Butcher, "to work with other scientists on our own atomic project."

Ike shrugged. "Then get Donovan or someone to talk with him and report back to me." He chuckled, and everyone in the room relaxed a little. "Things have changed a lot, gentlemen," he said, "since the days when we could just send in the cavalry to get the job done."

There was much muttering of agreement, but no one ventured any comment. The meeting room soon turned to a discussion of the continuing campaign in Italy, but every now and then Eisenhower would look over to General Smith and nod as if to communicate how much he was counting on Smith to help in this matter. General Smith could think of little else other than the fact that the newly named Supreme Commander of the biggest military venture in history was counting on him to answer what might be an unanswerable question.

Smith wasn't sure what he could do, but he knew he had to do something.

15

General Bernard Law Montgomery had set up his command headquarters for the planning stage of the invasion at St. Paul's School in the West Kensington section of London.

As a boy Montgomery had been a rather indifferent student at St. Paul's, and so it was doubly satisfying for him to return to his old school in this position of tremendous responsibility.

In the private rooms of the high master he began planning the land attack that was intended to sweep the Nazis from the French coast back to the borders of their own nation.

The dining hall at St. Paul's, a long, rectangular, high-ceilinged room, had been converted to a meeting room for the Combined Chiefs of Staff. At the front of the room a huge map of northern Europe covered the entire wall, and rows of chairs had been arranged to accommodate the field commanders who would soon attend the briefings held here.

On this day, however, there were fewer than ten men sitting around a green-felt-covered dining table. Those present included: General Dwight D. Eisenhower, General Omar Bradley, General Walter Beddel Smith, General Bernard Law Montgomery, Admiral Bertram Ramsay, Air Chief Marshal Arthur Tedder, and Air Chief Marshal Trafford Leigh-Mallory. These men constituted the Allied leadership for Operation Overlord, the invasion of northern France.

Also present were General Hastings "Pug" Ismay and Professor Frederick Lindemann, Churchill's military and scientific advisers. At the conclusion of the meeting, these two men would report directly to the prime minister. Eisenhower himself would prepare a report for President Roosevelt, which would be dispatched immediately by military courier.

At the table the men had formed small groups engaged in informal conversation, awaiting the signal that the meeting itself was to begin. Although this was the room where the cooperative decisions for the conduct of the war were made, the British talked with the British and the Americans talked with the Americans before the meeting began.

Finally, with a quick glance at his watch, Eisenhower stood up at his end of the table. "Gentlemen," he said, clearing his throat for emphasis. The others quickly fell into silence. "I'll come right to the point of this meeting." He looked around the table, making eye-contact with each man. "All of you in this room have access to most classified communications about the conduct of the war, including the plans for the coming invasion. What you may not be aware of is the race for the development of what has been called the atomic bomb." Ike smiled and shrugged his shoulders in that engagingly deferential manner of his that suggested he was in over his head on this one.

"If the reports I get are accurate," he said, "one B-17 bomber"—he nodded to Leigh-Mallory and Tedder—

"or a Lancaster could devastate Berlin or any other German city with a single bomb."

The men were silent, as if imagining the force of such a weapon, until Montgomery chimed in. "I hope you're going to tell us that you have the bloody thing in your back pocket and we can all go home to tinkering in our gardens."

"No," said Ike, "I'm afraid I'm not going to tell you that."

"You're not going to tell us that Gerry's got his hands on this thing?" asked Monty.

Ike hesitated just long enough to see the look of dismay begin to spread around the room. "No," he said finally. "Fortunately, I don't have to tell you that either."

The men around the table gave a collective sigh of relief.

"That is, however, the subject of today's meeting." Ike continued. "We have been receiving some disturbing intelligence reports in the last few weeks. Sources within the German intelligence community itself—sources which, I am assured, have been extremely accurate in the past—have reported that rumors are running wild among the German military that the Germans have come up with a new wonder weapon."

"We've heard such rumors before," scoffed Professor Lindemann, "and nothing ever happens."

Ike nodded. "True, but this time these rumors are coupled with another distressing piece of intelligence information."

The room was silent as Ike paused dramatically.

"German agents, who were captured upon entering England and who now work for us, have been informed by Berlin to avoid major population centers after May fifteenth."

Someone gasped, and the British looked guiltily at each other.

"There is also the possibility," Eisenhower went on, "that the Germans have discovered some vital scientific information that might"—he paused and repeated for emphasis—"*might* help them unlock the secrets of the atomic bomb." He looked directly at Professor Lindemann.

"Professor," he said, "you are aware that Niels Bohr, the Danish scientist, is now in America working on the Allied atomic project."

Lindemann nodded.

"What you might not be aware of is that Bohr left behind all of his scientific papers in Denmark."

Lindemann's eyes widened slightly.

"Recent intelligence reports lead us to consider the possibility that the Germans have discovered the hiding place of the documents he left behind."

"Good God," Lindemann muttered under his breath.

Ike ignored him and went on. "I have asked one of your"—he corrected himself quickly—"*our* English scientists, who until just a few weeks ago was in New York working on the joint British-American nuclear project, to join us this morning and speak to us about the possibility—hopefully remote—that the Germans will develop an atomic bomb before we do." He studied the sober faces around him. "If that does happen, we would have no recourse but to sue for peace under the most favorable terms that Hitler was willing to give us."

After waiting for that to sink in, Eisenhower went to a side door, opened it, and motioned for someone to enter.

Dr. Robert Duncan was surprisingly young. At thirty-seven, he was already one of England's foremost nuclear physicists. He and several other British scientists had just returned from Columbia University in New York, where it had been decided that the best contribution the British could make in this joint venture was on the theory of the gas-diffusion process. Duncan and some of his colleagues had returned to the University of Birmingham, where this research had originated before the war.

Now he stepped to the front of the room, smiling nervously at the small assemblage of dignitaries. His hair was dark and unkempt, but his suit was meticulously pressed, giving him the appearance of one who was in some minor way at war with himself. He cleared his throat and nodded in the direction of General Eisenhower, who had retaken his seat at the head of the table.

"Gentlemen," he said, "I will not attempt today to explain the mechanics of nuclear fission, nor will I try to relay to you our own great strides in this endeavor. General Eisenhower has asked me to give you a comparative view of our advances as opposed to the advances made in Germany in this same field, and I can tell you at the outset that in the opinion of the majority of scientists working on the project, the German research is at least as advanced as our own." He slipped a finger inside his collar, moved his head from side to side as if he were terribly uncomfortable in a shirt and tie. "I should also tell you that a sizable minority believes that the German research program is more advanced than ours."

"How can they know that?" barked one of the men at the table.

Duncan smiled, relieved that someone had asked a question he was prepared to answer. "We have the benefit in our program of working with many refugee scientists, men who were often well aware of developments in the German research program before being forced to leave the country. We know, therefore, that no line of research currently pursued is unknown to our counterparts in Germany."

"Dr. Duncan," said Admiral Ramsey, "you speak of 'benefits' that we have in our program. If indeed these are benefits, why are we not far ahead of the Germans in research?"

Duncan scratched his forehead and began a stammered reply, but Eisenhower interrupted him. "Perhaps I could help with that one, Doctor," he said. "I think we should understand, gentlemen, that although we have the benefit of many of these refugee scientists, the Germans have the benefit of those scientists who were unable to escape as well as the complete research facilities of the occupied nations. It is my understanding that several priceless pieces of equipment were captured by the Germans in France in 1940."

"Yes," said Duncan, grateful for the opening. "The cyclotron at Professor Joliet's laboratory at the College de France fell into their hands when they occupied Paris."

"Cyclotron?" asked Montgomery.

"Yes. A cyclotron is a particle accelerator used to drive atomic particles to the extreme speeds necessary to precipitate an atomic explosion."

His explanation was greeted by a sea of blank faces.

"If I can explain it to you this way," began Dr. Duncan.

Ike interrupted. "Not necessary, Doctor." Ike, smiling, looked around the table. "Most of us don't understand anything more complicated than a horse and saber." While the others laughed quietly, Eisenhower looked at some notes in front of him. "We also know that the Germans have available to them facilities in Norway and Belgium for gathering the necessary raw materials."

"Are we talking about the Norsk Hydro plant in Trondheim?" asked Montgomery.

Ike looked down at his notes. "That's correct."

"My information is that that plant was put out of operation in 1943," said Montgomery, "and that it won't return to full-time operation for at least two years."

Professor Lindemann spoke for the first time since Duncan had entered the room. "Initial estimates of damage were too high. The plant was damaged in February of last year, restored to partial operation by March, and, as far as we can tell, by June was operating at its usual capacity."

Eisenhower nodded, then turned to Dr. Duncan. "Is there anything else, Doctor?"

"Let me conclude by saying that the process which we now feel is the key to the development of the bomb—that is, the enriching of uranium by gaseous diffusion—was developed in Germany by Gustav Herz in the 1930s. Also, in 1938 two German physicists, Otto Hahn and Fritz Strassman, were the first to achieve atomic fission. The Germans have always been advanced in atomic research."

Duncan put his hands in his pockets. Now that he was almost finished he seemed more relaxed. "Just before I left New York, I talked with Niels Bohr, the Danish physicist who escaped from Europe only three months ago. He had talked with German scientists as recently as five months ago." He paused for effect, then said, "Dr. Bohr seems to feel that the Germans are very close to the construction of a nuclear device."

"When will they have it?" asked Montgomery.

"Difficult to say."

"Guess," said Monty sharply.

Dr. Duncan shifted his papers. "Eighteen months . . . a year . . . maybe less."

"This Bohr fellow, isn't he the one who left all of his scientific papers behind when we got him out of Denmark?"

"Yes."

"Do your colleagues think these papers will be of help to the Germans?"

"If the Germans have those papers," said Duncan, "there is no telling how much their program may be accelerated."

Except for a few embarrassed coughs, the room was quiet. These men, most of whom had fought this war for four years and in the beginning had despaired of ever achieving victory, had begun to hope that perhaps 1944 would see the conclusion of this disastrous war. From defeat they had begun to dream visions of overwhelming success. Now in a few short moments this stranger had once again raised the possibility of the unthinkable. For the British it was especially galling. Once on the brink of disaster, now on the edge of success, the sweet fruit of salvation had been whisked away. Again the specter of disastrous defeat cast a shadow across their souls.

As usual, Ike spoke first. "Thank you very much, Doctor. I'm sure you will make yourself available to any member of the committee who has any further questions on this matter."

Dr. Duncan nodded agreeably, and then, realizing he had been dismissed, gathered his papers into his briefcase and quickly left the room.

Ike lit another cigarette. "Well," he said, "that seems

to sum up the situation pretty well. Anyone like to comment?"

Montgomery was the first to accept the invitation. "It seems painfully obvious to me that we can't go on in such uncertainty. The problem is—how soon will it be before they have this atomic bomb?"

Leigh-Mallory chimed in. "According to Dr. Duncan, the evidence seems to be that there is a good possibility they will have the bomb before we do."

"We can't be sure of that," said Ike.

Monty chuckled, "Ike, old boy, you can't bring in one of your experts to tell us one thing and then bloody well disagree with him."

Ike's face darkened. "I just wanted you to have the facts before we proceeded with—"

"Proceeded!" boomed Montgomery in a voice that startled everyone. "How can we *proceed* with this. The British people have been bled dry in this conflict, General Eisenhower. We have little more to give. I remind you that if these atomic bombs begin to rain down upon us, it will be British cities that stagger under the blows." As he spoke his sharp eyes darted around the table. "I know what is said about me in some quarters. Unless Monty has a two hundred percent superiority in men and armament and a one hundred percent chance of victory, he will not engage in battle." His eyes narrowed, and the others at the table recoiled as he slammed his palm against the table top. "I will not and cannot ask the British nation to be bled to the point of extinction." He threw back his shoulders, and the others knew what was coming. "In the First World War," he said, "Britain suffered over three million casualties. One million of our young men left their lives and their nation's fortunes on the battlefield." He fixed the Americans in his steely gaze. "You lost one hundred thousand . . . a drop in your vast bucket. And then, while still in the process of recovery from that earlier blow, we took on—by ourselves—the defense of Western Civilization against a foe so Satanic that other nations rushed to lick his bootheels. We fought for—"

"Monty," Ike interrupted gently but firmly, "we are

all aware of the tremendous sacrifices made by the British people. What we want to do is end this conflict as quickly as possible. You know what that means."

Monty's head was shaking vigorously even before Ike had finished. "If there is any chance the Nazis are going to have this bomb at any time soon, we cannot proceed with the invasion."

"Our best chance," said Ike, "is invasion and a quick run for Berlin."

Monty smiled grimly. "A quick run? A quick run through sixty divisions of the toughest, most fanatic troops in the world?" Montgomery could have added that none of the American divisions scheduled to invade the Continent had been involved in combat. "Even with overwhelming strength," he said, "our best estimates are for a nine-month campaign from the beaches to the Rhine." He paused to stare at Ike. "I wouldn't be surprised if it took twice that long. And what then? Suppose a year from now we are slogging it out somewhere in northern France. We have overwhelming superiority, but they're hanging on as they always do. They know that it's just a matter of time before we overwhelm them with numbers, just as the Russians are doing in the east. What if on that day, a year from now, one of their scientists says to Hitler, "We've got your bloody bomb for you, mein Führer. What should we do with it?" He looked up at the intricate carvings on the ceiling. "What do you think that evil man is going to say?"

There was silence. No one looked at anyone else, much less Montgomery.

"What do you suggest, Monty?" asked Ike. "Peace talks?"

"Absolutely not," snapped Montgomery angrily. "I say, let's find out what they've got. If they've got this fellow Bohr's notes, then we know we're in a pickle. With his notes they might have the bomb in less than a year. If that's true, we may just have to rethink our strategy. If they don't have the notes, then maybe, just maybe, we can get to Berlin before all hell breaks loose."

Everyone nodded their agreement at the reasonableness of Montgomery's suggestion.

"All right then," said Ike. "It's agreed that we'll try to discover the location of Dr. Bohr's notes and attempt their recovery from Axis territory."

"One more thing," said Montgomery. Everyone fell into silence again. "What I don't understand is why the Germans didn't pick up this Bohr fellow and force him to their side."

Ike shrugged.

"Another thing," Montgomery went on. "Why didn't we send someone in to kill him before they had the chance?"

16

It was the next morning, and a weak English sun struggled to break through the heavy haze. Three soldiers sat in front of a warming fireplace at Hayes House.

"It's a bluff, Ike," said Montgomery. "I'm sure of it."

Eisenhower seemed surprised. He looked to General Bradley, who sat in an easy chair next to Montgomery, and fought to keep the exasperation from his face. "You didn't seem so sure yesterday."

Monty nodded. "Yes, but I've been talking to some of *our* scientific chaps since then." The emphasis on the *our* left no doubt that Montgomery meant British scientists. "Our boys are not quite so sure that the Germans are as advanced in their research as *your* boys seem to think."

Eisenhower sighed. "Professor Duncan is one of your boys."

Montgomery waved that fact aside as if it were of no importance.

Bradley chimed in. "What about the intercepts warning their agents to stay clear of London?"

Monty shrugged. "Part of the game. Fact is, in 1940 we tried to make the Germans believe that we had a secret weapon we would use if they tried invasion." He chuckled. "What we had was a few old men with pitchforks."

"What about the radioactive canisters on the beaches?" asked Ike. "Is that part of a bluff, too?"

"Who can tell?" said Monty with a shrug. "At this point we can't be sure."

The two leaders were a contrast in military decorum. Eisenhower was sharp and neat, every crease in his uniform ironed to perfection. He wore the famous waist-cut battle jacket that had come to be called the "Ike" field jacket. There were four gold stars on each epaulet and a blaze of campaign ribbons above his left breast pocket. His plain, midwestern face was as usual open, smiling, and without guile.

Montgomery, in contrast, was in baggy fatigue trousers and a misshapen olive-drab sweater. His sharp, craggy features and long slender nose gave him a look of constant suspicion. His attire made him seem the poor relation of his well-dressed American cousins.

Eisenhower thought that Montgomery was an ill-tempered pain in the neck who happened to be a good soldier.

Montgomery thought that Eisenhower was an affable fool who knew nothing about being a soldier.

Ike lit another cigarette, masking his exasperation in a long exhalation of smoke. He was thinking how typical this turnabout was of Montgomery. Yesterday he wouldn't hear of proceeding with the invasion plans until the matter was settled. Now that everyone else agreed with him, he had changed his mind.

Ike watched his cigarette smoke wander to the ceiling. "What about Bohr's notes?" he said. "What if they have fallen into enemy hands?"

"Other than the intercepts, we have no proof of that."

"But," Ike insisted, "what if they have?"

Monty slumped forward, hands together, elbows on knees. "That would make quite a difference, wouldn't it? The scientific people tell me that Bohr's calculations might hand the Germans the bomb on a silver platter."

"It will still take time to construct it," said Bradley helpfully.

Ike smiled. "Yes, but we can't be sure how much time, can we?"

The three men fell into silence. Ike got up and walked to the window, pulling back the curtains and staring out into the gray English morning. For some reason he'd never been able to fathom, this weather made him think of Kansas cornfields and blazing summer sun. Perhaps it was the contrast. Somehow he found himself thinking about home a lot lately.

He turned back to the other two. "So what do we do? Sit back and wait or plow ahead?" He was looking at Bradley, but the questions were directed at Montgomery.

"I think," said Montgomery, "that our decision to recover the notes is our only course of action."

Ike stifled a smile, feeling that he had led Montgomery to the desired response. "Fine," he said. "But how do we do it?"

Monty shrugged. "We'll send some of our Special Operations chaps in there to bring back the documents."

"Why not let the resistance find them and destroy them?" said Bradley. "It might be easier."

"The resistance," said Montgomery, "is unreliable—riddled with informers. It's too risky to trust anyone but our own people. The SO boys can take care of it."

"I'd want the OSS in on this too," said Ike.

Monty was about to protest but changed his mind. He'd fought this battle too many times and was tired of the constant skirmishing. The Americans were slowly, surely, and inexorably wielding their power in all areas of the war. "Fine," he said with a small sigh. "Our boys can take one of your chaps along with them."

Ike's eyes narrowed momentarily. This was the typical lopsided arrangement always proposed by the British. They didn't seem willing to accept the fact that their power was no longer supreme in the alliance. He smiled and gave a quick nod. "Then it's settled. As soon as possible, we send in a team to recover the documents."

Monty was silent.

"If the documents are still there, we're home free. If not"—Ike shrugged—"then we're back to square one."

Ike looked to Bradley, who nodded in agreement and slapped his palms to his knees as he rose from his chair. "That's it then," he said.

The meeting was apparently over, but Montgomery did not seem to notice that both Americans were on their feet. He sat, face stern, lips pursed, doubt spreading across his craggy features.

Ike tried to ignore him. "I'll have Donovan at the OSS send the American participant as quickly as possible. The sooner this is taken care of, the better." He looked at Bradley. Good Lord, he thought, what is it now? He forced a smile. "What is it, Monty? What's troubling you? Isn't this what you recommended?"

Montgomery sighed and caught Eisenhower in a hard stare. He knew that part of the American's success lay in letting others think they had made the decisions that he had wanted in the first place. "Yes," he said sarcastically. "I think this is what *we* wanted." His hard look turned into a smile. "I wonder, however, if this isn't what Gerry wants."

Bradley turned to Eisenhower with a shrug. "I don't get it."

Ike nodded, in accord with Montgomery. "We know where the documents are hidden. The Germans either have them or don't know where they are. Maybe they are trying to force us to lead them to the hiding place."

"Precisely," said Montgomery, nodding.

"Do we have any other choices?" asked Ike.

Montgomery looked away for a moment. Outside the sun was fighting to break through the haze. "I'm afraid we don't," he said. "I'm afraid there are no other choices."

17

The noise was deafening—absolutely mind boggling. The four great Packard-Merlin two-thousand horsepower engines of the B-17 droned in synchronized mayhem, the pounding vibration a constant physical presence.

The young army lieutenant pulled his wool cap over his ears and tugged at the strings on the fur-lined hood of his borrowed flight parka in a fruitless attempt to block out the noise and the bone-chilling cold. He had never been more uncomfortable in his life. In combination, the noise, the cold, and the vibration were almost unbearable. He shifted on the metal frame seat that someone had obligingly fitted with a cushion. It didn't help. His rear end and back were stiff and sore.

"Coffee, Lieutenant Chapman," said a voice above the sound of the engines, and the lieutenant opened his eyes to see an airman standing in front of him with a steaming mug of coffee.

Slowly, he removed one of his gloves. "Thanks," he said, reaching for the mug, enjoying the pain as the warmth attacked his frozen fingers.

Hands on hips, the airman—one Angelo De Rosa of Jersey City—grinned arrogantly at his passenger. He had made this ferry trip several times and considered himself an old hand at the business of transporting warplanes from the United States to Europe. His was the northern route, which took him from New York to Labrador to Iceland, and on to Prestwick, Scotland. The outside temperature at fifteen thousand feet was twenty below zero, and the inside temperature, even with the B-17's glycol heating system at full blast, hovered around freezing.

Besides Airman De Rosa and the passenger, there

was only a pilot and copilot aboard. The B-17 had been stripped of all armament to reduce the weight of the aircraft, and all Plexiglas windows and openings had been sealed to keep out the cold and reduce wind drag. Upon arrival in Scotland the B-17 would be refitted with fourteen .50-caliber machine guns and readied to join one of the Eighth Air Force's bases in England.

"How's the coffee, Lieutenant Chapman?" asked De Rosa, grinning stupidly. He was enjoying the officer's apparent discomfort.

"Hot," said Chapman. Even with the fleece-lined coat and gloves, he was freezing.

The airman snorted a laugh. "That's what everybody says." He moved toward the bulkhead door leading to the radio compartment. "There's more if you want it. Just holler."

"How much longer?" Chapman yelled as the airman disappeared through the door.

De Rosa's head reappeared in the doorway. "Not much," he grinned. "About six hours." His smile broadened. There was nothing like seeing an officer uncomfortable. Especially one who had hitched a last minute ride.

The lieutenant leaned back in his seat, holding the mug against his frozen cheeks. Six hours, he thought, then what? The last few days had been a jumble of orders, travel plans, and hasty decisions made by strangers.

Lieutenant Andrew Chapman had been selected from a small pool of agents-in-training and hurriedly sent on to New York to make the first available flight to Scotland. He had been assigned to the Special Operations training school and Number 7 Commando at Galloway in Scotland.

He knew from the intensity of the OSS training in the past few days that the men were being groomed for something important. Activity had reached a feverish level, and anticipation had hung over them like a maiden aunt. The ritual of the selection process—men gathered together, commanding officer listing qualifications, Chapman being singled out—had only enhanced the feeling that something important was happening.

Chapman had been allowed a stopover in Scranton to see his parents on his way to New York, but it had been a too brief, unsatisfying encounter. The tranquility of his hometown and the ridiculous ordinariness of his own home had been too much for him to bear. Almost as soon as he had arrived he was preparing to leave. He had told his parents that he had to meet a friend in New York, and two days after his arrival they had accompanied him to the train station to see him off.

The young lieutenant, who now sat freezing in an unbearably uncomfortable chair, was young and blond and handsome. He had the body of an athlete, long, lean, and muscular, and the quick mind of the superior student. In his young life he had enjoyed the best that his country could offer, and he was now on his way to pay her back.

Other than a vague feeling of its importance, he was not certain what his mission would be. Training exercises had given him and the others some idea of the type of mission, but in the absence of concrete orders, he could not be sure.

He smiled, thinking of the Hollywood salute that Colonel Goodwin had given him after presenting him with his travel orders. It was the same kind of salute that Tyrone Power and Errol Flynn received from their commanding officers when they breezed off on another secret mission.

The other men in the training group had received two-week passes, while Chapman had immediate travel orders.

So much for the fruits of success.

He chuckled at the irony. At least, he thought, the winner had received a more impressive send-off than the losers.

Colonel Goodwin had personally escorted Chapman to his ground transport and then had snapped off another beautiful Hollywood salute, which had been returned just as snappily.

MORITURI TE SALUTAMUS.

Soldiers respected death, and those who volunteered for hazardous duty were usually held in high esteem only by those whose job it was to send them off. The ordinary foot soldier laughed at the volunteer and thought he was slightly crazy. But the commanders, those who sat behind a desk and planned the next suicide mission, were always impressed with the man who was foolish enough to volunteer.

The lieutenant drained his mug, put his glove back on, and tried to settle down in the flimsy chair. He could have used the rest, but the incessant drumming of the engines proved more powerful than sleep.

■

Ernst Luddeck waited in the rose garden in Tiergarten Park. Even at ease he seemed to be holding himself at attention as he paced back and forth across the paths around the rose beds. In his magnificent field-gray Waffen-SS uniform with the silver piping that he often wore to distinguish himself from the dark uniformed desk jockeys of the regular SS, he was a formidable figure.

He checked his watch again and expelled a short exasperated sigh. At a sound behind him, he turned to find Brigadeführer Schellenberg approaching him on the path. Luddeck resisted the temptation to give another reproachful glance at his watch to indicate how late Schellenberg was.

"The admiral was very talkative this morning," said Schellenberg, and Luddeck assumed that that was as close to an apology as he was going to get.

Luddeck clicked his heels and gave a half nod in salute.

Schellenberg smiled. "I feel like walking, do you?" He seemed ebullient this morning.

Luddeck fell into step without comment, and the two men walked through the park, exiting on Tiergarten Strasse near Bendler.

Still Schellenberg had said nothing. Luddeck was content to wait for the Brigadeführer to begin.

They walked down Bendler Strasse past a vast complex of modernistic concrete buildings with tan, stucco walls and high rows of identical windows. Wing after wing branched out from the main building, forming several sunlit courtyards. This was the headquarters of the Army General Staff.

Schellenberg motioned toward the building with a jerk of his head and spoke for the first time in almost ten minutes. "Inside they are trying to formulate excuses for the Russian disaster."

Luddeck was discreetly silent.

"Our plan goes forward," said Schellenberg. "If we are successful, we will save them all from the hangman."

Now they were walking past the offices of the Naval High Command, a more conventional building with huge gray granite columns supporting a squat ugly facade.

"Do you have any news for me from the Reichsführer's office, Ernst?" It was the first time that Schellenberg had ever called Luddeck by his given name.

"Yes, Herr Brigadeführer," said Luddeck, maintaining the formalities between the two.

Schellenberg didn't seem particularly interested in whatever information Luddeck had. He stopped at a street corner and peered down a side street. Standing alongside the waters of a narrow canal was a row of gray stone townhouses. "Tirpitz Ufer," said Schellenberg, as if in a trance.

Luddeck nodded matter-of-factly. He knew that this was the home of the Abwehr and the seat of power for Admiral Canaris.

"If our plan works, Ernst, the Abwehr will soon be under my jurisdiction."

"Yes, Herr Brigadeführer," said Luddeck obediently.

"I will need someone to run it for me," said Schellenberg, smiling broadly at Luddeck.

Luddeck's eyes widened and his back stiffened.

"Do you think you could handle such a responsibility, Ernst?"

"Me, Brigadeführer?"

"It is one of the most prestigious jobs in the Reich."

Luddeck's casual attitude was gone. "It would be a great honor, Brigadeführer."

Schellenberg smiled, thinking that he knew how to reach the heart of every man he had ever known. "If we do our job now," he said, "there will be honors enough for both of us."

Turning quickly, Schellenberg began to retrace his steps back toward the park. He had shown the bait, no need to overdo it. If Reichsführer Himmler wanted to plant a man in the middle of this operation, that was fine with Schellenberg. Schellenberg just wanted to make sure that the man worked for him.

Luddeck rushed to keep himself at his new master's side.

"You were going to tell me the news from the Reichsführer's office," said Schellenberg pleasantly, continuing his brisk pace.

"Yes. It seems that the Allies have taken the bait. A team is being prepared to recover the documents."

Schellenberg's eyes sparkled. "Excellent. They are doing exactly as we hoped."

They walked for a bit in silence, and then he said, "Does the Reichsführer get this information from the Red Lady?"

Luddeck cleared his throat. He had not been instructed to tell how the information was obtained. He decided quickly. "Yes."

"And where do you think the Red Lady gets his information?" asked Schellenberg, who pursued an advantage wherever he found it.

Luddeck took a deep breath. "It seems that the Russians have a spy very well placed in Section five of the British Secret Intelligence Service. The minute the decision was made, the Russians knew about it." Luddeck smiled with satisfaction. "And of course when they know about it, so do we."

"It's too bad," said Schellenberg, "that the Red Lady

can't tell us where the documents are hidden. That would certainly make things a lot easier."

"We will find them," said Luddeck confidently. "The mouse has already taken the bait."

Schellenberg laughed, but it was a laugh without mirth. "A mouse?" he questioned as he walked, his hands behind his back, his open greatcoat flapping in the breeze. "You might take care, Ernst, that your mouse doesn't smell like a rat."

Luddeck stopped, his eyebrows lifting in surprise at Schellenberg's sudden change in manner. He fell behind Schellenberg and had to quick step to catch up before the Brigadeführer disappeared through the Tiergarten gate.

■

A staff car waited on the tarmac as the B-17, wings glinting silver in the pale Scottish sunlight, banked into an approach at Prestwick's airfield. At the far end of the field, in long, straight rows like Kansas corn, sat the earlier arrivals, most still in their factory silver.

Row after magnificent row of factory-fresh Boeing B-17s awaited the arrival and fitting of the armament that would complete their preparation and speed their delivery to the Eighth Air Force, where they would join the already huge and growing air armada that daily struck at the heart of Fortress Europe. Like huge stingless hornets they sat, lacking only venom to send them swarming.

A rear door of the staff car opened and an American officer stepped out. He put his elbows on the door and watched the B-17 touch down at the end of the far runway and hurtle toward his car. The wheels touched before the sound of the squeal reached him, and he watched the huge craft bounce slightly and almost become airborne again before settling down to race down the runway.

He shrugged absently. Ferry pilots, he thought, weren't always the best available.

As the huge plane taxied past him he got back into the car, and his driver began to follow the B-17. He could see clearly the sealed Plexiglas gunports that would soon bristle with .50-caliber machine guns and the new chin turret whose twin fifties would surely surprise any German fighter pilot who tried the traditional head-on pass at the B-17s in formation.

The car pulled up on the right side of the plane next to the tail section, and once again the officer got out. A small door on the rear fuselage opened, and a lieutenant, looking skyward as though thankful for his deliverance, stepped out.

"Lieutenant Chapman?" the waiting officer called out, and the young lieutenant turned with a nod.

"That's me," he said, reaching back inside the plane to extract a large duffel bag.

"I'm Lieutenant Rollins," said the other. "Colonel asked me to provide transportation." He turned to the man in the driver's seat of the staff car. "Corporal, get the lieutenant's gear."

"Yes, sir," mumbled the corporal and went to Chapman's aid. He yanked at Chapman's duffel bag, which was almost too large to get through the door.

"Better let me do it," said Chapman. "I dragged this stuff four thousand miles. Why destroy it now?" He smiled to show that he was only half serious, but the corporal shrugged and backed away to let him finish the job himself.

"I thought you might want to grab some lunch and get cleaned up before we send you off to your next stop," Rollins suggested.

"Fine with me," said Chapman as he slumped in the seat, luxuriating in the soft comfort of the cushions.

"We'll get you fixed up and on your way by early afternoon. I understand you're off to one of the British camps south of here."

Chapman nodded but added nothing.

"Should have you there by early evening," said Rollins.

"Fine."

"Sounds very hush-hush," Rollins said, his unspoken question hanging in the air between them.

"Yes," said Chapman. "I suppose it is."

18

Less than an hour from Prestwick the terrain turned bleak and inhospitable, a misty rain drenching everything in sight, and Chapman huddled in the backseat of the staff car, clutching the collar of his coat beneath his chin as if shielding himself from the desolation outside.

"It's like this all along the coast," said the driver, a British corporal who had been assigned to transport him to his destination. "Be a little less desolate where we're going."

Soon the landscape did indeed change, and the car plowed on through lush green countryside. On both sides of the single-lane road were slope-shouldered green hills with purple heathery garlands around their crests. Between the hills lay long meadows crisscrossed by low stone walls and populated at every turn by herds of sheep. Every once in a while the car whisked past a small stone cottage with a thatched roof and smoke curling skyward from a tall chimney. These and the sheep were the only signs of life.

In another half hour they pulled off the road onto a gravel driveway that led to a large, three story, gray granite building with wings on either side.

"It's a mansion," said Chapman in amazement. He had expected rows of Quonset huts and had found instead an eighteenth century palace.

"Yes," said the driver. "This is the ancestral home of the fifth earl of Galloway. It's called Galloway House."

"Where is he now?"

The driver shrugged as he pulled the car to a stop in front of the main entrance. "Edinburgh, I suppose.

Nice enough to let us have the run of the place for the duration."

"It's not quite what I expected," said Chapman.

"It's big enough to house the staff and trainees, and the grounds provide room for training exercises."

Chapman stepped out of the car and looked up at the house. "Quite a place," he said admiringly.

The driver chuckled as he climbed out of the car and retrieved the lieutenant's gear from the trunk. "Don't expect to live like the landed gentry," he said. "Most of the earl's furniture is in storage. We've brought in our own stuff."

They went in through the double-doored entrance into a spacious vestibule with a wide staircase to the upper floors. The corporal led him into a room on the left, where Chapman was surprised to see a woman in uniform. She turned to face them as they entered, a pretty woman in her late twenties dressed in the khaki uniform of the First Aid Nursing Yeomanry. On the shoulder straps of her blouse were the single markings denoting a second lieutenant.

"Evening, Lieutenant," said the driver. "This is Lieutenant Chapman. He'll be staying with us for a short time. Could you fix him up?"

The woman smiled a greeting. She was, thought Chapman, damned good-looking. She wore her brown hair short and swept back to one side. Her cheeks were rosy, and beneath long lashes her brown eyes were large and seductive. "Be glad to, Corporal," she said and then turned her attention to Chapman. "Welcome to Galloway," she said, extending her hand.

Chapman, speechless in her presence, shook her hand. "Thank you," he managed to mumble.

"Follow me," she said, and Chapman went with her to what turned out to be a supply room. As he walked behind her into the room he took stock of her assets. Nice legs, he thought. Good slim ankles. He was beginning to recover from the surprise of seeing a beautiful woman in what he had thought would be a desolate training outpost. A smile formed on his lips as he observed her shape beneath the well-fitting uniform skirt.

The woman turned and eyed him as if she had read his mind. "By the way," she said, "I'm Margaret Brown. How long will you be with us?"

"I'm not really sure," he answered truthfully.

"You with Bishop's bunch?"

He shrugged. "I don't know. So far, no one has told me anything."

She smiled. "Don't worry. I'll get you fixed up, and I'm sure someone will be in to see you."

She handed him sheets and a thick brown blanket from metal racks where such supplies were stacked, then turned to look him up and down.

Chapman felt himself blush at her blatant stare.

"These should do," she said, pulling down a heavy wool khaki uniform without markings. It was the standard British battle dress.

"I have my own fatigues," said Chapman.

She shrugged. "Everybody wears these here." She smiled. "Nice and warm."

He started to protest, but the woman simply placed a green commando beret on top of the pile of clothing. "You're attached to Number Seven Commando now, Lieutenant." Her face broke into a wide smile. "Enjoy the experience, Yank."

Chapman made a face. He had been called "Yank" at least ten times since his arrival, and it was beginning to grate on him. It wasn't so much the term "Yank" as the way the British said it—derisively, as if they were making a joke at his expense.

Margaret Brown caught his expression. "Something wrong?" she asked.

"Name's Andrew Chapman," he said quietly.

"You told me that," she began before it dawned on her. "Oh. You don't like being called Yank?"

"Not much," he said.

She smiled. "Get used to it"—she paused—"Andrew. That's what everyone around here will call you . . . except me."

"Thanks," he said. Their eyes met for a little longer than either intended.

She seemed flustered for the first time, her cool, confident air dissipating in the heat of his stare. "Let me get the rest of your things, and then I'll have one of my girls show you to your quarters."

"How many women are stationed here?"

"Eight of us," she said from behind a stack of shelves, where she gathered socks and a shirt and a sweater. She came back to the table. "There's Captain Welles, who's in charge of the FANY contingent"—she grinned foolishly—"and there's me. Then there is a sergeant and five corporals. All assigned to administrative duties."

"No privates?"

She laughed, displaying white, even teeth. "We have to have rank on somebody." She walked to the door and called to someone in the hallway. "Corporal Wilson, in here please."

Corporal Wilson, a chunky block of a girl in her early twenties, entered. Her hair was cut short and she wore a pasty smile on her face. "Yes, Lieutenant?"

"This is Lieutenant Chapman. He has been assigned to room thirty-two. Would you show him the way?"

Chapman grimaced at this vision in uniform and thought he detected a sly smile on Margaret Brown's face. Chapman turned his back on the waiting corporal. "How about if I come back when I get settled in?"

Margaret Brown seemed puzzled. "Don't you have everything?"

"Maybe we could have a drink—or a coffee or something?"

Her eyes widened as she understood his meaning. "Oh, I see." She smiled sympathetically. "I don't think so Lieutenant. I've got lots of paperwork to handle before I turn in. Besides there's no place to get a drink around here and our coffee is dreadful."

"I've got a bottle of Scotch in my bag."

"Don't tell me you brought nylons and chocolates to entice the little English girls too?"

He didn't understand her sarcasm. "No, just the Scotch."

She thought about it, and he found himself praying fervently that she would say yes.

"I do have work to do," she said, cautioning him.

"I'll wait," he said. "I never go to sleep early."

She laughed. "That'll change after tomorrow. Everybody around here is asleep early."

He shrugged. "Whattya say?" he asked boyishly.

Lieutenant Brown looked at Corporal Wilson, who was observing all this in embarrassed silence. Finally she made up her mind. "Eleven o'clock too late?"

"No," he said quickly.

"Meet me in the second floor lounge. It's about the only place left in this monstrosity with some comfortable chairs."

"See you then," Chapman said and turned to face Corporal Wilson.

"Follow me," the corporal said and started for the stairs.

On the third floor there were two small rooms and four dormitory-style large ones, where enlisted men were billeted. Chapman found that he was sharing his room with two other officers.

One stood up and offered his hand. "John Iverson," he said. "You must be Chapman."

"Yes," said Chapman, looking to the third man, who remained sitting on his bed leafing through a magazine.

"That's Madsen," said Iverson. He shrugged. "Doesn't say much."

Madsen nodded a lukewarm greeting.

"Danish," said Iverson by way of explanation.

Chapman dropped his things on the one remaining bed and looked around the room. It would have been reasonable for one, adequate for two, but was definitely overcrowded with three. Other than the three cots, there was only one dresser and one hard-backed chair. Beside each bed was a small cabinet with a drawer and a lamp.

Chapman switched on his lamp and rummaged through his duffel bag. "Anyone like a drink?" he asked, holding aloft the Scotch.

"You Yanks are bloody marvelous," said Iverson, cup already in hand. Chapman poured him a good hefty drink, and Iverson sipped it reverently. Looking over at the Dane, Chapman raised the bottle encouragingly, but Madsen merely turned another page in the magazine.

"Does he speak English?" Chapman asked Iverson.

"I speak English quite well," said Madsen, the accent thick but the words clear.

"Are you here for training?" asked Chapman.

Madsen stood up. He was tall and muscular. His light hair hung across his forehead, and his face seemed set in a perpetual frown. "*You* are here for training," he said. "I am here to ensure that you are trained well." He stomped across the room, his boots rattling like machine gun fire on the tile floor, opened the door and left.

"What's his problem?" asked Chapman.

Iverson shrugged. "Who knows? He's just not a very friendly fellow. From what I understand he and this Major Bishop have been a special reconnaissance team with Number Seven Commando since Madsen got out of Denmark. Rumor has it that they've made over fifty trips behind enemy lines since 1942."

"I thought that foreigners were all in their own units."

"Most are," said Iverson. "But I guess those that have special skills get assigned to special units." He smiled. "Just like us."

"What's his special skill?"

Iverson drew his finger along his throat in a slashing motion and made a belching noise. "Likes to kill Germans, I think."

Chapman returned to his unpacking, spreading his clothing out on the bed.

"You can have one of the drawers in the dresser," said Iverson. "I'll move my things."

"Thanks," said Chapman without comment.

He opened his bedside cabinet, found a water pitcher and basin inside, and put the Scotch behind the basin. "What's the story on the girl downstairs?"

"Which one?" asked Iverson.

"Brown—the good-looking one."

"Oh, her. Forget it. You can't get near her. She acts as if she's God's gift to the armed forces."

"I'm supposed to meet her at eleven for a drink," said Chapman, trying to hide a pleased smile.

"Well, I'll be... You Yanks really are something," said Iverson admiringly. "I've got my eyes on Doris, the little corporal with the big knockers, but Margaret Brown is the prime target around here. So far no one has gotten as far as first base."

"She's not married, is she?"

"A widow, they say. Her old man was with the BEF in France. He was one of the unlucky ones who didn't get out at Dunkirk. They say she hasn't let anyone near her since."

A slow smile spread across Chapman's face. He plumped up his pillow. It was hard as a rock. "We'll see," he said, thinking about Margaret Brown. "We'll see about that."

"Lieutenant Chapman?" boomed a voice.

The lieutenant stood up quickly. "Yes, sir," he said, looking into the steady eyes of the man who had just entered the room.

"I'm Major Bishop, attached to the Number Seven Commando. I am in charge of the special reconnaissance group to which you have been assigned."

"Pleased to meet you, sir," said Chapman, carefully eyeing this mountain of a man, who seemed to fill the room. Bishop was tall and lean, his hard expression seemingly set in concrete. The face was young—no more than late twenties, Chapman imagined, but the eyes were ancient, and Chapman could not help but wonder what this man had been through to give him such world-weary eyes.

His motions swift and sure and graceful, he went to the dresser and sat on its edge, his arms folded across his chest. "I understand you went through OSS training at the British training camp in Canada."

"Yes," said Chapman. "Lots of British there. They run a pretty tough program."

Bishop's eyebrows lifted. "We'll see," he said quietly. "How much did they tell you about this operation?"

"Not much," said Chapman with a shrug. "I was hoping that you'd fill me in."

"Not yet. Twenty-four hours before we're scheduled to leave we'll be quarantined and then given all the details. If you want to back out then, you can."

"I won't back out," said Chapman confidently.

"We'll see," said Bishop. The two men stared quietly at each other for a moment, Chapman feeling that Bishop was giving him a spot evaluation.

Bishop looked at his watch. "You'd better turn in. We start our training program bright and early."

Chapman's face fell. "More training. I can't believe it."

Bishop showed little sympathy. "It's not that we don't trust your OSS training, Lieutenant. It's just that we have some time before our scheduled departure." A smile crossed Bishop's craggy features. "We don't want anyone growing stale in the meantime."

"I was hoping I'd get to see London before we left," said Chapman, his voice rising to a whine.

"Glasgow is not exactly London," Bishop said, "but it's a lot closer. Some of the men manage, somehow, to get there once in a while for some relaxation. I would think that most of them would be too tired after what we put them through here, but I guess part of soldiering is raising a wee bit of hell."

Chapman nodded. "How much time do we have?"

Bishop seemed not to understand.

"When are we going in?" asked Chapman.

Bishop's face was blank. "Going in where?"

Chapman laughed. "Look, I know that this is all hush-hush and everything, but it's fairly obvious that we're going behind enemy lines. I could even venture a pretty good guess at where we're going."

Bishop said nothing.

"Yes, those of us who were in training at the camp were obviously selected for—among other things— proficiency in Danish."

"What else can you venture a pretty good guess at?"

Chapman shrugged. "Well, by the training exercises we ran through constantly at the camp, I'd say we're going on some kind of recovery mission. Our training in sabotage was minimal, so I'd say we're going into occupied territory not to destroy something but to bring something back."

Bishop nodded. "I don't suppose it would be possible to select and train intelligent people without giving them some inkling of what's going on." He paused. "But let me warn you about being overly inquisitive about this mission. I think it would be to your benefit not to know too much about the purpose of our"—he paused—"recovery, as you so aptly put it."

"Why not? If I'm going, I should know what I'm getting into."

Bishop walked to the door. "I suppose you should," he said. "But let me warn you about an excess of knowledge. I know all about this mission, only because I have to in order to lead it. Because I know all about it, one of your responsibilities and the task of anyone else who accompanies us will be to shoot me if it appears that we might fall into enemy hands."

Chapman's eyes bulged. He could think of nothing to say.

Bishop stood, his hand on the doorknob, smiling sadly. "Sometimes knowledge is indeed dangerous." He opened the door. "See you at o-five-hundred hours. You'd better get some sleep."

At eleven o'clock Chapman tucked the Scotch under his arm and made his way down to the second-floor lounge, where Margaret Brown, kneeling in front of a huge fireplace, poker in hand, was stoking the fire.

She turned when she heard his approach. "Fire's almost gone out," she said. She was wearing a heavy olive sweater over her regulation blouse.

"Let me," said Chapman, taking the poker from her hand. He managed to turn the charred log that remained, took the small bellows from the hearth, and got the flames going again. He added some smaller pieces from a box at the side of the fireplace, and soon the fire was burning brightly.

"That should do it," he said.

Margaret was sitting on the sofa, watching him. Her eyes seemed to dance with the fire, and Chapman thought that at that moment she was one of the loveliest looking women he had ever seen.

"How about that drink?" he asked.

She nodded, pointing to the glasses and a water pitcher on the table behind the couch.

He poured two stiff drinks. "Water?" he asked.

She nodded, and he poured water into her glass but none into his own. He sat beside her, and they clinked glasses. "To new friends," he said, and Margaret Brown looked at him over the top of her glass. For a minute he thought she was going to laugh. "What is it?" he said. "What's so funny?"

"You Yanks," she said. "You think you're so smooth."

"I thought you weren't going to call me a Yank," he said.

Her face turned serious. "Do me a favor?" she asked.

"Anything."

"Don't make a pass at me right away." She shook her head sadly. "I'm really rather tired of that."

"Did I look like I was going to?"

She stared at him directly. "I don't know. I just thought it would be pleasant to have a drink and a chat with a nice young man without having to worry about what's going to happen."

Chapman touched his glass to hers. "No problem. A drink and a chat sounds fine to me."

They talked for over two hours, Chapman frequently stopping to stoke and replenish the fire. The house was so quiet that it might have been deserted. The fire cast long, dancing shadows on the dark, mahogany paneling, and they found themselves increasingly talking in whispered tones.

He had started by saying, "Tell me about yourself," and after insisting there was nothing to say, she had gone on for over an hour telling him about her life. The story seemed to flow out of her as if she'd had no one to tell it to for years.

She had been born in Belfast in 1920, and her father, unable to find work, had brought the family to England in 1924. In 1939 she had met and married Sergeant William Brown, who in 1940 had been part of Montgomery's 3rd Division with the BEF in France. Sergeant Brown had been one of the first casualties of the German offensive, and Margaret Brown, at twenty, had become one of the war's first young widows. In November of 1940, she told him, her family—father, mother, sisters, and a brother—had been lost in the great raid on Coventry. Another brother was a POW in Germany.

Chapman listened patiently as she went on. "After that," she said, "I sort of threw myself wholeheartedly into the war effort."

She had joined the First Aid Nursing Yeomanry and had first been assigned to the Royal Artillery with the 1st Anti-Aircraft Division. During that first summer of the war she and hundreds like her had been heavily engaged in the daily battles over London. In 1942 she had become part of the administrative staff of the Commando Training Center and had been assigned to Galloway House on the Solway Firth in Scotland.

"And," she said, raising her glass in salute, "here I am."

He was silent for a moment, thinking. Compared to her, the war had barely touched him. She had been battered and pounded and suffered blows that would have crushed a lesser person, but all she said was, ". . . here I am."

Chapman sipped his drink. "I think you're marvelous," he said.

"Oh, Yank," she said, smiling. "You're doing it again."

"What?" he asked innocently.

"Being so terribly smooth." Imitating his accent, she said, "I think you're marvelous," then laughed quietly.

He blushed. "It does sound dopey when you say it like that, but I meant it."

"Tell me about you," she said quickly as if she wanted to change the subject. "Tell me about Lieutenant Andrew Chapman."

"Nothing much to tell. Born in Scranton, Pennsylvania . . . attended Rutgers University . . . graduated

1941 . . . joined the army 1942 . . . officer's training school . . . I spent a year as an artillery instructor in Oklahoma and then volunteered for this operation. Had some special training and"—he smiled—"here I am."

He swallowed hard, her gaze made him slightly uncomfortable.

"Another drink," he said, breaking the long silence.

She stood up, straightening her skirt, pulling at her sweater. "No, thank you, Andrew. It's much too late." She smiled down at him. "You'll be cursing me tomorrow morning at o-five-hundred when you have to get up."

"I'd never do that."

She shook her head. "You're doing it again."

He stood up. "I guess I am." He swallowed. "Can I walk you to your room?"

Her eyes met his. "Yes, but I think you should know that I share a room with Captain Welles."

Chapman shrugged. "Life is filled with small disappointments."

Her room was on the same floor as the lounge, and they walked together in silence. The hallways were darkly quiet and, except for the low murmur of a conversation at the foot of the stairwell, the house seemed deserted. They walked down a carpeted hallway, and Margaret Brown stopped in front of the first door.

"This is it," she whispered.

He nodded, unsure of how to proceed.

"I had a lovely evening," Margaret said, moving imperceptibly closer to him so that their bodies were almost touching. She was looking up at him, her eyes bright as beacons, her lips wet and parted.

"So did I," he said and kissed her on the mouth.

For just an instant he felt her body melt into his before she stiffened and pulled back.

"Please," she whispered. "It's late. I've got to go."

He tried to kiss her again, but her lips avoided his until he realized that she was serious. "Okay," he said. "Will I see you tomorrow?"

She was looking somewhere past him. "Pretty hard not to, I suppose."

"I mean can we get together sometime tomorrow?"

She shook her head in sharp rapid strokes. "I don't know if that's wise." She looked up at him. "You'd better let me think about it."

He nodded. "All right."

Without another word she opened her door and slipped inside, leaving Chapman standing in the hallway.

Inside, Captain Lauren Welles turned to face her as she entered. Margaret, her back against the door, placed a finger over her lips to communicate that Welles should be silent. She listened at the door until she heard Chapman's footsteps on the bare floor at the end of the hallway.

"Okay, he's gone," she said.

"How did it go?" asked Welles.

"All right, I suppose," said Margaret. "He seems like a nice enough chap." She pulled her sweater over her head and threw it on the bed. Welles looked at her questioningly. "I hate this bloody job," said Margaret Brown with vehemence.

Welles shrugged. "I know it's difficult," she said, "but it's got to be done."

O-five-hundred hours came disgustingly soon, and Andrew Chapman found himself bleary-eyed and with a huge headache, standing in formation in the courtyard with twenty-four other men in training. It was not yet fully light. He was wearing the British battle dress he had been given the day before and was further encumbered by a full equipment pack that weighed close to forty pounds. Each man carried the standard British Enfield rifle, and every fourth man carried a rope and grappling hook for cliff scaling.

Chapman looked down the line. Every man stood rock still, bright and alert and eager. He could only think about getting back to bed.

"Little too early for you, Lieutenant?" barked the commando sergeant in charge of the training exercise.

Sergeant Major MacKenzie was a tall, broad-shouldered Scot with a thick brogue. His face was hard, his back ramrod straight. He eyed Chapman through eyes narrowed to suspicious slits. "We seem a wee bit red-eyed this mornin', Mr. Chapman," he said, with little respect for rank in evidence.

Chapman felt every eye on him. "No, Sergeant," he said pleasantly. "I just can't wait to get going."

The men laughed, and even the sergeant smiled a little before he led them, in double time, their boots clattering like animal hooves on the cobblestones, out of the courtyard and into the countryside for a full-equipment run.

Bishop watched from a ground-floor window as the column hiked its way down the driveway, past the gate, and left toward the shoreline. He let the curtain fall back into place and turned away from the view.

"What do you think?" said Madsen, who sat in a chair, teacup in hand, in the center of the room.

"Seems in good enough condition."

Madsen snorted derisively. "Seems soft to me."

Bishop went to the low table in front of Madsen and poured himself some more tea. "We'll find out how soft he is in these next few days. If he's not tough enough—he doesn't go. It's that simple."

Madsen made another guttural noise. "He goes because he's American. You and I both know that. It'll take more than doubts about his conditioning to get him off this mission."

Bishop sipped his tea. "We'll see, my friend. We'll see."

After a ten-mile run with full equipment, the men were led, without rest, in a mock assault on an abandoned farmhouse. Bullet holes on the heavy front door and pockmarks on the stone walls attested to the fact that this was not the first assault the farmhouse had suffered.

Afterward, the sergeant declared a rest period, and everyone ate in the field. Although there were the customary complaints about the American-provided C rations, the men seemed to devour every last morsel. Sergeant MacKenzie made a fire and brewed tea, and Chapman and the others luxuriated in the simple act of relaxing over a strong cup of the incredibly dark brew.

For the rest of the morning the sergeant demonstrated some of the weapons that they might expect to use in an assault on enemy shores. One weapon that Chapman found particularly intriguing was a kind of "sticky" hand grenade. It looked like a round glass ball with a short handle protruding from one end. The object was to throw the ball against an enemy tank or other armored vehicle. On impact the glass broke and an extremely sticky substance on the inside caused the explosives to stick to whatever they had struck.

"It is hoped," said Sergeant MacKenzie, his eyes rolling heavenward to show what he thought of this invention, "that this device will enable a ground soldier to destroy an enemy tank. Tests have demonstrated that the weapon actually works." He looked around the circle of men before adding, "So they say." He lowered his voice to something less than his usual bark. "If I were you, laddies, I'd as soon hit a Panzer tank with my bloody helmet as firing one of these popguns at it."

At noon they loaded up their equipment and marched back to the big house, where they enjoyed a hot lunch, Chapman marveling at how good simple food could taste.

That afternoon they ran an obstacle course—crawling under barbed wire, climbing walls, leaping ditches, fording an icy stream. All the while, MacKenzie barked orders—"Keep your head down! Move it! Faster, man, faster! Move it!" Chapman thought he would drop from exhaustion, but the others went on, so he called on some hidden reservoir of strength and continued.

It was already growing dark when they returned again to the house. Chapman had never been so tired in his life. Even a brief encounter with Margaret Brown, who passed the men in the courtyard as they entered, failed to revive him. A few of the men managed whistles, but Chapman's mouth was too dry to even venture a greeting.

Margaret Brown shook her head and passed him with an I-told-you-so smile on her face.

By seven P.M. Chapman was sprawled in his bed, dead to the world.

This was how it went for the next three days. He did see Margaret Brown each day—once even managing to engage her in a brief conversation, but she seemed cool, and Chapman was at a loss to explain the change in her attitude.

19

Nicholas Falzetti was deep in some paperwork at the beginning of the evening shift when he sensed that someone was standing next to his desk.

He looked up.

"Hello, Lieutenant," said a young patrolman who was vaguely familiar.

Falzetti squinted. "What can I do for you?"

The patrolman realized that Falzetti did not remember him. "Kevin Powers, Lieutenant." He waited and then added, "I was the officer on the scene at that murder-suicide over at the Hallmark."

Falzetti pretended he had known all along. "Sure, Kevin. How are you?"

"Fine, Lieutenant. The reason I stopped by is to tell you how I've been doing on that case."

At first Falzetti was puzzled, but suddenly it came to him. He had asked this kid, who seemed so eager to please, to do some legwork for him on the investigation and had then forgotten all about it. Now Falzetti was off the case, and this poor kid had been running around for nothing.

Too embarrassed to tell the kid the truth, he chomped on his cigar. "Come up with anything?"

"Well, I talked with a few of the neighborhood working girls—as you suggested."

"And?"

Powers shook his head. "Not much. One thought she might have seen the soldier with one of the men in the hotel room that night, but she didn't get a good look at him."

"She describe him at all?"

"Young, blond, well built, good-looking."

Falzetti sighed. "Could be him—but then again that could be a lot of people."

Powers smiled. "She said he was a second lieutenant."

Falzetti laughed. "How'd she know that?"

"This girl has a lot of experience with the military," said Powers, breaking into a wide grin.

"Did you test her?"

"Sure did. This girl could identify rank all the way up to a bird colonel."

Falzetti was still laughing. "She couldn't tell you what outfit he was with, could she?"

"Afraid not, Lieutenant," Powers said.

"Girl with that kind of experience could be a security risk if she fell into the wrong hands."

Both men were grinning foolishly now, the way that men usually do when the undercurrent of the conversation was about sex.

"Well, I guess that's it then," said Falzetti, who was toying with the idea of telling Powers that the FBI had taken jurisdiction over the case.

The patrolman didn't say anything, but a serious look came over his face.

"There's something else?" Falzetti said.

Powers seemed uncertain. "Maybe. It might be nothing."

"Let's have it."

"I've got a buddy up at the Twenty-third Precinct. He tells me that they pulled a body out of the East River a few days ago. Seems to me, he might have been our soldier boy from the Hallmark."

"What makes you say that?"

"Young, blond, well built . . ."

"Good-looking?"

"Hard to say. Somebody had worked him over pretty good before they dumped him. His face was pretty badly bruised. One thing though, Lieutenant."

"What's that?"

"He was a second lieutenant."

"Did they get a positive ID on the guy?"

Powers nodded. "Yeah. He was still wearing his dog tags."

"Anything else to tie him to the Hallmark?"

"Well, the detectives at the Twenty-third think it might be drug-related. The guy had needle marks in his arm."

Falzetti's eyes narrowed for a moment, then he got up and walked Kevin Powers to the door. "Thanks, Kevin," he said. "You just might be onto something. If you hear anything else let me know."

He watched Powers disappear down the stairs and then went back to his desk and picked up the phone.

When the Medical Examiner's Office answered, he asked for Frank Downes.

"What can I do for you, Nick?"

"Frank, remember that jumper over at the Hallmark?"

"Sure. I thought you were off that one."

"I am. This is unofficial. My curiosity has been killin' me. Sometimes I think that's why I became a cop. I can't stand loose ends."

"If you don't like loose ends, you're in the wrong business, Nick."

Falzetti forced a laugh. "You're right, Frank. But what about this Hallmark business? The last time we talked, you said something about the guy being loaded with drugs. Did you ever find out what it was?"

"Sure. I told the FBI all about it."

"So tell me."

"It was sodium thiopental."

"Which is?"

"It's a barbiturate that can be used to induce a kind of hypnotic state. No wonder the guy thought he could fly from that ledge."

"Frank, is this stuff anything like a truth serum?"

"Well, there actually isn't any such thing as a truth

serum, but somebody who was really doped up on this stuff might be more likely to be cooperative."

"Somebody wanted this top-security-clearance scientist to talk—so they stuck him full of the serum?"

"Seems that way. At least the FBI was very interested in that possibility."

"Did the FBI ever say what this guy was working on?"

"No. I asked, but they wouldn't say a word. I doubt if even they know what the guy was working on. One thing I did hear them say though . . ."

"What's that?"

"The other guy—Marcovic—was a commie."

"That right?"

"Yeah. I overheard one of the FBI people say that this Marcovic was 'One dead red.' The guy laughed when he said it. Thought it was real funny."

Falzetti was silent, thinking for a moment. "This is off the subject, Frank, but I heard about the body you got from the East River a few days ago."

"Last Friday," said Downes. "That's not in your precinct either, Nick. What, are you covering the whole city now?"

"It might have something to do with a case I'm working on. How long was he dead?"

"Hard to say. The river is almost freezing. It's like keeping a body on ice. You don't get the normal deterioration."

"How about an educated guess?"

"Anywhere from a few days to a week."

"Not any longer?"

"Definitely not."

"Why so definite?"

Downes chuckled. "Nothing scientific. The guy has been identified. His name was Karl Streetman, and he was known to have been alive a week before he was pulled out."

"I understand he was a soldier."

"That's right. Stationed in Virginia."

"What was he doing in New York?"

"Lived on Long Island, somewhere."

"Frank, send me anything you've got on this guy, will you? Name, address, anything."

"You got it."

"And, Frank?"

"Yes."

"I understand this guy had needle marks on his arm."

"That's right," said Downes, his voice betraying surprise at the extent of Falzetti's knowledge. "Detectives on the case suspected a drug-related motive."

"Did anybody test him for that sodium thiopental?"

"What? No . . . Is there any reason to suspect—"

"I don't know, Frank, but I'll keep in touch."

Falzetti sat at his desk for a long time after he hung up, staring absentmindedly. He relit his cigar and blew a ring of smoke, adding to the blue haze hanging in the room. Letting his mind roam freely over the details of the case, he could sense the excitement of the hunt begin to build. I don't like the feel of this one, he thought. He took out his small notebook and flipped back to the day of the murder-suicide, read through his notes, and made a few additions at the bottom of the page.

Then he closed the book. This isn't my case, he thought, let the FBI handle it. He almost laughed. It was difficult for him to think of the FBI without doing that. Bunch of college boys, he often called them. Running around pretending they knew about police work. What the FBI was really good at, he thought with a measure of bitterness, was showing up in time for the arrest and in time to take most of the credit from the cops who had solved the case.

Shit, he said to himself. If I leave this to the FBI, they'll diddle around for months before they do anything.

He put his notebook in his jacket pocket and leaned back, hands behind his head, blowing smoke rings at a furious pace.

20

The twenty-four men of the Commando Training Group sat on the rocks below the cliff that lined the shore. The beach itself was covered with smooth stones, and at brief intervals large outcroppings of rock jutted skyward. The sun was a dull orange ball of muted fire that emitted no heat through the covering mist, and the ocean was a dark bone-chilling gray.

Chapman looked around and caught Lieutenant Iverson's eye. "Nice day for the beach," he said. "Just like Coney Island in August."

Iverson laughed while holding his collar around his chin.

They had run to this spot from the courtyard of the great house and now sat gathering their collective breaths as the sergeant prepared for the exercise. They watched him standing beneath the cliff selecting the spot from which they would scale this vertical precipice.

"Good God," said Iverson. "Do you really think he's going to make us climb that cliff?"

"It certainly looks that way," said Chapman, leaning back on his pack. He turned away from the sergeant and looked out to the sea.

Two hundred yards off the beach, aground in the center of the bay, sat a rusting hulk—an old freighter that looked as if it might have come to disaster there twenty years ago.

When the tide was out, as it was now, almost the entire hull was visible from the shore and the derelict tipped at an extreme angle.

"What's that all about?" asked Chapman, pointing to the ship.

"They ran her aground in the shallows so that we can practice boarding exercises," Iverson replied.

"Looks like she's been there forever."

Iverson shrugged. "Two years." When Chapman seemed disbelieving, Iverson added, "In this war two years is forever."

The sergeant barked an order, interrupting their conversation, and the men rose and gathered around him while he explained the exercise.

"You men who have been with us for some time," he said, "are familiar with the rope-climb exercise on our obstacle course, where each man climbs a one-hundred-foot rope to the top of a tower." He paused and looked toward Iverson and Chapman. "Those of you who have joined us in the last few days are reported to have undergone similar physical training before your arrival. So today we will begin the more practical application of your training."

Chapman eyed Iverson, who gave a quick grin in response.

The sergeant took one of the climbing ropes and dropped it onto the rocks. "The rope is coiled," he said, holding one end, "and you must make sure that there is no snag when it is dropped to the ground." He removed a large grappling hook from a hitch on his belt and skillfully attached the end of the rope to the handle end of the hook.

He tested the security of the knot, then, satisfied, began to whirl the hook over his head in ever widening arcs.

"This is the fun part," he said as the rope made whooshing noises against the wind, "but you'd better be careful you don't wind up with this hook in your arse."

The man laughed, and the sergeant released the rope, flinging the hook high into the air. The rope at his feet played out swiftly as the hook disappeared over the top of the cliff.

The sergeant pulled hard on the line and the hook caught firmly. "This cliff is about sixty feet high," he said, "so it should take less than a minute to get to the top." He sprang forward and, to Chapman's amazement, practically ran up the sheer face of the cliff. Scrambling over the top, he stood on the edge, hands on hips.

"Nothing to it, laddies," he called from above. "It's like running up a flight of stairs."

In a matter of seconds he was back down on the beach. "All right, let's all give it a try," he barked. "Split up into groups of four. Spread out and get those ropes ready."

The men shuffled into position, Chapman and Iverson managing to get into the same group. Everyone stood back as the rope-men twirled the hooks in ever expanding circles above their heads.

"Be ready," called the sergeant. "When I give the word, I want you to release the hooks at the same time."

He waited as the rope sounds whipped through the wind, then screamed, "Now!"

Five of the six hooks actually went sailing over the top of the cliff. One fell short and clattered back onto the rocks. The sergeant glared at the man whose toss had been found wanting.

"Let's get it up there," he yelled and the trainee scrambled for the hook while his group struggled to coil the rope in preparation for the next throw.

In just a few minutes the hook was whirling overhead and on its way. This time the toss was successful.

The sergeant went down the line, tugging at each rope, testing the strength of the hold. Two of the ropes did not test to his satisfaction, and he tied a large loop in the bottom of each rope. "Stay away from these," he cautioned. "Not secure." He returned to the men. "Any questions before we proceed?"

Chapman's hand shot up and the sergeant gave him a withering look. "Yes?"

"You said these cliffs are about sixty feet, Sergeant." The sergeant was nodding, his lips pursed impatiently. "What happens if we encounter cliffs higher than these—let's say one hundred feet—like some of the cliffs on the

French coast? I don't think you can throw a hook that high with any reasonable degree of consistency."

"Right you are, Lieutenant. In that case we have a nicely modified mortar that will launch our hook just as high as we want it to go."

Chapman nodded. "Thank you, Sarge."

The sergeant smiled. "Now, how would you like to be the first one up the rope?"

Chapman shrugged, pulling on the gloves that each man had looped through his belt. The sergeant selected three others to lead their groups aloft. "You four men will go up top, check the security of the hooks and their position. When you have done that, wave your group aloft." He looked around, scanning the faces in front of him. His power was absolute. The men knew he had done this in combat—he had been one of the few to return from Dieppe. "Ready," he called, and the four men crouched, ready to race for the ropes. At the yell of "Go!" they plunged forward, Chapman getting to his rope first and heaving himself aloft the way he had observed the sergeant.

Muscles straining against the rope, boots slipping against the rocks, the men struggled to heave themselves into the air. Where the sergeant had seemed to bound from foothold to foothold, the other men moved forward fitfully, looking for a secure place for each giant step.

One man slipped, slamming face-first into the cliff and almost losing his grip on the rope. The others continued the struggle upward. Chapman was the first to the top, pulling himself over the edge and rolling over onto his back in exhaustion. The earth was soft, and the smell of the grass filled his lungs. He could have stayed here forever.

"Check the hook," he heard the sergeant bellow from below, and Chapman rolled over onto all fours and struggled to his feet. Parallel to and about ten feet back from the edge of the cliff was a row of logs. Each log was held in place by stakes driven into the ground at each end. It was to these logs that the grappling hooks had held. The two hooks that the sergeant had judged insecure had fallen short of the logs and were imbedded in the short grass. Chapman could see the gouge in the earth that had been made when the sergeant had tugged on the rope.

He checked the security of his hook as two of the others pulled themselves over the top. Chapman raced to the edge to wave on the rest of his group from below.

That's how it went for the rest of the afternoon—up and down the sheer face of the cliff. Soon the men were bounding and leaping and driving themselves to the top, and Chapman found that it now took him half the time and energy that it had on his first try.

After each man had ascended and descended a half-dozen times, they turned it into a game—a relay race in which the object was to transport an entire team and its equipment to the top of the cliff before any of the others could do likewise. Knowing that such competition relieved boredom and instilled team spirit, the sergeant did not object.

The technique, first developed by Chapman's team, was to send a single man aloft to check the hook, then the second man would go. When he reached the top, the first would grab him and pull him up. As soon as the first two touched hands at the top, the third man would start his ascent. The pattern would be repeated until all four men in the group were on top. Then they would pull up their equipment, which had been secured to the end of the rope.

Late in the afternoon Sergeant MacKenzie decided that the men, now resting at the top of the cliff, had had enough. He stood up. "Gather up your equipment, laddies," he bellowed. "It's time we started back." He was pleased with the way the day had gone. The men had accepted his direction and, by competing, had driven themselves further than he had dared to hope.

"How about one more go, Sergeant MacKenzie?" said Hawkins, one of the men from group three. Hawkins was the youngest of the trainees and had an infectious enthusiasm that pleased MacKenzie. The other men, seeing the sergeant smile, took up the cry.

MacKenzie smiled. "Okay. One more go. Then that's it."

The men spread out into their six groups, and one by one lowered themselves back down to the beach. The sergeant loosened the hooks and threw them back over the edge, then waited for the hooks to come flying back. This time, he observed with satisfaction, all six hooks sailed across the logs and lodged securely when the men below pulled on them. He saw all six ropes grow taut and knew that the first climbers were on the way up. In less than a minute Chapman's head appeared over the edge, and the sergeant gave him a nod of approval as he scrambled over. In rapid succession first one, then two, then all of the others appeared, pulling themselves to the top. The men below were yelling encouragement as the second group of climbers started from below. Soon, the second group appeared at the edge and were helped over the top, the ropes momentarily going slack before again growing taut with the weight of the third climber.

It was at this point, when each team had two men on the top and one midway that everyone heard a loud crack. It happened so suddenly that most of those on the top gave different versions of the incident. But one thing was certain: the first thing out of the ordinary had been the loud noise—some said like a gunshot, others like a small explosion—when the grappling hook of group three had ripped through the log and sprung loose. Everyone reacted to the sharp crack, heads jerking around in unison in the direction of the sound. The two men of group three who had already scaled the cliff turned toward the noise. One stood at cliff's edge, straddling the rope, prepared to pull the next man aloft; the other, Hawkins, was about six feet behind him. He turned just in time to see the hook hurtling toward him. Hawkins had no time to duck or react in any way. The flying hook caught him in the shoulder, the lower barb imbedding itself under his collarbone, another barb just missing his face.

The man straddling the rope was lifted off his feet as

the rope snapped upwards into his groin, propelling him over the edge.

He did the only thing he could do and grabbed on to the rope as he plummeted into space, adding his weight to the hook, which dragged his impaled teammate to the edge.

It was a frozen moment—everything happening in slow motion but with no time for reaction. Everyone remembered with photographic precision the look of shocked surprise on the face of the head man as he went over the edge and the blood-curdling shriek of Hawkins impaled by the hook.

The sergeant was the first to react, but he was too far away to be of any assistance. Chapman was not the closest, but of those in the vicinity he was the only one to snap out of his shocked stupor. The American was standing at the edge of the cliff prepared to haul his man over the top when he heard the sharp crack and almost instantaneously Hawkins' scream as he took the full force of the hook in the chest. As the other man disappeared over the edge, Chapman dove for the rope. The rope whirred through his hands, burning a track through his gloves and into his palms. He screamed in pain, but he held on. Hawkins, flat on his back, thrashing helplessly like a hooked fish was beside him now, and both were being dragged to the edge when Chapman felt someone grab at his legs. MacKenzie had grabbed him just as he was about to go over.

"Hold on, laddie," he heard the sergeant call. In a flash the sergeant had the rope, and suddenly the weight was bearable.

It had happened in an instant, and in seconds it was over. Chapman rolled away from the rope as the others held on until the two men below could lower themselves to the beach. Then the sergeant ripped open the injured man's tunic, grimacing at the ugly blue point of impact where the hook had stuck.

"Dressing," he called, and one of the men gave him some rolled bandages. He made a compress to halt the flow of blood while the other men made a stretcher with their garrison belts. Hawkins was unconscious most of the time.

The sergeant stood up. "All right. I want this boy back at HQ as fast as possible. You, Murchison." He pointed to the man who always led on their ten-mile morning run. "I want you to run ahead and tell them to get things ready."

Murchison was gone, racing off like the wind through the tall grass.

The others slipped the net of belts under the injured man and gently raised him off the ground.

"All right," bellowed the sergeant. "Hop to it. I don't want this lad to bleed to death."

Six men raced off after Murchison.

The sergeant watched them go, then turned to Chapman, who sat on the ground, his bleeding palms face up in his lap. "You all right, Lieutenant?"

Chapman nodded. He held out his hands. "They'll be okay. Nothing serious."

"Good," said the sergeant, then paused as if he wanted to say more. He was a man who did not give or receive praise easily. "I want you to take charge of the men on the beach. I'm going after the lads," he said. "Get these men back. Then we'll see to those rope burns of yours."

Chapman struggled to his feet without using his hands to assist him. "Okay, Sarge. I'll see you back at the house."

MacKenzie hesitated once again. "Lieutenant?"

"Yes, Sergeant?" said Chapman.

"Damn good job, sir."

Chapman shrugged. He started to say, "Thank you, Sarge," but MacKenzie was already running after his men.

By the time Chapman returned to the manor house, Bishop was waiting for him. The men who had carried back the injured boy were sitting on the steps of the house as Chapman led his men into the courtyard.

"I understand you made a good showing out there," said Bishop.

Chapman grimaced. "Instinctive reaction, Major. Nothing terribly heroic."

"None of us are heroic if we take the time to think about it. It's instinctive reaction that shows what we're made of."

"How is the man who was hurt?" said Chapman, realizing for the first time that he didn't even know the injured man's name.

"Hawkins? Doctor thinks he'll be fine. Be out of action for a few months, but no permanent damage." Bishop looked at the way Chapman held his hands away from his body. "We'd better get someone to look at those hands. Get some ointment and bandages on them." His eyes narrowed. "Anything serious?"

Chapman shook his head. "I think they'll be all right. Lucky I was wearing my gloves."

"Very good then. I'll let you get in to see the doctor. He's probably going to be busy with Hawkins for a bit, but I'm sure he can fix you up in no time." He stepped back, and Chapman hoped he wasn't going to salute. He didn't. He gave a brief wink. "Damn good job, Lieutenant," he said and tramped off across the courtyard.

As soon as he was gone, Chapman was surrounded by the other men, who slapped him on the back for a job well done. The two men who had dangled on the rope approached him sheepishly. The one who had gone over the edge, still ashen-faced from his brush with disaster, spoke for them both. "Jack and me, we just want to thank you for what you did, Lieutenant. When I went off that edge, I thought the game was up for sure."

Jack nodded eagerly in agreement.

"I'm just glad that no one was seriously hurt," said Chapman. "I'm sure that you'd have done the same for me."

Both men answered in unison. "Anytime, sir. Anytime."

Chapman addressed the group that had gathered around him in a semi-circle. "I would like to make one request of you," he said. "While I'm here in training, I'd like to just be part of the group. I'd prefer not to be called 'sir' or 'lieutenant.' My name is Andrew Chapman. You can call me Chapman or Andy"—he smiled—"you can even call me 'bloody Yank' if you like."

The men burst into laughter and cries of "bloody Yank" filled the courtyard as Chapman strode through the group to make his way into the house.

He was waiting in the doctor's office—the nurse who had dressed his burns now sat at her desk across from him, working—when Margaret Brown entered.

She was wearing a heavy fisherman's knit sweater over her regulation blouse and tie. Chapman decided that it wasn't easy to look sexy in government-issue heavy black shoes, opaque cotton stockings, and a FANY uniform skirt, but Margaret Brown had done it. She shook her head as if she were about to reprimand him for something foolish. "I hear you've been quite the hero," she said.

"Tales of my derring-do are quite exaggerated," he said. "I merely grabbed hold of a rope and was almost dragged off the edge of a cliff. If the others hadn't caught me, you'd be looking at a mashed Yank."

"Modesty too," she said teasingly, then her face softened. "The way it's being told you saved three men from falling to their deaths."

Chapman shrugged without comment.

Margaret Brown smiled. "I've got to get back to work," she said. "I just wanted to stop by and see how you were doing." She went to the door, pausing with her hand on the handle. "Got any of that Scotch left?"

Chapman caught her gaze for a moment before answering, "Yes."

Her eyes flashed and her tongue touched her lips. "Same time, same place?"

Chapman sneaked a glance at the nurse, who sat head down at her desk, pretending not to be taking all of this in.

"Same time, same place," he said. "I'll see you later."

Without another word, Margaret slipped out and was gone.

The nurse, a frail young woman with alabaster skin that never seemed to have seen sunlight, looked up and smiled in recognition of Chapman's singular achievement.

He shrugged and smiled back.

21

Bishop had appropriated a small room in the rear section of the house for a temporary office and living quarters. It had a large glass window that looked out on the neatly manicured lawns and shrubbery that surrounded the back of the house.

Sergeant Major Duncan MacKenzie stood at ease in front of Bishop's desk. Bishop, sitting, perused the written report that the sergeant had recently placed in his hands while Lieutenant Madsen, smoked a cigarette and gazed absently through the window.

Bishop looked up. "I think you're being too harsh on yourself in this report, Sergeant Major MacKenzie."

"It was my fault, sir. Periodically I should check the condition of the logs. I didn't."

Bishop put the report on his desk. He could tell by the typing that MacKenzie had painstakingly typed the report himself, which probably meant that he did not want anyone else to see it.

That probably meant that while he was willing to accept the responsibility, he was hoping he wouldn't have to.

"I've been doing this job for over a year, sir—ever since Dieppe—and I haven't lost a man yet." He sighed. "But I came damn close today. If it hadn't been for Lieutenant Chapman, I'd be standing in front of you now with two or three dead men on my hands."

"Commando training is inherently dangerous, Sergeant," said Bishop. "We all understand that. Last year we lost over thirty men in training accidents—four of them on one parachute jump."

"I know that, sir, but—"

Bishop cut him off. "I want you to redo your report, eliminating all reference to your negligence. I don't want to put a black mark on an otherwise fine record. Is that clear?"

"Yes, sir," said the sergeant major, pulling back his shoulders so that even at ease he appeared to be at attention. "Thank you, sir," he added, drawing himself up and snapping off his best salute.

Bishop waited until the sergeant had gone before turning to Madsen. "Well, Eric. What do you think?"

Madsen blew a long stream of smoke toward the window. "He's right. He should have checked the logs. He knew that if he accepted the responsibility, you'd let him off the hook. If he had tried to evade accountability, you'd have—"

"That's not what I'm talking about."

Madsen's face grew puzzled. "What then?"

"Chapman? What do you think of his performance?"

Madsen paused for a moment before answering. "Can't fault his instincts."

"According to MacKenzie, the men responded to his leadership—and not because he is an officer. He performed the physical tasks as well—or better—than any of the other men. 'Consistently first' was how MacKenzie put it."

Madsen sighed. He looked at the burning end of his cigarette. Finally he spoke. "You know how I feel about this. The man seems fine, but I don't like going on an operation like this with someone I don't really know. How can we depend on him?"

"We don't have much choice. The Americans insist that one of their boys go with us."

"Typical of the OSS to send someone who is completely untried in operations of this sort. All the training in the world means nothing when bullets fly. Why couldn't we take that Johnson of the First Ranger Battalion? We've worked with him before. We know we can count on him."

"Unavailable," said Bishop.

Madsen shook his head in disappointment. "What about the rope burns? Will he be ready to go?"

Bishop smiled, knowing that Madsen was clutching at straws. "Doctor says he'll be fine in a day or two. Superficial burns—the gloves saved him from being seriously injured." He saw the glum look on Madsen's face and laughed to lighten the mood. "C'mon, Eric my boy, I think we're lucky with this one. He's fit, he's smart and—if this incident on the cliff is any indication—he'll risk his life for his team. What more can we ask?"

"We can ask that we know him better. We've taken men behind enemy lines before—good, brave men—and watched them come undone under the constant pressure."

Bishop tapped his fingers on the desk. He and Madsen had been together for almost two years. Although Bishop was the senior officer and in command, they were a team, and as such, rank meant little between them. He felt that in some way he had to satisfy the Dane's uncertainties. "What do you suggest?" he asked.

Madsen smiled slyly. He knew that sooner or later Bishop would ask. "The girl," he said. "He seems to be smitten with her."

"Isn't everyone?" said Bishop, raising an eyebrow. "She is rather lovely."

Madsen shrugged as if that meant nothing to him.

"I was going to suggest," continued Bishop, "that she discontinue her surveillance—but if you don't think so . . ." He let the sentence trail off into emptiness.

"Perhaps," said Madsen, "she could entice him into some small indiscretion."

"The Americans will have a fit if we try to get rid of their man like that."

Smiling, Madsen went to the window. "What they don't know won't worry them."

Margaret Brown's jaw was set in a hard line, her eyes dancing fire. "I really must protest, Major," she said. "What do you think I would have to do to get a man to agree to such a thing?"

"That, of course, would be up to you," said Bishop. He was perched on the edge of his desk looking down at Brown, who sat in one of the chairs before him. "I would not—could not—request that you do anything that would be against your religious or moral principles."

"Fine. That's settled, then." She got up as if to leave, then her anger spilled over. "I don't know what's wrong with you people. Andrew Chapman seems like a really fine young man. I talked with him that first night—as you asked me to—and I gave you my impressions of him." Her eyes burned into Bishop's. "Then today, he risks his life and saves three of our boys from going over a cliff—and you still doubt his fitness . . ." She paused and then a look of understanding came over her face. "Or is it just because he's an American and you don't want him? Is that it?"

Bishop seemed embarrassed by her anger and her questions.

"That's not it at all," he said. "It's just that we're putting our lives on the line with each mission and I think we have a right to know about the people who go with us."

"He could have been killed today," she said. "I think he showed what he's made of."

Bishop nodded. "You are probably right. We just want to be sure."

He saw her weaken and pursued his advantage. "I remind you that you are in training as a special operations agent."

"As a wireless operator," said Margaret Brown. "Not as some kind of bloody Mata Hari."

"All I ask is that you give him this letter—how you do it is up to you. You can walk up to him in broad daylight and hand it to him if you like."

The anger returned to her eyes. "But it would obviously be more effective if I gave it to him in bed?"

"I would never suggest such a thing," said Bishop with a shrug. He held out the envelope, and Margaret Brown snatched it away from him.

"Tell me something, Major," she said, the sarcasm heavy in her voice. "If I wasn't a little Irish lass from Belfast but one of your prim and proper English ladies who had gone to the best schools—would you even think of suggesting such a thing?"

Bishop tried to mumble a reply, but Margaret Brown cut him off. "I'll tell you one thing," she said defiantly. "I'll do my part in this war, but I won't become a whore for England—or anyone else for that matter."

While Bishop searched for a suitable reply, she slammed the door behind her.

Immediately, the door opened and Madsen came in. "She's got fire, that woman," he said. "I thought she was going to knock me over in the hallway."

"Did you hear?"

"Only when she yelled at you." He was smiling, as if he had enjoyed the whole scene. The plan had been his, but it was left to Bishop to carry it out.

"She refused," said Bishop, "As well she should."

"She didn't refuse," said Madsen.

"What?"

"She thinks you were a bastard to ask her, but she didn't refuse."

"But you heard how she—"

"Major," said Madsen, shaking his head sadly, "you've been at war so long you don't know much about women. Haven't you seen the way this woman looks at Chapman? I've watched her. Every day she waits for him to return from the training exercises. In the past year every man who has been to this center has dreamed about taking this girl to bed, and she hasn't given one of them a second look. Yet look how she defends this American. How concerned she is for his welfare."

"But that doesn't mean—"

Madsen held up his hand and Bishop stopped talking. "We have given her an excuse to do what she wants to do. Years from now, when this war is long over, she'll look back and think of the sacrifices she made for her country." He chuckled. "She'll probably tell her grandchildren how she helped win the war."

Bishop snorted disbelievingly. "I doubt that." He was lost in thought for a moment. "Besides there really isn't enough time for them to build the kind of relationship where they could reasonably be expected to trust each other."

"Captain," said Madsen, shaking his head. "Time is

relative. In war, hours are like months, months are like years." He picked up the calendar on Bishop's desk, then threw it back. It landed with a loud thump. "Especially," he said, looking at a spot just beyond the office window, "since we could all be dead in ten days."

At just after eleven that evening Chapman entered the second-floor lounge and saw that Margaret Brown was not there. A man in a captain's uniform was sitting on the couch by the rapidly dying fire, reading a book, an empty tea mug before him.

Chapman approached and sat in one of the lounge chairs. The officer looked up and, noticing the light bandages wrapped around Chapman's palms, said, "I say, you're the American fellow everyone's talking about."

Chapman nodded. "Andrew Chapman," he said, showing his bandaged palms as excuse for not offering his hand.

"Archie Collins. A pleasure to meet you." His eyes went to the bottle in Chapman's left hand.

"Like a drink?" said Chapman. "I was just about to have a nightcap."

"I'd enjoy that," said Collins, holding out his mug.

Chapman poured for each of them, and Collins raised his glass. "Victory," he said sincerely.

"Yes, victory," said Chapman. "I'll drink to that."

When Margaret Brown entered the room, both men turned to look at her. She wore a blue sweater and a navy blue skirt and nylon stockings instead of the regulation issue. Her hair was up, and she had obviously spent some time getting ready.

"Sorry I'm late," she said.

"I just got here myself," said Chapman. He looked to Collins. "Captain Collins and I were having a drink."

Collins took his cue. He stood up, draining his glass. "That's it for me," he said. "I've really got to get some sleep." He turned to go. "Thanks for the drink, Chapman. It was a pleasure meeting you."

Chapman nodded politely, but his eyes were on Margaret Brown. She went to the fire and threw on some kindling and two larger logs.

"I'll do that," said Chapman, kneeling beside her.

"No," she said. "Let me. I enjoy making a wood fire." She smiled. "Don't care much for coal, but wood is nice and clean."

Chapman went back and sat on the couch, watching her minister to the fire. He pulled the extra glass from his cardigan pocket and poured her a drink and then sat back, both arms outstretched on the back of the sofa.

Soon the fire was blazing happily, shadows dancing around the darkened room.

Margaret Brown stood up, straightening her skirt. "That should do for a bit," she said, coming over to the couch. She sat very close to him, her hip touching his, and it seemed the most natural thing in the world that he should slip his arm around her shoulders. They sat in silence for what seemed like a long time until Chapman said softly, "This is very nice."

"Yes, it is," she said quietly, and then suddenly, as if the thought had just occurred to her, she asked, "Are you married?"

Chapman laughed. "No," he said. "I'm not married."

She finished her drink and refused another, seemingly content to sit with his arm around her and watch the fire.

After a bit she kicked off her shoes and put her feet up on the low table. "These are my last pair of nylons," she said, apropos of nothing. "If I get even the tiniest run in them I shall absolutely kill myself."

"I'll get you some," he said quietly.

"Don't bother," she said. "Every American who comes through here has two extra pairs of nylons—along with his chocolate and chewing gum. If you see an English girl wearing American nylons, you know she probably slept with a sailor to get them."

"No one would think that of you."

She laughed softly. "How would you know what anyone thinks of me?"

He was surprised by the emotion in her voice. "I can tell just by the way they look at you."

She looked up at him, their faces so close they were almost touching. Then her eyes closed and her lips parted and Chapman was kissing her. Her arms went around his neck and Chapman could feel the warmth emanating from her.

His hand slipped to the inside of her knee, just beneath the hem of her skirt.

She pulled back a little. "We shouldn't be doing this," she said. Then she was kissing him again. His hand moved higher on her thigh, stroking her gently, moving steadily upward.

Still kissing him, she grabbed his wrist. "This is madness," she said. "It isn't the right place."

"Name the place and let's go," he said.

"There isn't anyplace."

"How about one of the offices downstairs? Or a storeroom?"

She pushed his hand away and sat up. "I don't intend to be screwed like some schoolgirl standing in a corner or spread-eagled across a desk."

Chapman tried to keep the urgency from his voice. "Maybe we could fly to New York and go to the Waldorf."

If she thought his joke was funny, she didn't show it. She stood up, fixing her hair. "I'm sorry, Andrew. I really am. But I just can't." There was no conviction in her voice. "I can't."

He was silent.

"You probably won't believe me when I tell you this but I've been with only one man since my husband. He was a Navy pilot. Killed in Malta."

"I'm sorry," he said. "And I do believe you."

She pulled her hair back from her face, holding her head in both hands as if she could crush it. "Why should you believe me? I've only known you for a few days, and here I am ready to jump into your bed."

He stood up and, grabbing her wrists, pulled her hands away from her face. "I said, I believe you. Sometimes a few days is long enough to get to know someone, and I think I know you. I know it sounds crazy, but I can't think of anything but you."

She was crying silently, huge tears rolling down her cheeks.

"What is it?" he asked.

She pulled away from him. "It's this bloody war," she said, "It fouls up everything. Nothing is like it's supposed to be."

He pulled her close to him, hugging the breath from her, until she pushed him away. Her tears had stopped. She took both his hands in hers. "In my storeroom," she said, "there's a nice stack of government regulation blankets. We can lay them out on the floor. Have you ever made love on a mattress of army blankets?"

He kissed her. "I'll try anything once . . . or twice," he said as she pulled him toward the door.

22

On Sunday afternoon Nick Falzetti drove over to Brooklyn across the Williamsburg Bridge. There were few cars on the road, as Sunday driving was generally nonessential and most people wouldn't waste their gas coupons on joyriding. Those who did probably got their coupons on the flourishing black market.

As a cop, Falzetti had no such concerns.

Once across the bridge, he drove to Havemeyer Street and on to Union Avenue, where he parked his car across from the Italian American Social Club. The club was a storefront, formerly a dry cleaner, that had been converted into a card room and meeting place for the neighborhood. In the back was a large room where the Italian Democrats held their meetings. When not used for meetings, the room was used for gambling.

Every eye turned to meet Falzetti as he entered. Most of the men were in their sixties and seventies, some even older. They sat around small tables, playing cards or dominoes, and drinking coffee and bottled beer.

"Hey, Nicky," boomed a voice from a corner table, "over here."

Smiling, Falzetti went over to the table. "Uncle Tony," he said, shaking hands. "How are you?"

Tony Calabrese, in his late seventies with thick, silver hair and a face split in a broad smile, responded with a shrug. "How's anybody my age?" He guided his nephew into a seat. "You know Junie Golini and Mario Frattaroli?" he asked by way of introduction, and Falzetti nodded and shook hands.

An old man from another table came over to say hello. "Nicky," he said, "you remember me?"

Falzetti looked at him carefully, then his face broke into a wide grin. "Mr. Manocchio," he said, standing up. "It's good to see you."

They exchanged pleasantries in Italian.

"Franco," said Calabrese to the newcomer, "get my nephew a cup of coffee."

As Franco Manocchio, almost eighty, nodded and turned away, Falzetti stopped him. "Sit down, Mr. Manocchio. I'll get my own coffee."

Manocchio frowned. "You think I'm too old to get coffee for you?" He shook his head as if terribly disappointed. "It's my pleasure, Nicky, to get you a cup of coffee. So shut up and sit—*capisce*?"

Falzetti smiled and sat. "Thank you, Mr. Manocchio."

Tony Calabrese lit a cigar. "You want one, Nick?" he asked, holding a tin of twisted black cigars toward his nephew. "It'll put hair on your chest."

Falzetti made a face and held up a hand. "No thanks, Uncle Tony. I'm not ready for those yet." He took out one of his own, and Calabrese sighed.

"Those are cigars for women," he said. "When you gonna smoke a man's cigar?" He laughed a big belly laugh that had his whole body shaking and ended in a huge, hacking cough. Red-faced, he wiped his brow with a handkerchief. "Don't tell your Aunt Tessie you saw me smoking these things. She'd have a fit."

Tony Calabrese was the first of his family to be born in America. The rest, including Falzetti's mother, had been born in Calabria, Italy.

Mr. Manocchio came back with the coffee. "Didn't spill a drop," he said, wiping his hand on his shirt.

"You still go to the ball park, Mr. Manocchio?" asked Falzetti.

The old man smiled. "Every day I can," he said. He shook his head sadly. "They're going in the wrong direction," he said. "First in forty-one . . . second in forty-two, and third in forty-three."

Mr. Manocchio loved baseball, especially the Dodgers. Many of the kids in the neighborhood had been taken to their first game at Ebbets Field by the old man.

"Half the team is in the service," said Falzetti consolingly.

Manocchio shrugged. "So is DiMaggio. So is Rizzuto. You don't see those Yankees in third place."

The old man was about to continue, but Tony Calabrese interrupted. "So tell me, Nick, what brings you over to Brooklyn?"

"I came over to see you, Uncle Tony."

Beaming with pleasure, Calabrese said, "Me? How'd you know where to find me?"

Falzetti smiled. "Where else would you be on a Sunday afternoon?"

Calabrese bellowed a laugh that filled the room and caused every head to look in his direction. "You didn't stop by the house?"

"No. I came straight here."

"Then you'll come home with me for dinner." It wasn't a question.

"I'd love to Uncle Tony, but I'm working on a case and—"

"If I tell your Aunt Tessie that you were here and I didn't bring you home with me, she'll kick my ass up and down Union Avenue. Then she'll come over to Manhattan looking for you and kick your ass up and down Mulberry Street."

Falzetti, smiling, shook his head in defeat. "Okay, Uncle Tony, I'll come home for dinner."

Tony Calabrese was Falzetti's mother's youngest brother. For fifty years he had been involved in Democratic party politics in Brooklyn and, although he had never run for elective office, had been one of the most powerful politicians in the city for almost thirty years. There were rumors that Nick Falzetti owed his rapid rise through the police ranks to the political influence of his uncle, and Falzetti himself had no reason to doubt it. If it was true, however, Tony Calabrese had never mentioned it. Once Falzetti had broached the subject, but Tony had laughed his huge laugh, slapped his nephew playfully on the cheek and adroitly turned the conversation to other areas.

Even now, retired and aging, Tony Calabrese was not without influence in Brooklyn.

His voice turned serious. "So tell me—what can I do for my sister's son?"

Falzetti, slightly embarrassed, looked at the other men at the table. "I've got to talk to you about something, Uncle Tony. It can wait."

Calabrese didn't take his eyes off his nephew. "Why don't you fellows enjoy another cup of coffee?" he said. "I see Louie Vitale over there. He'd probably enjoy the company."

Without a word the others rose and left.

"Now," said Calabrese, "what do you need?"

"Information."

Calabrese laughed. "Information I got. Not too much of anything else. But information I got."

Falzetti leaned over his coffee. "I need to get a line on a guy named Marcovic. He was killed two weeks ago in my precinct, and I need to know a little bit about him."

"This guy from Brooklyn?"

"Yeah. Rutledge Street. You know him?"

Calabrese smiled. "I know him."

Falzetti shook his head admiringly. His uncle knew everyone.

"Troublemaker," Calabrese said flatly.

"Troublemaker?"

"Yeah. I had him kicked out of the party fifteen, maybe eighteen, years ago."

"The party?"

"Yeah, the Democratic party. You know any other party? Say yes and I'll slap your face."

Falzetti ignored his uncle's joke. "Tell me—what kind of troublemaker?"

"Communist."

"That's it? You had him kicked out because he was a communist? Uncle Tony, you know and I know that there are plenty of communists in the Democratic party.

"I know that. My brother—your Uncle Phil—was a communist. When he worked for the longshoremen's union, he was the biggest red on the docks. But the difference was he loved this country. He thought he could make this country better. He would never have hurt his country."

"And Marcovic?"

"He didn't give a shit for America. He only worried about Russia. He'd sell America down the drain if Uncle Joe told him to. He's a Yugoslavian, Nicky. Those Serbians have no soul, no sense of family. What the hell do they care about this country?"

Falzetti pondered that for a moment. "Anything else, Uncle Tony?"

Tony puffed on his cigar. He shook his head. "He's got a brother who runs some kind of trucking business over on Atlantic Avenue. I'll see if I can find out anything, and let you know."

"I'd appreciate it."

Calabrese started to get up. "And now you come along home with me. You look like you could use a good meal."

23

A few days after the meeting with his uncle, Nick Falzetti received a phone call from Marcovic's brother, George, and a meeting was arranged.

They met on Flatbush Avenue in the shadow of the

Manhattan Bridge. Falzetti arrived first and watched George Marcovic approach. Marcovic was a small man, wrapped in a huge, dark overcoat. He wore a thick scarf around his neck and a gray homburg that seemed too large for his small head.

Falzetti rose from the bench in greeting, but Marcovic ignored the policeman's outstretched hand and, without taking his own hands out of his pockets, sat down on the bench.

Falzetti looked for a moment at his empty hand as if wondering how it had offended, then gave a small shrug and sat down next to Marcovic, whose face was almost buried in his chest. "I appreciate your coming to see me, Mr. Marcovic."

Marcovic hesitated before answering. When he did, his accent was pronounced. He did not look up at Falzetti, and his lips barely moved when he spoke. "Your uncle informed me that it would be in my best interests to speak with you," he said coldly. "That is why I am here."

Falzetti sighed. This wasn't going to be as easy as he had hoped. "I can understand why you don't want to get involved in this thing, Mr. Marcovic. That's why I thought it would be better if we didn't meet at the station. This makes it . . . less official. If you know what I mean?"

For the first time Marcovic turned to look at Falzetti. Instead of the hatred that Falzetti had expected to see in the man's eyes, he could see only tiredness and a hint of sadness. "I told the FBI—over and over again—everything I know about my brother's activities."

"Did you know that he was a spy?"

Marcovic shot an angry glance at Falzetti. "No, I did not," he said emphatically. "I assumed he was involved in something that was not quite legal, but I never imagined that he was a spy." He looked around as if admiring the skyline across the river. "My brother and I were quite different, Lieutenant. I have made a success of my life here. I married an American girl. I have two sons in the army. I would never do anything to hurt this country."

"And your brother?"

Marcovic, his eyes sad, shook his head. "Things always went wrong for him. He was a failure in everything he tried. I think his failure made him bitter—made him do things that he never really believed in."

"Like joining the Communist party?"

Marcovic said nothing.

"What about you, Mr. Marcovic? Did you ever join the party?"

Marcovic looked at Falzetti again. His eyes were steady. "I can assure you that the FBI has done a complete check on my background, Lieutenant." He waited for a response, but the policeman said nothing. "In 1928 I started a scrap-iron business. When the Depression came, I, like many others, experienced hard times, and in 1932 I lost my business. My brother had similar experiences. I, however, started over again a few years later in a new business, and now I am once again reasonably comfortable." He looked down at his hands. "My brother gave in to bitterness and rejection and associated with those who told him that it was the system and not he who had failed."

"Can you tell me anything about the people he associated with?"

"Not really. My brother and I were not close. We did not travel in the same circles. We never saw each other."

"How about Weissman, the man who died with him?"

"I knew him twenty-five years ago in Vienna. Just after the first war. Although we are Yugoslavs, Lieutenant, my family lived in Austria for many years. Weissman was a professor at the university in Vienna when I knew him. He and my brother were acquaintances, and he was a visitor to our home on several occasions until my father forbade my brother to associate with him."

"Why?"

"Weissman was a Jew, and Vienna was a hotbed of anti-Semitism. Many Austrians blamed the Jews for the catastrophes of the war. 'Profit-mongers,' they called them." Marcovic stopped, expecting Falzetti to say something, but the policeman merely waited for him to continue. "In addition to being a Jew," he went on,

"Weissman was a radical. Even then he was involved in communist activities."

"I see," said Falzetti.

"Of course, I told all of this to the FBI. They asked precisely the same questions that you did."

"Did they ask about the soldier your brother was with?"

Marcovic's eyes widened as if he had just understood something.

"Your brother went into the Hallmark Hotel with a soldier. An army officer. I think he is the man who killed your brother."

"The FBI didn't say anything about that."

"The description I have is: young, blond, good-looking. Did you ever see your brother with someone in uniform who looked like that?"

Marcovic hesitated before answering, his eyes darting back and forth. "Yes."

"How often?"

"Twice. Once about six months ago, and the second time about three or four days before he died."

"Do you have a name to go along with this description?"

"We were never introduced, but I heard my brother call him Karl." Marcovic shook his head. "I thought that they must have been involved with the black market or something. It never occurred to me that they were spies. I thought . . ." He shrugged and fell into silence.

"Thought what?"

"—now that America and Russia were on the same side, my brother would feel more warmth towards this country."

"Did you tell the FBI about this man?"

Marcovic said sheepishly, "It didn't seem important."

Falzetti watched him for a moment. "What else didn't you tell them?"

Marcovic sat up straight, his mouth forming a small circle of displeasure. "I told them everything I knew."

"You also said you never saw your brother, but now you tell me that you saw him at least twice in the past six months."

Marcovic looked around like a wounded bird looking for an escape.

Falzetti knew there was something else. "I'm not trying to involve you or implicate you in any way, Mr. Marcovic," he said gently. "I'm just trying to find out what happened. I'm hoping you can help me."

"I told them everything," Marcovic repeated.

Falzetti said nothing. He knew enough about interrogation to keep quiet and let the subject hang himself. Often it wasn't the question a policeman asked that got him the answer he was looking for but the question he didn't ask. He stared hard into Marcovic's eyes until Marcovic had to drop his gaze and look away.

They sat in silence for a long time, and then Marcovic, in a hesitant voice, said, "There is one other thing."

"Tell me," said Falzetti, holding his voice steady.

"My brother left a small notebook with me for safekeeping. I don't know if it is of any importance."

"Why didn't you tell the FBI?"

Marcovic thought for a moment. "Quite frankly, I thought it had something to do with the black market and I didn't want them to think that I was involved."

"Where's the notebook now?"

"It is still in my office. I have never looked at it."

Falzetti's face registered his disbelief, and Marcovic, caught in an obvious lie, shrugged. "Well, at least not until I was told that he was dead."

"What's in it?"

"I don't know," he said, and when Falzetti gave him the look again, he protested, "I'm serious. It seems to be in a code of some kind." He stretched out his hands, palms up, in an appeal for mercy. "What should I do?"

"You should turn it over to the FBI."

"But they'll think I'm involved." He was desperate.

"Not if you tell them that you just discovered this notebook among some things that belonged to your brother."

Smiling hopefully, Marcovic said, "Do you think so?"

"Yes," said Falzetti. "But one thing first. I want you to copy everything in that book and give it to me before you hand it over to the FBI. . . . And don't tell them I have a copy."

Marcovic's eyes narrowed as he struggled to comprehend.

"Don't worry about it," said Falzetti. "Just do as I say. The FBI is interested in the information that your brother had—I'm more interested in who killed him."

Later that evening, Nick Falzetti was alone in his apartment, listening to music on the radio. Although he knew that he shouldn't, Falzetti still lived in the same three-bedroom apartment that he had lived in when his wife was alive and all his children still lived at home. It was too big for him now, and friends had tried to get him to move, but everything he wanted to remember was here.

Tommy Dorsey's trombone was sounding a mellow but mournful tune that suited Falzetti's mood perfectly as he sat in his old stuffed chair and thought about the way things used to be. He'd already had a few beers and was well on his way to a pretty good melancholy buzz when the phone rang. He got up, staggering just a little, took a long swig from the beer bottle and picked up the phone on the fourth ring.

With the first word, Falzetti recognized the thick accent of George Marcovic.

"Lieutenant?" he said. "I am sorry to bother you at home, but I had to get in touch with you."

"What's the problem, Mr. Marcovic?"

"A man was here to see me about my brother."

"FBI?"

"No. This man said he was an associate of my brother."

"What did he want?"

"He knew about the notebook. Asked me if I knew of its whereabouts." He paused. "I told him I didn't."

"Did he say why he wanted it?"

"No. Only that he and my brother were"—he paused as if trying to remember—" 'in the same business,' was how he put it."

"Did he leave a name?"

"No. But I don't think he believed me about the notebook."

Falzetti could almost smell the fear in George Marcovic's voice. "What makes you say that? How could he know?"

"He said that my brother had told him to get in touch with me if anything ever happened to him."

"Did you make my copy of the notebook yet?"

"I'm working on it now. That's why I'm at the office so late."

"I want you to call the FBI and tell them that you've found the notebook—also that someone has contacted you. They'll be pretty interested in that. I still want you to send me a copy."

Marcovic's voice was a whine. "Is there anything else I should do? I mean to protect myself."

"Did this man threaten you in any way?"

"No, but . . ."

"But what?"

"I don't know. I'm very nervous about all of it. I never bargained for anything like this."

Falzetti shrugged. "I wouldn't worry about it, Mr. Marcovic. It's probably not all that important." He reassured Marcovic that everything would be all right and hung up.

But later, even in his semi-drunken state, he felt slightly guilty about his lack of response to the nervous sound of George Marcovic's voice.

24

That casual response to the fearful tone of George Marcovic's voice was the first thing Nicolas Falzetti remembered when Tom Brownmiller of the FBI called to tell him that Marcovic had been murdered.

"I thought I told you to stay out of this," said Brownmiller.

"What makes you think I didn't?"

"I'm looking at an envelope on Marcovic's desk that has your name and address on it."

"Oh," said Falzetti.

"At least I think it's your name and address. It's kinda hard to read with Mr. Marcovic's brains all over it."

"Is there anything in the envelope?"

"No." Brownmiller's voice was cold. "Were you expecting a birthday card or something?"

"No, not really," said Falzetti, slightly embarrassed.

"Why don't you come on over to Marcovic's office—I assume you know where it is—and maybe we can talk about what you were expecting."

Falzetti started to say that he could not be there for at least an hour, but Brownmiller hung up in his ear, so he decided he'd better get over there right away. The problem with the FBI, thought Falzetti, was that even though they managed to screw up almost every investigation in which they were involved, they wielded tremendous political influence in Washington. That influence filtered down to every precinct in the country and the typical street cop had learned to keep out of the way of the FBI. An agent who felt he was not getting complete cooperation from a police department or individual officer could bring down the holy wrath of higher authority. The FBI had a way of making law enforcement agencies lean on each other. If an agent felt slighted, the next thing you knew the mayor had received a call from Washington, the police commissioner had received a call from the mayor, the precinct captain had received a call from the chief, the various departments were dressed down by the captain, and so on down the line until some rookie cop found himself walking a beat in Coney Island.

Falzetti, deciding that discretion was the better part of valor, left for Brooklyn immediately.

When he arrived he was ushered into Marcovic's office by a uniformed patrolman who stood guard at the door. The tearful secretary who had discovered the body sat at her desk in the outer office, her head in her hands, bewildered by this turn of events.

The office itself was large but far from opulent. Other than the desk and chair, the only furniture was a line of file cabinets along one wall and two chairs. In front of the desk was a well-worn Oriental rug that at one time might have been impressive. Marcovic lay on it face-down, a dark burgundy stain, like a halo in a Greek Orthodox religious mural, circling his head.

The room was filled with people, one of whom was Captain Bill Howser, commander of the Brooklyn North Detective Command. There were at least six detectives from Brooklyn North, whom Falzetti recognized, and three men from the county coroner's, who hovered over the corpse as if they could bring it back to life. Huddling in the corner, looking for all the world like the Yale Glee Club, was the FBI contingent, talking with a soldier in uniform.

Brownmiller stared at Falzetti for a full minute, allowing the weight of his credentials as bureau chief of the FBI to fall on Falzetti's shoulders, before he said anything. Falzetti chewed on an unlit cigar, knowing that Brownmiller was about to put on a performance for the assembled police officers of Brooklyn North who had been called in to investigate the scene of the crime.

"Well, Detective Falzetti," began Brownmiller, sarcasm oozing from his voice, "did you come to help us in our investigation?"

Falzetti picked a flake of cigar from his tongue and looked at it as if he were reading a label. "Always glad to give a hand to the boys from the FBI," he said.

Brownmiller approached him. "Weren't you told to stay out of this?" His voice was loud enough for everyone to hear.

"That's right." Falzetti nodded a greeting to the detectives of Brooklyn North, who had stopped what they were doing to watch Brownmiller's impending tirade.

"Then why did you get yourself involved in this matter?" Brownmiller's jaw was set, his neck muscles straining.

Falzetti stuck his cigar back in his mouth. "You got a light?" he said, his eyes boring into Brownmiller's.

Brownmiller blinked. "What?"

"Oh, I forgot. You don't smoke." Falzetti turned to the audience. "Anybody got a light?"

Captain Howser stepped forward. "Sure, Nick," he said. "Here ya go."

"Thanks, Howser," Falzetti said with a wink. Then he turned back to Brownmiller. "You ever find out who killed those guys at the Hallmark?" he asked casually.

"Not yet. But we're close."

"Gee, you shoulda called me," said Falzetti innocently. "I figured you guys must know already—being FBI and all that."

Brownmiller's face fell. He cleared his throat and said angrily, "What's that supposed to mean?"

Falzetti puffed on his cigar, sending billows of acrid smoke in Brownmiller's direction. "I just thought you'd know, so I didn't bother calling you."

His face turning red, Brownmiller lowered his voice to a dangerous growl. "You mean, you know who it is?"

Falzetti shrugged. "I think so." He looked around the room. The cops from Brooklyn North seemed to be enjoying the show. "I didn't really follow it up," Falzetti went on, "because I figured that you guys were right on top of it and I was off the case. The suspect's name is Karl Streetman."

"You were supposed to stay out of this," Brownmiller said icily.

"I did. I didn't even try. The guy just fell into my lap." He smiled innocently. "That happens sometimes."

Brownmiller's brow was furrowed in a frown. He was genuinely interested now, his show of anger forgotten. "Who is he?"

"We can't be sure it's him, but we fished a soldier out of the East River last week who fits the general description of the soldier who was in the room when Marcovic was killed and the old guy went for a walk on the ledge."

Brownmiller thought for a moment, then turned and motioned to the young man in army uniform to approach. "This is Captain Green of army intelligence. He works out of Fort Jay on Governors Island," said Brownmiller as Falzetti and the soldier shook hands.

"He has been assigned by the army to assist us in this matter."

"Captain, huh?" said Falzetti. "Must be easier to make captain in the army. I've been a cop for almost thirty years, and I doubt if I'll ever make it."

Green smiled pleasantly. "If it wasn't for the war, Lieutenant Falzetti, I'd still be a lieutenant myself."

Captain Green appeared to Falzetti to be in his late twenties—certainly no more than thirty. He was tall and wore his light brown hair slightly longer than a regular military cut. His square-jawed, regular features gave him the look of the typical handsome American soldier depicted in the recruiting posters that were plastered everywhere.

Brownmiller interrupted their greeting. "I want you to tell me what you know about this George Marcovic, and then you can fill in Captain Green on the suspect."

Falzetti told Brownmiller about his meeting with Marcovic and how Marcovic had called him about the notebook, adding, "I told him to call you about that. To turn it over to you right away."

Brownmiller's face twitched, and he cleared his throat a little.

"Did he get in touch with you?"

"Yes, he did. Earlier today."

Falzetti's eyes narrowed. "How much earlier? I talked with him last night, and he said he was going to call you. When did he call?"

"I am not exactly sure of the time," said Brownmiller, looking away quickly.

Falzetti waited until Brownmiller had turned back to face him before he said in a very quiet voice, "So he called you last night, and you—or one of your three-piece suits—told him to sit on it. Right? Probably told him that you'd get in touch with him the next day. Right?" Falzetti blew a stream of cigar smoke in Brownmiller's direction. "And next day he's dead—and the notebook is gone."

"It didn't happen quite like that."

"He must've called you last night if his secretary

found him dead this morning—unless he placed the call with a hole in his head."

Brownmiller shrugged. "Why don't you talk to Captain Green now?" he said and stomped away.

When Falzetti turned to Green the captain was smiling. "You were pretty rough on him. Could've happened to anybody."

"I know," said Falzetti. "It happened to me. Marcovic called me and I told him the same thing Brownmiller did."

Green's face broke into a wide grin. "Let's go out into the outer office and talk. I'd like to hear about this suspect of yours."

They sat on a couch in the outer room, and Marcovic's secretary brought them some coffee. Falzetti told the captain everything he knew about the dead soldier and about the rest of the case. Green, nodded occasionally until Falzetti was finished and then said, "You certainly seem to know more about what's going on than the Bureau."

Falzetti shrugged. "The bureau is good for *Pathe News* and not much else. They're desk jockeys, college boys who really don't know their way around the city."

Green smiled, somewhat self-consciously, but said nothing.

"Okay. I've given you all I've got," said Falzetti. "Now I want you to tell me something."

"If I can."

"What is going on here? I mean, I figure that Marcovic was trying to get some kind of information from Weissman. Marcovic was a red, so it's easy enough to figure who the information was going to. But other than that, I don't know what the hell is happening."

Green thought for a moment. "Well, I'll tell you as much as I can." He looked around the room to see if the secretary and the policeman were paying attention to this conversation. They seemed to be paying more attention to each other than to anything else, so Green began talking in a quiet voice. "Dr. Weissman was working on a top-secret government project. If I knew what it was I couldn't tell you, but I don't have any idea—only that it had the highest priority of secrecy. Obviously we don't want the Russians or anyone else to know about this. We assume Marcovic was in the process of getting that information from Weissman to give to his Soviet contacts. We also assume that Weissman was not a willing participant in this exchange of information because of the large amounts of drugs found in his body."

Falzetti nodded, then asked, with a nod towards the other room, "What about the guy who killed George Marcovic?"

"That's a good question. Until you told us about the body in the river, I had assumed that the same man killed both Marcovics."

"I'm not sure about the involvement of the guy in the river. Right now that is just a hunch."

"Which still leaves us," said Green, "wondering who killed the guy in the next office."

"He told me someone called him about his brother's notebook. The notebook isn't here, so I assume that had something to do with it. Do you think he was involved in this?"

Green shook his head. "No. We don't think he was involved. The FBI had both of the Marcovics under surveillance for the last several months. Theodore has been suspected of being a Soviet agent for years. In 1939 he worked at the Grumman factory on Long Island. Plans were missing for a new propeller that they were developing. No one ever found out what happened to them. In 1940 he moved over to the Sperry Corporation here in Brooklyn. Six months later a gyroscope was missing. Once again it was never recovered. In 1942 he moved to the Sikorsky plant in Farmingdale, Long Island. With the war in Europe it was easy for people in the aircraft industry to move around—they were in short supply. Anyway, a few months after he was at Sikorsky, some drawings for a new plane under development were lost—and never recovered."

"How did they know it was Marcovic?"

"They didn't. They simply studied the personnel lists, and his name showed up on several lists where there were missing documents or equipment. They put a tail on him and found that he had regular meetings with a member of the Soviet diplomatic legation here in New York."

"Why didn't they just pick him up?"

Green shrugged. "We were hoping to get him in the act with some big cheese from the Russian Consulate or something."

"Then you must have known that he met with Weissman several times?"

Green's face went blank and his jaw sagged a little.

Falzetti raised his eyebrows. "I guess you didn't."

"Is this true?"

"The hotel manager said that they met there at least three times. It was in the report that I turned over to Brownmiller. Didn't you get a copy?"

Green turned to look at the office door, where he could see Brownmiller and his agents directing the harried-looking policemen. "Seems as if the FBI doesn't always tell everything it knows."

Falzetti nodded. "They can be hard to work with because they want credit for everything. They want all you've got, but they only tell you what they want."

"I'm finding that out," said Green, looking back toward the other office. "I don't have too much confidence in our friends from the bureau."

"Why don't we work together?" said Falzetti.

"How?"

"I want to know about this dead soldier—this Karl Streetman. If we find out about him, we might figure out exactly what is going on here. It would be a lot easier for you to find out from the army than it would be for me."

Green nodded noncommittally.

Falzetti said, "I'll try his family—he lived on Long Island somewhere—and see what I can come up with. Then we can get together and trade information."

Green hesitated for a moment, wondering if this was his best course of action. He knew nothing about this gruff-talking, cigar-smoking policeman. Why did he have to get involved with the police anyway? The FBI was a big enough pain in the neck. He needed someone who could help him solve the case and get the army and his commanding officer off his back. From the other room he heard Brownmiller snarl an order to someone. Green made up his mind. He stood up. "I'll start working on it tomorrow. I'll call you in a day or two."

Falzetti smiled. "Good," he said. "We'll meet in a coupla days and get this whole thing straightened out."

25

The surf pounded on the rocky beach below the cliffs. The sky was dark gray and dangerous, and the threat of rain hung heavy like a portent of things to come.

"We're going to catch it soon," said Margaret Brown, looking up.

"I don't care," Chapman said. "Nothing can bother me today."

Chapman had been excused from most of the exercises for the day. In the morning he had performed the warm-up calisthenics with his group and then gone on a full-gear hike. Just before lunch break he had stood around watching as the trainees practiced a mock assault on another abandoned building on the estate, and then reported to the doctor, who changed the dressings on his hands and told him that he was coming along just fine.

After lunch Sergeant Major MacKenzie, who had become overly solicitous of the man who had saved his job, informed him that since the "boys" would be digging a few holes that afternoon, Chapman could take the rest of the day off. Amidst the good-natured groans and jeers of his group, Chapman had waved a cheerful good-bye and raced off before anyone could have a change of heart. His first stop was the motor pool, where he cajoled the sergeant in charge into letting him borrow a jeep for a few hours. Then he drove up to the front door of the house and went looking for Margaret Brown.

Thirty minutes later the jeep was parked off to the side of the beach road, and they were walking on the path above the cliffs with a view of the ocean.

Margaret Brown disengaged her arm from his and started running along the dirt path that meandered along the edge of the cliffs. She ran flat out, head back, hair flying in the wind. She was like a gazelle—at any moment he expected her to bound high into the air in one marvelous leap and soar across the meadow.

"Be careful," he yelled, but the wind whipped his words from his lips and sent them off in the other direction.

She stopped anyway and turned to look back at him. From thirty yards away he could see that she was embarrassed by her own exuberance. Her eyes dropped to the path, and she stood still, hands clasped in front of her, waiting for him to catch up.

"What's the matter?" he asked as he approached her.

She linked her arm with his. "You must think I'm daft," she said. "Prancing around like a schoolgirl."

He only laughed.

"I'm almost twenty-five years old," she went on. "I should know better than this."

"Better than what?"

She left the path and walked closer to the edge of the cliff, where, looking down, she could see the rock-strewn beach. It curled off into the distance in a gentle curve, disappearing into a misty fog where land and water became one.

He stood next to her. "Better than what?" he said again.

"This," she said, suddenly serious. "Us." She looked out into the bay. The tide was high, and the old, rusted freighter bobbed at anchor in the chop. "It's all right," she said, forcing a smile. "Really. I know that it's a wartime fling. This is what happens in wartime. It's fun for a while, but I shouldn't get carried away."

"I'll be back," Chapman said. "I—"

She knew what he was going to say and put her fingers to his lips to silence him. "Don't promise me anything. You don't have to do that. You couldn't, even if you wanted to."

His face showed his puzzlement.

"People can't make promises to each other anymore. That's what this bloody war has done. Until it's over, there can't be any promises."

His face was hard; the line of his mouth was straight across. "If I'm alive when this war is over," he said, "I'll come back for you. By then you might not want me, but I'll find you anyway just to be sure."

She put her arms around him, and he held her.

"Don't say that," she said. And then in a lower voice, "Unless you mean it."

"I'll come back for you," he repeated.

She pulled away from him, breathing deeply, and he knew that she was trying not to cry. "Let's walk," she said gently, taking one of his injured hands in hers.

They returned to the path. The dark clouds blotted out the sun, and across the horizon there was a flash of light, and moments later, a low rumble of distant thunder.

"We're going to get soaked," said Chapman.

Margaret Brown shrugged her shoulders nonchalantly. "How old are you?" she asked.

"Twenty-eight," he said.

"Hmm." she said. "That's a problem. I'm fifty-nine."

He laughed. "Well preserved," he said.

"I was nineteen when the war started," she began, her eyes squinting as she calculated, "and that was at least forty years ago. So I must be at least fifty-nine. I'm probably in my sixties."

"By those calculations," he said, "I must be close to seventy."

"No," she said quite seriously, "you didn't get into this mess until two years after we did. That makes you considerably younger."

"I like older women," he said, trying to keep the

conversation light, but knowing that in some strange way she was serious.

"Do you understand what I'm saying?" she asked.

He forced a smile. "Sure."

"I mean, do you ever get the feeling that time is so terribly compressed—because of the war, I mean? As if we're all racing to a sudden end like those funny little creatures that follow their leaders over a cliff and dash themselves on the rocks below. . . . They say the war will be over next year. I'm afraid that when it ends I'll be too old to enjoy much of anything."

"You'll be young again—you'll see."

"My grandfather died when he was eighty-four—my grandmother was a widow at eighty-two and lived to be ninety. She lost two children in childbirth, but the other seven were there with her when she died. I can't help but feel that that's how God intended life to be." She laughed a little, but Chapman saw the large tears rolling down her cheeks. "He must be on holiday."

Chapman wanted to stop her but realized that he had to let her get it out.

The tears did not seem to affect her in any way. Her voice was strong, her shoulders didn't shake. If Chapman weren't seeing them, he would never have been able to imagine the volume of those tears.

"I was widowed at twenty," she said. "Lost my parents, who were in their early forties, when I was twenty-one. I've lost two sisters and a brother. Another brother is supposed to be a POW, but I haven't heard from him in over six months."

Chapman put his arm around her. "It's all right," he said soothingly. "Get it all out if you want to."

"I've had this bottled up inside, with no one to tell it to. I'm afraid all the time. Afraid I've lost the best years of my life and when this damn war is over no one will be able to give them back. No one will say, 'Okay, that's it. You can be nineteen again.' "

"One good thing," said Chapman, "I've known you for only days and I'm absolutely crazy about you. If there weren't a war, it would have taken at least a week."

Margaret threw herself into his arms. "And I love you too," she whispered.

A huge raindrop plopped onto Chapman's arm, then another. "Here it is," he said.

Margaret Brown wiped her tears away with a finger. "We'll have to make a run for it," she said.

"Too late," he said, pulling her closer and kissing her lips. The skies opened and the rain came down in torrents as the two of them stood holding each other in the meadow above the rocky beach.

They walked back to the jeep, ignoring the rain that had drenched them and still pummeled them without mercy.

"You know what I wish," said Margaret in his ear, above the crescendo of the falling rain. "I wish that big old house were ours and nobody else were there. And that we could go and take off our wet clothes and lie in front of the fire."

"Let's do it anyway," he yelled, laughing at the thought.

They were both hysterical with laughter when they got back to the jeep and began the drive back in the rain.

They were still laughing when the jeep pulled into the courtyard of Galloway House and Chapman ran around to help Margaret down from her seat. As she stepped down Chapman saw her eyes focus somewhere over his shoulder and her smile freeze like a photograph of a remembered moment. He looked back quickly and saw Bishop standing in the doorway, smiling pleasantly.

"Lovely day for a drive in the country," he called to them. There seemed to be no suggestion of innuendo in his tone.

Chapman nodded and turned back to Margaret. "You're not in any trouble for leaving with me this afternoon, are you?" he asked in a low voice.

She had already recovered and her smile was dazzling. "Not at all," she said. "What ever gave you that idea?"

Chapman began to mumble something, but she interrupted him. "You'd better let me run inside and change." She looked to Bishop, then kissed Chapman quickly on the lips. "I'll see you at dinner," she said and started up the steps to the house. For a fraction of a minute Chapman thought that she hesitated just as she reached Bishop, whose eyes seemed to ask some unspoken question. If there was an answer, Margaret Brown did not give it. She merely brushed past Bishop and disappeared into the house.

Chapman, soaked to the skin, stood in the rain, unsure how to proceed. "I hope you're not upset that I took off in the jeep today. Just thought I'd get out for a while."

"Not at all," said Bishop. "Good idea, I'd think. How are the hands?"

Chapman looked at his bandaged palms. "Fine. Ready for full duty by tomorrow, I'd say."

"Don't rush yourself," said Bishop. "You've nothing else to prove here. Day after tomorrow will be fine."

Chapman started to smile, then stopped. "What's the day after tomorrow?"

Bishop leaned against the brickwork that surrounded the huge front door. "Don't you want to get out of the rain?"

"I want to take the jeep back to the motor pool." He caught Bishop's eyes and held them, "What's the day after tomorrow?"

"Jumping practice. Some of us are going over to the aerodrome in Dumfries for a few practice jumps. I'd like you to come along."

Chapman smiled, "I'll be there."

"Splendid," said Bishop, his smile growing.

The rain ran down Chapman's face, and his hair was plastered in clumps across his forehead. He pushed the drops from his eyes with a quick wipe of a finger. "It's going to be soon," he said, "isn't it?"

Bishop was still for a moment, and Chapman thought at first that he wasn't going to speak. "I'm not at liberty to say that it's going to be soon," he said slowly, "but I will say that it's not going to be terribly long either."

With that, Bishop went inside the house and Chapman clambered back into the open jeep. Puddles had formed on the floor, and the seats were soaked. He started the engine and put the transmission in gear, but before he engaged the clutch, he sat for a moment, thinking about what Bishop had said but also about how Bishop had looked at Margaret Brown and how the laughter had died in her throat when she saw him in the doorway.

He released the clutch and the jeep lurched off across the courtyard. As he turned the corner toward the garage area the rain stopped and the sun broke through a gap in the clouds, spilling light across the lush green gardens.

Chapman was pushing some lumpy mashed potatoes across his plate when Margaret Brown entered the dining hall. She was wearing her service uniform and had her hair pulled straight back. Every man in the dining hall took at least one surreptitious look in her direction. Some looked quickly at Chapman, then back to Margaret Brown.

Apparently unaware that she was the object of such scrutiny, she paused in the doorway, looking around the room until her gaze fell upon Chapman. She gave a small grin and a half wave with her fingers that no one missed.

Iverson, sitting next to Chapman, said, "At this very moment you're probably the most hated man in the British Empire."

Margaret filled a mug with tea, took milk and sugar, and turned to face the dining hall again. She caught Chapman's eyes and gave a slight nod of her head toward the door.

As Chapman got up to leave, Iverson mumbled, "You Yanks are bloody amazing. When this war's over there won't be a decent-looking woman left in England."

Chapman left his tray near the stack at the front door and went into the hallway. "What's up?" he asked as

Margaret took his hand and led him down the hall. She was smiling devilishly.

"I hope you're satisfied with what you've done to my hair," she said, running her palm across the back of her head.

"Looks wonderful," he said.

"Wonderful, my eye," she said, laughter bubbling up in her throat. "I look like something the cat dragged in."

She was still pulling him down the long hallway when Chapman asked, "What was all that about between you and Bishop today?"

She stopped. "All what?"

He shrugged. "Just seeing him seemed to upset you. I thought for a minute that you were in some kind of trouble."

She shook her head. "I just don't care for him, that's all. He makes me nervous."

"Did he ever try—"

Her laugh interrupted him. "Bishop? Never. I think he must have taken a vow of celibacy for the duration," she said. "The war is too bloody important for him to worry about earthly pleasures."

"I just thought you acted kind of funny."

"Men like Bishop scare me," she said seriously. "They'd kill all of us to see their final victory."

"Someone's got to be like that," Chapman said.

Margaret's face hardened and her eyes narrowed. "What good is victory if we're all dead when it comes?"

They crossed the foyer, and she led him into her storeroom. "Let's forget about that," she said. "I've got some good news I want to tell you."

Chapman smiled. "New shipment of army blankets that you want me to help you inspect?"

She punched him lightly on the arm and gave him a brief kiss. "Something better," she said, grinning.

"What could be better?"

Margaret Brown's eyes were dancing. "Upon returning from our little underwater outing today, I found that Captain Welles, my commanding officer and roommate, has been called away to London for three days, leaving me in charge of the FANY contingent and sole occupant of a lovely room on the second floor."

A stupid grin spread across Chapman's face.

"Wipe that look off your face," said Margaret playfully, "or I'll take you for the lecher you really are."

Chapman pulled her close, and Margaret Brown nervously eyed the door. He kissed her. "When?" he whispered.

She pushed him away. "Twenty-three-hundred hours. I'll leave the door unlocked." She started to leave, but Chapman stopped her.

"I don't know if I can wait," he said, pulling her close.

She let him kiss her once, then pulled away. "Twenty-three-hundred hours," she said. "And please be careful. Don't let anyone see you coming. I'd die of embarrassment if someone saw you at my door."

"Not to worry. I'm an expert at surreptitious entry."

"I'll just bet you are," she said and hurried off.

Chapman waited a few minutes, then followed. In the foyer a large clock on the wall showed ten past seven. He exhaled a long sigh, wondering what he was going to do with himself until eleven o'clock.

Chapman waited until five minutes past the hour before swinging his legs off the bed and onto the floor. He had lain there, fully clothed, pretending to read a year-old *Life* magazine while counting the minutes until eleven. Iverson, exhausted from a hard day in training, had gone to sleep the minute he put his head on the pillow, but Madsen, still in uniform, lay on his bed, cigarette in his mouth, staring silently at the ceiling.

When Chapman got up, Madsen looked over once, then wordlessly resumed his ceiling watch.

Chapman considered offering some explanation to Madsen, but then decided against it. The Dane hadn't said ten words to him since he arrived, so why, he thought, should he favor him with an explanation? He gathered up the Scotch—there was still enough left for a few drinks—and went quietly to the door.

The hallway was empty, and he went quickly to the

stairs and down to the second floor. He moved stealthily, smiling to think that his special training was useful at a time like this, and made it to the hallway without being seen by anyone.

He paused at Margaret's door, listening for a moment to the quiet. He considered a gentle knock, but instead, with a quick look around, he opened the door and slipped inside.

The room was dark. Only a faint cloud-shrouded moonlight shone through the single window.

He let his eyes adjust to the darkness. "I hope this is the right room," he said.

Margaret Brown gave a low laugh. "I'm over here," came her voice. Gradually Chapman began to make out some of the darkened shapes.

From the bed on the left he saw the dim, red glow of a cigarette grow brighter as Margaret took a long drag. Briefly he could make out her features, and then the light was gone and he heard her give a long sigh.

He felt his way across the room and sat next to her. Touching her hand, he let his fingers run up her arm to her shoulder. She took his hand and brought it to her lips, kissing his palm. "No bandages," she whispered, kissing him again.

"All better," he said.

She brought his head down across her throat and under the blanket to her breasts. She was naked.

He leaned forward to kiss her, and her arm went around his neck.

He stood up and began to undress, and she leaned over and put her cigarette in the ashtray. He dropped his clothes in a heap on the floor and slipped in beside her, feeling the warmth of her flesh next to his. They kissed, holding each other, and Chapman ran his hands down her back, stroking her gently.

"I was beginning to wonder if you were coming," she said.

"Is this Margaret Brown?" asked Chapman, a low lecherous chuckle in his throat.

She laughed. "Who do you think it is?"

"It's so dark in here, I'm not sure. But I just came to tell you that Lieutenant Chapman couldn't make it."

"You rat," she said, biting him on the shoulder. "When you get back, you be sure to tell Lieutenant Chapman that he missed the time of his life."

She rolled on top of him, straddling him. "I was looking forward to seeing him," she whispered in his ear, "but I think I'm going to like you even better."

The moon passed between clouds, and in the sudden rush of light, Chapman saw, in the wide eyes and parted lips, the hunger on Margaret Brown's face. He pulled her down and moved easily inside her. She drew a sharp breath as if he had touched her with a hot iron, and then she began to move. "I like you even better," she said over and over, repeating the words in rhythm with her movements.

Chapman was awakened by the sound of a match scraping across a rough surface. He squinted in the sudden flare of light and saw Margaret leaning against the window, lighting a cigarette.

She had a blanket wrapped around her, oblivious to the fact that he was awake.

He watched her, smiling, thinking how beautiful she was and how lucky he was to have found her.

She rested her forehead against a windowpane and drew almost savagely on the cigarette, as if to rid her soul of a terrible burden.

The smile slipped from Chapman's face as he noticed the deep frown and the almost demented rhythm of her movements.

He sat up. "What is it?"

She jumped, startled by the sound of his voice. "What?" she asked sharply.

"What is it? What's bothering you?"

She shook her head fiercely, her eyes closed. "Nothing."

Chapman pulled back the sheets and climbed out of bed. The floor was icy on his feet as he went to her. "Something is wrong. What is it?"

She was silent.

He opened the blanket that she held and moved inside with her. "Is it something I've done?"

She kissed his chest. "No—it's nothing you've done."

"Tell me then. I'd like to help."

She hesitated, then took another drag on her cigarette. "I was just thinking about my brother," she said.

"The one in the POW camp?"

She nodded. "I haven't heard from him in six months."

"If anything happened to him, the Red Cross would let you know."

"I suppose," she said doubtfully, then began again. "But—" She stopped herself.

"What is it?"

"Never mind," she said, kissing him. "It was a silly thought."

"Are you going to tell me?" he asked playfully.

She took a final drag on her cigarette and stubbed it out in the ashtray. Holding him tightly, she kissed his shoulder. "I know where you're going," she said. "I just found out today."

"You do? Where?"

"Captain Welles was talking with Bishop just before she left. I overheard them talking about your mission."

"Where are we going?"

"If anyone found out I told you, it would be big trouble for me."

"Where?"

"Holland."

Chapman seemed surprised. "Holland?"

"That's what they said."

She went on. "My brother, if he is still alive, is in the POW camp near Bentheim." She hesitated. "That's only ten miles from Holland."

"Should I stop by and say hello?" said Chapman with mock seriousness. He didn't like the drift of the conversation.

"No, but you could help me."

His brow was furrowed in a frown. "How?"

"You'll be meeting with resistance group Jordan."

Chapman's voice was wary. "Yes?"

"They would be able to find out if my brother was still alive."

"But how can—"

She cut him off, her words coming in a torrent, as if now that she had decided to ask, she could not hold back the words. "I will give you a letter for the resistance. They will contact my brother and then report to England by radio whether he is alive or dead."

"But if you waited?"

"I can't wait," she sobbed. "I've waited for months."

He looked down at the floor.

"Will you do it . . . for me?" she said. "I'll understand if you don't. It won't make any difference."

He knew it *would* make a difference. He thought about it. "All right," he said. "If I can do it without risking the mission, I will."

She kissed him. "Thank you. I'll write the letter tomorrow and give it to you after dinner." She stiffened. "You won't change your mind?"

"No, I won't change my mind," he said softly.

"One thing," she said, biting her lip. "Don't let Bishop or anyone know that I've given you the letter. If they find out, I'll be in big trouble."

"Don't worry. I won't tell anyone."

She hugged him. "I love you," she said almost sadly. "I knew I could count on you."

He thought it strange that she did not seem happy that he had elected to deliver her letter.

"Do you want to go back to bed?" she asked.

"Do you?"

"Yes," she said. "Oh, yes."

He thought she was going to cry again.

26

On Monday morning Captain Howard Green rode the train to Richmond, Virginia. During the long ride he had time to reflect on the course of the war and on his own career. The war was over, he said to himself, everyone knew that. It was just a matter of convincing the Germans and the Japs that the die was cast. The people on the street knew that victory was almost theirs. The blackouts had been lifted, and foods that had been rationed were readily available—as a matter of fact there had been such a surplus of eggs in the stores that one would have thought even the chickens knew that the war was almost over.

New Year's Eve, for the first time in three years of war, had been a genuine, joyful celebration. The crowds had once again gathered in Times Square, and when the clock ushered in the new year of 1944, the people, sensing that this would be the final year of the long and grueling war, had exploded in triumphant jubilation.

It was time, thought Green, to start thinking about what he would do when the war was over and he could leave the army and escape from his dull, boring routine at Fort Jay on Governors Island. Army intelligence had sounded like a good idea when his father had suggested it, but the reality had been mindless routine. William H. Green, senior partner in the Washington law firm of Green, Herschfeld and Walters, had enough influence to get his son placed wherever he chose. "Someplace safe," he had said, "where we don't have to worry about you getting your ass shot off, but also the kind of job that can be a political asset in the future." Howard's father had very early on determined that Howard would be the family politician.

The family still maintained a residence in Manhattan, and it would be from there that Howard would begin his political career. A few years on city commissions, a term or two in Congress, a run for the Senate, and then . . . who knew?

Howard Green laughed to himself as he thought of his father's plans. After the war he would be happy to go back to work with his father's law firm—or some other law firm. When he thought of the politicians he had met through his father, he could not think of a group of people whose ranks he would be less willing to join. Unless, of course, one included the army. My

God, he thought, how could anyone make a career of the army? Whenever he told someone that he was with army intelligence, he had to force himself not to add, "I know that's a contradiction in terms."

Generally he used the army term "G-2" to describe his role as a military intelligence officer. Most of his duties consisted of paperwork having to do with the immense amount of material leaving the Third District Supply Area of the Port of New York.

It was not exactly what he'd had in mind when he graduated *cum laude* from Harvard Law School in 1939. After two years with his father's New York office he was ready for something different. Then the war came along. At his father's urging he had enlisted, gone to officer candidate school, and been commissioned a second lieutenant. "No one will be able to get into politics without having served in this war," his father had said. And then William H. Green had used his influence to make sure that his son's service did not involve any possible threat to life or limb. When the son had made a somewhat feeble objection to his father's plans for his safety, he had been told, "If anything happened to you, your mother would ruin me."

That had been enough to end the conversation. And so Howard Green, feeling that he had put up a convincing display of courage, went off gladly to command a desk and three enlisted men for the duration of the war.

Then the boredom had set in.

This case with the two dead men at the Hallmark Hotel and the dead second lieutenant in the East River had been the most exciting thing to come along in the eleven months he had been assigned to Fort Jay. His commanding officer, Major Grogan, had been happy to assign him to the case and had voiced no objections when Green had said he was going to Camp Lee, near Richmond, where the dead officer had been stationed. When Howard thought about it, it seemed that the major had been pleased to get him out of the office for a day or two.

Camp Lee was a Quartermaster Center that had been demolished after the First World War and then gradually rebuilt in 1940 and 1941 when it began to appear likely that the United States would have need for a QM Replacement Training Center. The facility had blossomed since December 1941. A once ramshackle assortment of makeshift buildings and Quonset huts that had appeared to be abandoned and disowned by any administrating authority had been replaced by neat rows of squat, solid structures that showed solidity and permanence.

Fort Lee, like other army posts across the nation, symbolized the miraculous metamorphosis that had occurred in America since Pearl Harbor. The United States Army had been transformed almost overnight from the nation's neglected cousin, represented by the old, now abandoned, dilapidated buildings, to the trusted brother who was given everything he required to get the job done.

Howard Green showed his identification card to the guard on duty at the gate and was waved inside. The corporal who had picked him up at the station and who had bored him with a brief history of Richmond on the short drive to Fort Lee now gave him a brief, guided tour of the camp as he drove to the parking lot of the administrative building.

Green was happy to get out of the car and wave good-bye to the gregarious corporal.

He went up the stairs of the administration building, down a short corridor lined on either side by doors with smoked glass panels, and stopped in front of one that read "Colonel Arthur P. French." He knocked and went inside.

"Captain Howard Green to see Colonel French," he explained to the largely uninterested sergeant who sat at a desk in the small outer office.

The sergeant looked at a list on his desk. "Right on time, Captain," he said. "The colonel is expecting you. I'll just check to make sure he's ready."

He slipped through the door and returned in a few seconds. "You can go right in, Captain." As Green headed for the door the sergeant added, "Can I get you a cup of coffee, Captain?"

Green smiled. "Thank you, Sergeant. Black, one sugar."

Colonel Arthur French turned from the window as Green entered. He was a big man, with a huge smile and a shock of red hair dangling in his face. "Good to see you, Howard," he said with genuine warmth. "How long has it been?"

"1940," said Green. "I believe it was at a cocktail party my father gave for the secretary of defense."

"That's right," said French. "How is your father?"

"Just fine, thank you, Colonel. He's still making life miserable for everyone in Washington."

The Colonel laughed. "He is a tough, old buzzard, isn't he?" He motioned Green to a chair in front of his desk as the sergeant entered with two mugs of coffee.

French opened a lower desk drawer. "Like a little something extra in it?"

"No thanks, Colonel. Black is just fine."

Green watched French's face calculating before he decided. "Yeah. It is a little early anyway." He smiled somewhat self-consciously and closed the drawer. "Now what can I do for you?"

"Well, as I told you on the phone, I want to know about this Lieutenant Karl Streetman, who was assigned here for much of last year."

French slapped the desk top with the palm of his hand. "Got his records right here." He handed Green a folder. "Can you tell me what this is all about? I know you G-2 types thrive on secrecy, but I just wondered."

"Routine investigation," said Green with a shrug. "Streetman got himself killed in New York a few weeks ago. Some of the facts about the case are somewhat puzzling so I've decided to do a little legwork on him."

"That record," said French pointing to the folder in Green's hand, "will only take you up to December forty-three. After that he was designated for special assignment."

"Special assignment?"

"Yes. OSS was looking for a man with certain skills, and Streetman seemed to fill the bill pretty well."

"What kind of special skills?"

"Language mostly. He speaks—spoke—a couple of languages. It's in his file."

"He volunteered?"

"Absolutely. Jumped at it as I recall."

"Do you know what they needed him for?"

"You'd have to ask them that."

Green leafed through the personnel file. It showed that Karl Streetman had been born in New York City in 1917, that he had attended private schools there and had graduated from Columbia University. In January 1942 he had joined the army and attended officers' training school at Fort Benning in Georgia. From July 1942 until May of 1943 he had been assigned to Camp Kilmer in New Jersey and then to Fort Lee. His service record seemed exemplary, and every commanding officer had found him to be a "hard-working competent officer." Knowing how army personnel ratings worked, Green was aware that these were rather ordinary recommendations and did not indicate the kind of officer who had impressed his superiors with his verve and dedication.

"Says here," said Green, "that Streetman had twice applied for transfer. Once in June 1943 and again in August 1943."

French nodded without comment.

"Any idea why?"

French shrugged. "I'm not sure. Perhaps he thought we were a little too dull for his liking here."

"Any idea where he wanted assignment?"

French smiled almost wickedly. "He wanted G-2, I think. He thought you guys had all the glamour, I guess."

Green returned the grin. "Yeah," he said, "lots of glamour. That's why I'm sitting here with you."

They both laughed, but Green was vaguely troubled by the fact that Streetman had sought assignment to army intelligence and then jumped at the opportunity for an OSS assignment. He decided to call Major Grogan at Fort Jay and tell him that he had decided to pay a visit to OSS headquarters in Washington.

* * *

Howard Green spent the evening with his parents in their Georgetown home. He had a pleasant visit with his mother, but his father spent the evening bombarding him with questions about his postwar plans.

William H. Green was a small man, slight in build and with sharp linear features. Howard did not in the slightest resemble his father. After listening to his father ramble on through dinner and for an hour after, Howard had decided that when the war ended, he would find a job with another law firm in any city but Washington. By ten o'clock he had had enough, and, pleading overtiredness and a splitting headache, he escaped to his upstairs bedroom.

Early the next morning he went to the OSS headquarters on 25th and East Streets. The building that housed the Office of Strategic Services was described by its architects and its occupants as modernistic, but most of those who saw it for the first time described it as either "plain and dull" or just "ugly." In contrast with the many government buildings in the neoclassical style that dotted the area, the OSS building was indeed an ugly duckling in a neighborhood of swans.

Captain Howard Green was shown into the office of a Major Harold Cowan, who greeted him without warmth.

He wasted no time in establishing the limits of his cooperation. "Maybe you'd better tell me," he said, "why army intelligence is interested in this Lieutenant Streetman."

"The man died in unusual circumstances, Major. We have reason to suspect that he was involved in the deaths of two other men."

Major Cowan's mouth looked as if he had just tasted a lemon. He said nothing.

"It is my understanding that Lieutenant Streetman had been selected for some sort of OSS mission." Watching Cowan's expression, Green decided to stretch the truth somewhat. "My commanding officer, Major Grogan, feels that if we knew the nature of this mission, we might be able to determine if there was any connection between that and the several deaths I mentioned before."

Major Cowan made a noise with his tongue against his teeth, and Green realized that he was not making much headway. "The army would appreciate whatever cooperation the OSS is willing to give us on this, Major."

There was little love lost between the OSS and army intelligence. When the OSS had been formed in 1941, the army had felt that one of its basic functions, the gathering of military intelligence, was being appropriated by an outside agency. The army, jealous of its prerogatives, had been notoriously uncooperative while the OSS was struggling to establish itself in the labyrinthine world of espionage. It was no secret that the army and the ONI and the FBI had tried to throttle the fledgling agency before it could leave the nest.

Consequently, Howard Green's plea for interagency cooperation fell on understandably deaf ears.

Major Cowan sat back in his chair and emitted a long sigh. "Lieutenant Streetman was merely an OSS trainee, Lieutenant. He was never, as you suggest, selected for any OSS mission. As a matter of fact, he was rejected for the particular mission he was in training for."

"Any particular reason?"

Cowan looked puzzled.

"That he was rejected, I mean."

The major shrugged. "There were several men in training for a particular mission. He was not the best available. It was that simple."

"Can you tell me anything about the mission?"

Cowan shook his head. "I'm afraid not, Captain."

The two men stared at each other—Cowan smiling slightly at Green's lack of progress.

For all intents and purposes the meeting was over, and Cowan stood up to indicate that fact.

"Can I ask you one more question?" asked Green.

Cowan sighed. "Go ahead." He sat down.

"Does the name Theodore Marcovic mean anything to you?"

"Not off hand. Should it?"

"He is one of the men that Streetman is believed to have murdered."

Cowan shook his head slowly. "Can't say that the name means anything to me." He started to rise again.

"What about Weissman. Dr. Adam Weissman."

Cowan's eyes widened slightly in surprise and then narrowed suspiciously. "Weissman? I understood that his death was a suicide. I have a report to that effect from the FBI."

"I am in contact with a New York City policeman who doesn't think very much of the FBI's investigative capabilities."

"He's not alone there," said Cowan, "but I thought this was cut and dried. The man jumped from a window."

"That's true," nodded Green, "but according to the medical examiner, his body was pumped full of sodium thiopental."

"Truth serum."

"Someone apparently had been trying to make Weissman talk before he jumped. My police contact thinks that someone was Lieutenant Karl Streetman."

"That makes no sense."

"Why not?"

"For what possible reason?"

"That's what I'm trying to find out. With Streetman dead there's no way to find out what information he forced from Weissman."

Cowan got up from his chair and walked around his desk. "Captain, I want you to keep me informed of your findings."

Now it was Green's turn to play hard to get. He scratched the top of his head and looked down at the floor.

Cowan went on. "I'll let you know what—if anything—I come up with."

"Can you tell me anything about the mission that might help me understand what is going on?"

Cowan sighed and after a long pause said, "I'm going

to tell you as much as I can without revealing the exact nature of the mission."

"Fair enough," said Green.

"We had been looking for some American to send on a joint venture with the British behind enemy lines. We felt that it was important that we be represented on this particular mission and that we not let the British handle it alone. Unfortunately there was a rather strict deadline, and we had to make our selection in a hurry. We were given very little time to prepare." He paused to gauge Green's reaction, but the Captain merely nodded agreeably. "One of the problems," continued Cowan, "was that there were some stringent language requirements that we couldn't fill with any of our regular people, so—as we often do in these cases—we had army people go through their personnel files and come up with some candidates for us. Streetman was one of about six or seven people recommended to us by the army."

Green was wondering if Cowan was trying to shift some of the responsibility away from his own agency. Typical, he thought, no one even knows if there is anything to take responsibility for, but already people are trying to duck it. "All of these men were regular soldiers, picked because of some specific skill?"

"That is my understanding of the situation. Yes."

"How did Streetman do on the OSS evaluation?"

Cowan thought for a moment then shrugged a little. "He wasn't selected. If that's what you mean."

"Can you tell me anything about that? Why wasn't he selected?"

Cowan sighed as if this whole thing was bringing him a great deal of pain. "You must understand that I am not personally familiar with the case . . . but I did look over the file when I was told that you were coming."

"Fine," said Green. "I understand that." The bastard, he thought, is trying to get as much distance as he can between himself and this case.

"In many ways, Streetman was superior to the other candidates. Physically he was in better shape, intellectually he was superior to all but the top candidate. He also had a sense of the con man in him, which for an agent can be an important advantage. He was aggressive, forceful, confident. All in all he had many of the qualities which his evaluator felt would make him an excellent agent. In fact he had been promised a future assignment."

"But," said Green, "he didn't get this one."

"It seems," said Cowan, shaking his head, "that he wasn't as strong in the language requirement as some of the others—and the British were very insistent on absolute fluency. He did speak several languages and was actually quite good in the one essential language, but one of the other top candidates spoke the language like a native and that tipped the scales in his favor."

Howard Green thought for a moment and could think of nothing else to ask. It was obvious that Cowan had told him all that he could—or was willing to tell. "That's it then, I suppose," he said.

Both men stood up and shook hands.

"Remember," said Cowan, "to keep me informed. . . . I would greatly appreciate it."

"I'm not sure how important all this really is," said Green with a shrug.

Cowan's face grew serious. "If we can find out what information was taken from Weissman, it may be the most important thing that either of us ever do."

27

While Howard Green was busy at OSS headquarters in Washington, Nick Falzetti drove out to Port Washington to talk with the father of Karl Streetman. As he drove along Horace Harding Boulevard he wasn't quite sure what he was going to ask Mr. Streetman, but he had a feeling that if he was ever going to get to the bottom of this case, he had to talk to someone who had known the dead man.

The Streetman residence was a large, rambling Victorian structure surrounded by porches on three sides. To the left of the long driveway that intersected the grounds was a red clay tennis court and a small covered patio. The property was wooded and from the rear afforded a good view of Manhasset Bay in the distance.

As Falzetti got out of his car he heard a dull thumping sound from beyond the tennis court. His eyes went in that direction, and he saw someone there splitting wood. Falzetti slammed the car door shut, and the man paused in midstroke—his axe poised above his head. When he saw that he had company, the man drove the axe down with tremendous force, splitting the log with a single blow.

After driving the axe into a tree stump, he approached Falzetti, who stood next to his car, puffing on his cigar. The man was in his mid-fifties, well built, and ruggedly handsome. Falzetti could tell by the look on his face that he did not welcome visitors. When he spoke, there was a slight trace of some accent.

"This is private property," said the man coolly as Falzetti moved toward him.

Falzetti displayed his gold shield. "Lieutenant Nicholas Falzetti, N.Y.P.D.," he said, chomping on his cigar. "I'm here to see Mr. Streetman. I talked with him yesterday on the phone."

The man's expression changed immediately. "Yes, of course," he said, extending a huge hand. "I'm Jon Streetman. I was not expecting you so early, Lieutenant."

Falzetti shook his hand, feeling the power in the man's grip. "I know this isn't easy for you, Mr. Streetman, and you've been through it all before, but I'd like to ask you some questions about your son."

Streetman nodded. "Very well. Why don't we go inside? Perhaps you'd enjoy some coffee while we talk."

Falzetti followed Streetman into the house to a tastefully decorated sitting room.

"I'll take your coat," said Streetman, peeling off his

own jacket. "Sit down. My housekeeper will fetch us some coffee."

He disappeared, and Falzetti took the opportunity to look around the room, which was large with a high, ornamented ceiling. A fireplace dominated one wall, and the oak plank floors were covered with dark Oriental rugs. Thick draperies hung from the room's two full-length windows, and Falzetti had the impression that if the drapes had been drawn, the room would have been plunged into total darkness. Streetman returned. "The coffee will be here shortly," he said. "And now, Lieutenant, what can I do for you?"

"I'd like you to tell me about your son. What he was like. Who his friends were. I'm afraid we're not making much progress in finding whoever killed him. Anything you can contribute might help."

Streetman went to the fireplace and started to make a fire. He began talking, his back to Falzetti, as he stacked the logs on top of the kindling. It was a fairly typical story and one that Falzetti had heard many times from bereaved parents. "Good boy . . . respectful . . . never in any trouble . . . plans for the future . . . who can understand?" It was at this point that most parents broke down or choked back a sob, but Streetman lit his fire, turned to face Falzetti and said, "There, that ought to take the chill off the room."

"Perhaps," said Falzetti, "if we had some more information about your son's activities—particularly those around the time he was killed—we might be able to do something."

"I'm afraid I really can't help you, Lieutenant. I saw my son about two weeks before he was reported dead. I really don't know anything about his activities or who he might have seen after that." Streetman poked at the fire. "The next time I saw him was when I identified his body at your morgue in Manhattan."

"You identified the body?"

"Yes. He was wearing his dog tags, but when I got the call at two A.M., naturally I wanted to be sure. So I went into the city immediately."

The door opened, and a very young woman, dark-haired and plain, entered with a tray bearing a silver coffee service and two cups. Streetman, as if used to silence in the woman's presence, said nothing until she had served the coffee and left.

"That was the last time I saw him," he said.

"When your son was here, did he say or do anything that, now that you think about it, might have seemed odd or out of place?"

Streetman shrugged. "No. He told me that he had been in training for an overseas mission. He volunteered for that," he said proudly. "But then for some reason the mission was canceled, and he was returning for reassignment."

"Did he tell you about the assignment?"

"No," said Streetman quickly. "He either didn't know what it was or didn't want me to know. I assumed that if he could have told me, he would have."

Falzetti sipped his coffee. "Did he tell you where he was going when he left here for the last time?"

"No. I thought he was returning to base. We Streetmans have always done our duty for our country, Lieutenant."

Falzetti looked at Streetman over the top of his coffee cup. "You served in the last war, Mr. Streetman?"

"No. I was not fortunate enough to have that opportunity."

Falzetti watched him carefully, sensing instinctively that there was some kind of evasion in that answer. "Did you know or did you ever hear your son mention a Professor Weissman or a Theodore Marcovic?"

Streetman paused for a moment as if considering, and Falzetti watched his eyes, but they revealed nothing. "Those names mean nothing to me," he said.

Falzetti asked a few more questions, but the answers were never illuminating. He pulled himself up from the chair. "Well, I won't take any more of your time, Mr. Streetman. I'm very sorry about your son, and I hope we will have some answers for you soon."

Streetman shrugged as if it were of no consequence.

Later, on the ride back to the city, Falzetti realized that it had been that indifferent shrug, more than anything else, that had convinced him that Streetman was hiding something. He knew, thought Falzetti, more than he was telling, and for some reason he was covering up. How could a father shrug aside the murder of a son? Most parents would scream at the police, demanding that justice be done, that the killer be punished.

Streetman had led Falzetti to the front door and out onto the porch. Neither man had spoken until Falzetti was halfway down the front steps.

"Mr. Streetman—if you don't mind my asking—what country are you from? I couldn't help but notice your accent."

Streetman smiled as if he knew what Falzetti was thinking. "I'm Dutch, Lieutenant. My family came from Nieueschans, but I have lived in America for forty-two years. My son was born here in 1917. We are not German, Lieutenant."

Falzetti smiled foolishly as if apprehended in a lie and accepted Streetman's hand.

In a few minutes he was in his car, heading back to the city.

■

By that evening, Howard Green was back in New York. He went directly to his father's townhouse on West 54th Street just off Fifth Avenue. William H. Green used the family residence only on his infrequent visits to the city, and for all practical purposes the residence was Howard's.

He had hoped that his girlfriend, Janice, might be there when he arrived, but the house was deserted. He made himself a martini and sat in the darkened den, unwinding from the day's travel.

After sitting in the dark for a while, he decided to call her.

"Hello," she answered. Her voice, as usual, was bright and cheerful.

"'S'me," he said. "How are you?"

"Fine. How did your trip go?"

"I'm not sure. Okay, I guess." He did not want to think about it. "Had dinner yet?"

"I'm just making myself an omelette." She laughed. "I bought so many eggs this week."

"C'mon over," he said, "I'll take you to 'Twenty-one'."

"And what about my omelette?"

"Throw it away," he said. "Eggs are plentiful."

"I will not," she said indignantly. "You Americans are so extravagant. There are people in Britain who haven't had a fresh egg in years."

"Please," he said. "Not again. I'll send my eggs to London first chance I get."

"I'm going to come over and make us both an omelette," she said, and before he could reply, she hung up.

Janice Porter was Canadian and worked as a secretary for the British Security Coordination at Rockefeller Center. Green, and almost everyone else, was well aware that the BSC was a front for British intelligence in the United States. The BSC had come to New York in 1940 in order to counter threats of sabotage by German nationals who were reportedly trying to disrupt shipment of American supplies to a beleaguered Britain. The British had placed guards, whom they called consular security officers, at each New York docking facility where British ships were being loaded with supplies.

As the staff of BSC grew, it was found that there was a need for women with secretarial skills. Rather than bring in women from Britain, the directors of the operation decided to import them from Canada.

Janice Porter, a secretary at a bank in Hamilton, Ontario, had jumped at the opportunity to come to New York and work for British intelligence. The young women who came down from Canada were all aware that this was not just another run-of-the-mill secretarial position. They were carefully screened, and only those who were prepared to make a real contribution to the war effort had been selected. Sometimes the women were used to follow suspected agents or saboteurs when a male agent might have aroused suspicion or as couriers to transport secret information. In addition the "secretaries" were trained as telegraphists and were given additional training in coding and deciphering.

Janice Porter had worked in New York for over two years and had met Howard Green a little over a year ago at a cocktail party given by the English-Speaking Union. Since then they had become quite close. Although she still maintained a small apartment with two other secretaries on West 61st Street, she actually spent most nights at Howard's townhouse and had many of her clothes stored in one of the upstairs bedroom closets.

He heard her knock at the door, and when he opened it, found her fumbling for a key in her pocketbook while trying to balance a package.

He looked at her and burst out laughing.

"Dinner," she said, motioning with her head to the package.

He took the package and looked inside, then made a face. "What is it?"

She feigned anger. "It's my omelette—and my frying pan." She came inside and closed the door.

"You brought it with you?"

"What did you want me to do with it? I couldn't let it go to waste. Don't worry. I brought some more eggs. We'll have a lovely dinner."

Watching her as she took off her coat and hung it on the rack in the foyer, Howard Green marveled, as he always did, at the strength and beauty of her body.

Janice was almost as tall as he was, with long legs, a narrow waist, and small but firm breasts. She wore her blond hair long and straight. Her eyes were a steely blue, and seemed always on the verge of surprise.

She planted a kiss on his lips and gave him a big smile, revealing her dazzling white teeth. He thought—as he had thought a thousand times since he met her—that she was the picture of health. Someone should have put her picture on a cereal box.

When they had met in late 1942, he had assumed that she was younger than he was, but in actuality she was more than a year older. In December of 1943 she had turned thirty.

He had found the fact that she was older slightly disconcerting at first but had soon dismissed the fact that he was dating an "older woman" as inconsequential. He had to admit to himself, however, that he had neglected to tell his mother the difference in their ages. It was a small, unimportant deception, he thought, but still it left him vaguely disturbed at his own cowardice. Somewhere in the back of his mind a little voice told him that he should be older—even if only by a day—than the women he dated. He knew that it made no sense, but the voice was there anyway.

He had to be satisfied with the fact that she looked younger than he did.

"Wanta drink?" he asked as they walked toward the den.

"Yes, got any gin left?"

He nodded and went to the liquor cabinet.

"I missed you today," she said. This was one of their signals for sex but if Howard heard her, he did not answer. She shrugged, wondering what could possibly have him so preoccupied. "Tough day?" she asked as he poured her drink.

"I don't know," he said absently. "Just one of those days."

"Top secret?" she asked, her voice gently mocking him.

One of their inside jokes was that the work that he did for Army intelligence, although often labeled secret was so mundane it was laughable that anyone could consider it important enough to be worth concealing. A considerable source of irritation to him was that her work seemed to be infinitely more important than his.

He told her everything that crossed his desk and assumed that she did the same. In fact, she told him very little of what she encountered on her job.

"Not too secret," he said, giving her a drink and sitting beside her on the couch. "It's probably nothing," he said.

"Can you tell me about it?"

Without hesitation, he told her everything that he knew. He hoped that her quick, logical mind might bring some order out of the chaos he had formulated.

When he was finished, she sat still for a moment, thinking about what he had said. "Have the FBI said anything?"

"Nothing. They're as closemouthed as usual."

"Russian spies," she said confidently. "They're into everything. They trust no one. They were probably trying to find out about whatever project this Weissman was working on."

"That's what I think," said Green. "Marcovic was a known red, so it seems logical. But what were they after? What is worth killing two—three—men for? What is Streetman's role in all this?"

Janice shook her head slowly. "The Russians are deathly afraid that we'll abandon them to the Germans. They have an intrinsic distrust of Western cultures. We've sent them billions of dollars in aid, lost thousands of lives to deliver it, and still they don't trust us. They still think we're out to get them."

Howard nodded. "Washington is crawling with Russian spies. There are more spies per employee in their embassy than in any other embassy in the capital. They're everywhere—into everything."

"It has to be them," Janice agreed.

"That's all fine," said Howard, "but what about Lieutenant Streetman? What's his part in all this? He's an American—the other two are foreigners."

"He wouldn't be the first American to sell information to a foreign government."

"Selling information is one thing, but if the information is correct—and right now it's only circumstantial—and he *was* the other man in that hotel room, he killed one of the men in that room and maybe was responsible for the other man's fall from that ledge."

"That's a lot of 'maybe,'" said Janice. "As you said, the evidence is only circumstantial. Maybe he wasn't the one who was in that room. Or maybe he followed them there for reasons only he will ever know. Maybe someone else killed the others, and he saw who it was.

That could be why he is dead now." She looked at Howard, her lips in a pout. "You can build a lot of bridges with *maybe*."

"You're right," he said. "So what should I do?"

She thought for a moment. "Have you thought of taking off my clothes and carrying me to the bedroom?"

Howard Green laughed. "Seriously. D'you think I've got enough here to merit going on with this?"

Her face was serious again. "Yes, I do. I think you should find out everything you can about this dead soldier and about the people he might have killed."

He smiled, glad that she had agreed with him. "You're right, as usual," he said, kissing her and pulling her close. He reached for the buttons on her blouse. "Now I think I'll take your clothes off and carry you to the bedroom."

"Oh, my," she said, laughing. "I just love a man who doesn't have to be told what to do but just does it."

"That's me," he said, his voice husky. "You might have to walk the last flight of stairs by yourself," he added.

Janice jumped up. "I'll race you," she said and was off for the stairs.

■

At first Falzetti didn't recognize the woman when the sergeant led her to his desk.

"Says she's gotta talk to you, Nick. Says it's urgent."

With that the sergeant left, and Falzetti looked up into the vaguely familiar face of the young woman who stood in front of his desk. He looked longingly at the half-eaten pastrami sandwich and lukewarm cup of coffee in front of him before he waved the woman into a chair. "Sit down . . . Miss . . . ?"

The woman sat. "Gretchen Vandervort," she said, her accent thick. "I'm sorry to interrupt your lunch."

Suddenly it came to Falzetti who the woman was.

She had served the coffee at Streetman's house. "You are Mr. Streetman's housekeeper," he said.

She nodded and seemed pleased that he had remembered her. "Please, Lieutenant," she said, "continue with your lunch."

Gratefully Falzetti picked up his sandwich. "What can I do for you, Miss Vandervort?" He wasn't sure if he had pronounced her name properly.

"I cannot stay long," she began haltingly. "The chauffeur drove me into town, and I took the train to the city. I must return as quickly as possible. If Mr. Streetman ever found out that I was here . . ." Her voice trailed off into uncertainty.

Falzetti tried to be as reassuring as possible. "Why don't you tell me why you've come?"

She looked around the squad room as if searching for a more private spot.

"Don't worry," said Falzetti, "no one here is paying any attention. They're all too busy with their own problems."

Miss Vandervort looked down at her hands, which she held in her lap. "I'm not really sure where to begin."

"Is it about Streetman?"

She nodded, then sat silently, unable to proceed.

Falzetti took another bite of his sandwich. She needed coaxing. "How long have you worked for him?"

"Almost four years. I am from Holland. My family sent me to New York when the war broke out. I lived with an aunt in Manhattan for almost a year, but she died, and I had to find work. I was fortunate to find a position with Mr. Streetman."

"What is it about your employer that disturbs you, Miss Vandervort?" said Falzetti, taking a closer look at the young woman, who continued to look down and had begun to wring her hands as if in despair. She was plain-looking—her beefy face had not one attractive feature—but she carried herself with a certain amount of dignity.

"When I first began working for Mr. Streetman, he was visited every Sunday afternoon by two men whose names he never mentioned. Usually they would go outside to talk—down by the tennis court, where no one could hear them. But if the weather was bad, they would come into the house, and I would serve them coffee."

"And you overheard what they said?"

"No," she said, shaking her head helplessly, "they never spoke when I was in the room."

Falzetti encouraged her. "But when you were not in the room?"

"I do not eavesdrop, Lieutenant, but sometimes I did overhear what they were talking about."

"Which was?"

"I heard them talking about aircraft from some of the factories on Long Island and sometimes about ships in New York harbor."

"What did they say?"

"I never heard enough of their conversation to really know."

Falzetti disguised a sigh behind his sandwich. When the war started, the police had been inundated with scores of people who reported suspicious behavior of their neighbors, their friends, their employers. Everyone was sure that he was reporting a German spy. Falzetti hadn't had one of these stories for more than a year.

Miss Vandervort gave an embarrassed smile as if what she was about to say was foolish. "But once or twice I overheard them speaking in German."

Falzetti paused in midbite. "Are you sure?"

"I'm positive."

Falzetti thought about it, then shrugged. There were over one hundred thousand people in New York City who spoke German. A walk along East 86th Street would convince anyone of that.

"You said, when you 'first' went to work there. Do these men still visit?"

"Not since America entered the war. That ended their visits. Now Mr. Streetman gets in his car and goes for a ride once a week—every Friday. It's the only time he ever drives himself. He is gone most of the day. I think he visits them now."

So far, thought Falzetti, she had given him exactly nothing: Now instead of having company on Sunday, Streetman goes for a drive on Friday.

"Can you tell me anything about Karl Streetman?" he asked her.

"They hated each other."

"The father and the son?"

"Yes."

Falzetti's eyebrows went up. "Yeah?"

She nodded. "They fought all the time. That boy could never please his father, no matter what he did. Just a week before his body was found, they had a terrible fight. It was awful. You could hear them screaming at each other all over the house."

"Did you say a week?" Streetman had said that he had seen his son two weeks before he identified the body. If what this woman said was true, Streetman had seen his son much later, perhaps even on the night he had been killed.

"Yes. I remember it was on a Friday and the next Friday was when they called to say the boy was dead."

"You saw him in the house on that Friday?"

Miss Vandervort frowned. "I didn't see him. It was late when he arrived. But I heard his voice. I heard them yelling at each other."

"Sometimes when people yell, it's difficult to distinguish voices. It might have been someone else."

Gretchen Vandervort looked down at the floor. She hadn't expected to be challenged. "It was him," she said softly. "They left the house together close to midnight. The next morning Mr. Streetman was back. I don't know what time he came in. I never saw young Mr. Streetman again."

"You don't think that Streetman had anything to do with his son's death?"

She shrugged. "I don't know. As I said, he hated that boy. He was a cruel father."

"Lots of fathers have strained relationships with their sons. It doesn't mean—"

"I don't think he has ever visited his son's grave."

Falzetti flapped his hands helplessly on his desk. He wondered how a homicide investigation had turned into a discussion of father-son relationships. "Lots of people can't bear to visit the grave of a loved one."

"Loved one?" Gretchen Vandervort almost laughed. "He doesn't care . . . for anyone."

Falzetti was beginning to wonder about Miss Vandervort's relationship with her employer. She was beginning to sound more and more like a scorned lover.

"At the funeral," she said, her anger growing, "he sat like a lump of stone. No emotion—nothing."

Falzetti shrugged. He'd had enough of this. "Everyone doesn't act the same way at—"

She cut him off. "That night, after the funeral, when he came home, he went into his study for a while by himself." She closed her eyes as if picturing the scene.

"And?" Falzetti said. He was looking around the room to give someone a signal to get him out of this. As usual, no one was paying any attention.

"I walked past his door," she said, "and he was whistling."

"Whistling?"

"Yes. And not sad but happy. As if he didn't have a care in the world. And his only son just put in the ground."

Falzetti could not help the sigh that escaped his lips. He was imagining Jon Streetman as the first man ever convicted of whistling after a funeral. So he was whistling. Unusual? Perhaps, but certainly not an indication of anything criminal.

Gretchen Vandervort looked nervously at her watch. "I really must go," she said.

Falzetti jumped up. "I'll let you know if anything comes up."

"I don't know who else to talk to," she said. "I just feel that something is wrong in that house—somebody is hiding something."

Falzetti watched her trudge across the room, take a tentative look back in his direction, and then disappear through the door.

Falzetti shook his head and picked up his coffee cup.

He sipped, but it was cold, leaving a bad taste in his mouth.

28

The old lorry bounced and bustled its way along the narrow country road, squeaking like an angry crow. The six men in the back of the truck were exhausted. They had left the main house at six A.M. and boarded the antiquated lorry that someone said had been used to deliver bread before the war. They had driven to the airfield in Dumfries almost thirty miles away and spent the better part of the morning with a paratroop instructor who had given them a brief but intensive course in the art of parachuting.

He had walked them through the large hangar, where men were hunched over long tables like elves at work on Christmas toys, carefully folding the long silk fabric and cords of the parachutes.

"We still use silk," said the instructor, "even though it's in short supply. We tried cotton, but it's not as good and"—he chuckled—"it's in short supply too."

He moved over to the tables, watching the men work. "One of these boys will go with us when we jump," the instructor said. "It keeps them from getting careless with other people's parachutes."

They were led outside to a wooden scaffold and ordered to the top. There they attached lines to a cable and jumped off into space. This, they were told, simulated the effect—but not the hazard—of leaping from an airplane.

Chapman, who had made several jumps while in training in Canada, performed flawlessly. Some of the others were not so lucky, although ankle sprains were the most serious injury.

In the afternoon they made four jumps from an old

Douglas Boston that had been converted for training duty. Bishop accompanied them aloft but made only the first jump. On the other jumps he stood by the open door and slapped each man on the shoulder as his turn came.

On the final jump the wind picked up, and two of the men were dragged along the ground. Although their harness was of the quick release type, the wind tumbled them about so much that they were, for a time, unable to release the chute. One of the two suffered a broken arm; the other, various cuts and bruises.

After that, Bishop decided they had had enough for the day. They piled wearily back into the lorry, leaving behind their comrade who had been taken to the hospital with his broken arm.

The commandos' usual enthusiasm seemed dampened by the incident and by the generally grueling physical hardships of the training. Most were content to smoke a cigarette in silence and bounce along with the cadence of their vehicle. Bishop kept his eye on Chapman, who seemed particularly lacking in spirit. His head was down, and he made no attempt at conversation. Mere eye contact with the others in the truck seemed beyond his capabilities.

In fact, his mind was filled with thoughts of Margaret Brown and the letter she had asked him to deliver. Why, he wondered, had she put him in such a position? Was this some kind of loyalty test? Her concern for her brother was genuine, but what she had suggested could conceivably threaten the entire mission. A thought hummed in his brain for one brief moment: was it possible that that could be her intention? Was she trying to jeopardize the mission? Or was she trying to use him as a courier to the Nazis? What did he know about her, he asked himself. Not much. How much can you know about someone in a few days? She was Irish, and although many Irish in Britain served with distinction in the war, others, he knew, would just as soon let the British stew in their own juices. Some would even welcome a German victory. There were many of Irish descent in America who had been openly hostile to the

British, at least until Hitler had declared war on the United States.

He looked up and saw Bishop watching him with interest. I should tell Bishop, he thought. Even if it's nothing, I should tell him. Then what? If the letter was indeed a message to her brother, Margaret Brown would probably be court-martialed, or at the very least severely reprimanded and reduced in rank. They would probably never trust her again. And what if the message proved to be more than just a simple letter from a worried sister to a missing brother? What if the message was in code and was meant to betray the mission? What then? Margaret Brown would be arrested, imprisoned, and in all probability hanged for treason.

He closed his eyes. The image of Margaret Brown twitching convulsively on the end of a rope was too strong for him to face. He shuddered, his shoulders gyrating involuntarily, and when he opened his eyes, Bishop was watching him, a question on his face.

"Something wrong?"

"No," said Chapman, "just a sudden chill. I'm all right."

They rode the rest of the trip in silence.

Long before they arrived back at Galloway House Chapman had made his decision. The mission must be paramount. He knew that he was in the grip of a power stronger than love. Nothing must jeopardize the mission.

Margaret Brown studied his anguished expression and waited for him to speak. They were walking in the lower of the two gardens behind the main house.

"I can't do it," he said. Instead of the expected disappointment he saw something else in her eyes.

"You said you wouldn't change your mind," she said, but her voice seemed more relieved than troubled.

"I know I did, but I just think it's a foolish idea. The success of this mission cannot be jeopardized by any—" He saw the dim glow of a half smile on her face and stopped in midsentence. She was relieved that he was not going to go through with it, happy that he had refused her.

She struggled to keep her face steady, but her eyes betrayed her.

His eyes narrowed. "You never wanted me to take the letter, did you?"

Surprise was written across her features. "That's not true. I told you I'm desperately worried about my brother."

"Then why are you glad I won't do it?"

"I'm not glad," she stammered. "I just think that you're probably right. I have no right to jeopardize your mission or to involve you in my personal affairs."

He said nothing. His eyes were a hard ice-blue peering through narrow slits. For the first time she found him just a little frightening.

"Let's forget about it," she said, forcing a smile. "It was a bad idea anyway."

The look stayed in his eyes, and his voice was incredibly cold. "You set me up, didn't you?"

"What are you talking about?"

"It was some kind of test, wasn't it? Just like everything else around here is a test."

"Don't be—"

"Some kind of loyalty test—or a test of judgment—or—or—something. Wasn't it?"

Her eyes couldn't meet his. Her hands fluttered to her throat and then, as if unable to find a suitable perch, dropped to her sides. "Yes," she said finally, then looked up, "and you passed with flying colors." She tried to smile, but her lips would not move in the required pattern, and her attempt looked more like the beginning of an anguished sob.

He thrust his hands into his pockets, and she imagined that it was so he would not strike her. "Thanks," he said, turning away from her.

"I'm sorry," she said. "It wasn't my idea."

"Just doing your job, I suppose." He stopped suddenly, seized by a thought. "Just what is your job? Do you take care of all the outsiders who pass through here? Are you the pretty girl who seduces men into giving up all their secrets? A sort of reverse Mata Hari?"

"Please," she began. "I never wanted this to happen. I wanted everything to be truth between us."

"*Truth*!" he shot back. "Where does the truth begin? How many men have you given your truth to?"

She recoiled as if she had been slapped, and he thought for a moment that she would run away from him, but she held her ground. Her voice quivered a little as she spoke. "I don't blame you for feeling the way you do. What I did was unforgivable. I thought I was doing my duty, but I realize that I was only hurting you for no good reason." She paused, then forced herself to look up at him. "But I want you to know that everything I ever said to you—everything up until that letter business—was the absolute truth."

"You told me that you loved me," he said.

She was calmer now. "That was true—and it's still true."

"I don't know if I can believe you," he told her.

She shrugged helplessly. "How can I make you understand?"

He turned quickly and walked away from her, his speed increasing with the distance until he was running, his head down, his arms flying, and his legs driving him as fast as he could go.

Margaret Brown sat quietly, smoking a cigarette. Her shoes were off and her legs were curled under her as she sat on her bed, her shoulders back against the wall. In an uncommon act of carelessness she flicked the ashes from her cigarette onto the floor as she stared absently at the window to her left. From her vantage point she could see only a patch of gray sky and the granite corner of the sleeping wing of the house.

As she stared into space her thoughts ran to the events of the day and to how she had been an idiot to let Bishop talk her into such foolishness. There was a sharp rap on her door—a staccato pounding that signified that the visitor was either very angry or very sure of himself.

Andrew, she thought as she raced to the door.

She whipped open the door to find Major Bishop standing on the threshhold.

He seemed taken aback by her surprised expression, his left eyebrow shooting up. They glared at each other for a moment. "Well?" he asked.

"Well what?" snapped Margaret Brown.

Bishop looked up and down the hall. "May I come in for just a moment, Lieutenant Brown? I think we have something to discuss."

Margaret drew herself up to her full height. "I would prefer not to discuss it here in my private quarters."

Bishop nodded an acceptance. "My office? Five minutes?"

"I'll be there," said Margaret, closing the door in his face.

When she entered Bishop's office, Margaret noted that Eric Madsen was sitting in front of Bishop's desk.

Feeling her unasked question, Bishop said, "Lieutenant Madsen has an interest in this conversation. I hope you don't mind if he sits in." He motioned her to a seat.

Margaret Brown sat, and Bishop, not knowing where to begin, drummed his fingers on his desk. He took a deep breath. "First of all let me say that I know how difficult this has been for you—"

"You don't know that at all, Major," said Margaret Brown quietly.

"—and"—Bishop plunged on as if he had not heard—"we deeply appreciate your assistance in this"—he hesitated—"delicate matter."

"May I smoke?" she asked, taking out a cigarette.

"Of course," said Bishop, leaning forward with his lighter.

Margaret Brown lit her own cigarette, and Bishop sighed and put his lighter back into his pocket. He sneaked a glance at Madsen, his eyes rolling to the ceiling to show his exasperation. Madsen did not seem concerned. He sat, elbows on the arms of the chair, chin resting in his right hand, carefully watching Brown.

Bishop turned back to her. "Did you give Chapman the letter?" he asked.

"No." She hesitated. "I didn't get the chance."

"I'm not sure I understand. When I inquired earlier, you said—"

"I asked him about it last night, and he said that he would deliver the letter for me, but today he told me that he could not—that he was afraid it might threaten the mission."

Bishop chewed on his lower lip. "But he did accept at first?"

Margaret Brown chuckled softly. "A man will say lots of things he doesn't mean when he's in bed with a woman, Captain."

Her eyes held his. Bishop cleared his throat and looked away. He opened his mouth several times to speak, but the words would not come.

Margaret Brown was pleased that she had shocked him. She looked to Madsen, but except for a wry smile, his expression had not changed. "I don't want you to think," Margaret Brown said to Bishop, "that I let him into my bed because of your little scheme."

"Of course not," sputtered Bishop. "I would never dream of such a thing."

Margaret Brown stood up. "Anyway, I think you can stop worrying about the American's loyalty. I've done my bit for England," she added sarcastically.

"I'm sorry," said Bishop. "I never intended that you would become so . . . personally involved in this."

Margaret Brown said nothing, only stared into Bishop's eyes. There was something there—something missing or far away—that made her suddenly sorry for him. "May I go now?" she asked.

"Yes, of course," he said, looking away. "Thank you for your help, Lieutenant."

Margaret Brown nodded, looked at Madsen, and quickly left.

As she closed the door behind her Bishop emitted a long sigh. "Too bad we can't fight this war without women," he said. An officer—a male officer—would never have dared to be so disrespectful to a superior. "What do you think?" he asked, turning to Madsen.

Madsen's eyes were still on the door. "Magnificent. You English have magnificent women."

Bishop was puzzled. "She's Irish, actually."

Madsen shrugged. "No matter. She's wonderful."

"I meant, what did you think of the result of our little charade with Chapman?"

"Inconclusive," said Madsen.

Bishop thought for a minute. "Instead of refusing her, he should have come to me and reported what she had asked him."

"Perhaps you're right," said Madsen, sitting back in his chair and thrusting his hands deep into his pockets, "but if I were sharing her bed and she asked me to deliver this letter, knowing that she could be imprisoned or severely disciplined, I don't know if I would report her either."

Bishop seemed mystified, as if Madsen's statement was beyond comprehension. "You wouldn't?"

Madsen laughed. "I'd probably deliver the damn letter."

Bishop laughed halfheartedly, not sure if Madsen was only joking. He waited for some sign from Madsen that the joke was over, but the Dane said nothing.

The smile dropped from Bishop's face. "Well, I don't think we have any other options now. The American goes with us. Even the psychologists on the Students' Assessment Board have given him a clean bill of health."

Madsen nodded.

"You agree?" said Bishop, with some surprise evident in his voice.

"My earlier doubts about his inexperience have been laid to rest. He's obviously fit and is instinctively courageous. He's the best choice we can make at this point."

Bishop beamed. "That makes things much easier. I was dreading having to report to the Americans that we didn't want their boy along with us. This small-scale raiding force has to have American participation." He made a brief note on a pad in front of him. "Who else?" he asked, without looking up.

"Iverson," Madsen said immediately.

Bishop made another note. "I like him too. Seems quite calm. I think he'll handle himself well if things get a bit sticky."

Madsen smiled at Bishop's English idiom. "Yes," he said, "and things just might."

29

When the phone rang in Howard Green's bedroom, he pulled the covers over his head and waited for Janice to answer it. On the sixth or seventh ring he began to think that she might not, so he reached over to nudge her, but her side of the bed was empty. Sleepily, he picked up the phone and was surprised to hear her voice on the other end of the line.

"Aren't you up yet?"

"Where are you?" he asked, his dulled brain too disoriented to understand how she could be with him and talking to him on the phone at the same time.

"I'm at work," she said. "I got up early and left while you were still sleeping." The BSC offices at Rockefeller Center were only a few blocks from Green's house. A hint of recrimination crept into her voice. "I thought you'd be up by now."

"What time is it?"

"Almost nine. Don't you have to check in with Uncle Sam or something?" He heard her laugh. "You *are* still in the army, aren't you?"

"They don't even know I'm back yet. I'll go in after lunch. I've got some things to do this morning."

"Listen to this," said Janice. "I decided to check through our files here in the office and see if we had anything on this Karl Streetman—you know, Communist party, German-American Bund, leftist, fascist, anything I could find." She paused to let him ask the question.

"And?"

"Nothing."

"Shit. You didn't wake me up to tell me that."

"Of course not," she said, her voice gleeful. "His father is in our files as a possible German sympathizer."

Green was wide awake now. He sat up and swung his legs onto the floor. "Go on," he said brusquely.

"It's all here in his file," she said. "Do you remember the big to-do when all those American millionaires and industrialists got together at the Waldorf-Astoria to celebrate the German victories in Europe?"

"Yes," said Green. "I think it was right after the surrender of France."

"June 26, 1940, to be exact," said Janice. "Big shots from Ford, General Motors, Texaco, ITT, and scores of others were there. Prospects of trade with the new supreme power in Europe had them drooling."

"What does this all have to do with—"

"He was there," she interrupted. "Jon Streetman—Lieutenant Streetman's father. He was there, cheering with the rest of them."

"Are you sure?"

"It's right here in his file." Her voice dropped to a whisper. "I'll get canned if anyone finds out, but I'll bring the file to you after work. There's lots of good stuff in here."

"Meet me for lunch," he said, his voice growing more urgent. "Bring it with you."

"If I can. Where shall we meet."

"How about the Rainbow Room?"

"Right here in the same building? I'm going to give you documents that could get me fired, in the same building where I work? Not likely!"

His mind was racing. "'Twenty-one' then. At noon."

"Fine," she said. "I'll be there."

Janice hung up and looked at the man who sat on the corner of her desk. He was her boss, Jonathan Blakely, one of the top three men in British intelligence in the United States.

"He sounded interested?" he asked.

"Very," said Janice, with a smile that soon faded into a frown.

"What is it?" asked Blakely.

She shrugged. "Why couldn't I just give him the information? Why the subterfuge?"

Blakely stood up and stuffed his hands in his pockets. "We don't want the Americans to think that we're feeding them information. It makes them feel as if they're not doing their part when we just dump it in their lap. We'd rather let them think they got the information by their own devices." He smiled. "Good for morale."

Janice made a face. "What about my morale?"

"Come on now, Janice. Let's not be foolish. He's really quite a nice young chap, your Howard Green." He punched her lightly on the arm. "What's the harm if we give his career a little boost once in a while?"

Falzetti whistled when Green called to tell him about the Waldorf celebration. "That sure puts things in a different light, doesn't it?" he said.

"Yes," said Green. "We're thinking Russians, and suddenly the Germans are in the picture."

"I talked with Streetman yesterday," Falzetti said. "I thought there was something funny about him."

"We've got to talk," Green said. "I've got lots to tell you."

"I can meet you at lunch time."

Green thought. "Okay. 'Twenty-one' at twelve-thirty."

"'Twenty-one!'"

"Yeah, you got anything against good food?"

"You buying?" asked Falzetti.

Green laughed. He was caught up in the excitement of the unraveling mystery. "You bet, Nick," he said, still laughing.

While he waited for Janice Porter to arrive, Howard Green admired the Frederic Remington painting in the foyer of The "21" Club on West 52nd Street.

The maitre d' approached him. "Captain Green," he said. "It's good to see you again."

"Thanks, George," said Green. "I'm waiting for someone. She'll be here shortly."

"Miss Porter, I hope?"

Green smiled and nodded. George didn't miss much.

"I'll have a nice table ready for you when she gets here."

He started to walk away, but Howard stopped him. "George. Someone else will be joining us in about"—he looked at his watch; Janice was late—"twenty minutes."

"No problem, Captain Green. I'll take care of it."

Janice arrived, bursting through the door like a cyclone. "Sorry I'm late," she whispered, kissing Howard on the cheek. "I had to wait 'til I could sneak this file out." She held up a large, brown envelope. "I think you'll find it interesting."

They were led to a small table in the corner of the dining room, and Howard Green ordered drinks. "Someone else is joining us for lunch," he said to Janice.

Her expression was puzzled. "Who?"

"This New York City cop that I'm working with on this Streetman thing. I told you about him."

She shrugged. "You didn't tell me much."

"I told him to be here at twelve-thirty because I wanted to talk with you first. I want him to see this file too."

She bit her lower lip as she thought about that.

"He doesn't have to know where the information came from," he said.

She nodded slowly. "All right."

Howard smiled, glad to have her agreement. "You'll like him, I think. Kind of rough around the edges but a good cop. He knew a lot more about this case than the FBI—and he wasn't even trying."

Janice nodded. "The investigative abilities of Mr. Hoover's boys are positively amazing."

Their drinks arrived, and Howard took a long sip. "Let me see the file," he said.

"You want it now?" she said, looking around as if the room were filled with enemy agents.

He shook his head. "You wake me up to tell me about

this, and now you want me to wait." He smiled. "Let's have it."

She forced a smile. She really liked Howard, but sometimes his naiveté was appalling. Either one of them might have been followed by a German agent or a Russian agent or—God forbid—by the FBI. She looked around the room at all the businessmen in three-piece suits. If anything, it was more likely that they had been followed by the FBI than by anyone else. Thinking this way made her feel slightly paranoid, but she knew that in wartime New York, anything was possible. Three weeks earlier, one of the BSC agents in her office had left the office to check on a report by one of the consular security officers at Pier 90. He had boarded a British vessel that was being loaded with machinery. Three hours later he was found lying at the foot of a ladder. His neck was broken. The official explanation had been "accidental death," and the BSC had, of course, avoided any publicity, but everyone had become a little more aware that this, too, was part of a shooting war.

Janice shrugged and slipped the envelope to him across the table.

He grabbed it greedily, opened it, and took out the file. He opened the folder and, while Janice sipped her drink and looked around the room for suspicious faces, began to read.

She watched him. Every few seconds his eyebrows would go up or he would nod as if the file confirmed something he had suspected. Sometimes he would make little noises and move his lips, and she smiled, thinking that this was the same thing he did in bed.

In some ways, she thought, he was like a little boy. That was part of his charm. He was good and kind and fun to be with. But innocence was a two-way street. He didn't seem to understand her fervor about the war; he treated it as a temporary, personal inconvenience that would soon be over, letting them all get on with their lives. He laughed at her refusal to ride on the East River Drive Extension, which had been built on rubble from bombed British cities. British freighters had used the rubble as ballast as they made the trip to New York Harbor to load up with supplies.

He had finished reading the file and was looking back over a few interesting points when Janice noticed someone talking to the maitre d'—a fiftyish man in a baggy gray suit that contrasted with the neat suits around her. "I think your friend's here," she said, smiling.

Howard Green waved, and Falzetti shook hands warmly with the maitre d' and came over to the table. Green introduced Janice and could see that Falzetti was impressed with her. The cop couldn't take his eyes off her.

"So what do you do, Janice?" Falzetti asked.

Howard Green looked guiltily from one to the other. "She is a secretary," he began, his voice betraying his uncertainty.

Falzetti picked up on the hesitation right away, but Janice broke in with a smile. "I work for a British import-export firm over at Rockefeller Center," she said. "It's called British Sales Coordination."

"I see," said Falzetti with a nod, and Janice had the feeling that he could see right through her. If he called Rockefeller Center, he would find that there really was a British Sales Coordination, but she doubted that such a subterfuge would deter Lieutenant Falzetti.

As they ordered, the owner of the restaurant came over to their table. Howard Green was all smiles. As long as he had been coming to "21", the owner had never come over to his table. As soon as he arrived it was obvious, however, that he had come to say hello to Falzetti.

"Nicky," he said, "how are you?"

"I'm fine, Jack, how are you? I don't know if you know Miss Porter and Captain Green."

"Captain Green I've seen here many times." He smiled and shook hands with Green. "I don't see you here too often, Nick."

"Your prices aren't quite what they used to be when you ran the Red Head, Jack."

Jack's smile grew. "That was a long time ago."

After a brief conversation, the owner slapped Falzetti

on the back and said, "Well, I hope you enjoy your lunch. Nice meeting you, Miss Porter." He nodded to Howard Green, "Captain Green. Take care of yourself, Nick. Don't be a stranger."

When he had left the table, Howard Green looked at Falzetti. "I'm impressed. You know the owner of 'Twenty-one'?"

Falzetti laughed. "Jack Krendler and his partner Charlie Berns used to run a speakeasy back in the Twenties. So did Billingsly of the Stork Club and Perma of El Morocco. That's how they got started and that's how I got to know them. Jack and Charlie owned the Red Head in Greenwich Village . . . When you're a cop you get to know all kinds of people."

Janice chimed in. "Police work must be very interesting."

Falzetti smiled. His eyes caught hers and held on. "Not really," he said, shaking his head. "I'll bet your work at—what did you call it"—British Sales Coordination is just as interesting."

Janice felt herself blush. She knew that he had seen through her fabrication. She composed herself and said in a firm voice, "You're probably quite right, Lieutenant."

After lunch, Janice rose from her chair. "I have to get back to the office. I'll let you boys talk about whatever it is you have to talk about." She kissed Howard on the cheek and shook Falzetti's hand. "Nice meeting you, Lieutenant," she said. "I'm sure we'll meet again."

Both men sat in silence, watching her as she made her way to the door.

Falzetti was the first to speak. "That's quite a girl you've got yourself, Howard."

Pleased with himself, Howard smiled. "Yes," he said simply.

"Now," said Falzetti, "tell me what else you found out about Streetman."

Howard Green looked around the restaurant. "Let's go for a walk," he said. "It's a little close in here."

Green took care of the bill, and they went out onto 52nd Street. They walked down Fifth Avenue and took a right onto 51st, then cut through Rockefeller Plaza, stopping above the sunken plaza to watch the skaters perform on the ice below.

"Well," said Falzetti. "What about it? What do you have?"

Green handed him the brown envelope. Falzetti slid out the folder and began to read.

Jon Streetman had been born in Holland in 1889. He had two older brothers. His father was Dutch, his mother German. When he was seven, the family moved to South Africa. They settled in Transvaal, one of the Boer republics, and his father was active in the Boer insurrection against the British. In 1901 Streetman's father and his two brothers—sixteen and eighteen—had been hanged by the British. Apparently Streetman's age had been all that had saved him from the noose.

After the war Streetman—now thirteen—and his mother left South Africa and settled in Germany, where they lived until 1905. His mother remarried a German named Karl Odet, and the new family emigrated to the United States in 1906. Odet opened a hardware store in Bridgeport, Pennsylvania, in 1908 and for a time seemed relatively prosperous. In 1917, however, shortly after the United States declared war on Germany, the hardware store was burned to the ground. Karl Odet, it seemed, had been a little too outspoken in his pro-German views. After the war Odet and Streetman's mother moved back to Germany.

By this time Jon Streetman had already established himself in the booming oil business, first as a wildcatter and then as an oil trader. Before he was twenty-five, he had made and lost several fortunes.

He had married in 1916, a year before his stepfather's store had burned. He was then twenty-seven, his wife nearly forty. Their son Karl was born the next year. His wife, the former Johanna Ritter, had been the only unmarried daughter of a fairly wealthy Houston businessman who was well connected in shipping and oil.

Streetman concentrated on the oil business, and through his father-in-law, he developed extensive contacts in Mexico. In 1923 he founded his own company, which he called Eagle Oil Company, and by 1930 he was well established as an independent operator. By 1936 his company had extensive holdings in Texas and Mexico. Streetman, now in his late forties, was a wealthy man. His wife died in 1935 and Streetman had not remarried.

In those years he traveled extensively in Europe, ostensibly seeking new markets for his oil. It was now believed that the Germans were buying everything he could produce.

He was known to have been the guest of honor at a Berlin party in 1938 at the home of Dr. Hjalmar Schacht, president of the Reichsbank. Present at the party were Hermann Goering of the Luftwaffe; Admiral Erich Raeder, commander in chief of the German Navy; and Dr. Joseph Goebbels, the propaganda minister. It was also rumored that Streetman had had a personal audience with the Führer himself on the day following the party.

Falzetti looked up from the material he was reading. "Sounds as if this guy should have been arrested the day war was declared."

Green shook his head. "If we interned every businessman who tried to do business with the Nazis in the thirties, there'd be nobody left on the streets." He looked at the page in Falzetti's hand. "Read on," he said. "It gets better."

Through a complicated currency credit scheme, financed through the Reichsbank, Streetman traded oil for German-made machinery and oil tankers to transport the oil. Through personal contacts with Grand Admiral Raeder, Streetman's company became a major provider of oil to the revitalized German navy. His dealings with Nazi Germany rapidly made Streetman a very wealthy man, with a home in Houston and an estate on Long Island.

Until 1940 nothing that Streetman had done could be considered illegal, but when war came to Europe, his dealings with the Germans became more difficult. Even though President Roosevelt had imposed sanctions on delivery of war materials, Streetman apparently had tried to get around the sanctions and the British blockade by routing his deliveries through Mexico to Sweden, where the oil was switched to other vessels and shipped to Germany. The British caught on to his little scheme, and soon after, the State Department confronted him with the evidence.

Streetman denied any complicity, claiming that he had delivered his products to a neutral nation and was not responsible for what was done subsequently. No charges were made, but since then Streetman had confined his business activities to strictly domestic markets.

He was under FBI surveillance for some time in 1941 and again after war was declared, but apparently the bureau was satisfied that Streetman was not involved in any subversive activities. Since 1941 the Long Island home had been his principal residence.

A footnote to the report stated that Streetman had been a major contributor to Franklyn Delano Roosevelt's reelection campaign of 1940 and was expected to be a heavy contributor again in 1944 if the president chose to run.

Falzetti leafed through the pages of the brief report once more before looking up at Green. "So what have we got?" he asked.

Green shrugged. "A man with close business and family ties to Germany; a man with a good reason to hate the British—"

"And maybe not too many reasons to like Americans," interrupted Falzetti.

Green nodded. "Perhaps that's true. His mother and stepfather were treated poorly while they were here."

"And he did name his son after his stepfather."

"Right."

Falzetti looked puzzled. "But what does it all add up to? Where does the son, Karl, fit into the picture?" Green was unable to answer. "What did you find out about him?" Falzetti asked.

"Born in New York in 1917; graduated from Columbia University; worked for his father in the oil business for a few years; joined the army in early 1942; attended officers' training school at Fort Benning, Georgia." He shrugged. "Last year he volunteered for an OSS mission, but although he went through the training program, he never got to go through with it."

Falzetti turned his back to the ice rink and, leaning against the low wall that ran around the sunken plaza, looked down at the sidewalk. After a brief silence he said, "Do you think that Karl might have gone to Germany with his father during those early visits?"

"Possible," said Green. "We can find out through the State Department."

"What if," said Falzetti, as though he hadn't heard Green's comment, "he had been with his father when he met Hitler?" He looked up at Green. "What if this Karl Streetman had been very impressed with Hitler? What if he had been a real Hitler fanatic?"

Green looked around before answering. The skaters were twirling on the ice, and the war seemed a million miles away. "Then we'd have a pretty good idea what he was doing in that hotel room with Professor Weissman."

"And," added Falzetti, "where the information he got from Weissman was supposed to go."

Green pulled up the collar on his army coat. The wind whipping down Rockefeller Plaza had brought a sudden, more intense chill to his bones.

30

Police Sergeant Tim O'Connor sat behind the wheel of the '37 Plymouth. The car, unmarked and unobtrusive, was parked a hundred yards away from the driveway of the home of Jon Streetman. O'Connor was red-faced and overweight, his belly rubbing uncomfortably against the lower rim of the steering wheel. He was too old for this kind of work, and he knew it, but, as with every other kind of industry, the New York Police Department had its wartime manpower shortages, and even overage, overweight cops who should have been behind a desk— or retired to a cottage in Canarsie— were still in harness.

He had been waiting for Streetman since early morning. The coffee stain on his white shirt and the white confectioners' sugar on his blue suit were testament to his vigil.

Falzetti had told him to be here at 7 A.M., and he had been—well, 7:12 really. He had driven past the house once. All had been in darkness, and the car was still in the driveway. O'Connor had then picked a suitable spot where he could watch the house and not arouse the suspicions of any nosy neighbors. He knew why Falzetti had assigned him to do this job. O'Connor was reputed to be the best "tail" in the precinct, and he was proud of that reputation. He could follow a man for a month without giving himself away. The other cops attributed his success to some uncanny sixth sense, and some joked that he must have Indian blood in his veins. But O'Connor knew that the reason was preparation, pure and simple. When he followed someone, he always tried to know the area as intimately as possible so that he wasn't led into any blind alleys where discovery was assured. If his target entered a building with only one exit, O'Connor knew it and stayed outside and waited for him to reappear. Following someone was simple, he had often told the other cops. "Just stay back and stay loose."

This particular tail worried him a little. He didn't know the area as well as he would have liked and wondered why Falzetti didn't get some help from the local police. He passed the time as he waited by studying a road map of the town and the North Shore of Long Island, sipping coffee from his thermos and finishing off the last of the half dozen donuts he had brought with him from the bakery on Grand Street in Brooklyn.

At 8:15 he heard a car start down the street, and he dropped his map onto the seat beside him. He lowered his considerable bulk over onto his right side so that if his car were seen from the street, it would appear to be empty.

The nose of Streetman's car appeared, and O'Connor lay as flat as he could while watching it. If Streetman turned right, toward him, he would simply lie down on the seat. Streetman could drive past him without seeing a thing. Instead, he turned left and drove away in the other direction.

O'Connor smiled as he sat up and started the car. That makes things a little easier, he thought. He didn't have to worry about Streetman driving directly past his car and remembering it if he happened to see it later.

It was Friday morning and the roads were fairly clear, so O'Connor stayed well behind Streetman. Soon they left the narrow roads and back streets of rural Port Washington and were heading south on a main thoroughfare. There were more cars on the road now, and O'Connor closed the gap a little between himself and his prey.

Streetman stayed on this main road for about fifteen minutes and then turned right into Northern Boulevard and headed toward the city. They passed through Manhasset and on into Thomaston, where Streetman exited the boulevard at Middle Neck Road and headed north into Great Neck.

O'Connor followed cautiously. This was the dangerous part now. It was obvious that Streetman was going to stop somewhere along here, and O'Connor didn't want to be taken by surprise.

Less than ten minutes after leaving Northern Boulevard, Streetman pulled into the Great Neck Train Station, parked his car and went into the small red brick building that sat alongside the tracks.

O'Connor parked some distance from Streetman's car but in a spot where he could watch the station house. He wondered for a moment if this was the rendezvous point or if Streetman was taking the train. If it was the latter, he knew that Streetman could have taken the train from several stations closer to his home. Perhaps, thought O'Connor, he wouldn't want anyone who knew him to see his car parked at his local station.

When Streetman emerged from the station house and went to stand on the platform next to three other passengers, O'Connor stayed in his car. Five minutes later the train appeared, rumbling into the station sending billows of steam cascading across the platform and causing the few waiting travelers to step back.

O'Connor waited until Streetman had boarded. Then he walked quickly to the platform and climbed aboard the car directly behind. Through the door between the two cars he could see Streetman, sitting near the middle, his back to O'Connor.

"Tickets!" called a voice behind him and O'Connor turned to see the conductor, punch in hand, standing in front of him. O'Connor flashed his badge. "Official business," he said unnecessarily, and the conductor shrugged and nodded.

The conductor was old. Probably past retirement, like me, thought O'Connor. His navy blue uniform was well worn, and threads hung from the sleeves like fringes.

O'Connor sized him up and decided to take a chance. "There's a man in the next car," he said, pointing through the glass. "Tall, mustache, tweed overcoat."

The conductor's expression didn't change.

"When you punch his ticket, I want you to let me know where he's going."

The old man nodded, and O'Connor stepped aside to let him pass. O'Connor watched through the window as the conductor made his way up the aisle. He went all the way to the front of the car and then worked his way back. When he had finished punching tickets, he pulled back the heavy door and reentered the car where O'Connor waited.

"Penn Station," he said.

O'Connor thought for a minute. "When do we arrive?"

Without hesitation the old man said, "Nine-forty-three."

O'Connor scribbled on a piece of paper. "At the next stop I want you to give the stationmaster this note and tell him to call this number."

He ripped the piece of paper from his small notebook. "Okay?" he asked.

The conductor took the note, looked at it and shrugged, then put it in his pocket. "Next stop is Little Neck," he said. "In about five minutes. I'll take care of it."

O'Connor thanked him and, after sitting down in the first seat of the car, watched Long Island rush past him from the window.

Falzetti waited at the upper level of Pennsylvania Station, his eyes glued to the doors where the passengers from the Great Neck train would emerge into the main floor of the station. O'Connor's message had been relayed to him almost twenty minutes ago, and he had left for Penn Station immediately.

Every once in a while he looked around at the crowds on the huge open floor of the main terminal. It seemed that every other person, man or woman, was in uniform. The terminal was a mass of movement. Thinking of his son, he watched the men in uniform. Everyone seemed so young. We're a nation of children in uniform, he thought sadly.

He thought of the photograph he had seen the day before in the *Times* of a young B-17 pilot who had just finished his thirteenth bombing mission over Germany. The young pilot was twenty years old. *Twenty*, Falzetti had thought with amazement. In a world that had not gone mad, a twenty-year-old would be in college, or starting a new job, or chasing girls at Childs.

The gates opened and soon passengers streamed into the terminal. Falzetti stayed across on the other side, not wanting Streetman to see him. He watched, but neither Streetman nor O'Connor appeared.

Soon the stream flowed to a trickle. Falzetti was beginning to worry about O'Connor when suddenly he saw him exit from the gate. O'Connor stopped, his eyes swinging around the floor.

Falzetti pushed his way through the crowd and caught up with O'Connor. "Where's Streetman?" was his first question.

"He never got off the train," said O'Connor, taking his arm and drawing him along with him. "I think he's just going to turn around and go back."

Falzetti's eyes narrowed. He looked puzzled. "Why'd you get off?"

O'Connor pointed ahead of him. "See the short guy

at the top of the steps? The one in the gray coat and dark hat?"

Falzetti looked and nodded.

"When the train pulled in, Streetman stayed in his seat. That guy came aboard my car, right behind Streetman's. Then he walked through Streetman's car, and as he walked past him, he dropped a newspaper on the seat next to Streetman. Streetman picks up the paper and starts to read. This guy just keeps walking and gets off with the other passengers."

By this time they had left the station at Eighth Avenue near West 33rd Street.

"Streetman make you yet?" Falzetti asked, already knowing the answer.

O'Connor smiled proudly. "Not a chance."

"Good work, Tim. I'll follow this guy, you get back on the train with Streetman."

"Good," said O'Connor. "My car's back in Great Neck."

O'Connor spun around and with surprising quickness moved back inside the terminal and bounded down the steps. Falzetti watched him for a moment, then turned and began his pursuit of the man in the gray coat.

Outside the station the man hailed a cab, and Falzetti quickly did the same.

"Follow that taxi ahead of us," he said.

The cabbie groaned. "Whatta you? Humphrey Bogart?"

"Police," said Falzetti, flashing his badge to the driver, who watched him in the rearview mirror. "Just stay back, but keep him in sight."

The cab ahead went north on Eighth Avenue and then east on 42nd Street. Just across Fifth Avenue, the first cab pulled over to the curb, and Falzetti, half a block behind, said to his driver, "Pull over here."

He got out at the public library and waited to see which way his quarry would go.

After a brief look around, the man crossed 42nd Street and headed north on the east side of Fifth Avenue.

Falzetti followed on the other side.

At 44th Street the man crossed Fifth Avenue, and

Falzetti ducked into a clothing store to stay safely behind.

After crossing Fifth Avenue the man continued on 44th, past the Harvard Club, the New York Yacht Club, and the Algonquin Hotel. He crossed Sixth Avenue, and Falzetti, still on the opposite side of 44th Street, followed at a safe distance. At the Belasco Theatre the man stopped and seemed to admire the posters on the wall. Again he glanced back as if to see if anyone was following. He looked across the street, and Falzetti just kept on walking.

When Falzetti passed the Belasco, he kept his face turned away so that the man would not recognize him if he saw him again. Twenty yards past the theater, Falzetti came to a church, climbed the steps, and went inside.

From just inside the door, he watched the man take one last look around, then retrace his steps back toward Sixth Avenue, turn left, and disappear around the corner. Falzetti waited a few minutes to see if the man would double back again, and when he did not, Falzetti left the church and quickly went after him.

He saw him a block ahead at 45th and slowed his pace to match the man's leisurely stroll. The man turned left on West 47th Street, and near the middle of the block entered the Hotel Barmore, a small hotel which seemed lost among the larger buildings on either side.

From outside Falzetti watched him converse for a moment with the desk clerk, then head for the elevator.

Falzetti walked across the lobby in time to see his target enter the elevator and turn to face him.

The man was small and narrow faced. He wore thick, wire-rimmed glasses and had a small, well-trimmed moustache. He was whistling as the elevator doors closed, seemingly very pleased with himself.

The arrow above the elevator doors indicated that the man had gone directly to the fifth floor.

Falzetti went to the desk, where the clerk looked up for the first time from his newspaper.

"That man who just talked with you and then went to the fifth floor," said Falzetti, "what's his name?"

The clerk eyed him coldly. "I'm sorry, sir, we are not at liberty to give out the names of our guests."

Falzetti flipped open his wallet, displaying his badge without comment.

The clerk's eyes widened at the sight, and he seemed flustered for a moment. "That's different," he said, leafing through a small stack of index cards. He stopped at one, started to smile, and then Falzetti saw the smile slip from his face. He looked up. "I'll have to speak with the day manager."

Falzetti shrugged. "Speak with whoever you like. I want that guy's name." He lit a cigar while the clerk went to a door behind the desk.

The clerk disappeared, taking the offending card with him, and in a moment returned with an older man, whom Falzetti assumed was the manager.

Without being asked, Falzetti showed the badge.

The manager barely gave it a passing glance.

"I'm Mr. Thornhill," he said. "May I help you?"

Mr. Thornhill was very dignified. His black hair—obviously dyed—was slicked straight back, and a smile was frozen on his face. His dark blue suit was neatly pressed, as if just done for this occasion, and his nails were neatly manicured.

"Simple," said Falzetti. "The guy who just came in—I want to know who he is."

"Might I ask the nature of your business with our guest? Perhaps if you made it clear, we could take care of the problem."

Falzetti blew cigar smoke in Thornhill's face. "Perhaps," he said, mimicking the manager, "I haven't made myself clear. If I don't get that name in ten seconds, I'm going to arrest you and that twerp behind you. Then I'm going to call for a squad of detectives, who will bang on every door on the fifth floor until we get to the right one. Then we'll all take a little trip downtown and play twenty questions." He blew some more cigar smoke. "Is that clear enough?"

Thornhill, struggling to maintain his dignity, cleared his throat. "Quite," he said. He took a small square of paper from the desk and scribbled something on it, then handed the paper to Falzetti. "Before you decide to do all that," he said, "perhaps you might call this number first."

Falzetti's face darkened. "Look," he said, "I'm beginning to get a little tired of"—he noticed the number. He held the paper closer to be sure, then looked up at Thornhill. "This is the FBI."

"Why, yes," said Thornhill. "So it is."

A frown came to Falzetti's face. "What's this all about?"

"Perhaps you should call the number."

"You were told that if anyone asked about the guy on the fifth floor, you were to give him this number?"

"No," said Thornhill curtly. "We were supposed to refuse information and report any inquiries to the FBI." He bowed slightly. "I think that under the circumstances you can make your own inquiries to the FBI."

Falzetti looked again in bewilderment at the number while the manager and the desk clerk smirked at each other.

In an effort to regain the upper hand, Falzetti growled, "Don't mention to your guest that I was here."

The day manager smiled malevolently. "I wouldn't dream of it," he said, as Falzetti, his head reeling, made for the door.

Falzetti was at his desk, rummaging through a drawer, when one of his fellow detectives called out to him. "FBI on the phone, Nick."

A pained look flashed across Falzetti's face. "Who is it?"

"Brownmiller, I think."

Falzetti winced again. "Tell him I'm out."

The detective, Joe Wheeler, obediently relayed the message into the phone, then called out, "Sounds a little hot under the collar. Wants you to get right back to him."

Falzetti nodded absently and went back to the paperwork on his desk. He wasn't in the mood to listen to Brownmiller.

Wheeler went on. "Wonder who elected the FBI as

the top dog in the city? I'm tired of them ordering everybody around. You'd think we worked for them, for Chrissakes."

Falzetti shrugged. There was plenty he wanted to say about the FBI—their officious manner, their bungling of cases, their arrogance. The list went on and on, but he decided he didn't want to get himself going. Brownmiller wasn't really so bad, but lately he had become a regular pain in the ass.

He looked at his watch. "Anybody heard from O'Connor?" he called out to the few detectives who were at their desks.

Somebody laughed. "Indian's hot on the trail again. We won't hear from him until spring.

Everyone laughed, and Falzetti forced a smile, but he was growing concerned. By this time O'Connor should have called him from the train station in Great Neck.

Falzetti had made a few phone calls and sorted out some loose ends on a number of minor cases when he noticed a man in a dark trench coat talking to one of the detectives. Brownmiller!

The detective started to point towards Falzetti's desk, and Falzetti looked away just as Brownmiller turned toward him. He picked up the phone and held it to his ear. Shading his eyes with his left hand as he sensed Brownmiller approach his desk, he spoke into the receiver, "Agent Brownmiller, please. This is Lieutenant Nick Falzetti returning his call." He looked up and saw a grim-faced Brownmiller standing over his desk. "Never mind," he said and hung up.

"I was just calling you, Tom," he said pleasantly. "I just got in."

Brownmiller's face seemed carved in stone. He sat down across from Falzetti and eyed the policeman with a trained, intimidating glare. "You've been very troublesome to me lately, Nick."

Falzetti feigned surprise. "How's that?"

"First the situation at the Hallmark. I told you to stay out of it, that it was a national security matter, a problem for the bureau—not the New York Police Department."

Falzetti said nothing, moving his hands in contrite circles above his desk.

"Now I find you getting your nose into another, more delicate bureau matter."

"What's that?" Falzetti said innocently.

"The man you followed to the Barmore Hotel today."

"Why don't you put a sign on him: OFF LIMITS—FBI?"

Brownmiller's eyes narrowed. "I want to know why you followed him."

"I followed Mr. . . . what's his name?" He paused, giving Brownmiller time to fill in the name but getting no response. "I followed your friend because he was seen conversing with a suspect in a criminal investigation. I just wanted to talk with him, that's all."

"Forget it. He is out of your jurisdiction," said Brownmiller flatly.

Falzetti took a half cigar from his ashtray and stuck it between his teeth. "Pretty soon most of the city will be out of my jurisdiction. Is it all right if we continue to prosecute traffic violations?"

Brownmiller sighed and his attitude seemed to soften. "Nick, you'll just have to trust me on this one. It is absolutely essential that you keep away from this man. We cannot have even the suspicion that he is under police surveillance. My men are watching him closely. If he were into anything, we would know about it."

"You got him twenty-four hours a day?" asked Falzetti. "That takes a lot of manpower."

Brownmiller shifted uncomfortably.

"That's three shifts, two men to a shift, seven days a week. You can get away with one man when the subject is sleeping, but that still means—figuring your men get days off—six or seven agents working full-time to cover one man. You got that kind of manpower to spend on one guy?"

Brownmiller shook his head slowly. "No, but I can assure you we have him adequately covered."

"Who is he, Tom?"

Brownmiller looked at his fingernails. "I can't give you that information."

"Can you tell me his name?"

Brownmiller was shaking his head slowly when Falzetti interjected, "What if he runs afoul of one of my other men? How are we supposed to know he's your boy?"

Brownmiller shrugged reluctantly. "He goes by the name of Frank Smith, and he resides on a permanent basis at the Hotel Barmore."

"Paid for by the FBI, of course?"

Brownmiller nodded. "You know all you have to know."

Falzetti chomped on his unlit cigar. "That's it, then. No problem from this end, Tom."

Brownmiller seemed surprised by Falzetti's easy acquiescence. He stood up, and they shook hands. "I hope not, Nick," he said. He stared into Falzetti's eyes for a second, then nodded. "I'll be talking to you."

Falzetti watched him leave and then bellowed across the open room. "Anybody hear from O'Connor?"

His call was greeted with shrugs and silence.

O'Connor was lying on his belly in the sand, propped up on his elbows, a pair of field glasses pressed firmly to his eyes. He was staring out to sea, letting the binoculars sweep the horizon.

He had successfully and without incident followed Jon Streetman back to the Great Neck train station and had decided on a hunch to track him back to his house before reporting to Falzetti. To O'Connor's surprise, Streetman had passed Northern Boulevard and gone on to the Northern State Parkway, heading east.

At first O'Connor had assumed that Streetman was merely taking another route home, but soon they passed the interchange that would have taken them to Port Washington. Streetman had some other destination in mind. O'Connor settled in, one hundred yards behind, trying to keep at least two cars between himself and his quarry.

They continued on, O'Connor's 1937 Plymouth a poor cousin to Streetman's 1941 Continental, taking

Northern State's big southern detour, where Robert Moses and Governor Roosevelt had sold out to the land barons of the North Shore in 1929, and then swinging east again five miles later.

On they went, through Nassau and into Suffolk County. Fifteen miles later the road narrowed and pursuit became more difficult. Traffic was very light, and O'Connor knew that his chances of detection were increasing. At some points O'Connor would stop the car just below the crest of a hill, get out and walk to the top, where he would watch Streetman's car through his field glasses for a while before running back to his car and continuing the chase.

Soon, despite the almost freezing temperatures, O'Connor was drenched in sweat.

Finally, almost an hour after leaving Great Neck, Streetman had pulled off the main road, somewhere past Port Jefferson, and turned north to drive along the shoreline on a country road. O'Connor stopped the car and let Streetman go on alone. It was impossible to tail someone on this kind of road.

He waited five minutes, then followed along the now empty road. He passed a Yacht Club, and there, sitting at the edge of the parking lot, was Streetman's blue Continental. O'Connor drove past the gate and parked several hundred yards down the road, pulling off the shoulder as far as he could. He crossed the road and found a vantage point in the sand where he could watch the club and the parking lot and settled down to wait for Streetman to appear.

The yacht club was small—one main building, the parking lot, and the boat moorings in a protected cove. From his position O'Connor had a good view of the moorings and the open sound beyond.

He didn't have long to wait. About ten minutes later Streetman appeared, carrying a satchel of some kind, and O'Connor watched him stroll casually toward the boats. Streetman went down a walkway that wound amidst the moored boats. At the end Streetman stepped aboard what must have been the largest yacht in the anchorage—over fifty feet, O'Connor estimated. He watched Streetman take a key, open a padlock, and disappear below.

O'Connor lay in the sand, teeth chattering from the bone-chilling dampness. He cursed himself for leaving his metal whiskey flask at home. He had been trying to do less drinking on the job, but now he was furious at his lack of foresight. He could use the fortification, he muttered as he lay watching the yacht through the binoculars.

Less than fifteen minutes later, Streetman reappeared on deck. He walked around the boat, apparently checking lines and hatches, and at one point he thumped the palm of his hand on one of the forward hatches as if checking for soundness. Then, apparently satisfied, he spent some time checking the mast. He returned to the hatch that led to the lower compartments, and O'Connor watched him secure the doorway with the large padlock, tugging to test if it was secure.

From the boat he went directly to his car, pausing only to chat briefly with a man who sat in a small guard post at the gate before driving off in the direction from which he had come.

O'Connor stood up shivering, wiping off the sand that clung to his clothing. With his field glasses he watched the Continental disappear down the road. It was useless to follow. He couldn't possibly escape detection again on these roads.

He lowered the field glasses as lines of puzzlement etched a path across his beefy face.

"Get back in here, Tim," said Falzetti, practically yelling into the phone. "I've been worried sick about you. Why the hell didn't you call?"

O'Connor laughed. He had stopped at the first bar he had seen in Queens to make his call and warm his bones. "Don't worry about me, Nick. I'm fine. I've just been freezing my ass off out in the boondocks."

He went on to explain what had happened and why he was late.

Falzetti grew puzzled as he listened. "That's it?" he

said. "He just went on the boat for ten—fifteen minutes and drove off?"

"That's it. I don't have the slightest idea what he was doing."

"Maybe we ought to check out that boat."

"Get somebody else," pleaded O'Connor. "I thought I was gonna freeze to death out there."

"Come on in, Tim," said Falzetti. "You can give me all the details when you get here. Find something to eat, and I'll see you later." He looked around the squad room. "And Tim"—he lowered his voice against the possibility of eavesdroppers—"I don't want any written report on this one. This is just between you and me, okay?"

O'Connor was puzzled but agreeable. "Anything you say, Nick. I don't need the paperwork."

Minutes after talking with O'Connor, Falzetti was on the phone with Howard Green. "We've got to talk," he said.

"Talk," Green replied.

Falzetti told him about the events of the day and how he had followed the man he now knew only as Frank Smith to the Hotel Barmore. "And then," he said, "the FBI came down on me with both feet."

"And they wouldn't tell you who he was or why they were protecting him?"

"Nothing. All they told me was stay away from him."

"Someone they're keeping undercover for some reason?"

"Obviously," said Falzetti. "But I want to know who he is . . . It's important. I can feel it." He waited for Green to say something, then added, "Can you find out?"

Green cleared his throat. "Let me work on it. I'll see if I can figure out what the hell is going on there. I'll check with some of the other G-2 people and get back to you tomorrow."

"Okay." Falzetti sighed. "But come up with something, Howard. This one is starting to burn a hole in my gut."

31

"We'll be leaving here tomorrow," Bishop said to Chapman.

"I'm going then?" Chapman answered.

Bishop nodded. "We'll go to a holding center in southern England for a few days for final briefings before we leave for our destination."

Chapman didn't ask what that destination was. "Who else is going?"

"You, me, Madsen, and Iverson."

"Iverson?" Chapman seemed surprised.

"Any objections?"

Chapman shook his head. "No."

"He was with the Second Saskatchewan Regiment at Dieppe." Bishop waited for some response from Chapman, then added, "Decorated for bravery during that operation. For what we have in mind, he'll be fine."

Chapman raised his eyebrows but did not comment. "We're a regular international brigade, aren't we?"

Bishop's eyes narrowed. "How's that?"

"A Canadian, an American, a Dane, and an Englishman."

Bishop shrugged and smiled. "Like one of those bloody awful war pictures I see from time to time."

They sat looking at each other, and an embarrassed silence engulfed them. It was fairly obvious that they had little in common and even less to talk about.

Bishop looked down at his hands. "I'm sorry about that foolish testing business," he said. "Sometimes I think we go a little too far in the name of security."

Chapman's face was expressionless. "Perhaps," he said, leaving the suggestion of what he might have replied hanging in the air like the smell of cordite.

Bishop stood up from his desk and walked to the window overlooking the gardens. His back was to Chapman. "I hope our little"—he paused momentarily, groping for the right word—"procedure didn't affect your relationship with Lieutenant Brown."

Chapman said nothing.

Bishop turned to face him. "I saw her go down into the lower garden about fifteen minutes before you arrived." He averted his eyes from Chapman's steely gaze. Matchmaking was not his forte. "Perhaps," he said, "now that we're leaving, you two might be able to patch things up." He shrugged. "She was only doing what she had been told to do—and I might add, she did it against her will."

Chapman stood up. "May I be excused, Major?"

"Of course," said Bishop. "If you take the door to the left of this office, you'll find it leads to the garden."

Chapman smiled. "Thank you, sir."

When the Earl of Galloway had ceded his estate to the military, he had left explicit instructions that these two acres of garden and the hedge that surrounded them were not to be touched. His exact words to the commander of the first group of commandos trained at the site were, "Blow up the bloody place if you like, but do not tamper with my garden."

Now, in winter, the flower beds lay bare, like recently closed but unmarked graves. The tall hedges were magnificently full, providing an uninterrupted wall of privacy on all sides for anyone who chose to wander within.

Margaret Brown had seen what a magnificent place the garden was in summertime. Dressed in a profusion of summer flowers and enclosed by the dark green hedge, it was a world apart—peaceful and serene, a perfect spot for quiet reflection. Even in winter, without the flowers, Margaret still found that the garden afforded her the privacy that she craved, the seclusion that she needed.

Since her confrontation with Chapman, she had come here every afternoon.

Today she had gone down into the lower garden to her usual seat on the bench that circled the huge oak in the center of the grounds. She sat back, eyes closed, shoulders against the trunk of the tree. She thought about lighting a cigarette but knew that she could never bring herself to desecrate this place.

And then, even with her eyes closed, she could feel that someone else was there. Before he spoke she sensed that it was Andrew Chapman, standing close to her.

"Hello," she said, her eyes still closed.

His voice betrayed his surprise. "I thought I could sneak up on you."

She opened her eyes. "I didn't know you liked walking in gardens."

Chapman looked around as if just realizing where he was. "I don't," he said. "I followed you."

"I've been here for a while."

He smiled. "I've been watching you from back there," he said, indicating the opening in the shrubbery that divided the upper and lower garden. "I was standing there for about five minutes trying to get up the courage to come here and talk with you."

She looked down at the ground. "You don't need courage to talk to me."

He shrugged. "I just talked with Bishop. He told me that we'll be leaving here soon."

"I guess that means you're on the mission."

"Yes."

She nodded her head slowly. "I'm very glad for you. I know it's what you want."

"It's not the only thing I want."

She looked up at him. She wondered if she should tell him that the letter was Bishop's idea, but she realized that he must know that by now.

He sat next to her. "I didn't want to leave things the way they were."

"Can I say something first?" she asked. "I want you to believe me when I tell you that everything that happened between us—everything I told you—was genuine. None of what happened had anything to do with that beastly little trick I was asked to play on you." Her eyes were damp. "I'm sorry," she said tonelessly. "I never should have agreed to it."

"It's all right," he said. "And I do believe you."

"Are you sure?"

"Yes. I thought about it, and I realized that it was just some stupid kind of test that they put people through. I passed it, and I'm just glad that—"

Her laugh interrupted him. "I don't think you passed it," she said.

His eyes narrowed. "What do you mean?"

"You refused to do it. But if I had been a spy, I would have found someone else. You should have turned me in."

"I thought about it. But if you had been a spy, they would've hanged you."

She made a face. "Yes, I suppose they would have."

"That's why I couldn't do it. Even if you were a spy, I couldn't let anything happen to you. In spite of everything, I still love you."

Her eyes grew moist. She took his hand. "You don't have to tell me that. I know enough not to expect too much from a wartime romance."

"The war can't last forever," he said. "It's going to be over soon—sooner, perhaps, than any of us think." He looked into her eyes.

"I'll wait for you," she said, kissing him. "I promise."

He smiled and pulled her close to him. "I thought you said there couldn't be any promises in this war."

She put her head on his shoulder. "For the first time in a long time, I feel the need for promises."

They sat for a long time, holding each other.

"When do you leave?" she asked.

He hesitated before saying, "Tomorrow."

She pulled away. "Tomorrow!" Tears leapt into her eyes.

He nodded. "Bishop just told me before I came out to find you."

She closed her eyes and a tear rolled down each cheek.

He wiped them away.

"I'm sorry," he said.

She looked up at him. "We've still got tonight."

Ernst Luddeck was waiting for Schellenberg outside the modernistic building that housed Department VI of the Reich Security Administration. He paced impatiently on the sidewalk, stomping back and forth like a caged animal. He was angry and his anger showed. He had called Schellenberg's office earlier that morning and had been told that, as usual, Brigadeführer Schellenberg was riding with Admiral Canaris.

Captain Luddeck was incredulous. The night before, Berlin had suffered one of the worst air raids of the war. British bombers had dropped thousands of tons of explosives and incendiaries in a raid that had lasted almost until morning. Even at this moment fire departments all over the city were still fighting to control the flames. He couldn't believe that Schellenberg was off riding through the Tiergarten, chatting with Canaris as if nothing had happened.

He saw Schellenberg's car approach and pull to a halt in front of the building. Schellenberg opened the rear door and stepped out before his driver could make it around the big Mercedes.

"Ernst," said Schellenberg brightly as if this were a happy surprise. "You're out and about early this morning."

Luddeck looked at his watch. It was almost nine-thirty.

Schellenberg pointed a thumb skyward. "Did our friends keep you awake last night?"

"It's a disaster," said Luddeck. "The Americans by day, the British at night."

Schellenberg smiled. "I stopped by to see Ribbentrop over at Wilhelm Strasse on my way here. He will announce later today that the British lost fifty bombers to our night fighters and that the damage inflicted was minimal."

Luddeck looked to the north. In the distance great billows of smoke poured from a multitude of still raging fires. "Minimal?"

Schellenberg shrugged. "Anyway, it wasn't as bad as the raid on January twenty-first."

"How many bombers *did* they lose?"

"Probably no more than twenty. Our air defenses are crumbling. Now that the Americans are sending their day bombers with long-range fighter escorts, we can only hold out for so long. Our factories at Brunswick, Halberstadt, and Oschersleben have been hit so many times that fighter production has slowed to a trickle."

Luddeck followed Schellenberg into the office building. "Did you enjoy your ride?" he asked sarcastically.

"Yes," said Schellenberg, either not noticing Luddeck's tone or choosing to ignore it. "The admiral had some nice juicy tidbits of information for me."

They went up the stairs and down the hallway to Schellenberg's office. "Did you know," Schellenberg said, "that the Abwehr is preparing to move to Maibach Two—their concrete fortress at Zossen? They'll be able to conduct their business underground, safe from the bombings. The Army General Staff is also preparing to move underground."

"Underground?" said Luddeck disbelievingly. "The greatest war machine the world has ever known is forced to move underground?"

"The Führer has promised new wonder weapons that will drive the enemy from the skies," said Schellenberg with a cynical smile.

Luddeck's eyes brightened. "The Führer will keep his promise," he said.

Schellenberg shook his head slowly. There was no discouraging a man like Luddeck. "Don't forget Omega," he said. "That's our own little wonder weapon. If we do our job, we may yet save the Fatherland."

Luddeck leaned forward. "Is there any news of your deception?"

"Ah hah!" said Schellenberg. "I thought you'd never ask." He sat behind his desk and waved Luddeck into a seat in front of him. "I talked with Werner Best in Copenhagen last night. His resistance informers have told him that something is afoot. A silence has descended upon most of the resistance groups, and they are operating very cautiously."

Luddeck scoffed. "That could mean anything."

Schellenberg gave a knowing smile. "The Copenhagen group is expecting an arrival within days," he said. "Best is convinced that this is it. They are coming for Bohr's papers."

Luddeck's eyes flashed. "Our salvation is at hand," he said.

"I want you to go to Copenhagen and take charge of the operation. I don't want any mistakes at that end."

Luddeck stood up. "I will leave immediately."

"Sit, sit, there is time. I received another intriguing piece of information from Canaris this morning. It seems that one of his agents in New York has actually managed to acquire some valuable information about the American atomic bomb project. His radio transmission was monitored at Wohldorf in Hamburg."

"And this information—is it of real value?"

Schellenberg shrugged. "According to Canaris it was too lengthy to be transmitted without giving away the location of the radio. The message merely stated that the information was in the agent's hands and that he was arranging for its shipment to Germany aboard a Spanish freighter. It also mentioned something about a personal courier."

"What does that mean?"

"Canaris either did not know or would not say," said Schellenberg. "One thing is for certain, though. If that information is as valuable as Canaris says it is, I don't trust the Abwehr to see that it is delivered safely to Germany."

"The SS should meet that Spanish ship and personally escort the information to Berlin."

Schellenberg laughed. "Maybe that's what Canaris's man in New York meant by personal courier. Maybe he doesn't trust Admiral Willie either."

Luddeck agreed, smiling at the idea. Then his mind turned to more personal matters. "When do I leave for Copenhagen?"

"Tonight will be soon enough. Check in with Best

when you arrive. He is in titular command, but he knows that you are to run the show."

Luddeck stood up, his back straight, his chest fully expanded. "I will do my best, Brigadeführer."

Schellenberg rose too and slapped both hands to Luddeck's upper arms in a paternalistic gesture. "I know you can be counted on," he said. Both men gave the fascist salute.

"Heil Hitler," said Schellenberg.

"Heil Hitler," repeated Luddeck.

Schellenberg sat at his desk for a while after Luddeck had left his office. He opened his top drawer and removed two leather-bound folders, both identical, with the seal of the RSHA prominently displayed on each.

Schellenberg opened the first and read the contents carefully. He had spent most of last night composing the report, which stated that the idea for the Omega deception had been the brainchild of Ernst Luddeck. He went on to praise the young officer and declare that although the operation had been one about which he had great reservations, he had acceded to Luddeck's personal pleas and his plan. As the superior officer he took full responsibility, but he did hope that Luddeck would exercise the caution that he, Schellenberg, had demanded. It was very probable, Schellenberg concluded, that Luddeck's Omega Deception would come to nothing.

He closed the report and sealed the folder. Not bad, he thought, as he locked the report in the top left-hand drawer of his desk.

In the right hand drawer he locked the other folder. That was the one where he claimed that none other than Walter Schellenberg had been responsible for the planning and execution of the Omega Deception.

32

Captain Howard Green had not been able to find any information about the man in the Hotel Barmore. Not one of his contacts or fellow G-2 officers knew anything about a "Frank Smith" under FBI protection. As far as they were concerned, the man did not exist.

As usual, he told Janice Porter what was troubling him—he rarely if ever held anything back from her. Her face was a mask of indifference. "Can't we forget about the war for tonight?" she said. "I'd like to go to the Paramount. Tommy Dorsey's playing."

Green looked at her with amazement. "Aren't you the one who's always saying that Americans don't take the war seriously enough?"

"Yes," she said, her eyes sparkling with humor, "but I just love Tommy Dorsey."

They went, but Green was preoccupied during the show. Afterward, Janice, still exuberant over Dorsey's music, felt like dancing. "Let's go to the Stork Club," she said when they reached the street. "Or Elmo's." She saw he didn't care much for that. "I'll settle for Childs," she added.

Green shook his head indifferently. "Let's just go get a bite to eat," he said.

She shrugged. "Okay, where?"

"Let's try Sardi's."

"It's late. We might not get a table."

He was already hailing a cab. "Let's go anyway," he said.

On the way downtown Janice tried to keep up a barrage of lighthearted chatter. Broadway had returned to some of its prewar brightness since November of 1943, when the wartime blackout had been partially lifted. Even at forty percent of its former brilliance, Broadway seemed incredibly dazzling in a world plunged into wartime darkness.

As they passed the Winter Garden Theater, Janice pointed to the marquee. "We should try the *Ziegfeld Follies* one of these nights. They say Milton Berle is marvelous." She sneaked a look at Howard, brooding in the backseat of the taxi. "It might cheer you up some."

Green grunted an unintelligible reply.

The taxi dropped them off at 44th Street in front of Sardi's. The theaters were already closed, and the marquees had been dimmed. Across the street from the restaurant, at the Shubert, Paul Robeson was appearing in *Othello*. On the same side as Sardi's, the long running hit *Oklahoma* was still packing them in at the St. James Theater.

"You can really forget that there's a war going on," said Janice hopefully as they headed into Sardi's.

"Sure," said Green sarcastically.

Janice put her hand on his arm, stopping him. They were in the foyer of the restaurant, surrounded by caricatures of the season's stars. "What's bothering you so much?" she asked. "Is it that man at the Barmore?"

He nodded. "I just can't get it out of my head. I know there's a connection between that man and the killings at the Hallmark, but I just can't figure out what."

"I know someone who might be able to help you," she said casually.

"Who?"

"My boss at BSC. Jonathan Blakely."

"Jonathan?" said Green with surprise. "How could he help?"

Janice smiled. "He has resources that you couldn't begin to imagine."

"I know that," said Green. "But do you think he could help on this one?"

"Absolutely. Call him tomorrow." She paused, letting him think about it. "I'll even tell him you want to speak with him."

"Great," said Green enthusiastically. "That would be

great." He looked around as if noticing where he was for the first time. "It's too crowded here," he said. "Let's go someplace where we can dance."

The next day he called the BSC offices at Rockefeller Center from his office at Fort Jay on Governors Island. The line went dead for thirty seconds as he was put on hold, and then came the strong, cheerful voice that Green recognized as Jonathan Blakely's.

"Howard," the voice boomed, "how are you?"

"Just fine, Jonathan, but I'm afraid I'm going to have to ask for your help with a little problem I'm having."

"Oh, yes," Blakely said casually. "Janice said you might be giving me a call. If there is anything I can do, I'll be glad to."

"Did she tell you what the problem is?"

"Only the barest details. Why don't you fill me in?"

Green explained the situation to Blakely, leaving out nothing, including Falzetti's participation. If he was embarrassed that an American intelligence officer had to turn to an agent of another government for assistance, he did not show it. The American intelligence community had only limited experience in the field—spying had always been considered un-American, while the British had long understood the benefit, indeed, the necessity, of gathering intelligence information about one's enemies.

The British Secret Intelligence Service had a well-established network of agents in the United States to protect their interests against the large number of Germans there who were sympathetic to the Nazi cause. Many of these sympathizers were German nationals, but an even greater number were first- or second-generation German Americans who still had emotional or familial ties to the fatherland. Some had engaged in nothing more disruptive than questioning American aid to Britain during the early stages of the war. Others, however, were actively involved in acts of sabotage, particularly in the factories where war material for the British war effort was manufactured.

From the beginning of the war it had been in the

best interests of the British to give as much aid and assistance to the American authorities as possible in their attempts to prevent the clandestine activities of the German sympathizers. Some of the early FBI breakthroughs in the destruction of German spy rings had actually been the work of British agents, who had then turned the information over to the bureau. The British did the work, the bureau made the arrests, and Hoover took the credit. This fact was acknowledged throughout the Allied intelligence services, but for propaganda reasons it was deemed preferable to let the American public believe that J. Edgar Hoover's men were as ruthlessly efficient in the pursuit of German spies as they had been in the elimination of John Dillinger and other criminals.

The arrangement worked well for the British, who found that Hoover's ego allowed him to be easily manipulated, but with the formation of the OSS—an American intelligence organization—the British found themselves trapped between competing political foes. The fledgling OSS wanted access to British expertise, but Hoover, as always, jealously guarded his sources. If the British were going to operate on American soil, then, he demanded, they should operate through his agency. And Hoover had the political clout to make his demands stick.

The British now had the unenviable task of trying to please Hoover while at the same time giving as much help to the OSS and other American intelligence agencies as possible without alerting the FBI director. Sometimes an agent would receive an anonymous tip in the mail or in a late-night phone call. Sometimes, as with Howard Green, a suggestion would be made in casual conversation that help just might be available at the BSC offices in Rockefeller Center.

When Howard Green had finished his story, Blakely thought for a minute and said, "Very interesting problem, Howard. I can see why you might be interested in who this Mr. Smith is and why the FBI is protecting him."

"Do you think you can help?"

Blakely coughed, and Howard Green could almost see the noncommittal expression on his face. "Of course I can't guarantee anything," he said, "but I think I might be able to talk to someone about this situation. Can you give me until tomorrow?"

"Of course," said Green, laughing. "Let me give you my number."

Blakely jotted down the phone number, then said, "One more thing, Howard. I'd like to meet this policeman friend of yours. He sounds like the kind of man we might be interested in talking to. He might be a good contact for us at BSC."

For a moment Green did not say anything.

"Do you think that might be possible?" asked Blakely.

"I'm not sure," said Green. "He's kind of a strange bird. He might not go for the idea."

"If I find the information about your Mr. Smith, he might change his mind."

"He might."

"You will ask him for me, won't you?"

Howard Green agreed, and they decided to meet the next day at a location to be decided.

When he had hung up the phone, Jonathan Blakely turned to his secretary. "Meg," he said, "would you get me the file on Rudolph Krueger—alias Frank Smith? He's that German chap the FBI has over at the Hotel Barmore."

The three men met the next morning on the Staten Island Ferry. Green introduced Falzetti and Blakely, and each man sized up the other carefully before saying anything.

Blakely was tall, red-faced, and sported a bushy moustache that reminded Falzetti of the fake moustaches that police decoys sometimes wore to alter their appearance. He wore a wool suit and a heavy overcoat and scarf. As a precaution against the stiff wind of the Upper New York Bay, he had removed his hat, holding it safely ensconsed in his left hand.

"Nothing like an ocean breeze to clear the mind," Blakely said cheerfully. His eyes twinkled, and Falzetti, who was freezing, decided that the Englishman's smile was genuine.

There were only a few dozen passengers on board, and most of them stayed inside to avoid the chill, so the three men had little trouble finding a quiet spot on the stern rail for their conversation.

Blakely began. "Captain Green tells me that you and he are looking for some information that I might or might not be able to provide. If I am able to help, I would expect to be informed of any action resulting from the use of that information."

Falzetti turned to look at Blakely. "I'll have to be the judge of that."

Blakely coughed politely. "We are on the same side, you know."

Falzetti examined his cigar, which had gone out. "Mr. Blakely, I don't know what side you guys are talking about. I'm a cop, trying to get to the bottom of a murder case. So far I'm involved with two different intelligence agencies from my own country." He looked at Howard Green. "No one tells me anything. One of them even gets in my way. Now I find out I'm involved with a third intelligence agency from a foreign country."

"I have reason to believe," Blakely broke in, "that you are also involved with a fourth intelligence agency—also from a foreign country." He smiled saccharinely. "An agency, I might add, that is not quite as friendly or as cooperative as some of the others."

"If you want information," said Falzetti, "you should talk to the FBI. They seem to have all the answers."

"Unfortunately," Blakely said, "as I think you may have already found, the FBI is willing to take information but is often reluctant to give it."

"I don't think it's my job to give out information to an agent of a foreign government."

"To an ally," Blakely said quickly.

Falzetti stared into Blakely's eyes, and the Englishman knew that this was a man not easily persuaded. Blakely shrugged deliberately and looked out over Governors Island. Several navy vessels, including a DE, were tied up in the Buttermilk Channel close to the eastern end of the island.

They sat in silence, all three men staring at the New York skyline as if none expected ever to see it again.

Blakely looked at Green, who offered a silent signal of helplessness. Falzetti tried to light his cigar, but the winds of the bay whipping across the deck made the task impossible.

"Would you have any objection to giving this information to Captain Green and letting him decide whether to pass it along to me?" Blakely finally said.

Falzetti looked at Green, who shifted uncomfortably as if expecting a blow to his ego.

"I'd have no problem with that," said Falzetti.

Green seemed to sigh with relief as though he had just been saved from embarrassment.

"Then we are in agreement," said Blakely. "I am perfectly willing to let Captain Green tell me what he deems appropriate. Is that arrangement suitable to you?"

Falzetti nodded, turning his back to the wind in another attempt to light his cigar.

"Let's sit down inside," said Blakely, "and I'll tell you what, I think, is a very interesting story."

They went inside, out of the wind, and selected a bench as far away from any other passenger as they could get. Howard Green sat next to Blakely, with Falzetti, happily puffing on his now lit cigar, across from them.

"Since 1940," Blakely began, "the British Secret Intelligence Service has helped the American authorities arrest more than one hundred and fifty German agents—most of them right here in the New York area. Thirty-seven of these agents had been sent from Germany to infiltrate American defense plants or to transmit classified information back to Germany. The others were Germans who were already residents of the United States, naturalized citizens who had lived in this country for as many as forty years."

He looked at Falzetti as if the policeman should be

impressed with this revelation, but Falzetti sat still, his face expressionless.

"Before America entered the war," Blakely continued, "it was relatively easy to bring in agents. But since December eleventh, 1941, all the legal avenues of entry have been closed. Now, instead of landing agents by freighter or luxury liner right here in the Port of New York, or even by Pan Am's flying boats out in Port Washington, German agents have to be transported by submarine—a hazardous and time-consuming passage. Last year four agents were landed on Long Island and four in Florida. Their intent was to join up and attempt sabotage in the many defense plants on Long Island and in the New York area. Unfortunately for them, they were rather quickly discovered and captured. Six were executed before the year was over."

"I read all about it in the papers," Falzetti said sarcastically.

Blakely shrugged good-naturedly. "The Germans are having immense difficulties planting agents on enemy soil, and in their desperation they often select men who are poorly suited for the job. In England, as fantastic as it seems, it is not unknown for the Germans to land agents who cannot speak English. Often they are picked up on the afternoon of their arrival."

Falzetti was shuffling his feet impatiently, anxious for Blakely to get on with it.

Blakely's eyes were sparkling. He was obviously enjoying his role as storyteller. He pointed a thumb toward the window and to the bay beyond. "You are aware, of course, Lieutenant, that right now we are in the center of the most important port in the world."

Falzetti shrugged indifferently.

Blakely went on, "I say that only because it is sometimes difficult to perceive the importance of something when you see it everyday. New York Harbor is the lifeline that keeps the war effort afloat. Almost within view of where we sit there are enough shipyards to rebuild a navy larger than the prewar U.S. Navy. Since 1941, the major yards in this harbor have built more tonnage than the combined tonnage of the Axis forces.

He pointed back across the bay to Brooklyn. "At the Brooklyn yards they have just launched the battleship *Missouri*, bigger than anything afloat. Under construction—two slips away from where the *Missouri* was launched—is a battle cruiser that will probably be launched within the year. A hundred yards from that, two fleet carriers of the *Essex* class are almost completed, and next to them a new battle carrier of the *Midway* class is underway—bigger than anything the world has ever seen." He paused, shaking his head admiringly. "And that's just in one yard. Over on Staten Island at the Bethlehem yards, they're stamping out destroyers like they were automobiles. They've launched five since August."

Blakely's eyes scanned the harbor as he rattled off the figures. Shipping was everywhere. Freighters in line, waiting for dock space, dull-gray warships slipping slowly past the freighters on their way to anchorages farther up the Hudson. And as far as the eye could see—Brooklyn, Staten Island, Bayonne, Manhattan, Governors Island, Jersey City—the panorama bristled with the masts and funnels of ships already docked. New York Harbor was one mass anchorage.

"Eighty percent of the war materials that eventually wind up in England is shipped from this port. I mean food, medical supplies, tanks, planes, ammunition—you name it and it's from New York. Over a million men have sailed from this port to fight overseas. Over—"

"I get the point," Falzetti interrupted.

"My point is that," Blakely went on as if Falzetti had not spoken, "any reasonably observant person could furnish the enemy with a tremendous amount of invaluable information just by keeping his eyes and ears open in this port."

Falzetti nodded. "I suppose you're right."

Blakely laughed. "I know I'm right. It is not inconceivable that the same diligent agent could make a reasonable guess as to the date of the impending invasion just by the flow of men and materiel from here."

Falzetti sighed and chomped on his cigar. "I assume

this lengthy buildup has some connection with the man at the Hotel Barmore."

Blakely shook his head, smiling at Falzetti's impatience. "You Americans always want to get right down to the problem," he said.

Falzetti nodded. "So let's get right down to it."

Blakely paused, the smile slipping from his face. He looked across the bay, eyes on the statue in the distance behind them. When he began, his pace was deliberate and Falzetti knew that he was carefully considering each word. "What I am about to tell you, Lieutenant, is classified information. If my government or yours ever found out I had revealed this to you, I would be immediately recalled." He smiled again. "I might even go to prison. I tell you this only to impress upon you how important I think this information is." He turned to Green. "Captain Green has vouched for your integrity, so I have decided to tell you as much as I think is necessary."

Falzetti took the cigar from his mouth. "I love the buildup. Now can we get to the punch line?"

Blakely shook his head sadly. "I can see you are not a man who is easily impressed."

Falzetti sighed and looked to Howard Green. "Can you ask him to get on with this? There's a good chance the war will be over before he tells us anything."

Blakely looked heavenward, then began. "Frank Smith's real name is Rudolf Krueger. He is an Abwehr agent—" Falzetti's eyes had narrowed in a question; Blakely explained, "—an agent of the German High Command. He was recruited in Hamburg and trained at the Abwehr training facility in Zossen. According to Krueger, he was recruited because he had lived in the U.S. since 1930 and is reasonably familiar with the language and customs of this country. During his stay in the U.S. he was employed by both the Grumman and Brewster companies on Long Island."

"When did he go back to Germany?" asked Falzetti.

"Again, according to Krueger, he returned in August of 1941 because his brother was in some kind of political trouble. When he arrived, he was coerced by the

German secret police into returning to America as a spy. He was told that the best way for him to help his brother was to spy against his adopted country.

"He was given training, money, all the necessary documents and a shortwave radio of the very latest design. Because war had broken out between the U.S. and Germany, he could not return by traditional methods of travel, so passage was booked for him on a freighter from Lisbon to Buenos Aires. Once in Argentina he was supposed to arrange his own passage to New York and set up his espionage operation."

He paused dramatically, and Falzetti asked, "So what happened?"

Blakely turned to Howard Green. "Perhaps Captain Green would like to tell you the rest?"

Green shook his head and motioned for Blakely to continue.

"In July of 1942 Krueger traveled as ordered to Lisbon, where his passage to Argentina was preparing to sail. On his first day in Lisbon, however, he went directly to the American Consulate and admitted that he was an Abwehr agent. He said that he had agreed to spy against America only under great duress because of the vague threats made against members of his family still in Germany. He showed them his forged documents, his spy apparatus, and his radio.

"As you might imagine, Lieutenant, an agent who turns on his employers can be a very valuable tool. The consul in Lisbon reported the conversation to Washington, and the FBI became very interested in Mr. Krueger. Said consul was instructed to tell Krueger to leave for Buenos Aires as planned, but when he arrived he was greeted by two FBI men who had already arranged his passage to Washington.

"The FBI confiscated his radio and documents, and after a period of careful evaluation they set him up in a hotel in New York City. Now once each week he transmits a message to his employers in Hamburg—a message prepared for him by the FBI.

"The reasons are obvious. By providing the Germans with as much misleading information as possible—while mixing in enough factual material to make the reports seem authentic—the FBI hopes to confuse the German High Command."

"Sounds like a good idea," said Falzetti. "I can see why they didn't want me interfering."

Blakely smiled. "Now that you have discovered a link between Mr. Krueger and someone who is a suspect in another crime, it might not be such a good idea. Especially since the other crime might also include espionage."

Falzetti looked from Blakely to Green. He seemed puzzled. "So what does all this mean?"

Blakely shrugged. "If your suspicions about Streetman are correct, it is quite possible that the Abwehr and Krueger have put one over on the FBI. By pretending to be a turned agent Krueger has gained entry into the U.S., and with the cooperation and protection of the FBI he is living in the most strategically important port in the world."

Falzetti still looked perplexed. "But you said the FBI confiscated his radio. How does he get his messages out?"

"With another radio—or through another agent who has a radio."

"Streetman!"

Blakely nodded. "Now that you have linked them together, it seems possible."

"What now?" asked Falzetti. "The FBI will have my head if I roust this Smith/Krueger guy."

"I'll put a couple of my men on him for a few days," said Blakely. "We'll find out how he spends his idle moments."

Falzetti nodded, his hands stuck in the pockets of his overcoat. There didn't seem to be much to say. He was thinking about Streetman and why he had gone to a yacht at Port Jefferson after meeting with Krueger. "If there's a radio," he said, "I think I know where it is."

"Excellent," said Blakely, and for the rest of the trip he talked about how Americans still did not have any real concept of what war was like. "The worst thing that happened last year," he said, "if you believe the man in the street, was that the *Amos 'n' Andy* show was taken off the air for most of the year." He shook his head sadly, a gesture that Falzetti was already tired of. "Quite a tragedy," he said. "Don't you agree, Lieutenant Falzetti?"

Falzetti, deep in thought, was no longer listening.

33

Training completed, members selected, the small-scale raiding force moved into what was called an operational holding school—in actuality a small country manor—near the East Anglian airfields from which the team would depart on its mission.

The excitement level was high. At any moment Chapman and Iverson expected Bishop to announce that they would leave, but as each evening approached, he would shrug and announce, "Not tonight."

On the first evening of their arrival they had been told by Bishop that their destination would be Copenhagen, and since then they had worked diligently on memorizing locations and street names so that they would be as familiar as possible with the city. Madsen tested them constantly, and sometimes Chapman and Iverson were forced to admit that they found the rigors of their commando training easier than Madsen's insistent demands.

A former officer of the Danish navy who had escaped from Denmark when his resistance group had been penetrated and destroyed by the Germans was brought in to go over some of the items they would have to know in case they were subjected to scrutiny by German security forces.

"If your identity papers are not perfect," he said, "or if your answers to any of their questions are not satisfactory, or they just don't like the way you look, you will be taken to Gestapo headquarters at Shell House. If you cannot convince them that you are Danish and innocent of whatever they think you have done, you will not leave that place alive."

On the third evening at the holding center, the four-man team gathered in the main room of the house. Three of the men—Chapman, Iverson, and Madsen—sat in comfortable chairs, facing a map-covered wall. Bishop stood facing them, a pointer stick in his hand.

In one corner a fire burned merrily, casting long shadows across the expectant faces of the men.

"This is a simple recovery operation," said Bishop. "We're looking for a quick in-and-out." He looked each man in the eye. "It is possible, however, that we might have to remain in Denmark for as long as three or four days. The longer we remain, the greater the chance of discovery. Therefore we should be prepared to pass as Danish citizens." He smiled in Madsen's direction. "That shouldn't be too hard for some of us."

Iverson's hand shot up. "I take it then that we won't be in uniform?"

Bishop shook his head. "No, we won't." Iverson raised his eyebrows and Bishop asked, "Does that bother you in some way?"

Iverson shrugged. "Only to the extent that out of uniform we are not covered under the rules of the Geneva Convention."

Bishop scratched his nose. "Are you aware of Hitler's commando order of October eighteenth, 1942?" he asked.

"I'm afraid not."

Bishop looked to Chapman. "Are you?"

Chapman shook his head, and Bishop sighed before going on. "Hitler has issued a directive to his commanders in western Europe. Any soldier in a small-scale raiding force such as ours—whether in or out of uniform—is to be summarily executed when captured. We already have reports of at least six incidents where commando groups in uniform were executed shortly after capture. This includes eighteen survivors of a glider that crashed during an operation in Norway. Partisans report that the men—including the wounded—were propped up against the nearest wall and executed by firing squad."

Iverson swallowed hard. His mouth had suddenly gone dry.

"So you can see," said Bishop, "the uniform is no protection against execution."

No one said anything. Iverson looked at Chapman, who shrugged and looked away. Madsen did not seem to be concerned one way or the other.

"Actually," said Bishop, smiling warmly as if he were explaining the rules of a complicated parlor game, "it makes things easier for us. We don't have to agonize over the decision to wear uniforms or not. The disadvantages of wearing a uniform in occupied territory are obvious, and since there is no advantage to it . . ."

He went on. Each man was to be provided with identity papers with an authentic seal of the German occupation administration. The identity papers certified each in some itinerant occupation—house painter, handyman, or plumber. "You will be independently employed," said Bishop. "We don't want a simple phone call to a nonexistent employer to trip us up and put a noose around our necks."

Iverson's hand went to his throat at this remark, but only Chapman saw the gesture.

Bishop had turned away and had placed the tip of his pointer on a detail map of the Danish island of Zealand and the southwestern coast of Sweden, from Göteborg in the north to where the Swedish town of Malmö sat on the narrow waters of the Oresund across from Copenhagen.

"We're fortunate that our area of operation is very close to a neutral country." He touched Malmö with the pointer. "As you can see, Malmö is only twenty miles from Copenhagen. We can use Sweden as a staging area, and then we can slip into Denmark under cover of darkness."

Chapman interrupted. "You said we might possibly remain in Denmark for three or four days.

"Only if our mission is delayed by unforeseen circumstances," said Bishop. "The plan is to get in and out as quickly as possible."

"Yes, but if we are delayed, wouldn't it be easier to cross back over into Sweden and then return to Denmark at the proper time?"

Madsen spoke for the first time, looking at Chapman and Iverson. "Don't think that you will be out of danger while we are in Sweden. The country is teeming with German agents—particularly along the coast where we will be setting up our operation."

Bishop nodded. "That's right. The Germans are well aware that neutral Sweden is the perfect jumping off spot for any kind of operation. You can expect that the towns close to Denmark will be crawling with German agents. His face was sympathetic. "And, while it might seem safer to spend any unavoidable waiting time in a neutral country, the crossing from Sweden to Denmark just might be the most dangerous part of the mission. The area is heavily patrolled, and if we are discovered it's curtains." He hesitated, placing the pointer under his arm like a riding crop, and Chapman suddenly saw an aristocratic British officer reviewing his troops.

"On the other hand," Bishop continued, "the Swedes are so deathly afraid of antagonizing the Germans that they patrol their side just as vigorously. And if we are caught by the Swedish patrols, we'll probably spend the rest of the war in internment." He smiled. "Slightly better than execution, but I have no desire to sit out this war in some Swedish prison."

Bishop turned back to the maps. "If there are no more questions," he said, "I will give you the details of our arrival and departure." He waited for a moment, but there was no response to his invitation. He removed the detail map from the wall and placed the pointer on the larger map of western Europe. "From our takeoff point in England," he said, "we will cross the North Sea and into the Skagerrak, keeping as far as possible from the German radar in Norway and Denmark. Our drop area in Sweden is just north of the town of Hindras. If there is any problem at this initial drop point, we will continue on into the interior to our secondary drop point at Ulricehamn, where a backup group will be waiting in case we need it.

"At the Hindras drop area we will be picked up by Swedes who are sympathetic to the Allied cause."

Chapman's hand shot up. "Can we trust them?"

Bishop made a small gesture of uncertainty with his hands. "In this business we don't trust anyone. We understand these people are extremely reliable, but we don't take chances. We don't tell them anything they don't have to know."

Madsen looked at Chapman. The Dane seemed sullen and resentful, and when he spoke his tone matched his expression. "I will vouch for these people."

"Enough said," added Bishop, but Madsen continued to stare at Chapman.

Bishop returned to his map. "This group will provde transport into Hindras and shelter for the night. They will also provide Swedish documentation: identity cards, working papers, and the like. These papers should spare you from internment if the Swedish authorities have reason to question us, but they will be left behind when we leave for Denmark and picked up again when we return. If the Germans found our Swedish papers, along with our Danish documentation, they would probably shoot us on the spot."

He continued to trace the route that they would follow. In the morning they would take a bus to the town of Boras, twenty miles away. From there, at eleven A.M. they would board a train for a 175-mile journey to Landskrona on the Swedish coast, a town ten miles across the Oresund from Denmark.

"There will be several stops along the way," said Bishop, tapping his pointer as he traced the route. "Falkenberg, Halmstad, Bästad, and Hälsingborg." Here he paused, tapping the last town with his stick several times, then pointing the stick at Iverson. "Here in Hälsingborg, Lieutenant Iverson, is where we will part company."

Iverson, his face puzzled, looked at the others.

Bishop went on. "You will leave the train, accompanied by one of the Swedes, and set up your wireless in a house situated on the coast. There you will wait for my transmission, which you will then relay to England."

Iverson was too stunned to speak.

"I couldn't tell you before, Iverson," said Bishop, "but you won't have to worry about carting that radio around enemy territory."

The radio had been something of a sore point ever since Bishop had assigned it to Iverson. The B mark II radio weighed thirty pounds and fitted into an ordinary suitcase, and Iverson had complained—mostly to Chapman—that it was rather bulky to be dragging around under the noses of the Germans.

"I'm not so sure I understand," said Iverson warily. "Am I not to go in with the rest of you?"

"The wireless stays in Sweden, and I'm afraid, old chap, that you'll wave to stay with it."

Iverson's eyes widened as the realization struck him, and then, like a condemned man given a last minute reprieve, his face burst into a radiant smile that he immediately but unsuccessfully tried to wipe from his face.

Bishop narrowed his eyes, surprised and somewhat disappointed in Iverson's joyous reaction to the news. Maybe Chapman was right to wonder about this fellow, he thought, but without comment he returned to his maps. He tacked the detail map back into the wall. "The rest of us will continue on to Landskrona, which is about another fifteen miles. That evening we will cross to a point on the Danish coast just ten miles north of Copenhagen."

Iverson asked, "Why don't you cross at Hälsingborg? It looks to be half the distance."

"True," said Bishop. "It is only five miles across at Hälsingborg and ten at Landskrona. That's why you'll set up your radio at Hälsingborg. But the crossing is much more heavily patrolled by the Germans at that point."

Iverson nodded and Bishop went on. "After crossing we will be met by members of the Danish resistance, who will take us to a safe house on the coast, from which point I can contact Iverson by S-phone." He opened a small suitcase and removed what appeared to be an ordinary telephone.

The S-phone was a microwave wireless set normally used for two-way voice communication between an agent on the ground and either an aircraft flying overhead or a ship at sea. The advertised range was fifty miles in the air and fifteen to twenty at sea, but experience had shown that actual reliability was approximately half of those figures.

"The range should be adequate," said Bishop. "The S-phone is extremely short range and almost impossible for the Germans to get a fix on with detection equipment."

This time he pointed to Chapman. "That's where you will come in, Chapman. Your job will be to maintain contact with Iverson and to protect our means of escape from Denmark."

Chapman only nodded.

"Madsen and I will go into Copenhagen," said Bishop, "and make the actual recovery of the documents. Then the three of us will retrace our route, picking up Iverson in Hälsingborg, return to Boras, radio our position, and a plane will be dispatched to pick us up."

"Sounds simple'" said Iverson, still euphoric over the decision to leave him in safe territory.

"Yes, doesn't it." said Bishop. His face was blank, without any discernible expression. "Unfortunately, almost nothing is as simple as it sounds."

He tapped the map with his pointer again. "That, basically, is it." He held his hands behind his back, rocking on his heels. "I want to tell you now to get your equipment in order." He looked down at his feet. "If you have letters to write, do it this evening." He paused dramatically, looking around the room as if it were filled with anxious soldiers preparing for an invasion instead of only three interested faces. "We go tomorrow night," he said and left immediately before Iverson and Chapman had the chance to ask more questions.

■

"They will be here within forty-eight hours," said the man. "I guarantee it."

SS Oberführer Best rocked back in his chair. "Please, Herr Jespersen," he said with a small, dangerous smile, "do not guarantee anything. You know how hazardous guarantees can be."

Best was in full SS uniform, his boots up on his desk. He was a small man with sharp, rodent eyes and a pointed head.

The man called Jespersen looked down at the thick Oriental rug on the floor of Best's office. He wondered how many others had wilted under Best's stare. "I believe," he stammered, "that the men you are looking for will be here within forty-eight hours."

"What makes you believe that?" asked Best, his expression wolfish in anticipation.

"The resistance is on alert. They are preparing for their arrival."

Best turned to Ernst Luddeck, who sat in a stuffed chair in a corner of the room. "Do you have any questions for Herr Jespersen?" asked Best. Although he had the rank of a brigadier general and Luddeck was merely a captain, Best had been cautiously deferential to the man from Berlin. Already rumors were flying in the SS ranks that Luddeck was a young man on the move. He was a personal favorite of Himmler's, and it seemed that even Schellenberg, who himself was destined for a major role in the SS organization, had taken a liking to this serious young officer.

Luddeck looked at Jespersen, who tried but could not look into the German's eyes. "Do you know which resistance group they will contact?"

Jespersen shrugged. "One of the Copenhagen groups . . . Hunter, I think."

"Do you know anything about their destination? Where they will go when they arrive?"

Jespersen looked up, trying valiantly to look into Luddeck's eyes. He could not. "From what I understand, the English know where they are going—the resistance does not. We are merely to help with transportation and shelter."

Luddeck nodded to Best. "It is as I thought. They would not give such important information to"—he waved a hand, in a gesture of dismissal, in Jespersen's direction—"rabble such as this."

Best's eyes twinkled. "Jespersen is not such a bad sort. Are you, Jespersen?"

Jespersen pulled his coat closed, as if to hold back the numbing cold of what he had done. He did not answer.

"You may go now, Jespersen," said Best. "Be careful you are not seen."

Jespersen, a tall thin man in his early fifties, stood up. "What about my son?" he said. "You said you would bring me a letter from him."

Best shrugged. "It did not arrive. Perhaps next time."

"But you promised," Jespersen protested.

The pasted smile slipped from Best's face. His expression was one of distaste. "You may go now, Herr Jespersen," he said again, but this time there was iron in his voice.

The man closed his eyes for a second as if to compose himself and then stood erect. With as much dignity as he could muster, he turned slowly, left the room, being careful not to slam the door.

"That's it, then," said Best to Luddeck. "It looks as if your guests are coming soon." He smiled and nodded toward the door. "Jespersen is rarely wrong. He has good contacts."

Luddeck was looking at the closed door. "What about his son?" he asked. "What did he do?"

"Some foolish thing," said Best with a shrug. Then he smiled. "He was executed months ago."

34

It had been a relatively simple matter for Blakely to find out the FBI's surveillance schedule on Krueger and then assign personnel to the off hours. It turned out that the FBI trailed him, sometimes quite openly, between five P.M. and midnight—or whatever time Krueger returned to his hotel. He was on no apparent curfew but never stayed out past one A.M. He did not leave his room until at least ten A.M. and, apparently the FBI had decided not to continue surveillance during the early morning and afternoon. During that time Krueger had the run of the city. BSC members followed him daily as he crawled across every inch of New York and its environs. He walked and took the subway everywhere. For a man of his apparent age, his stamina was remarkable, said more than one exhausted British agent.

His favorite place seemed to be the docks on the West Side, where freighters rushed in and out of port each day, loading and unloading the cargoes that were the lifeblood of Allied efforts around the world. He visited there almost every day and had become such a familiar figure in the area that he was able to walk almost anywhere he chose without challenge from the military guards who patrolled the west side of Twelfth Avenue. As one BSC agent put it in his daily report on his surveillance: "Krueger seems so secure and so much a part of the daily scene in that area that many of the personnel there must believe that he too has some official function. American security is, as usual, deplorable."

Another place under Krueger's scrutiny was the Brooklyn Navy Yard. Security in such a place was impossible. The world's busiest shipyard sat just across the East River from the world's busiest city. On any given day, scores of old men sat on benches along South Street, in the shadow of the Manhattan Bridge, and observed the construction across the river. It was a relatively simple matter for Krueger to join them. Because of the pace of construction, he obviously felt that a weekly visit to his South Street observation post was sufficient. On other days he would ride the Staten Island Ferry and walk all over the island—paying particular attention to the Bethlehem yards along the Shore Road.

On this particular day he had started his rounds at Pier 90 on 50th Street, then walked down Twelfth Avenue to where it intersected Eleventh Avenue and continued down into the lower West Side of Manhattan. At Liberty Street he cut over to Trinity Place, at which point the agent trailing him began to feel he was acting suspiciously. Krueger cut back and forth across the narrow lower Manhattan streets, at one point walking down Morris Street and then reversing himself and coming back on the other side of the same street. Finally he made his way through Battery Park and boarded the Staten Island Ferry for the trip across. The agent cautiously joined the throng of passengers. At the other side, as the gates opened and the crowd filed forward, Kreuger stood to one side, observing the departing passengers. The agent had no choice but to get off—to do otherwise would have aroused Kreuger's suspicions.

When the ferry left on the return trip with Krueger still on board, the agent frantically called BSC headquarters at Rockefeller Center.

"He's on his way back. Get someone down there to meet him!"

Janice Porter was the only one available and was hustled to a cab to pick up the trail. She arrived before the ferry and easily picked up Krueger, but this time, instead of taking his usual walk, he hailed a cab. Janice frantically chased after another to continue her pursuit.

Krueger's cab went directly to Penn Station, where Janice followed him inside. From the entrance tier she watched him walk across the main concourse, stop and read the arrivals-departures board, and then head over to the boarding gates.

She waited until he had selected a gate and let him enter before she followed. Casually, she went through too, pretending to be fumbling for something in her pocketbook. Below her on the platform she saw Krueger, his back to her, walking toward the train that sat at the siding. She watched him from the top of the stairs as he made his way down the nearly deserted platform. Finally he selected a car and entered. Only then did she descend the stairs and move toward the train. She was halfway down the platform when to her amazement she saw Krueger exit the train and begin to walk back toward her. He held a small package under his arm.

Fighting her rising panic she kept walking. If he tries anything she whispered to herself, I've got the pistol in my bag.

Krueger's eyes never met hers. His expression never changed. He walked past her without a glance.

Janice breathed a sigh of relief and kept going. She entered the train at the first open car, waited for a few minutes, then cautiously stuck her head out. The platform was deserted.

She exited and walked up the platform, her heartbeat matching the clip-clopping of her heels on the cement. As she approached the doorway of each darkened car she slowed, half expecting a form to come hurtling out of the blackness.

There was nothing.

She rushed up the stairway and reentered the terminal, knowing that even if she could find him it would be foolish to follow Krueger now. He had seen her once. To follow him now would only let him know that he was under surveillance.

She looked around. He was gone.

From a phone booth she called her office. "Blakely back from lunch yet?" she asked his secretary.

She waited until she heard his voice. "Janice, are you all right? I wish you had taken someone with you."

"I'm all right, but I lost him—or rather he lost me."

"What happened?'

"I followed him to Penn Station. He doubled back on me on one of the platforms. There was nothing I could do. He walked right past me. I had to let him go."

"Do you think he made a drop in the station?"

"I think he might have picked something up, but I didn't see anyone else. It was dark," she added, hoping that Blakely wouldn't perceive how frightened she had been.

"You were wise not to continue," said Blakely. "I'll talk to you when you come back in."

"Okay," she said, "but I'm going to get some lunch first."

"Take your time," he said. "I'll be here for the rest of the day."

Janice headed for the Eighth Avenue exit, unaware that Krueger was watching her from behind the circular information booth at the middle of the cavernous main floor of the terminal.

Detective Tim O'Connor and Jon Streetman had both been aboard the train that Krueger was on. Once again, O'Connor had followed his target from the Port Washington residence to the Great Neck Train Station and on into the city.

When the train arrived at Penn Station O'Connor, one car behind Streetman, stayed in his seat while the other passengers reached up and took packages and coats from the overhead racks, moving methodically toward the exit doors. In minutes the train was all but abandoned. A lone conductor moved through the cars, flipping the seats to the face-forward position for the return trip.

While Janice Porter stood at the top of the steps watching Krueger walk down the train platform, Tim O'Connor sat in the last car of the train.

O'Connor sat patiently waiting for something to happen—patience was the hallmark of a good tail. He was sure that Streetman's contact would make his appearance and that someone—Falzetti hadn't been too clear on that—would probably be tailing the contact.

Out of the corner of his eye he saw a figure pass by his window going down the platform in the other direction away from the main terminal. To his surprise it was Streetman.

Puzzled by Streetman's maneuver, O'Connor got up and prepared to follow. So far, no contact, he thought, and Streetman was leaving the platform but going in the wrong direction. At the doorway he poked his head outside and cautiously looked up and down the darkened platform. From his left, toward the main concourse, a single figure approached. It was too difficult to make out who it might be. In the other direction, he saw Streetman disappear at the top of a flight of stairs near the end of the platform.

O'Connor exited the train and went after Streetman.

At the top of the stairs, O'Connor found himself in a long narrow corridor lit by a row of naked bulbs along the ceiling. Streetman was nowhere in sight. O'Connor hurried along the corridor, and when he came to a corner, he peered cautiously around before proceeding. He caught a glimpse of Streetman's back and picked up his pace a little to keep up. The corridor, he knew, was part of the labryinth of hallways, tunnels, and side exits that literally honeycombed the terminal. What he didn't know was exactly where he was. He suspected that he was heading in the direction of 33rd Street, but it had been so long since O'Connor had used any of these passageways that he could not be sure. He picked up his pace. He had never lost a tail in thirty-two years, and he didn't intend to now.

Around the next corner he was surprised to see a man sitting on a blanket. The man was blind, and his hat sat brim up on the edge of his blanket. There were a few coins in the hat, evidence of previous passersby, and O'Connor had the fleeting thought that this corridor must have had heavier traffic at some point earlier in the day.

If the blind beggar heard his approach, he did not give any indication. He sat rock still, yellowed eyes staring directionless and out of focus into some dimly acknowledged darkness.

O'Connor kept his head down, his eyes on the beggar—some inner instinct telling him not to take anyone or anything for granted. He walked past, but the man sat motionless, and O'Connor watched him in perverse fascination until he reached the next turn.

Suddenly an arm was wrapped around his neck, and he felt himself lifted until his toes barely touched the ground.

"Who are you?" growled a voice in his ear, and O'Connor struggled helplessly to free himself. "Who are you?" repeated the voice.

"Cop," blurted O'Connor through his tortured throat. "I'm a cop." At first he did not realize that the blade had slipped in up inside the rib cage—the first great piercing pain came only when his assailant probed for his heart. O'Connor struggled frantically against the death grip, feeling the blade inside him as he moved, biting him like some tiny steel-toothed creature that slashed and withdrew, slashed and withdrew.

He reached for his police revolver, but his fingers fumbled as if the task were alien to them. He couldn't make them work properly, and Streetman slapped the gun away from him as easily as he might have done with a child.

O'Connor felt the blade withdraw, and for one fleeting instant he thought Streetman had changed his mind, that this was some terrible mistake, that Streetman hadn't meant to do it, wouldn't do it again.

Then he felt the knife plunge in at another angle and he knew the truth. He tried to scream but nothing happened. He heard Streetman grunting and cursing in his ear and instinctively knew that his murderer was not cursing at him but because the job of killing was so difficult. He felt a kind of sympathy for Streetman, doing such a bad job of something that should have been quick and clean.

Streetman released him, and O'Connor slumped heavily to the floor. Not dead yet, O'Connor thought, amazed at his own persistence. He lay sprawled in the narrow corridor, his head at an improbable angle against the wall. His eyes fought to focus on the figure standing over him, but it was impossible.

Streetman looked up and down the corridor. Except for the blind man, it was still empty, but who knew for how long. This was supposed to be quick and simple, the way they had taught him at the Abwehr school in Zossen, but somehow real victims never cooperated in their own demise the way they were supposed to.

Streetman looked down at O'Connor, who gasped for each shallow breath, blood running from his mouth, air gurgling in his throat. O'Connor's glazed eyes stared wide open, one hand reached out as if to grasp the air. Streetman stepped forward to finish the job.

The blind man listened intently to the scuffle down the corridor. He could tell by the sounds that life and death were being decided here. There was a thump, and then one man went down. After a brief pause he heard a long gurgling sigh and he knew that it was over. He waited, holding his breath as he heard the footsteps approach him. A man stopped in front of him, and he knew that his own fate was being decided. He drew himself erect, trying not to show his fear.

He waited and finally the man turned away, his footsteps echoing down the deserted corridor.

Outside the station Janice Porter hailed a cab and directed the driver to Howard Green's townhouse. She could have gone back to the office or to her own apartment but didn't feel like answering the thousand questions that would be thrown at her by Blakely or by any of her roommates. The fear she had felt on the platform still clung to her like her damp clothing, and she wanted to wash it away before she saw anyone.

It made her feel delightfully wicked to know that she kept extra clothing at a man's apartment.

Using her key, she let herself in, calling out to make sure that Howard was not at home. She smiled at the silence that greeted her call. She didn't want to talk to Howard either.

Janice walked through the spacious living room, marveling for the umpteenth time at the restrained luxuriousness of the furnishings. She didn't think she would ever get used to that. Leaving her coat and bag on the sofa, she went up the stairs to what Howard liked to call "our bedroom." Janice smiled at that thought as she undressed, draping her things across a chair. Before she crossed the hall to the bath, she took underwear from a drawer in the dresser and left it on the bed.

She spent fifteen marvelous minutes soaking in the oversized tub, allowing the tension to drain from her body. She could have used the bathroom in Howard's bedroom, but this was the master suite, and its bathroom was decorated with a conspicuous disregard for wartime shortages. If the communists ever got a look at this bathroom, she thought with a laugh, they'd shoot Howard's whole family—and me too, for luxuriating in the opulence of the big claw-footed, porcelain tub with gold fittings.

After a while she started thinking about Howard and how surprised he would be if he came home and found her naked, soaking in the tub. She almost laughed imagining how much he would enjoy it. She began to picture him coming up the stairs, his footsteps muffled by the thick carpeting, stopping halfway up to listen to the sound of her splashing. She could even see him stopping outside the bathroom door, listening quietly, wondering how he would surprise her.

At one point her imagination was so strong that she even thought she heard his step out in the hall. Her gaze went to the door handle, almost expecting to see it turn ever so slowly. It didn't.

"Howard," she called softly, "is that you?"

There was only silence.

Janice sat up in the tub and dried her hands on a towel before reaching for the pack of Lucky Strike and the cigarette lighter that Howard always left on the shelf at the foot of the bathtub. She shook out a cigarette from the olive green package, automatically thinking of the slogan, "Luckies have gone to war."

"Even the bloody cigarettes are in uniform," she said aloud.

She had flipped open the top of the Zippo lighter and had lit her cigarette before realizing that the lighter was hers. She read the inscription, her fingers caressing the cold, lifeless steel as if she might transfer some of her warmth and life.

She read aloud: "To Janice, Love Forever, Martin."

She lay back in the tub, her arms and hands resting on the sides, letting the warm water cover her breasts. She blew a cloud of smoke at the ceiling, trying to fight back the tightness in her throat and the tears in her eyes.

She fondled the lighter, turning it to where she could again read the inscription.

Forever wasn't a very long time these days, she thought.

Forever, as a matter of fact, had only been until August of 1942, when a large contingent of Canadians had landed on the French coast at Dieppe. The plan had been to test the German defenses. The German defenses had been even more formidable than expected, and the Canadians had been pinned down on the shore. Only half of the invaders had made it back to England. Lieutenant Martin Wilson, Janice Porter's fiance, had not been among the lucky half.

After toweling herself dry, she wrapped herself in Howard's terry cloth robe and then untied her hair and let it tumble about her shoulders. She leaned over the sink to observe herself closely in the cabinet mirror. Good bones, she thought, smiling. That's what her mother had always said. Her skin was pale with a shiny, almost translucent luminescence. It glowed as if from within. She considered herself rather ordinary looking, and in truth she was—nice eyes, nice nose, nice mouth. Nothing wrong with any of her component parts but nothing unusual either. Her legs were long, her body was slender and her breasts nicely rounded, but she had always wondered why men seemed to find her so attractive. In a roomful of women, most of whom she found to be infinitely more attractive than she, she invariably got most of the attention.

It was pleasant, she thought, but sometimes it was a nuisance.

She crossed the hall back into the bedroom, hoping to get dressed and on her way before Howard returned. She loosened the belt and was in the process of slipping off her robe when she noticed that the panties she had left on the bed were not there.

More puzzled than alarmed, she narrowed her eyes. Then she heard the door swing shut behind her.

She spun around, instinctively pulling the robe closed.

Krueger smiled. His back was against the door. "This what you're looking for?" He held her underwear in his left hand, a long-bladed knife in his right. There was a smile on his lips, but his eyes were cold. He was a short man—not much taller than she—but she could see that he was strongly built.

Janice fought her panic. "Who are you?" she said with all the outrage she could muster.

"That's my question," he said. "I want to know who you are—and why are you following me."

"Following you?" she said, forcing a laugh. "If I've stumbled into your bedroom sir, there's been a terrible mistake. It looks a lot like mine."

"I mean this afternoon—at the station."

"The station?" she struggled to compose her thoughts. Her brain kept running to the pistol in her bag in the living room.

"I was at Penn Station earlier. I was supposed to meet someone, but I'm afraid I was late and missed her."

"You followed me there."

"I've never laid eyes on you until this minute."

He thought for a moment—a flicker of doubt showing on his face. Then his face hardened, and Janice saw that he had decided not to believe her. He shrugged. "No matter," he said. "You're English?"

"Canadian," she said, clutching at her robe. "And you by the sound of you are German."

"Dutch," he said.

She laughed in his face. "If you prefer." She could be bold because she knew the bluff was over. Her story had caused him a moment's hesitation, but she saw in his expression and in his dismissive shrug that he had decided to kill her.

"No matter," he said again.

She surprised him by moving forward. "If you don't mind I'd like you to hand over my underwear," she said, extending her left hand toward him as if to take possession of the panties, her eyes never left his face. He pulled them back, reluctant to give them up. Watching him carefully, Janice allowed her robe to fall open. As she had expected, his eyes darted to the opening, and she took one swift step forward. Grasping the wrist of his right arm in her left hand, she drove her right elbow into his nose with as much force as she could.

Moving quickly, she put her right hand under his elbow, pulled him toward her and flipped him effortlessly over her right hip. He crashed onto the floor, but still held on to the knife. Stunned by the quickness of the assault, Krueger was slow in rising. In that moment Janice ripped open the door and raced out of the room. Only slightly hurt, Krueger recovered from his surprise and dashed after her. He hurtled down the stairs and came to a skidding halt in the living room, where Janice was leveling the barrel of her .22-caliber pistol at his midsection.

"Throw the knife over on the couch, Mr. Krueger," Janice said, "and then sit down in that chair to your right." He threw the knife aside. "I'm very nervous," said Janice, "and if you frighten me, even one tiny bit, I'm afraid I would have to shoot you."

Krueger sat down heavily. "I doubt very much," he said with a wistful smile, "that I could frighten you very much, madame, and I assure you that I have no intention of trying anything foolish."

Janice nodded and went to the telephone, keeping the gun trained on Krueger. She dialed.

"Bobbin, please," she said, using Blakely's code name, and waited. "It's me, Janice. I'm at Howard's apartment. I stopped in to freshen up on my way back to the office, and you'll never guess." She waited but Blakely said nothing. He was not the sort of man to engage in guessing games. "Krueger followed me here." She listened to his anger. "I'm sorry I made such a mess of it, but he got in here and tried to kill me." She looked at Krueger carefully. "No," she said. "I didn't kill him. Do you want me to?" she asked matter-of-factly, watching Krueger's eyes pop out. "Very well," she said. "I'll wait for you then. D'you remember the address?"

She hung up and said to Krueger, "I think he wants to kill you himself."

"Don't be ridiculous." Kreuger laughed. "I don't know who you people are, but you had better call Agent Brownmiller at the FBI office here in New York before you do anything foolish. I am under his jurisdiction and protection.

Janice shrugged. "We'll see about that."

35

"We'll see to it that you hang, Mr. Krueger," said Blakely with obvious conviction.

Krueger scoffed. "For what? For following a pretty girl back to her apartment?"

Blakely slapped him hard across the face, the sound reverberating around the room.

Krueger eyed him with contempt, then laughed again. "I wonder what the FBI will say when they find out that British intelligence is torturing one of their protected aliens." He was handcuffed to a chair.

Janice pulled Blakely away. "He's right, Jon," she whispered. "Hoover will have a fit when he finds out we've been interfering with one of his people."

Blakely's teeth were clenched, his jaw set in a hard line. "Damn them," he said. "I'd like to just . . ." He looked at Krueger, and his voice trailed off into nothingness.

Krueger grinned.

They heard a key in the door, and all three heads turned as the door swung open. Howard Green, newspaper under one arm, a small bag of groceries under the other stood in the doorway, a half-smile on his lips, a half-frown on his brow. "What's all this?" he asked.

"Come in, Howard, please," said Blakely as if he were the host and this were not Green's apartment. "And do close the door."

"Janice, what is this?" Green said again.

She explained that Krueger had followed her here and had tried to kill her.

"Jesus," said Green, looking at Krueger, who shrugged.

"It was all a mistake," said Krueger. "I thought merely to frighten her into telling me why she was following me. I suggest that you call the FBI immediately."

"We should call the FBI," said Green hopefully. "This is going to cause an awful mess."

Blakely motioned Green into the kitchen. Once inside he spoke in a low voice that could not be heard in the other room. "As you know, the relationship between Mr. Hoover's organization and mine is not always smooth. The FBI—and not without reason—thinks that we have overstepped our authority. We've stumbled into this rather awkward situation, and I think the only way to salvage it is to either make Mr. Krueger talk or dispose of him quietly."

Green's eyes widened. "Dispose of him?"

"War is hell and all that stuff, my boy," Blakely said regretfully.

"Now wait a minute," said Green. "Nobody is going to be disposed of in my apartment."

Blakely shrugged. "Then what do you suggest?"

"Call in the FBI."

"Out of the question. Without proof of his activities it would drive a wedge between our two agencies. Innocent or guilty—he's not worth that."

"Then let me call Falzetti. He'll know what to do."

Blakely thought about that for a second. "All right, let's call your friend Falzetti."

Green breathed a sigh of relief as he grabbed for the phone. Falzetti would know how to get out of this. These British were crazy. They were ready to kill this guy, "innocent or guilty," to preserve some insane arrangement they had with the FBI. He needed help to cool down Blakely. Falzetti would know what to do.

Falzetti listened grimly when Green explained the situation. Janice sat in the kitchen while the three men huddled in the living room with Krueger nearby. Every few seconds Falzetti glared at Krueger, who smiled confidently as if he were on a job interview.

"Kill him," said Falzetti, and Green blanched.

Blakely chimed in with a smile. "That's what I've

been trying to explain to Captain Green here. The man either talks or we have to kill him."

Falzetti shot a look at Blakely. "You don't understand either, Blakely. Whether or not he talks, I'm going to kill him."

Blakely's eyes widened. "Excuse me?"

"It's simple. One of my men is dead because of this slime, and I'm going to see him dead before the day is out."

Blakely stammered a little as he spoke. "But the information that we require?"

"I don't give a shit about that. That's your problem. I'll give you ten minutes, then I kill him."

Krueger's eyes began to widen as the conversation went on.

"Wait a minute," said Green.

Falzetti waved aside his protest. "Don't worry. I won't do it here. I'll take him with me to headquarters. I've got two men in a car outside." He turned to Kreuger. "You ever been to Police Headquarters on Centre Street, Mr. Krueger? We've got rooms in the basement that we keep just for cop-killers. We're going to break every bone in your body, then hang you up on a meathook. The record is twelve hours. But I don't think you've got more than five or six hours in you."

Kreuger's lips were suddenly very dry.

"See here," said Green in protest. "I can't believe that an American would act like this."

Falzetti took his cigar out of his mouth. "Green, if I were you, I'd put on my hat and coat and take that pretty little girl of yours out to dinner. Maybe Sardi's or "21." Then go dancing at the Persian Room. Have a good time. When you get back, you'll never know we've been here." He looked at Blakely. "You've only got eight minutes left."

Blakely walked over to Krueger, whose eyes were rolling around. "Well, Mr. Krueger," he said. "I gave you an opportunity . . ." He let the rest of the sentence hang in the air.

"Can't you do anything with that madman?" whispered Krueger.

Blakely shook his head slowly. "What can I do? I am a guest in his city."

"Can we talk?" said Krueger. "Alone?"

Blakely turned to Falzetti. "May I speak with Mr. Krueger in private, Lieutenant?"

Falzetti looked at his watch. "You got seven minutes," he said and went into the kitchen.

Both Krueger and Blakely stared at Green until he reluctantly followed Falzetti.

"Now what can I do for you, Mr. Krueger?"

Krueger smiled. "You and I, sir, are merely players in this game."

"Ah," said Blakely. "Shakespeare. I admire a man who knows Shakespeare."

"What I mean is—we know the risks involved in serving our respective countries. Being a spy is a dangerous business. The penalties for failure are extremely high."

"Six minutes," called Falzetti from the kitchen.

Krueger licked his lips. "But usually there are other options."

"Such as?"

"Captured agents very often—as you and I know—manage to save their lives in some exchange of information. But you offer nothing. If I talk to you, the FBI will have me hanged because I would be too much of an embarrassment to them." He almost smiled. "I made such asses of them."

"I could have interceded on your behalf—if you had been cooperative. I couldn't have guaranteed more than a long prison sentence, but I'm afraid it's too late to worry about that now."

"If you call the FBI, they'll come and get me," whispered Krueger, his eyes on the kitchen door. "Even if he takes me to Centre Street, they'll come and get me out."

"Why should I?"

Krueger licked his lips nervously, his eyes blinking rapidly.

"Five minutes," called Falzetti.

"I'll tell you everything," said Krueger, clearing his

throat, "but you've got to keep that madman away from me."

"Absolutely brilliant, Lieutenant," said Blakely. "The bastard's in there now sweating like a pig."

Falzetti stared blankly at Blakely.

"I mean the part about the meathook. My God it was wonderful."

"I meant it," said Falzetti simply. "Tim O'Connor was a good cop."

Blakely made a face. "Interesting," he said. "I'm going to get someone else from my office over here to help with the interrogation." He went back into the living room where Green was guarding Krueger.

"You didn't really mean that, did you?" asked Janice when Blakely had left.

Falzetti looked at her. They were sitting at opposite ends of the kitchen table, coffee cups in front of them. She was smoking a cigarette and still dressed only in her bathrobe.

"Yes, I did," he said.

She stared at him. Behind the hard exterior, she thought she detected a softness in his eyes.

He smiled. "Maybe not the part about the meathook, but I would have killed him and never given it a thought."

She nodded matter-of-factly and sipped her coffee.

"You did all right," Falzetti said.

Janice looked at him questioningly.

"With Krueger, I mean. You've got guts."

Janice smiled. Obviously, she thought, this was a high compliment from this gruff, hard-nosed cop. "Thanks," she said.

After making his phone call Blakely walked back to Krueger, who waited anxiously. "I think I can hold him off. I told him that this information was absolutely imperative to the Allied war effort."

"What did he say?"

"Quite frankly, I don't think he cares much, but he's agreed to let me have my way."

"After we talk—what then?"

"I turn you over to the FBI."

Krueger looked more confident.

"But," Blakely, added. "I assure you, the first time I think you're not answering my questions, I'll turn you over to the lieutenant."

Falzetti watched Janice Porter stub out the cigarette in the rim of her saucer. He couldn't help but think about the fact that she had nothing on under the robe. He also couldn't help envying Howard Green, who, he was now certain, was sleeping with the woman. It must be great, he thought, to have money and position and a nice place on West 54th Street. He smiled at his own frame of mind. Green really wasn't such a bad guy. Just a typical rich man's kid who didn't want to get his ass shot off in the war. Who could blame him? Except Falzetti's kid was out there somewhere, preparing, for the coming invasion.

Janice raised her eyes and saw him watching her. He looked away shyly and she studied his face as his eyes moved quickly around the room. It was a good face, she decided. A handsome face marked by experience. It was the kind of face that made her wonder how long Howard Green had been shaving.

"You married?" Janice asked suddenly.

"Wife died six years ago."

She didn't say anything, only nodded.

"My son is in England," he said apropos of nothing.

"Army?" she asked.

"Eighty-second Airborne."

She nodded, he thought with sympathy. "Probably having a good time with all the English girls," she said.

Falzetti laughed softly. "If I know my Frank, that's exactly what he's doing."

For a moment there was silence, then Falzetti stood up, his chair legs scraping loudly on the linoleum floor. "I'd better go outside and see how Blakely's doing with Krueger."

He walked past her quietly. Janice tugged her robe closed around her and dragged on her cigarette.

When Howard entered the kitchen, he was shaking his head in amazement. "I can't believe that this is happening in my apartment," he whined. "There's going to be big trouble over this."

"Excuse me, Howard." Janice stood up. "I have to get dressed."

"Well then, Mr. Krueger," said Blakely, "let's hear your tawdry little story." Janice Porter, her steno pad and pencil at the ready, sat poised behind him to take it all down. Blakely's new man sat across from Krueger. He was young with a hard, expressionless face.

Kreuger licked his lips, and with a glance at Falzetti, who sat in a corner, he began. He revealed that he was indeed an Abwehr spy and that he had been brought to the United States to report on shipping and transportation in the Port of New York.

Blakely nodded. It was as he had suspected. "Where's your radio?" he asked.

"I have no radio—other than the one that was confiscated by the FBI."

"Then how do you make your reports?"

"I pass the information to another agent at preselected drops. I assume that he radios the information to Hamburg."

"Who is this other agent?"

Krueger's face twitched. "I don't know his real name. I only know him as Conrad.

"He called me the first time, and each time we meet, we arrange the time and location of our next meeting."

"So you don't know who he is or how to contact him?"

"No," said Krueger.

Falzetti stood up. "Forget this shit," he said. "This bastard is lying through his teeth." He pulled out his .38 and picked up a cushion from the chair holding it in front of the weapon. "Stand back. Let me put one through his kneecap, and we'll see if he can remember 'Conrad's' phone number."

Krueger's eyes widened in fear as Falzetti approached. "You call him every Thursday," Falzetti screamed.

"Please sit down, Lieutenant," said Blakely. "Please let us handle this." He turned back to Krueger, shrugging his shoulders as if in apology for Falzetti's wild behavior. "You see, Mr. Krueger, we already know who your friend Conrad is. We have followed you and him to one of your little meetings at Penn Station."

Krueger's shoulder's slumped. "Streetman," he said. "Jon Streetman."

"Precisely," said Blakely. "Where is his radio?"

"I don't know," said Krueger. "Our only contact is when I pass him information." He looked desperately at Falzetti. "I swear," he said.

"Do you code it, or does he?"

"He does. I give him information in the clear."

They went on for another hour, Krueger answering each question in turn until finally there seemed nothing else to add.

"I've got a question," said Falzetti. He approached Krueger. "Who killed Tim O'Connor, the policeman who was following you and Streetman?"

Krueger, his eyes pleading, turned to Blakely, who merely looked away. "Streetman suspected that someone was following him. He told me at our last meeting to be careful. I told him he would ruin everything if he did something foolish." He looked at Falzetti. "I didn't want anyone killed. It was too dangerous. But Streetman is a fanatic. It must have been him."

"Who killed George Marcovic?" Falzetti's expression didn't change.

"Streetman again. He wanted some information that Marcovic had."

"Tell me about the Hallmark Hotel," said Falzetti. "Why did Weissman jump?"

"I wasn't there," said Krueger quickly. "I don't know anything."

Falzetti said nothing. Blakely motioned him aside. "There may be a security problem here. Dr. Weissman's project was top secret, and mere mention of his presence could compromise the project. We don't know that Krueger had any hand in it."

"Hand in it?" said Falzetti. "He's up to his balls in it."

Blakely smiled at Falzetti's language and pulled the

policeman aside. "We have no proof that he was involved. Streetman is the man we want. He's the one who killed your friend. He's the one whose son was in that hotel room."

Falzetti glared at Krueger. "This bastard knows," he hissed.

Blakely turned to Krueger. "Do you have anything to add, Mr. Krueger, before I turn you over to the FBI?"

"No," said Krueger, "that's everything." He looked around the room. "What will they do to me?"

"I'm sure they'll think of something," said Blakely. "I'll just give them a call." He picked up the phone, then hesitated. "On second thought"— he turned to his own agent, who stood poised over Krueger—"Johnson can escort you over there in person." He smiled at Johnson, who nodded grimly. "You can take care of this little job, can't you, Johnson?"

Johnson simple nodded.

Falzetti knew immediately that the British had decided to kill Krueger. It made sense. It was simpler that way. With Krueger out of the way, nothing had to be explained to the FBI. Krueger had confessed and implicated Streetman. There was no need to keep him alive.

"I think I'm going for a drink," said Blakely cheerfully as if Krueger were nonexistent. "Anyone care to join me?"

Falzetti smiled. "Sure," he said, then moved close to Blakely. "If you're going to dump this guy," he said in a soft whisper, "don't do it in my precinct."

"Wouldn't dream of it," said Blakely, smiling brightly.

Krueger was watching them carefully, his eyes and ears turned carefully for the nuances that would indicate whether he would survive or die. He knew that this was the critical moment.

Falzetti saw Krueger's eyes dart around the room, and he knew it too.

"Wait a minute," Falzetti said. "Why don't you let me drive him over to the FBI office? I've got a car outside with two men in it. Johnson shouldn't have to do this by himself."

Kreuger stiffened and his eyes went immediately to Blakely. "You promised," he said, his voice near breaking.

Blakely shrugged. "I am a guest in the lieutenant's city," he said. "What can I do?"

Kreuger squeezed his eyes shut. His breathing was rapid and shallow. Falzetti knew that he had just given up.

"My real name," said Krueger, "is Herman Lang." He spoke in a monotone, as though he had rehearsed this moment for years. "In the 1920s I was a member, for a time, of the Austrian Communist party. One of my acquaintances at that time was Dr. Adam Weissman."

Everyone in the room heard Blakely take a sharp breath.

"I was sent here by the Abwehr to contact Dr. Weissman and convince him that I was still a communist sympathizer."

"And?" asked Blakely.

Kreuger smiled for the first time in a long time. "It was easy. Communists always think that everyone will see the light and join them."

"Go on," said Blakely sternly.

"He introduced me to Theodore Marcovic, another communist. He had been passing information to him for months."

"Good God!" said Blakely. "I don't believe it."

Kreuger shrugged. "Weissman was a communist. He wanted the Russians to have everything he knew."

"This is impossible," said Blakely.

Krueger was calm in the face of Blakely's disbelief. "Does the Manhattan Project mean anything to you?"

Blakely was stunned into silence.

"I was sent here by the Abwehr to gather whatever information I could about the atomic bomb project." He gave a thin-lipped smile. "I have been reasonably successful, and I am sure that the Americans"—he nodded to Blakely—"and the British would like to know how successful." He knew that he had just saved his life. He wasn't sure for how long, but the prospect of sudden, chilling death had been pushed into the background for a time. Who knew, perhaps with luck and resourcefulness he could manage to survive even this.

Blakely seemed too shocked to speak, so Falzetti, to whom this conversation meant nothing, pushed past the Englishman and confronted Kreuger.

"I want to know what you knew about the Hallmark Hotel and who killed those two men."

Krueger looked around for help. He would have preferred not to speak with this policeman. "I wasn't there," he said quickly. "I was merely an intermediary."

"Intermediary?"

"I introduced Streetman's son to Theodore Marcovic. I told him the boy was ashamed of his capitalist father and that he was a communist who wanted to serve Russia."

"I don't care about that shit," said Falzetti explosively. "Tell me what happened in that hotel room."

Kreuger was becoming afraid again. "Streetman's son tried to convince Marcovic to let him take Weissman's information to the Russians in New York or Washington, but of course Marcovic wouldn't hear of it. So Streetman's son killed Marcovic and drugged Weissman to get everything that he could from him."

Blakely was back with a question. "How was this information to be delivered to Germany?"

"Streetman's radio."

"If Streetman ever tried to broadcast that much information by radio, the FBI would be on him in a matter of hours," said Blakely.

"Only parts of it. The rest was to be sent in microfilm," said Krueger. "Processed here in New York and shipped by freighter to South America and then on to Portugal. It's slow but it's secure."

"I'll want the name of that freighter."

"You don't have to worry," said Krueger. "Young Streetman was supposed to deliver the microfilm to the freighter. Unfortunately he wound up in the bottom of the East River."

"I still want the name of that ship."

Krueger shrugged. "As you wish. I'll give that information to the FBI."

"Who killed Streetman's son?" asked Falzetti.

Krueger shook his head as if the story amazed even him. "He was killed in some minor altercation in one of your waterfront bars. Something that had nothing to do with any of this."

Blakely interrupted. "I think we'd better call in the FBI," he said. "There's not much we can do now but try to gather up the pieces."

Falzetti nodded, but he watched Krueger steadily.

36

The twin engines of the Vickers Wellington bomber throbbed in a bone-numbing vibration that seemed to force the freezing air deep into the marrow of the four passengers huddled in the modified bomb-bay compartment just behind the pilot's cabin.

The passengers—Bishop, Madsen, Chapman, and Iverson—wore Irvin sheepskin jackets over heavy sweaters and wool trousers. The wool coats they would wear on the ground were now used as blankets around their legs. The men were strangely quiet, each alone with whatever thoughts he could muster. They had trained for this night, but the training had always been against some silent, invisible foe. Now that enemy began to seem more real, more dangerous.

Earlier Bishop had tried some light conversation to relieve the obvious tension, but after yelling over the insistent throb of the engines and being greeted with a lukewarm response, he had decided that it wasn't worth the effort. He could only hope now that the Special Operations training, conducted under commando cover, had been sufficient to turn his raiding force into an efficient unit.

Pictures of the training flashed before him like some bizarre family album projected on the living room wall for gathered relatives. He captioned each picture in his mind and rated the proficiency of the participants. Silent killing: Madsen, A+. Rope work, boat work, automatic weapons: Chapman, A−. Plastic explosives, map and paper work, wireless transmission: Iverson, A. Pistols and knife work: Madsen again, A+. What does that leave for me? he wondered. Leadership? Organization? He smiled, patting the small, flat package taped under his shirt, knowing that he would do whatever it took to get the job done. He let the drone of the Wellington's engines lull him into a drowsy wakefulness.

The plane, affectionately known throughout the RAF as the Wimpey, had once been the backbone of the RAF's bombing raids on Germany, but had long since been replaced as a front-line aircraft by subsequent generations of Lancasters, Halifaxes, and Stirlings. Although no longer considered a prime attack aircraft, the Wellington was still a serviceable flying platform suitable for many other less glamorous but still demanding areas of combat. The bomber had been found useful for long-range reconaissance with Coastal Command and for troop equipment transport. If a commander wanted a sure and reliable means of air transport, he was sure to remark, "Get a Wimpey."

Tonight, aircraft number G3572 of the 161 Bomber Squadron at Tempsford was engaged in another exercise for which the Wellington was ably suited. With only minor modifications—a small trapdoor cut in the floor of the fuselage, extended-range fuel tanks, a modified bomb-bay compartment with metal seats and overhead static lines—the Wellington was an excellent platform for dropping agents or supplies deep into occupied territory.

On this night, even though the target was neutral Sweden, the trip was just as arduous and just as filled with the expectation of interception and catastrophe. Leaving Tempsford at midnight, the plane had flown due east, then banked sharply left and followed the English coast for a short time before heading out across the North Sea. The greatest fear was that German radar posts in Holland would pick up the lone craft early in its flight and dispatch the feared Messerschmitt Bf 110G night fighter. Many a bomber crew had spent their last moments in shocked amazement as the almost invisible, black-shrouded, and radar-directed Bf 110 had slipped below an unwary bomber and raked the aircraft from bow to stern with its upward directed 20mm cannon.

As if in expectation of this disastrous occurrence, Iverson sat in his uncomfortable seat, his eyes locked on the floor. He had grown increasingly nervous in the past few days, even though his job was less hazardous than the others. His dreams had been filled with thoughts of Germans waiting in ambush, only this time, unlike Dieppe, he was certain that he would not come home. The sound of firing squads, which had haunted him for the last several days, now seemed suddenly closer and much more real. Only Iverson knew how much of his courage he had left behind in France with his shattered comrades.

He glanced round, his eyes darting nervously from face to face. Bishop, as imperturbable as ever, nodded reassuringly when their eyes met, but Iverson's eyes moved on. Madsen slept, his ususal stern expression softened in slumber. Finally his eyes found Chapman, who gave him an encouraging smile.

Chapman sat huddled against the cold but seemed immune to the tension that Iverson felt. A small smile played around his lips as he thought how lucky he was to be here. This was what he had been trained for. In fact, he thought, this is what he had been raised for. He took a deep breath and gave a long satisfied sigh. After the years of waiting his time had finally come. Soon he would have the chance to serve. The opportunity had come, as he had always known it would, but even in his wildest dreams he could not have imagined that it would be like this. When it was over, he would be a hero. His father would be proud of him.

Ninety minutes after takeoff, the Wellington banked right, on a course that would take the four-man crew and their four passengers across the seventy-five-mile stretch of the Skagerrak between the two occupied nations of Norway and Denmark.

The copilot came in from the forward cabin. Young and slender, he looked lost in the fur-lined flying jacket. In his floppy flying boots he looked like a child playing in his father's shoes. "A bit more than an hour, gents," he said casually, above the roar of the engines and with the usual airman's disdain for the proprieties of rank. "Gerry should get another chance to pick us up on his radar as we approach the coast, but there's a big raid on Wilhelmshaven tonight, and we're hoping that he's got all that he can handle trying to cope with that. No one's going to pay much attention to a single bomber when there are over four hundred of us just two hundred miles to the south."

The copilot, smooth-cheeked and barely out of his teens, seemed casual and unafraid as if what he was doing was commonplace. In point of fact, in a world gone mad, what he was doing *was* rather commonplace.

"This far north," he went on, "we hardly ever see night fighters anyway. Gerry keeps them further south defending the big German targets. Our only problem might be if some overzealous fighter pilot in Norway decides to come up and look for us." He shrugged, "It happens once in a while, but without radar his chances of finding us are almost nil. If we pick up anything on our radar, we'll play hide and seek in the clouds until he gets tired or runs low on fuel."

He waited, expecting questions, and when there were none, he turned to go back to the cockpit. "One more thing," he said, remembering. "In about twenty minutes we'll drop to about two hundred feet for the run in over the Skagerrak." He smiled. "Not to worry. It's a nice clear night—no problem with visibility." He waved a good-bye. "We'll give you plenty of warning before we approach the drop area."

Bishop nodded a thank-you as the copilot disappeared, then looked at the faces of his team. The copilot's little chat had been intended, he was sure, to reassure them, but talk of night fighters, flying low, and evasive tactics in the clouds had not been exactly what they had wanted to hear.

"All right, chaps," Bishop said. "Let's have a final equipment check."

Each man pulled out the duffel bag stuffed beneath his seat and, for what seemed like the tenth time, began the tedious task of going over the equipment.

"Drop area in sight," called the copilot, sticking his head into the passenger compartment.

Bishop waved his acknowledgment and patted Madsen on the shoulder. Madsen sat on the floor of the bomber facing the rear, his legs dangling through the trapdoor that had been hoisted open moments before. His parachute was attached by a strap and buckle to a steel cable that was stretched the width of the aircraft. This strap would automatically open the parachute when he left the plane. In his lap he held his equipment bag, which was attached to his ankle by another longer line. As he left the plane he would drop the equipment bag, which would then hit the ground before he did.

The others, chutes already attached to the overhead cable, clustered around the jump hole in the fuselage floor, ready to drop through when Madsen was clear. With the Wellington at five hundred feet, the trip from plane to ground would take less than thirty seconds.

"Get ready," called the copilot, raising his arm over his head. He kept one eye on the pilot through the open bulkhead door.

Bishop yelled at Iverson above the scream of the rushing air. "As soon as Madsen's chute opens, you follow."

Iverson's eyes were as wide as saucers, his head nodding up and down.

Everyone instinctively tugged at the shoulder straps of their parachutes. Madsen gave an extra shake with his shoulders as if to release the tension.

The copilot dropped his arm, and Madsen dropped through the hole. Iverson, next to go, scrambled into a sitting position over the trapdoor, anxiously peering into the darkness. "I don't see him," he yelled at

Bishop, who knelt next to him, staring disbelievingly into the black space beneath the rushing aircraft.

"What's happening?" Chapman yelled, seeing Iverson still sitting and Bishop holding the Canadian by the shoulders as if to prevent him from jumping.

The copilot looked in. "Tail gunner says he didn't see a chute open. What happened?"

Bishop pulled Iverson back from the jump hole and slammed the trapdoor shut. "Take us to the secondary drop area," he said, ignoring the copilot's question.

The copilot shrugged and returned to the cockpit.

Bishop sat on the floor. "I watched the packers prepare these chutes myself," he said. "They were perfect."

"You don't think someone has tampered with our chutes, do you?" asked Chapman.

Iverson touched the straps as though he were carrying an alien creature on his back.

"Check the static lines," said Bishop. "If someone is going to tamper with a chute, that would be the place to do it."

Each man struggled out of his chute and inspected the steel ring connections that pulled the chute free under pressure from the lines. Everything seemed in perfect working order.

"Ten minutes," called the copilot. "Secondary drop area coming up."

They strapped their chutes back on, Iverson and Chapman not saying anything.

"Sit for a few minutes," said Bishop, his eyes glazed as if he could not believe what had happened. "Try to relax," he said, more to himself than the others.

They flopped back in their seats. Iverson's breathing was short and rapid, his eyes darting back and forth. He was imagining Madsen imbedded in the hard turf of some Swedish field.

Chapman watched him, thinking that Iverson was on the verge of hysteria. "Captain," he said, "let me jump first."

Bishop looked at Iverson, then nodded at Chapman, "Okay," he said, "get ready."

At the signal from the cockpit they pulled up the trapdoor, and Chapman moved into a sitting position, his legs dangling into space. While he waited for the go signal, he winked at Iverson, who watched him anxiously.

At the next signal, Bishop yelled, "Go!" and tapped Chapman on the shoulder. Chapman dropped his equipment bag and launched himself into space.

Iverson scrambled into position, his eyes never leaving Chapman. "I see it," he yelled. "It opened."

With that Bishop gave him a slight shove, and he was gone, tumbling through the bitter night air, waiting breathlessly until the cord jerked him upright and his parachute blossomed behind him. He looked up to see the dark shape of the Wellington racing past and another smaller shape detach itself from the plane and come tumbling toward him as Bishop followed.

The ride was exhilarating and terrifying at the same time as Iverson watched the dark ground rush up to meet him. He held his legs together, bent his knees and at impact rolled forward.

It was over. He lay on the ground motionless for a moment, taking mental stock of all his body parts. He had made it. He was on firm ground. His fear vanished, and he jumped up in time to see Bishop hit the ground less than one hundred yards away.

As Iverson pulled in the lines of his chute he saw flashlights approach and heard voices calling in English.

"Over here," he yelled and was caught in the beam of light. He continued to pull in his chute, and two men helped him fold it and stuff it into a canvas bag. They shook hands with Iverson, and one of them picked up Iverson's equipment bag.

"This way," said the one with the bag on his shoulder and soon they were all standing in the middle of the field where they had landed. In addition to the three parachutists, there were seven Swedes.

"Everyone all right?" asked Bishop. "No sprains or injuries?" He took the silence for an affirmative.

The leader of the group introduced himself to Bishop. "My name is Lindquist," he said. "Two of these men are my sons. The others are trusted friends. We are all very pleased to be of assistance."

Bishop shook his hand and then introduced his men.

"My understanding," said Linquist, "was that there would be four of you."

Bishop stole a quick glance at his companions. "No," he said tonelessly. "There are only three of us."

Lindquist shrugged. "Tonight," he said, "we will take you to a house not far from here. Tomorrow morning we will take you to the train station in Jönköping. One of my sons and one of the others, who also speaks English, will accompany you to your destination on the coast."

The Swedes picked up the equipment and escorted the three soldiers across the field to a dirt road, where an ancient truck was parked. In minutes they were all aboard, bouncing in the back as the truck made its way along the darkened road.

Chapman, looking back, could barely make out the trees that lined the road. The field where they had landed had already slipped into darkness, and the night was full of silence.

Bishop lay back, his head resting on his equipment bag, eyes open and staring at the night sky. Chapman watched him, imagining what he must be thinking. In Chapman's mind's eye he saw a picture of Madsen, eyes open, staring sightlessly at the sky in another empty field, fifty miles away.

■

At the same time that Andrew Chapman was looking up at the night sky in Sweden, Lieutenant Nicolas Falzetti sat in the backseat of an unmarked car parked three hundred yards from the Long Island home of Jon Streetman. Seated beside him, in stony silence, was Tom Brownmiller. Two FBI men sat in the front.

As his price for the information, Falzetti had insisted upon being part of the arrest team. As the story had been related to Tom Brownmiller, the FBI man's face had run the gamut of emotions. First he had been incredulous, then furious, then dumbfounded, and finally he had succumbed to the emotionless silence that he now displayed. Falzetti wasn't sure whether Brownmiller was angry at him for going against his orders or embarrassed that Krueger had made his organization look so foolish.

Across the street from Brownmiller's car was another unmarked vehicle with four more agents waiting for the signal to surround Streetman's house. At the other end of the street, past the house, a third FBI car sat in the darkness, also waiting.

"Got enough firepower?" asked Falzetti, his voice ringing like a thunderclap in the silence.

Brownmiller turned his head away from the window and looked at the policeman, who sat next to him with thinly disguised contempt. For a moment Falzetti thought that Brownmiller was not going to say anything, but then he spoke, his voice carefully modulated to control his anger. "Don't worry about it," he said. "I've got ten men with me. Just keep out of our way and let us do our job."

A comment sprang to Falzetti's lips, but he decided it would be better to hold it back.

The radio crackled in the car. "Unit one, unit one. This is alpha-red. We have a confirm from unit five. Repeat: a confirm from unit five."

Brownmiller sighed. "Acknowledge that," he said to the man in the front seat. "That's it," he said to no one in particular.

"That's what?" asked Falzetti.

"Streetman's radio," said Brownmiller wearily as if the statement brought him pain. "We found it on his boat... where you said it would be," he added. The last admission was even more painful than the first.

"What now?"

"Now," said Brownmiller, opening the car door and stepping out, "we go get him."

"Let me do it," Falzetti said. "He knows me. I'll

knock on his door and say I want to ask him a few questions."

Brownmiller's look was scornful. "Do you know what time it is? I want you to stay right here until this is over." He called softly to the men across the street. "I want the house surrounded. Two men on each corner. Hazelton will go in the front with me."

Hazelton, the young man working the radio, hopped out of the car and stood nervously beside Brownmiller, who then turned to his driver. "As soon as you hear my voice, I want you to block the driveway with the car." He looked smugly at Falzetti. "I don't want him crashing out of here."

Falzetti got out of the car. "How many covering the rear?"

"Two on each corner gives me four men on any one side," said Brownmiller.

Falzetti nodded. "Mind if I go around back just in case?"

"Do what you like," Brownmiller snarled. "Just keep out of our way."

Falzetti smiled pleasantly, took a flashlight from the backseat, and waited for the FBI men to start moving.

"Unit three is ready to move," said the driver of Brownmiller's car.

"Okay," said Brownmiller, "let's do it."

Car doors opened at opposite ends of the street, and as if on signal, every dog in the neighborhood started to bark.

"Shit," said Brownmiller as he and his men began to move toward Streetman's house.

Falzetti went off at a right angle to the others. Listening to the dogs, he knew that Streetman would be alerted. Falzetti walked down a long driveway past a large colonial style house. None of the lights were on. He cut across several backyards and then came to a high brick wall. With some difficulty he hoisted himself up and, before dropping over to the other side, surveyed the scene. From his vantage point he could see Streetman's house to his right. Lights were on in several downstairs rooms. Except for a light that had just flicked off in an upstairs room, the upper floors were dark.

He saw the silhouetted shapes move stealthily around the house as Brownmiller's men moved to cut off all avenues of escape.

The house sat at the top of a slight slope, and fifty yards below the slope disappeared into thick woods. Just short of the woods was a small building that might have been a toolshed. Falzetti lowered himself down from the wall and, following the tree line of the woods, made his way across the property to the shed.

On the other side of the woods he caught a slimpse of reflected moonlight. Water! he thought, surprised. He had not realized that Streetman's property bordered on what must have been an inlet of Manhasset Bay.

He reached the shed and tried the handle on the door. It opened. He saw gardening tools and a wheelbarrow when he briefly snapped on the flashlight. He pulled the door closed and redirected his attention to the house, which was now directly in front of him.

At that moment his fantasy was that Streetman would somehow elude the FBI's encirclement and come running toward him from the back of the house. Even as he thought it, he knew it wouldn't happen.

Wondering about the inlet, he looked behind him to the woods. There seemed to be a path leading into the trees and a dark shape blocking the reflection from the water on the other side of the trees. Deciding quickly, Falzetti took the path and cut through the woods. Sure enough there was another larger building at the water's edge.

A boat shed, he thought, and for some reason his pulse quickened. He looked inside and gave a low whistle. Sitting there, rocking gently in the slight chop, sat a long, brutally powerful speedboat.

Falzetti went inside and let his flashlight beam rake the length of the mahogany and chrome monster, which was aimed like a missle toward the open sea.

"This baby," he said aloud, "could outrun anything."

He chuckled to himself, thinking that this was probably how Streetman, in the event of his discovery, planned to escape.

Brownmiller and Hazelton tiptoed their way onto the porch and approached the front door. Unknown to them, Streetman had watched their progress up his driveway from a darkened room on the second floor and then, Luger in hand, had made his way downstairs to wait in ambush. He could have started his escape at any time but preferred to create as much of a diversion as possible before making a run for it. Streetman had known that sooner or later this moment would come. Better now, he thought. South America is beautiful this time of year.

Brownmiller, on one side of the front door with Hazelton on the other, whispered to his partner, "Try the door. If it's locked, kick it in, and I'll go in first."

Hazelton nodded and reached for the handle. To his surprise the door was unlocked and swung open at his touch. He was just as surprised when Streetman, crouching behind the bannister of the stairs in the front hall, shot him once in the arm and again in the chest.

The young agent screamed in pain, stumbled back across the porch, and tumbled down the steps. Foolishly, Brownmiller went to his aid, momentarily putting himself in direct line with the still open front door. Streetman snapped off a quick round as his target passed across his narrow field of view. He was rewarded with a gasp as Brownmiller clutched at his leg and tumbled down the steps to land heavily atop the unconscious Hazelton.

Fortunately for both men, Streetman's Luger had belonged to his father and used the old 7.65mm cartridge rather than the newer version's 9mm. The older version was more accurate but lacked the explosive power of the newer model.

The sound of the shots galvanized the men around the house, and they rushed forward, weapons drawn, ready for anything. Brownmiller pointed to the open front door, and two Thompson submachine guns opened a murderous fire that devastated the front hall.

After the reverberations of the drum-loaded fifty-round Tommy Guns had ceased, there was only an eerie silence.

"I think we got him," whispered one agent hopefully to the moaning Brownmiller.

At the sound of the three shots Falzetti started back up the path through the woods. Halfway through he heard the explosive roar of the submachine guns and mentally began counting how many pieces Streetman had been cut into.

He slowed to a walk, and then he heard the noise. Dead ahead. A distinctive click as if a door had been open.

He stopped and listened. It had come from the toolshed. From *inside* the toolshed.

A tunnel, he thought. The bastard had a tunnel from the house to the shed. . . . And now he's going to— Falzetti started backtracking toward the boat shed.

Cautiously Streetman opened the door to the toolshed and, staying low in a running crouch, made his way to the edge of the woods. Once there he stopped and looked back at the house, wondering how long it would take them to discover the basement tunnel. He grinned, knowing that he could quietly paddle his speedboat down the inlet and be in the bay long before they discovered what had happened.

If he played his cards right, he thought, he could be back in New York before they were and aboard any one of several Spanish or South American freighters. All it would take was one phone call. He already had his forged passport and working papers. His money was in Mexico and Switzerland, so he would have no trouble drawing funds. He almost laughed out loud.

He resisted the temptation to wave to the house and the fools inside, who were by this time, scratching their heads in amazement, and turned toward the path through the woods.

At the boat shed he untied the spring lines that secured his boat to the dock. Still holding the ropes, he worked his way around to the other side of the boat, quickly slipping a paddle onto the front seat. He felt along the wall for the nail where he kept the key, his face registering a dull surprise when his fingers touched the bare nail.

He was turning to check the powerboat's ignition when he heard the voice. "This what you're looking for?" Falzetti said, holding up the key. He advanced out of the dark corner of the shed, the key in his outstretched left hand, a .38 Chief's Special leveled at Streetman's belly in his right. He stood next to the stern of the boat and dropped the key into the water. It made a loud plop and disappeared.

Streetman stayed calm, knowing the Luger was in his belt and another key hidden under the rear seat of the boat. All he had to do was rid himself of this meddlesome fool. He looked down into the water, hoping that the look of shocked disbelief on his face was visible in the darkness. "You've ruined everything," he whined. "I could have gotten away if not for you." His shoulders slumped dejectedly, but his eyes never left Falzetti.

"Put your hands on your head and start moving outside," Falzetti said. "And do everything real slow."

Streetman held up the rope. "Can I tie up my boat?" he asked. "I wouldn't want it to just float away."

"Where you're going," Falzetti said, "it won't make much difference."

Streetman waited, rope in hand, his posture one of total submission.

Falzetti shrugged. "Go ahead. Do it."

Smiling in the darkness Streetman turned to his boat, kneeling down and securing the line to the bow cleat. As he knelt he turned his body so that he shielded his right side as he reached for the Luger. When his hand touched the metal he felt the full rush of victory, then spun and fired at the spot, less than ten feet away, where Falzetti had stood.

Falzetti wasn't there anymore.

As Streetman had knelt and turned away, Falzetti had instinctively moved two paces to the side and into the shadows. Bewildered, Streetman fired one more round wildly at the darkness before Falzetti dropped him with a single shot in the center of the chest.

The Luger went flying and Streetman toppled backward into the boat, landing with a heavy thud across the front seat.

He lay there gasping, his lungs gurgling with every tortured breath. Falzetti heard the sound and knew that Streetman was finished.

He heard the sound of confused voices approaching, and Falzetti went outside to wait. The night was clear, and low clouds skipped across the moon, sending shadows racing.

"It's all right," Falzetti yelled as three or four of Brownmiller's men burst out of the woods. He was reluctant to be mistaken in the dark for Streetman and cut to shreds by some snot-nosed bureau kid with a Thompson. "It's all over."

"We found the tunnel," said one of the men breathlessly, then added, "You got him?"

"He's inside."

Brownmiller appeared, supported by a man on either side, a bloody tourniquet around his right thigh. "He's dead?" he asked.

Falzetti shrugged and lit a cigar. "Not yet, maybe. But soon."

They went inside, listening to Streetman's ragged breathing. He still lay where Falzetti had left him, the breaths slower and more agonized.

"Turn a light on him," said Brownmiller and someone snapped on a flashlight and directed the beam in Streetman's face.

"Jesus," said one of the men in a whisper. "The bastard looks as if he's laughing at us."

Streetman's face was deathly pale, but his eyes were firm and focused, and across his lips was a faint, mocking smile. With superhuman effort he moved his head to focus on Falzetti, and when he found the man who had killed him, his eyes widened and he struggled to speak. His lips moved, but his lungs were too badly shattered to force the words.

Then his eyes glazed over and the breathing stopped. In death he stared mockingly at his killer.

Falzetti shivered. "Turn that damn light off," he said, knowing that even in the darkness he would see those two haunting, strangely derisive eyes.

37

For what was left of that night, the three un-uniformed soldiers stayed in a barn, Chapman sleeping the deep sleep of the innocent, Iverson dreaming of Madsen's plunge into terror, Bishop dreaming of nothing. In the morning a plump woman in her fifties awakened them and by gesture bade them to follow her into the house. There she had prepared a huge breakfast, and she sat smiling as they gorged themselves on eggs and sausages and cheese.

A little after seven they heard the rattle and bang of Lindquist's ancient truck, and soon the man himself was banging on the kitchen door. Seen for the first time in the light, he was revealed to be tall with a ruddy, healthy complexion but a heavily-lined face.

"I see you are all enjoying your meal," he said, smiling. "I have with me your papers, and when you have finished eating, we can start on our way to Jönköping."

In the truck Bishop sat up front with Lindquist and his son, the driver, while Iverson and Chapman sat in the back with another man, who seemed pleasant but did not identify himself.

"I thought," said Linquist to Bishop, "when I heard you were coming that you were going to destroy the match company in Jönköping or the arms manufacturer in Huskvarna." He shook his head. "I am ashamed to say that both deal with the Nazis."

Bishop shrugged. "They don't have much choice, I suppose."

"No," Lindquist said sadly. "My government is in the

awkward position of not wishing to antagonize the savage beast. I do wish, however, that we did not have to lie in the same stall."

Bishop slapped him on the knee. "You are doing your part, my friend. It won't be forgotten."

The train station at Jönköping was an ancient affair with trains that seemed relics from the last century. Lindquist escorted the group onto the platform and saw them safely aboard. "Godspeed," he said to all and stood waving solemnly as the train pulled out of the station.

The five travelers claimed a compartment for eight, sitting three across from two. "If anyone else joins us," said Bishop to the Swedes, "we will say nothing."

The Swedes nodded, and all five settled down for the slow trip from the higher plains to the broad heather and finally to the lower ridges of the coastal area.

It was after six and dark when the train arrived in Hälsingborg. Wordlessly Iverson and the Swede known as Paul got up and gathered the heavy suitcase that contained the radio equipment. The Swede swung down onto the platform, and Iverson handed the case to him through the door, then turned and faced the others.

He seemed embarrassed by his parting, either from emotion or from guilt that the others were venturing into dangerous territory. Chapman could not be certain. Finally, after standing for a brief moment looking as if he might say something foolish, Iverson stuck out his hand. "Good luck," he said to Bishop and, "Godspeed," to Chapman.

Bishop smiled, "With any luck, we'll see you tomorrow night."

Then Iverson was gone, moving off down the platform without looking back.

Bishop smiled at Chapman as if in silent recognition of some previously acknowledged fact. Chapman was not sure what he meant but felt certain that it had something to do with Iverson's apparent relief at remaining on safe ground. Now he thought he knew what Bishop had meant when he had said, "For what we have in mind for him, Iverson will be fine."

The train pulled away, and once out of Hälsingborg, Chapman could see the coastline off to his right. Beyond was Denmark, lying across the narrow waters of the Oresund. Bishop looked up and followed Chapman's gaze. "That's it," he said. "Soon enough you'll get a closeup look."

Chapman looked away, clenching and unclenching his fists. For the first time in a long time his palms were sweating.

Iverson, carrying the suitcase, followed Paul, who carried Iverson's duffel bag, out of the station on to a main street. They walked for several blocks before Paul stopped and put down the bag.

"We wait here for a few minutes," he said. With a shrug, Iverson complied.

Fifteen minutes later, just as Iverson was about to express some impatience, an old man pulled up in a horse-drawn wagon with what were apparently grain sacks in the rear. The man must have been eighty, gaunt and gray, with deeply etched lines on his face as if carved by advancing glaciers. The horse, slope-backed and emaciated, seemed too old to carry even its own weight.

"*God afton,*" he said to Paul, whom he apparently recognized. The old man looked Iverson up and down, the expression on his face never changing. "Is this the English?" he asked Paul, without taking his eyes from Iverson.

"Yes," said Paul.

The old man spat. "God help us," he said.

"This is Peter Torkillus," said Paul, but the old man seemed busy with the reins.

Torkillus motioned them aboard and, after throwing the baggage in with his grain, they climbed up onto the seat beside him. The old man gave a gentle flick of his reins, and the old horse slowly began to move.

They crossed a long square, where at the far end, looming above them, stood a medieval tower, remnants of some ruined castle that had dominated the narrow stretch of water between Hälsingborg and the Danish coast.

Paul jerked his thumb over his shoulder, pointing in the direction of the other end of the square. "Across the sound is Helsingor," he said, "less than three miles away."

Iverson nodded, wondering what Shakespeare's melancholy Dane would think of what had happened to his Elsinore.

The horse clip-clopped across narrow streets with buildings jammed closely together, finally coming to rest outside a whitewashed, three-story building that housed a general store on the ground floor and apartments above.

The old man unlocked the door to the store and took them up a back stairwell to a small room on the top floor. The room was no bigger than a large closet and had one tiny window high up on the far wall. Boxes and crates lined one wall across from a cot and a wooden chair.

Paul shrugged apologetically. "The other rooms are occupied," he said.

"This will be fine," said Iverson unconvincingly.

"The toilet is on the ground floor," said the old man to Paul in Swedish, and Paul translated, unnecessarily, for Iverson.

Iverson stood on the chair and looked out the window. The building was one floor higher than those across the street, and over their rooftops he could see the sound and the Danish coast. He stepped down from the chair, smiling. "This is ideal," he said. "If I can get my antennae up on the roof, I'll have no problem at all."

Paul smiled, happy that Iverson seemed satisfied. "I will help you," he said. "Then I must be going. When your friends return from Denmark, someone else will take all of you back to your rendezvous point."

"Well then," said Iverson, "let's get this wireless hooked up and be done with it."

Bishop and Chapman were met in Landskrona by two men whom Lindquist introduced as Lars and Jan.

Both were dressed in the coarse clothing and heavy sweaters of fishermen. When they shook hands, Chapman could feel their rough, callused palms.

They were taken to a small house near the coast, where they finalized the arrangements over a meal.

The older of the two, Lars, did the talking for both. "Tonight at nine we'll take our boat out and run you as close to the Danish coast as we can. We've been on this schedule for weeks, so the Germans won't bother us. We'll return to Landskrona by early morning and then back out again tomorrow night. We'll keep this schedule for as long as it takes to pick you up or until . . ." His voice trailed off and Bishop knew what he meant.

"Not to worry," Bishop said. "We'll be back soon enough." Lars shrugged and nodded without certainty, and Chapman felt that he had taken people across before.

"We can probably get you within two miles of the shoreline," said Lars. "Then if all goes well, you will switch over to a smaller Danish boat and be taken ashore. After that," he said, stuffing bread into his mouth, "I don't need to know. The return will be made the same way."

"How safe is it?" asked Chapman. "I mean, the Germans do patrol these waters?"

Lars shrugged. "We bring Jews out all the time. The Germans don't seem to care. Most of the time they look the other way. Glad to get rid of them, I suppose."

"Most of the time?" asked Bishop.

"Once in a while they decide to get tough."

Bishop nodded, pushing his plate aside. "So," he said, "what do we do now?"

Lars looked around the room at each of the expectant faces. He shrugged. "We wait."

■

Falzetti couldn't sleep. Even though he was exhausted from the events of the day, some internal mechanism prevented him from slipping off into blissful, dreamless sleep.

Krueger was in jail, Streetman was dead. There should have been the relief of a job completed. But the feeling wasn't there.

He kept seeing Streetman's mocking stare, a stare that taunted him without mercy.

He lay, fully clothed, staring at the ceiling, the memory of Streetman's last moments running through his brain over and over like some movie projecter gone berserk.

Falzetti talked to himself as though he were two persons.

What was it that FBI agent had said? He looks like he's laughing at us. He did, the bastard. I put a hole in him big enough to drive the Third Avenue El through, and he laughs at me.

Weird.

Maybe he was just a weird guy.

Everything about him was peculiar. Even the way he reacted to his own son's death. What was it the maid said? He whistled like nothing had happened. And when I told him that we'd catch whoever did it, he shrugged like he didn't care one way or the other.

And then when I blow his chest away, Falzetti continued to himself, he grins at me—at all of us—as if he's just won a victory or something. Like he's pulled something off that none of us know about.

How could anyone who has lost a son act the way this guy did? I've never seen anything like it.

Weird.

Before the thought crossed into Falzetti's conscious mind his pulse began to race and his palms had started to sweat.

"Jesus, Mary, and Joseph," he said, sitting up. "The kid is still alive."

■

The steady rhythmic putt-putting of the diesel engines of the fishing boat *Bifrost* echoed across the dark water of the Oresund, the running lights casting eerie elongated reflections as the boat headed northwest across the narrow Oresund and out toward the Kattegat.

Chapman and Bishop sat in the darkened galley while Lars and two other men were on deck. Chapman peered through the portside windows, eyes squinting in the darkness.

"He said the boat would have a faulty running light, didn't he?"

"Yes," said Bishop, who seemed uninterested.

"I don't see anything," said Chapman. "One or two other boats near the Danish side. Nothing else."

"Let me know if you see any German patrol boats," Bishop said, a smile creasing his face.

Chapman looked at him. "I must say, Major, you take all of this rather calmly. By this time tomorrow we could both be dead."

Bishop shrugged. "Not much chance of that, Chapman. By this time tomorrow we'll be on this smelly boat heading back to Sweden."

Chapman considered a reply but decided against it. He turned his attention back to the window. The lights were closer now. "I think I see it," he said.

Bishop got up and came to the window just as Lars poked his head into the cabin. "Get ready," he said. "Danish boat coming alongside."

They gathered up their gear and went up onto the deck, where they stood next to Lars near the bow. The night was cold, the air heavy with moisture that hung in a fine mist clouding vision and muffling sound. Both men tucked their coat collars under their chins. The dark shape of the approaching fishing boat was visible against the lighter sea and sky. One of the running lights flickered sporadically as if it had a faulty connection.

Lars whistled, and his engines cut to a lower register of sound. "They won't stop," he said to Bishop. "We'll both slow down, then coast past each other. You'll have to jump."

The boats veered toward each other, dark shapes bound for collision.

Lars laughed. "This is the hard part. Trying not to sink each other."

The other boat loomed closer, engines cut back, coasting almost silently.

Chapman and Bishop hopped up on the port gunwale, supporting themselves by holding on to the heavy rope rigging. They began to make out the details of the approaching boat and finally could see the men on the other deck watching them approach as intently as they themselves peered back.

The boats slid alongside each other, bumping slightly, the heavy braided rope bumpers absorbing the shock of the minor collision.

Bishop sprang first, landing on the opposite foredeck on bent legs, then straightening up as easily as if he had merely stepped off a ladder.

Chapman looked down at the sea. The gap between the ships began to widen, and the white froth of churning sea was visible below.

"C'mon," hissed Bishop through clenched teeth, and Chapman launched himself into space. He landed heavily and rolled over on the deck, then hoisted himself up, brushing at his clothes with his hands while feeling to check if he was still in one piece.

The Swedes tossed their two small bags across, and Bishop caught the first one, which he dropped onto the deck, then the other.

"Look here," said Chapman, and directed Bishop's attention to the stern, where another transfer was taking place. A man leaped from it across to the bow of the Swedish boat, jumped up and ran quickly to the side, waving wildly for someone to follow. A boy jumped into the arms of a Swedish crewman, and then, as the ships rocked closer, Danish crewman passed an infant over to the father.

Only the mother remained on the Danish ship, poised on the gunwale, one hand on a supporting rope, gathering her courage for the leap. The gap between the ships grew with each wasted moment, and the woman seemed immobilized.

They could hear her husband pleading as he walked

the length of the *Bifrost* while the two boats passed each other. "Jump, please," he urged desperately in a voice that was half cry, half whisper. "Please jump."

He reached out for her, but the boats were already too far apart. The woman's eyes were fixed on the two children in the rapidly receding bow of the Swedish boat while the father's cries became more frantic. His arms were stretched out to his wife, but even he realized that the distance was too great for her to leap.

Bishop heard Lars whistle two short piercing blasts, and in the wheelhouse the pilot swung the wheel hard right. The stern of the *Bifrost* swung left, thumping hard against the Danish ship, the two ships scraping against each other. The man grabbed his wife's hand, and she stepped from one boat to the other as easily as from sidewalk to curb.

Bishop picked up his bag. "Let's get below," he said to Chapman, but Chapman seemed not to hear. He watched the woman hug her husband, then run to her children. Until the *Bifrost* finally disappeared into the darkness, Chapman watched the family huddled together on the stern of the fishing boat, arms around each other, oblivious to the cold and the wet of the dark Swedish night.

Two men were waiting for them on the dock as the boat pulled in. Bishop waved, and one of the men returned his gesture. Both came aboard as soon as the fishing boat was tied up at the pier.

One came forward and shook hands warmly with Bishop and Chapman.

"This is Peter Swensen," said Bishop. "We are old friends."

Swensen smiled. "Yes," he said, "and this is Harold Buhl. He is one of us and will be with us until your mission is completed."

Swensen was in his middle thirties, short and with a thick shock of dark hair. His face was unlined and handsome. He might have been a graduate student but was in actuality a former captain in the Danish navy who had retired after the occupation and now ran a bicycle shop in Copenhagen by day and operated a resistance group by night. He was the man British intelligence called Hunter.

Buhl was young and blond with the kind of openly honest face that only Scandanavians can have. His eyes were bright and incredibly blue and shone with unbridled enthusiasm.

"Any problems?" asked Bishop.

Swensen smiled as though the two shared some secret. Then he slapped Bishop on the back. "So far everything is just fine. We have a safe house for you to spend the night, and then tomorrow we will go about finding your documents."

Swensen and Buhl led them off the fishing boat and up a narrow street to a truck loaded with furniture. "If the Germans stop us," he said, "we are moving furniture for a friend."

They climbed up, Chapman sat on an old sofa, and Bishop sprawled on a huge lumpy mattress as the truck pulled away down the street, gears squawking in protest with each shift. The sound echoed down the streets and into alleys and across a wider boulevard, where, in a small cafe a group of German officers entertained the young women who had danced in the revue at the club next door.

Ernst Luddeck, sitting alone at a corner table, watched the officers with disgust. They were drunk and, as far as he was concerned, had compromised the integrity of their uniforms. He was about to go over and speak to them when he heard the shrieking transmission of Buhl's truck. At once the behavior of the other officers was far from his thoughts.

The truck moved up the coast, hooded headlights casting a dim yellow glow on the road ahead.

"As soon as we get to our destination," said Bishop, "I'll want to contact Iverson." He peered at the luminous dial on his watch. "He should be waiting for our transmission now."

Chapman nodded, huddling beneath the blanket with

which he had covered himself against the chill, and looked out over the water to where he knew Sweden would be. The southern coastal area of Sweden observed a wartime blackout in order to protect the Danes from the threat of any Allied bombing raids that the Germans claimed were planned. Peering into the darkness he thought he could make out shapes against the black background. Iverson is there, he thought. Safe and sound, and glad to be out of it.

The truck stopped at a small house overlooking the narrow sound, and Bishop and Swensen went inside while Chapman prepared the S-phone. When he was ready, he couldn't resist trying to contact Iverson himself. "Hello," he said in a whisper," "RF-two, this is RF-one. Do you read me?"

"That you Chapman?" said Iverson's voice, so clearly that Chapman was startled.

"Yes," he replied. "Everything all right on your end?"

"Yes. Could you speak up a little?" asked Iverson.

"If I were in Sweden and you were in occupied Denmark, I'd speak louder too, you bastard."

Iverson laughed good-naturedly.

Bishop came out of the house and approached Chapman, who handed him the phone. "I've got him loud and clear," he said to Bishop, who eyed him suspiciously. "Better than a long distance connection."

Bishop took the phone. "Iverson, Major Bishop here. Everything all right?" He paused. "Stand by, then. We will contact you tomorrow. By this time then we hope to be back with the goods." He handed Chapman the phone, then added, "Don't muck about with the phone, Chapman. We can't afford any silly mistakes."

Five miles back down the road, Ernst Luddeck hung up the captured S-phone that had been taken from an SOE operative in France.

He smiled as he gave the phone back to his sergeant.

"Very well, Sergeant," he said. "Leave the men on guard tonight and report any suspicious movements to me. I will return to Gentofte and await their movements tomorrow. Be careful that you are not spotted and that your observers report every movement they make." He turned and walked across the road to his waiting staff car, a smile frozen on his face. Nothing displayed his authority more than the big Mercedes, engine grumbling in protest at the cold.

■

It had taken more than seven hours, from the time that Falzetti had sat up in his bed and reached for the phone to call Howard Green, to assemble the principals and acquire the court order for the exhumation of Karl Streetman's body. It was after six and already dark when the small group gathered at the gravesite, watching the two grave diggers plunge pick and shovel into the hard frozen ground in the small Long Island cemetery.

Present were Falzetti, Green, and Brownmiller, who hobbled painfully on crutches, his leg in a thigh-to-ankle cast. Also there was Green's commanding officer, Major Grogan, the G-2 on Governors Island; Major Harold Cowan of the OSS, whom Green had called immediately after talking with Falzetti; and a Dr. Lloyd Tillis of the Nassau County Coroner's Office.

A hearse stood nearby, engine running, lights on to provide illumination for the two workers. The others milled around, hands in pockets, feet moving against the cold, icy breath swirling around their faces as the two grave diggers methodically went on about their gruesome task.

As the mound of dirt grew in size so did the various apprehensions of those gathered around the grave. If this was all for nothing, Falzetti would look like a fool and Howard Green would have a lot to explain. The others had their own secret fears.

Falzetti chomped on his cigar, the others puffed furiously on cigarettes as if the small fires could somehow keep them warm.

A shovel thumped on something solid, and each of

the gathered men jumped as if he had been touched by a chilly hand. Then they made embarrassed faces and smiled at each other.

"Got it," called a voice from the open grave.

Howard Green's breathing was very shallow, and his mouth was dry. He clenched and unclenched his fists as he listened to the scraping sounds as the workers cleared away the dirt around the coffin.

Finally the workers climbed out. "You guys wanna help? We'll get it out a lot easier."

The men moved forward, taking hold of the offered ropes.

"Okay," said the grave digger who had asked for help. "Pull nice and easy and up she comes."

The men pulled on the ropes, and once the initial movement had begun, the coffin was hoisted rapidly to the surface, where they moved back and maneuvered it to solid ground.

Someone snapped on a flashlight and played the beam over the box. The brass fittings were clogged with dirt but still shone in the light.

No one said anything for a moment, each man wondering how to handle the next step.

Major Cowan spoke first. "Open it up," he said. "There's no sense carting this thing all the way back to the mortuary if it's him inside."

The others nodded in agreement, and one of the workers moved forward to the coffin. He worked his way around the latches on the top half of the coffin and in minutes was prepared to open it.

He looked up, waiting for a signal.

"Do it," said Cowan, and the man swung the lid back.

The others moved forward to see the body, but Falzetti and Howard Green stayed behind.

"Some light," said Cowan, and the light was shone directly in the dead man's face.

Cowan stiffened and actually stumbled back a pace or two. The others looked to him as if awaiting a verdict. His face was pale, his eyes were staring wide, and his breath came in short hacking gasps.

Falzetti broke the silence. "It's not Karl Streetman," he said.

Cowan shook his head back and forth as if to clear his clouded brain. "No," he said, his voice hoarse and sounding far away. "It's Andrew Chapman."

The others looked at each other, puzzlement on their faces, then turned back to Cowan hoping for some kind of explanation, but Cowan had already spun around and started running to his staff car.

38

Iverson was bored. He had not left his room since he and Paul had returned from the roof, where they had attached the B mark II's antennae to a chimney and stretched it across the length of the roof. Paul's last words before leaving had been a warning.

"Don't think that just because you are in neutral Sweden you are safe from the Germans. They have agents and sympathizers everywhere." He pointed in the direction of the Danish coast. "Because of the proximity to occupied Denmark, there are many German agents right here in Hälsingborg."

Iverson had decided not to leave the tiny cubicle to which he had been brought. It was better, he reasoned, to stay cooped up for a day and a half than to risk confrontation with Germans on the street.

But what if it took longer?

He looked around at the four bare walls. He had nothing to read and could only look from his window by climbing onto a chair. He closed his eyes and lay back on the bed. My God, he thought. I hope they get this over with quickly.

His only apparent function on this mission was to receive messages from Bishop and then to relay those messages on to London.

He had received Bishop's first message and was waiting for eleven P.M.—when the receiving station would be expecting his transmission—to dutifully relay back to London the news of the team's arrival in Denmark.

This was to be the sum total of his participation, he thought wryly. All the training and hard work had come down to preparation for receiving and relaying messages. If all went well, he would get a second message from Bishop at five P.M. saying that the mission had been successful and that they would return the next morning. He would relay that message to London at eleven and then await the arrival of Bishop and Chapman.

He looked at his watch. Ten minutes until his transmission to London. He rolled out of bed and walked to the radio, which sat on the small table beneath the window. He turned it on to let it warm up, and the radio gave a soft hum and low whistle.

He went back to lie on the bed, his mind filled with conflicting thoughts.

He found himself regretting that he and not Chapman had been left behind. He could not deny the fact that he had been relieved and happy when Bishop had given him his assignment. He felt a little guilty that he had been pleased that others would be going into mortal danger, while he would merely be waiting for them to return. He consoled himself with the thought that his expertise with the radio had made him the logical candidate to handle the mission's transmissions. He had known that all along. He hadn't known that he would be left behind. When faced with danger, he had been tense and fearful. Now that he was in comparative safety, his courage had returned and he longed to be part of the mission.

Iverson imagined the group's triumphant return to England. As they stepped from the plane a band would begin to play and soldiers would be lined up to receive them. The soldiers would cheer as they came forward and generals would salute them. Churchill would be there, and he would present Chapman and Bishop with medals and shake their hands. Then the prime minister would turn to Iverson, who was squirming in the spotlight of inattention, and say, "Someone had to watch the radio, my boy."

The radio! He sat up and directed his gaze toward the dim glow of the box on the table. Again he got up and went over to it, this time sitting down on the hard wood chair next to the table. On a pad he checked the accuracy of his coded message.

It was simple: MADSEN DEAD, PARACHUTING MISHAP. BISHOP AND CHAPMAN ARRIVED TARGET AREA. AM AWAITING FURTHER MESSAGES.

The message would take him less than thirty seconds to transmit in a simple code from what was called a one-time pad. Rather than use a complicated coding system for all missions, British intelligence had devised a limitless supply of simple codes that were meant to be used once and discarded. Both the sender and receiver had the key on a note pad. After each message the top page was torn from the pad and destroyed. The next message would be sent in the next code on the pad.

At precisely eleven P.M. Iverson flipped up the transmitting switch and began to broadcast his call letters. He waited for the expected reply, which came momentarily.

Tapping out the brief message carefully, not wishing to make any mistakes, he waited for the expected brief sign-off. The incoming message caught him by surprise, and he was not prepared to jot it down. He caught the last half of the message and had to ask London to repeat.

The message was repeated, and then the sender declared that he was STANDING BY, which meant that he would be waiting for Iverson to decode and acknowledge.

He ripped off the top page of his pad and went to page two, wondering if perhaps the message had been coded from page one. A simple job and he was botching it up. The fact that an operator was standing by waiting for his reply seemed to put additional pressure on him. He cursed himself for being this unsteady.

Finally he had the correct code and the message

began to take form. URGENT... REPEAT... URGENT ... SUSPECTED GERMAN AGENT ON MISSION ... ANDREW CHAPMAN DEAD IN NEW YORK.

Chapman dead! Why, that was ridiculous. Hadn't he just talked with him an hour ago? There must be some mistake. Then it hit him: this man who claimed to be Chapman was someone else.

Good God, he thought as his fingers fumbled over the code. Then he was tapping, PLEASE ADVISE.

URGENT... REPEAT URGENT... WARN BISHOP.

ACKNOWLEDGED... WILL COMPLY.

Another message was coming. THIS RECEIVER WILL REMAIN OPEN AT ALL TIMES FOR YOUR CONFIRMATION OF SAME.

After sign-off Iverson sat with his head in his hands. He could not contact Bishop through the S-phone. Communication was possible only at the designated hours, when both machines were prepared to receive, and if he waited to hear from him, it would be too late. His only recourse was to go to Denmark and tell Bishop himself what he had learned.

It was ten past eleven. He could not wait until morning, he had to make the crossing tonight. But how? He would have to get the old man to make contact with someone who could get him across while it was still dark.

He got up. If I have to, he thought, I'll swim.

He closed the door behind him, leaving everything where it was, and went down the stairs. The door at the foot of the stairs that led into the store was locked, obviously to prevent any of the tenants who lived in the building from going inside after hours. The old man had to be inside. Iverson pounded on the door, reluctantly at first but with increased intensity.

There was no answer.

He pounded again.

Someone on the second floor opened a door and called down. "What's going on down there—it's almost midnight."

"The old man, Torkillus," yelled Iverson. "Where is he?"

"He lives on Kyrkogatan, number eleven," said the voice and slammed the door.

Iverson raced back upstairs, grabbed his coat, took his revolver from under his pillow, and put it in his pocket. He locked the door and ran back down the stairs and out the door into an alley behind the building. He looked right and left to get his bearings. Right was a dead end, a stone wall that separated the building from a structure on the other side; left led to the street.

Pulling up his collar and holding his coat closed, Iverson headed toward the street. When he was almost at the end of the alley, a form stepped out of the darkness, blocking his path.

The man spoke in English. "Good evening," he said, standing ten paces in front of Iverson.

Iverson stopped, his hand slipping into his pocket, fingers curling around the handle of the pistol.

The man, his face and form, shrouded in darkness, spoke again. His accent was heavily German, which he made no effort to disguise. "It is a lovely evening for a walk, isn't it?"

Iverson struggled to steady his breathing. So far the man had said nothing menacing but his manner was somehow threatening. "*Förlåt*," Iverson said, "*Jag förstår inte*."

"You don't understand?" said the faceless voice. "Are you quite sure?"

Slowly Iverson began to withdraw the pistol from his pocket.

"Perhaps," said the voice, "you will understand that there is a man behind you, armed with a machine pistol.

Iverson's head jerked back over his shoulder. In the shadows behind him he saw a figure standing against the brick wall.

"His orders are to shoot you if you draw your weapon. I hope that that won't be necessary now that we know you speak English."

"What do you want?" asked Iverson.

"I want you to place your hands on top of your head and walk toward me . . . very slowly."

"I remind you that we are in a neutral country."

The voice chuckled. "I need no reminder. May I remind you that our countries are engaged in a struggle to the death? If you do not comply with my request, we will leave you dead in this alley."

Iverson put his hands on his head and approached the figure. Another figure appeared out of the darkness, pointing a pistol at his chest. Iverson gulped; there were three of them. He was searched roughly and his pistol removed from his pocket.

The first man watched all of this without speaking. He lit a cigarette and in the flaming match, Iverson saw him for the first time. The man had a flabby face, with fat cheeks and multiple chins. The eyes were bulbous and seemed to look in different directions. He felt Iverson's eyes on him and looked up from his cigarette.

"I'm sorry," he said. "Would you like a cigarette?"

Iverson shook his head.

The man shrugged. "As you wish," he said, then turned and began to walk away. "Bring him," he called over his shoulder, and Iverson was pushed forward, forced to follow the figure disappearing down the alley.

At the intersection the man stopped, then raised a hand. An engine roared to life, and in seconds a car pulled up, blocking the alley. The man climbed in and left the door open for Iverson, who was shoved inside. One of the others climbed in beside him so that Iverson sat between the two. The other man got in next to the driver.

"Where are you taking me?" said Iverson, his voice quivering but strong.

The fat man, who had been gazing out the window, turned to look at him but said nothing.

Iverson's voice grew more demanding. "I insist that you tell me where I am being taken.

The fat man spoke in German for the first time. "Make him shut up," he said to the man on the other side of Iverson.

The man drove an elbow into Iverson's midsection, doubling him over, then grabbed his hair and jerked his face back and smashed a fist into his nose. Iverson slumped back in the seat, blood streaming from his nose, running onto his shirt.

The fat man turned back to the window, puffing casually on his cigarette. "No more questions, please," he said softly. "Soon there will be plenty of time for questions." He patted Iverson on the knee as if the two were old friends. "I hope you have some answers, my friend." He shook his head sadly. "If not, I'm afraid things will be most unpleasant for you."

39

Karl Streetman sat quietly, his eyes never leaving Major Bishop, who was busily engaged in filling his pipe with some tobacco he had discovered in the kitchen.

They both sat in large, overstuffed chairs, one on either side of a fireplace in the room that served as the living, dining,and sleeping room of the small cottage to which they had been brought. Through a door to the left was a small kitchen, and above them, reached by ladder, was a sleeping loft.

Streetman looked around the cottage, enjoying the smell of the burning wood and the pleasant aroma of Bishop's tobacco. He felt a vague twinge of sadness at what this mission had come to. Madsen was already dead so he no longer had to worry about the brooding and dangerous Dane. That thought brought him great relief. Madsen would have been a real problem. The Dane had displayed an instinctive animosity toward him, thought Karl Streetman, as if he had sensed the presence of a predator.

Iverson was, for the moment, safely ensconced in neutral Sweden. Streetman would have to think about what to do with him. Although Karl Streetman personally liked the Canadian, he could see through the man's inherent weakness. Iverson was brave and his instincts were good, but he lacked the strength of will that drove a man beyond mere courage. Iverson served because it was compulsory to do so. He couldn't wait for all of this to be over so that he could get back to whatever it was he had done before the war.

For Karl Streetman, what he had done before the war was insignificant, what he would do after was meaningless.

He looked again at Bishop. Karl Streetman's feelings toward Bishop were increasingly ambiguous. Bishop was British, and since childhood Karl Streetman had been taught to think of the British as the muck beneath his feet. But, somehow, Bishop did not seem like the villains he had pictured all his life. Then he thought of his father and the terrible stories that he had told him about men who were probably a lot like Bishop. He owed it to his father to carry out this mission. His pulse quickened when he thought how proud his father would be when the Führer pinned the Knight's Cross to his uniform.

"I think you should know, Chapman," said Bishop, puffing on his pipe as he tried to get it started, "that there is a very real possibility that the Germans know we are here."

Streetman was jerked from his reverie, his eyes widening in surprise. "How?" he asked, unable to believe that Bishop could be so calm if such a thing were true.

Elbow on the arm of the chair, Bishop rested his chin on his fist. When he spoke, Streetman could tell that he was choosing his words carefully so as not to reveal more than he had to. "I want you to know that my reluctance to tell you everything about this mission has nothing to do with a lack of trust," said Bishop, pausing to let his companion take this in. "It's only that, in the event of capture—the less you know the better."

Streetman nodded. "I understand that. But what about you?"

Bishop shrugged. "If we are captured and there is no possibility of escape, your job will be to see that the

Germans don't take me alive." He looked directly into Streetman's eyes. "Do you think you can do that?"

Streetman looked away. "I'm not sure—how am I to determine that there is no possibility of escape."

"Once we are in their grasp, there will be no possibility of escape . . . Can you do it?"

Streetman, unable to meet Bishop's steady gaze, kept his eyes on the fire. "If I have to," he mumbled, "yes."

Bishop smiled. He reached into his shirt breast pocket. "Not to worry," he said, removing a small capsule, which he held between thumb and forefinger. "Cyanide," he said, his smile becoming more forced. "If things look bad, I simply take one little nip of this—and our troubles are over."

"Could you do that?" said Streetman incredulously.

Bishop, equally incredulous at such a question, replied, "Absolutely. I assure you that if the Germans capture us, we will be dead within twenty-four hours. They will torture us to find out what we know before they kill us. I'd prefer to go out quickly, thank you."

"Maybe you should shoot me, before you take your capsule," said Streetman, trying to inject some humor into the grisly conversation.

Bishop never cracked a smile. "If you like," he said.

Streetman fixed him in a stare. "No thanks," he said. "I'll take my chances with the Germans."

Bishop shrugged. "As you prefer."

They sat without speaking for a moment. A shroudlike silence had enveloped them. Finally Streetman spoke. "Now maybe you'd like to tell me what makes you think that the Germans know we're here."

Before answering, Bishop checked his pipe. It had gone out again. He struck a match and held it to the pipe, drawing deep draughts into the bowl until the tobacco glowed bright red. "These documents that we are going after, as I'm sure you must have gathered, are"—he paused while he considered the right phrase—"extremely important. The Germans would give anything to have them."

"That," Streetman said, "is rather obvious."

"Very few people know of the existence of these documents and even fewer know their precise location."

"That still doesn't tell me how the Germans know that we are here."

"I'm coming to that. First we know that they are aware of the existence of the documents because the resistance has reported to us that German troops searching for something have practically demolished the homes and laboratories of the two scientists involved."

"How do we know that they haven't already found these documents?"

"Because for the past two months they've been trying to make us believe that they have found them."

Streetman's face wore a puzzled expression, and Bishop went on. "They've been leaking bits and pieces of information through various intelligence sources, trying to convince us that they've found the documents."

"But we don't believe them?"

"We can't take the chance of believing or not believing. We have no choice but to attempt recovery."

"Even though the Germans might already have discovered their location?"

Bishop smiled, his eyes staring into the fireplace as if he could read signs in the flickering flames. He thought carefully for a moment, then said, "An unusually reliable source, high within German intelligence circles, has reported to London that the Germans are looking for some very valuable documents here in Denmark. London feels reasonably certain that we're all after the same thing."

Streetman was quiet. The flames licked around the base of the glowing coal chunks.

"Putting these two facts together," Bishop went on, "we assume that the Germans know of the existence of the documents and their importance and are actively trying to find them."

Streetman sighed. "How do they know *we* are here?"

"The resistance," said Bishop with a shrug, as if that explained everything.

"The resistance?"

"Yes. We have known for some time that the Germans have infiltrated certain units of the Danish resistance—just as they have infiltrated most other resistance groups." He puffed on his pipe and said casually, "The people who brought us here are working with the Germans." He paused. "At least the Germans think they are."

Streetman's jaw fell, his mouth hanging open. Finally he sprang to his feet. "You mean the Germans know we're here—right now? They know we're in this house?"

"I suppose so. One can't be sure, of course, but I imagine they've got the place surrounded."

Streetman raced to the window, pulling back the curtains, peering into the night.

"You won't see them out there," said Bishop, chuckling. "They're probably a mile or so down the road."

Streetman turned back to look at Bishop. "If they've got us surrounded, why don't they just move in and pick us up?"

"Why? Torture is such a messy business. And even though the Germans are exceptionally talented in that area, sometimes people die before they can divulge their secrets. The Germans would much rather we lead them to what they want. Then they will move in."

Streetman was mystified. "But if they will be following us—how can we get the documents and then get away?"

Bishop puffed rapidly, sending small clouds of smoke to the ceiling. "We'll just have to lose them before we make the pickup."

Streetman waited for more, unwilling to believe that this was the totality of Bishop's plan.

"Afterward," said Bishop, smiling mischievously, "I suppose we'll just have to run like hell." He seemed to be enjoying Streetman's discomfort.

After a moment of silence while Streetman waited for Bishop to tell him that this was all a joke, Bishop reached down for the duffle bag that lay beside his chair. He rummaged inside, looking for something.

"I doubt if I'll get much sleep tonight," said Streetman. "After listening to your plan I feel like a doomed man."

"Not to worry," said Bishop, extracting a Sten gun from his bag. "We'll be all right."

He slipped a magazine clip into the side of the weapon and held it up for a close inspection. The Sten gun was a crude and overly simple submachine gun that looked like a metal tube with a trigger. A single rod, bent to shape, formed the shoulder stock, which could be hinged to swing out of the way for concealment. Cheaply produced, the weapon was efficient and reasonably reliable but looked somewhat like the creation of a demented child.

"Check the magazines," said Bishop. "Sometimes the loaders put in too many cartridges."

Streetman reached inside the bag and, after feeling around, removed four magazines.

"It'll hold thirty-two rounds," said Bishop. "But unless you want to worry about jamming, I'd make sure they're no more than twenty-nine or thirty."

"I know that," said Streetman glumly, pulling the Sten from his bag.

"Just checking," said Bishop, smiling with the face of a child who is having a great deal of fun at the expense of a playmate.

"If we have to use these damn things," said Streetman, "we'll really be in a fix."

Bishop reached into his bag and pulled out the Enfield Mk II revolver. He twirled the revolver cowboy style. "This may be more to your style, Yank."

Streetman gave him a vicious look, but Bishop chuckled and continued to twirl the Enfield. "I'm beginning to think," said Streetman, "that you're crazy. I'm beginning to think that everybody is crazy."

40

"You are being very foolish," said the fat man. "If you'll just tell us what we want to know, all of this unpleasantness can be over with."

Iverson struggled to laugh in the fat man's face. His own face was a mass of dark purple bruises and bright red blotches. His left eye was swollen shut, his nose was broken, and most of his front teeth had been knocked loose. His attempted laugh sounded more like a gasping cough.

Iverson was seated in a wooden chair in a small, bare room in a house on the outskirts of Hälsingborg. His arms were tied, at the wrists and elbows, to the arms of the chair.

"Look," said the fat man, "we know you have been sent here to pick up Professor Bohr's papers. We just want you to tell us where they have been hidden."

"Then you know more than I do," Iverson mumbled through swollen lips.

"Tell us the names of the men who came with you."

"Can't remember," said Iverson, bracing himself for the blow that came every time he had given that answer.

His head snapped back from the force of the fist slammed into his face, but his face, so numbed from previous blows, felt very little pain, only a vague throb that seemed like the prodding of heavy fingers.

Iverson groaned obligingly, sensing somehow that his captors would be more satisfied with what they had done if he demonstrated how efficient they had been. He slumped back in the chair, his one good eye focusing on the man who had been assigned the task of beating him. Iverson had heard the so-far-nameless fat man call the other man Max.

The fat man stood off to one side, munching on chocolates that he had in a small paper bag. A soft, almost sympathetic smile played about his mouth, but his eyes were dark and cold. Max stood in front of Iverson. He was almost a full head taller than his obese companion, and his face, dark and brutish, betrayed no hint of remorse or even of pleasure. It was a job, like many other similar jobs.

"This is such foolishness," said the fat man. "Right now at this very moment your friends are in a small cottage near Gentofte. Unknown to them, they are presently surrounded by units of the German security police. By morning they will be in the hands of the SS. Your refusal to tell us their names and where they are going is totally meaningless.

Iverson shifted his gaze and struggled to focus on the fat man. "So why ask?" he said, forcing the words past battered teeth and swollen lips.

The fat man's face hardened. "Because I want you to tell me . . . Now!"

"Don't know," mumbled Iverson, and Max drew back his fist to hit him again. Iverson thought that it was somehow funny that the man who beat him had put on a heavy leather glove to protect his knuckles from the pounding of Iverson's face. It reminded him of an old joke, but he couldn't remember how it went.

He waited for the blow, but it didn't come. He looked up and saw that the fat man held Max's arm. They were both looking at him. "Perhaps enough of this," said the fat man sympathetically, and Iverson felt the joy of relief surge through his veins. Now maybe they would just let him sleep.

"Perhaps it's time for more drastic measures," said the fat man. He turned to the brute with the glove. "Didn't I see a small axe near the woodpile?"

Max smiled and nodded, then looked at Iverson. He shook his head sadly as if he were suddenly sorry for this pitiful creature in front of him.

Max left, and the fat man leaned forward, hands on knees, to peer into Iverson's bloody face. "I'm really quite sorry about this uncivilized behavior, Lieutenant Iverson. I'm really quite fond of you English, you know. I lived in London for a number of years before the war."

Iverson tried to spit in the fat man's face but only succeeded in dribbling blood down his chin and onto his shirt.

"I'm afraid that now we are going to hurt you very badly," the fat man went on. "And it's so foolish. Eventually you will talk, so why not do it now before I have to do something I don't want to do?"

Max returned and Iverson could not stop himself from looking at the axe in his hand. It was a small hatchet, the kind used for splitting kindling, but the blade was gleaming sharp.

The fat man let Iverson stare at the axe for a moment. He knew the value of intimidation. He blew his nose loudly into his handkerchief. "Nasty cold," he said to Iverson as if the Canadian might care about the state of the German's health. "Now," he said, "I want you to tell me who and where your friends are, where Professor Bohr's papers are, and when your friends intend to pick them up."

"I don't know," said Iverson. "My job was merely to handle the radio. There was no need for me to know anything else."

"I hope that isn't true," the fat man said. "I'd hate to have you go through all this suffering for nothing." He turned to his companion. "Max, I'm afraid it's time for the axe."

Iverson, his one good eye fixed on the blade, began struggling violently in his chair. The fat man slapped him hard across the face. It was the first time the fat man had struck him.

"We will assume that you are right-handed and begin with the fingers of the left hand." The fat man knew from long experience in this kind of interrogation that if a man's dominant hand was rendered useless, he sometimes refused to cooperate because he thought his life was over anyway. But if his other hand was ruined and his dominant hand then was threatened, he would often talk. The fat man was beginning to think that this one really didn't know anything. He motioned to Max who raised the axe over his head. Soon, he thought, he would find out.

Iverson curled the fingers of his left hand into a tight fist and struggled against the bonds that secured his wrist to the chair arm. His face was screwed into a horrible grimace in expectation of pain beyond belief, his eye fixed on Max's raised arm and the axe poised over his head.

He sensed a movement and closed his eye as Max grunted into the force of the blow. The pain shot through Iverson's arm with electric intensity as Max dealt the back of his hand a crushing blow with the blunt end of the axe just below the knuckles.

Iverson screamed and passed out.

He was awakened by the excruciating pain as Max straightened out the fingers from beneath his fist. The fingers seemed limp and useless. Max laid them out on the chair arm like sausages in a butcher's window.

Iverson tried to curl them under his broken hand in an absurd attempt at concealment, but the fingers would not move, and the effort was horrifically painful.

"I give you one last chance to save yourself," said the fat man as Max raised the axe over his head. "Tell me something and perhaps I can stop this madness."

"I'll tell you something," said Iverson, his voice wracked with sobs.

The fat man smiled and moved closer. "Yes?"

"Hitler eats shit," said Iverson, managing a facsimile of a spit.

With a sigh the fat man signaled to Max, who prepared to drop the sharpened end of the axe on Iverson's fingers.

Iverson closed his eyes and tried to transport himself to some other place. He waited for the pain.

Then there was a sound of confused noise in the other room, doors slamming, voices shouting. Max hesitated, looking toward the door, as the fat man drew his Luger from his coat.

A shot rang out from outside the house, a window shattered, and Max clutched at his throat with his left hand, his right hand still poised over his head holding the axe, before he slumped to the floor.

The door was kicked in, and the fat man fired wildly. Automatic weapons' fire burst out, and the fat man went flying against the far wall, hesitated for a moment, then slid down.

Iverson sat uncomprehendingly, strapped to his chair, while the chaos suddenly burst around him and just as suddenly stopped. In seconds it was over, and the strange magnified silence that follows explosive noise enveloped the room. Hands were loosening his bonds, and a face peered close to his. "Iverson." said the voice. "Are you all right?"

Iverson struggled to focus on the face in front of him. It looked vaguely familiar, but that was impossible. His mind refused to accept the existence of the face in front of him. It was the face of a dead man.

"Am I dead too?" asked Iverson. "Did they kill me?"

"No," said Madsen. "You're not dead."

"Then what are you doing here?"

"Don't worry about that," Madsen said. "Did you tell them anything?"

"No," he answered simply.

"Good man," said Madsen.

Iverson laughed grotesquely. "I don't know anything," he said. "If I did, I would have told them."

Madsen looked around the shattered room. Max lay dead at Iverson's feet. Against the far wall the fat man slumped, his hands on his blood-soaked belly, his eyes empty, his breathing tortured. The Luger lay just beyond his reach.

Madsen motioned to the two armed men he had with him. "Let's get Iverson out of here," he said and they came forward to help lift Iverson from the chair.

"I've got to tell you something," Iverson whispered to Madsen.

"It can wait until we get you fixed up."

"No, no," said Iverson, resisting the hands that tried to lift him, a note of desperation creeping into his mangled speech. "It's important. I must tell you now."

Madsen nodded and leaned forward, his ear close to Iverson's lips.

"Message from London . . . received at eleven . . . Chapman is a German agent . . . Must warn Bishop."

Madsen recoiled. "Are you certain?"

Iverson nodded. "Positive."

Madsen turned to one of the others. "Can you get me back in there?"

The man shrugged. "It will be very difficult to get back before morning."

"It's imperative. The whole operation depends on it."

The man smiled resignedly. "Then we'd better try."

"Can one of your men get Iverson to a hospital?"

"Yes."

Iverson had paid no attention to this conversation. He had noticed that the fat man was still alive, his labored breathing making short raspy sounds as his great belly rose and fell.

"Madsen?" said Iverson without taking his eyes off the German.

"Yes?"

"Give me your pistol, please."

Madsen followed Iverson's stare over to the wall where the fat man sat. He thought for a moment, then picked up the Luger. He adjusted the sights for short range. "Here," he said, "use this."

Iverson steadied his arm on the chair and, resting his head on his arm, sighted down the long barrel until the fat man's wide open eyes were on either side of the high sight. He squeezed the trigger, and the fat man's head slammed back against the wall. A small hole had appeared in the center of his forehead.

41

For some it would be the last morning.

"Let's go," said Bishop, gently shaking the man he thought was Andrew Chapman. "It's time to get moving."

Streetman sat up quickly in the chair he had slept in, startled by the sound and the touch. He looked sheepishly at Bishop, embarrassed by his apparent skittishness. "What time is it?" he asked, his voice too loud.

Bishop smiled, thinking that he understood. He looked at his watch. "Almost seven," he said. "Three hours and it should be all over."

"Yes," said Streetman grimly as he stood up and stretched his arms to the ceiling. "Soon it will be over."

He went to the window, parting the curtains to look

out at the morning. The sky was an impenetrable blanket of gray, and a slight breeze off the Oresund swirled pockets of fog low to the ground. Visibility was no more than fifty yards in any direction.

A good day for dying, thought Streetman, looking back at Bishop, who busied himself with a frying pan and some eggs. Streetman thought of the condemned man preparing his own last meal.

While Streetman washed his face in a basin, Bishop put the eggs on plates and brought them to the small table. "As soon as Swensen and Buhl get here," he said, talking to Streetman's back, "we leave."

"How will they get us past the Germans?" asked Streetman. "If they do happen to be out there."

"Buhl is a delivery man—milk and eggs and cheese. He picks up fresh milk and eggs from the farmers every morning and delivers them to Copenhagen before the stores open. The Germans see him every day. Besides, they could have picked us up last night if they wanted to—they want us to lead them to the documents. They won't bother us."

"And if they do?"

Bishop shrugged. "Make sure your Sten is in proper working order."

They ate in silence, without conversation, Bishop engrossed in a map of Copenhagen, Streetman in brooding silence. Almost exactly at seven, a truck pulled up outside, and both men looked expectantly at each other.

"That's it," said Bishop.

Swensen knocked and entered quickly. "Cold, this morning," he said, rubbing his hands together. "Are we ready?"

"In a minute," said Bishop, pushing his seat back. His eyes went to the door. "Can we trust your man, Buhl?"

Swensen's face darkened, and for a moment Streetman thought that Swensen might strike at Bishop. But it passed. "The Germans killed his father in 1940," said Swensen with a shrug. "He was my sister's husband. I think you can trust him." He smiled. "He helped me get Bohr out of the country."

"How about the rest of your people?"

Swensen's head shook slowly back and forth. "The Hunter group has been badly infiltrated. There are only a few that I can count on."

Bishop turned to Streetman. "The Germans think that Peter is working for them. When this is over, he goes back to England with us."

"Buhl, too," said Swensen. "He's a dead man if he stays."

Streetman nodded but said nothing. None of these men will see England, he thought.

"We'd better hurry," said Swensen. "The Germans will follow us at a safe distance. But don't worry, we have devised a method to elude them for a while."

Bishop stood up. Using the strap, he hung the Sten gun over his right shoulder and let it hang down at his side. With the stock folded, it fit neatly under his arm. He then pulled on his coat, concealing the presence of the weapon. He threw a haversack over his left shoulder and filled his pockets with extra clips for the Sten.

Streetman did the same.

"I think that about does it," said Bishop.

"All set," said Streetman, falling in behind Swensen and Bishop as they went to the door.

Outside, the chill was even more penetrating, the icy fog slithering around their legs as they walked quickly to the truck. As they approached, the engine sprang to life, sputtered, almost died, then roared defiantly.

Swensen pulled back a canvas flap, and Bishop and Streetman climbed aboard. In the back of the truck they sat down behind a row of tall milk containers and made themselves as comfortable as possible for the ride to Copenhagen.

"What if the Germans decide not to go along with Swensen's plan?" asked Streetman in a whisper.

"We'll know in just a few minutes if they decide to stop us. If they do, take out as many as you can. Forget about surrender. They'll shoot us anyway."

The trip was uncomfortable but uneventful.

The truck stopped outside a brick, two-story building on a narrow street, and Swensen came around to the back and pulled back the canvas cover.

"All clear," he said as he pulled out a milk container. Buhl joined him, and they emptied the truck, stacking the containers in the street.

Swensen went to the door of the brick building and pounded on the door, which opened almost immediately. He waved to Buhl, who signaled to the two in the truck to climb out.

Swensen came back to the truck, and each of the four men lifted a milk container and carried it inside. Once inside they could hear the clatter of empty glass bottles bouncing against each other.

They followed Swensen up a flight of stairs and out onto a catwalk, where they looked out over the entire lower floor of the building. Bottles in cases moved on metal rollers, pushed along from station to station by workers wearing white smocks. Dominating the scene was a large tank that was almost as tall as the building itself.

Swensen led them to the tank, where a man wearing a white coat and holding a clipboard waited for them. As they approached he opened a hatch, and Swensen hoisted his container up to the opening and poured the contents inside.

The man made a check mark on his sheet.

The other three followed suit, pouring the milk into the tank, each rewarded with a check mark.

Back across the catwalk they went, Swensen in the lead. At the end, instead of turning right to the stairs, he turned left and went through a doorway into a small room stacked with milk crates. Four men waited inside.

"Give them your coats," he ordered and the others quickly slipped off their outerwear and handed it to the four men. The men put on the coats, relieved the four of the empty milk containers and, single file, the one wearing Swensen's coat in the lead, went back out onto the catwalk, down the stairs and out to the truck.

"We wait," said Swensen. He pointed to the four coats hanging on a wall rack, and they busied themselves with finding the best fit.

The replacements brought in the rest of the milk

while the four waited, sitting on milk crates in the small room.

Swensen, who watched by the door, counted each trip that was made to the tank. "That was their last trip," he said. "Soon we can go."

Even inside the room and above the clattering bottles, they heard the engine roar on the old truck and the noise diminish as it pulled away.

After a few minutes, Swensen nodded. "Let's go," he said.

He led them down the stairs and across the work floor. Not one worker looked up. It was as if these four were invisible. They exited through a side door, out onto an alley, and walked quickly out onto the main street.

"Here we separate," said Swensen. "The Germans will be suspicious if we travel in a group. Bishop, you come with me. Chapman, you go with Buhl. Where we are going is only a few minutes walk from here. If you see any German soldiers, ignore them. If they ask for identification, use the papers you have with you. Do not, for any reason, draw attention to yourselves."

Streetman chimed in. "And what if they decide to detain us?"

Swensen looked at Bishop, who patted the weapon inside his coat. "Kill them and disappear if you can. Split up and make your way back to the cottage if anything goes wrong. We cross back into Sweden tonight."

Streetman nodded and they parted, Swensen leading Bishop off to the right, Buhl heading across the street with Streetman following at his side.

By this hour, the morning sun had burned off the fog, and the day had become bright. Buhl and Streetman crossed another cobblestone street and turned a corner. Streetman drew in his breath sharply when he saw the German truck and five soldiers lounging outside a bakery.

"Not to worry," whispered Buhl. "Act naturally and they won't bother us."

As they moved past, Streetman saw that their officer

was inside the bakery, conducting an animated conversation with a man behind the counter.

Disregarding Swensen's orders not to draw attention to himself, Streetman stared closely into the faces of the German troops. The men were security police of the Waffen SS and wore standard German army uniforms, but Streetman was somewhat dismayed to notice what was to him a disturbing lack of uniformity in the dress of the soldiers. He had been told many times that the German war machine was crumbling and was unable to produce the materials necessary to fuel a modern fighting machine. It had been said that even the clothing manufacturers were unable to provide the necessary attire to uniformly clothe the German soldier. He had dismissed most of these stories as propaganda designed to bolster Allied morale, but his first view of German troops shockingly confirmed what he had heard.

Even the headgear showed a certain disarray. Three of the five wore the standard field cap, but one wore the old, discontinued side cap, and the fifth wore the peaked mountain cap issued to mountain troops.

Only one of the five carried a weapon—the Mauser 98k rifle. Two other rifles rested against the truck. The remaining two soldiers were either unarmed or had elected to leave their weapons inside the truck.

In dress and attitude the soldiers were, to Streetman's dismay, more slovenly than menacing. He could easily have cut all five down with his Sten before they had any inkling of what had happened.

One of the soldiers noticed Streetman's stare, and his face hardened into a look of arrogance that challenged Streetman to look away or face the consequences. But when he did not, the German merely turned back to his comrades without so much as a second glance in Streetman's direction.

Streetman and Buhl walked on past the small cluster of soldiers, and Streetman's shoulders slumped with the realization that these troops, although still masters of Europe, had the air of defeat about them. Perhaps, he thought hopefully, these are merely garrison troops and not up to the caliber of the fighting divisions in France and Belgium. They were certainly not the German supermen that his father had told him about.

He could not resist looking back over his shoulder at this motley crew slouched on the sidewalk, and he wondered why he and Buhl had not been challenged.

"What are you doing?" Buhl hissed. "Don't draw attention to yourself."

"They don't look so fearsome," said Streetman as they continued moving away from the Germans.

"There isn't much for them to do here," said Buhl. "But don't worry, if provoked they can get very nasty."

They crossed a wide boulevard lined with shops and apartments. At one end a domed church dominated the view. Buhl picked up his pace a little, turning down into a narrower street with three-story brick buildings on either side. Gradually the neighborhood grew shabbier, the buildings in various states of disrepair.

"Won't be long now," said Buhl.

They came to a corner and Buhl held up his hand. Streetman stopped beside him. "There," he said, pointing to what appeared to be an abandoned building.

Streetman looked. The building was of red brick and had a row of windows at street level. The glass was either dirty or translucent, and several of the panes were broken. There was a large, double-doored gate at the front, obviously to allow large vehicles to pass inside, and on the right half of the gate was a normal-sized door. A faded, painted sign proclaimed simply Municipal Storage.

As Streetman and Buhl watched, Bishop and Swensen appeared from around the corner at the other end of the street. They walked slowly toward the warehouse, talking as if they were two strollers on holiday, and Streetman marveled at Bishop's composure. When they reached the double doors, Swensen produced a key and opened the small door. Both disappeared inside.

"Let's go," said Buhl, and he and Streetman headed for the warehouse.

At any moment Streetman expected to hear the roar of an armored vehicle and to see German troops flood the area, but it was not to be. The street remained eerily quiet. Once inside they bolted the door, and then they were greeted by the first two.

"Any problems?" asked Bishop.

Streetman shook his head.

Buhl chimed in. "Walked through a detachment of Sipo outside Lippman's Bakery.

Swensen chuckled. "Having breakfast at old man Lippman's expense, no doubt."

"But no one followed you?"

"Positive," said Buhl. "We doubled back several times."

Streetman looked around. The warehouse, except for some crates on the floor, seemed deserted. Empty racks lined the walls.

Swensen saw his look. "This was once a garage used to store trucks, tires, repair equipment, and automotive supplies for the city." He shrugged. "The Germans took everything. Now there is nothing left."

The front half of the building was open from the floor to the second-story roof, but the back was split into two floors, a stairway at the side leading up to what appeared to be offices on the second floor.

"Escape route ready?" asked Bishop.

"Yes, the manhole cover is in one of the back rooms. I just left some cardboard boxes over it yesterday in case anyone happened to come in here."

Bishop chuckled, and the two smiled knowingly at each other as if sharing some private joke.

"Escape route?" asked Streetman mystified.

"Yes. This place is over the sewer line. If Gerry happens by, we can leave by the sewer and come up several blocks away."

Swensen smiled. "The truck will be waiting for us. Parked over the manhole cover."

Bishop pointed to Buhl and Streetman. "Chapman, cover the door with Buhl, just in case we have unexpected company. Swensen and I will get the documents."

Streetman pulled off his coat, revealing the Sten dangling from his shoulder. "Okay," he said to Buhl, "let's do it."

Bishop gave his weapon to Buhl, who followed Streetman to the front gate. They stood on either side of the double doors watching the street through the broken panes. Every few seconds Streetman turned his attention back to Bishop and Swensen, who were making their way up the stairs to the second floor. He waited until they had disappeared into the hallway at the top of the stairs, then called quietly to Buhl, "I have to see Bishop," he said. "I'll be right back."

Buhl looked at him strangely but said nothing as Streetman moved quickly away from his post and toward the stairs.

Streetman went up the stairs two at a time, careful not to make any noise. At the top he found himself looking down a short hallway, which was blocked from the view of anyone on the lower level. He moved stealthily down the hall, following the murmur of voices, his rubber-soled boots padding softly on the bare floor.

He paused outside the door that was ajar, listening carefully, then peered inside.

Both men had their backs to the door, Bishop moving cardboard boxes, Swensen holding a flashlight and aiming the beam at a stack of similar boxes on the floor. The boxes were open at the top and apparently crammed with papers, but Bishop methodically set one box after another aside. He knew what he was looking for.

Bishop gave a sound of triumph and hoisted one of the boxes onto a wood crate. "This the one?" he asked Swensen.

Swensen hesitated, letting the flashlight beam sweep across the box. "I marked it on the corner," he said, looking carefully. "Yes," he said as the light hit whatever small mark he had left on the box, "this is the one."

Streetman lifted the Sten gun to waist level and prepared to kick in the door.

Bishop rummaged quickly through the papers in the box and pulled out a well-worn leather folder. He examined the folder, his eyes shining, an expectant smile growing on his lips.

"That's it," said Swensen.

Streetman shifted his weight and took a deep breath as he poised to plunge into the room.

Bishop opened the folder, unfastening the thin ribbon that held it closed. He reached inside. Streetman started to move.

The folder was empty.

Streetman's face registered his dismay, but Bishop seemed unperturbed that the object of his mission had disappeared.

Bishop slipped his haversack from his shoulder, reached inside and removed a small, slim package. He unwrapped the package to reveal a thin stack of lined paper, held it up for a brief inspection, then slipped the paper inside the folder, which he resealed and then put back into the cardboard box. He placed the box on the floor again and put another on top.

"That should do it," said Bishop, smiling gleefully into the glare of the flashlight.

Swensen nodded and impulsively shook Bishop's hand. "Let's go," he said, shining the light on his watch. "The Germans will be here soon."

Streetman backed quickly down the hallway, prepared to fire if either of the two men emerged from the office before he made it to the stairs. His mind was racing, his heart pounding, his thoughts a shambles. They had come to recover important documents. But there had been nothing. Instead of being devastated at this discovery, Bishop had placed some kind of papers in the leather folder and left them behind. And they knew that the Germans were coming!

Streetman's brain was a jumble of confusion. Conflicting signals ran through him. Kill them now! said one voice. Wait! said another. He broke out in a sweat, hands damp and clammy on the Sten gun.

What has happened? He shrieked silently. The mission had been turned upside down. They had come to bring something back, not to leave something behind. He wished that someone could tell him what to do.

"Quickly," he heard Buhl yell as he reached the ground floor. "Get over here quickly."

Streetman ran to the door. "What is it?"

Buhl raised himself from a crouch and peered through one of the broken panes. "Armored cars at both ends of the street."

Streetman looked through an empty windowpane. The brutish, gray-colored, half-track vehicles that the Germans used to transport personnel, blocked any chance of exit. Both vehicles bristled with heavy machine guns.

At one end of the street, Streetman saw an officer signal to someone and knew that soldiers must be working their way down the street on his side, out of his line of sight.

Buhl nodded. He knew it, too.

Coming down the stairs, Bishop and Swensen saw the intensity on the faces of the two men at the door. "What is it?" said Bishop.

Buhl turned to face him. "Germans," he whispered. "Armored cars blocking the street. Troops working their way down this side."

"They're early," said Bishop, and Swensen shrugged helplessly as if to say that he was sorry.

Bishop ran to the windows and looked out. "Probably coming down both sides," he said. "Hold them for five minutes while we get the escape route ready. If they get in before we get out, we've had it."

Buhl nodded, and Streetman watched as Bishop moved quickly back to join Swensen. Then both men disappeared into the darkness at the back of the warehouse.

"Hope they come back for us," said Streetman warily.

Buhl smiled, full of boyish confidence. "Don't worry. I know the way out."

Streetman turned again, peering into the dark, empty space behind them, but he could see nothing, and Buhl had to slap him on the arm to get his attention.

"When I say 'go,' open the door quickly," Buhl said. He checked the Sten, thumping the magazine with his palm to make sure it was properly inserted. Then he took two deep breaths, his face set in a grim smile, and nodded to Streetman. "Go," he said softly.

Ernst Luddeck watched from the end of the street, standing next to the armored half-track vehicle he used as a command post. He had deployed an identical vehicle at the other end of the street and six men with a heavy machine gun and MP43 automatic carbines at the rear of the warehouse in case his quarry attempted escape from that side.

His reserves waited, crowding behind the armored cars, while, from each end of the street, a single file of soldiers worked their way toward the warehouse. This first assault group was composed of ten men—five from each side. They moved closer, crouching low, brushing the wall as they went.

So far there had been no indication that this advancing line of soldiers had been spotted by the men inside.

Suddenly the door popped open, and a man, machine gun at the ready, stepped one foot outside the door. For a split second there was only shocked surprise, and then the man began firing short, rapid bursts at the column of men who had worked their way down from Luddeck's end of the street.

In less than three seconds the door had been slammed shut, the man safely inside. On the street, all five of that advance group lay in a bloody huddle. Luddeck looked through his binoculars at the shattered group. Two of them were obviously dead—bodies smashed into grotesque contortions—one seemed seriously wounded, while the remaining two, fortunate enough to be at the end of the line and therefore shielded by their less fortunate comrades, had been only slightly wounded. Both were now trying to extricate themselves from the pile of shattered men and crawl to safety.

The group on the other side of the main door seemed paralyzed with indecision, frozen in their tracks, and Luddeck cursed the fact that these men were garrison troops who lacked the toughening experience of combat.

Luddeck knew what was coming next. He waved his arm in a quick chopping motion to the men in the street. "Move! Move!" he yelled, knowing that their only chance was to rapidly advance and throw grenades through the warehouse windows. Now that they had been discovered, their exposed position left them no option but to advance quickly to cover the doors.

The lead man of the group heard Luddeck yell and looked back over his shoulder as if to assure himself that the others were still behind him. At that moment the door swung open just enough to allow the Sten to protrude, and the staccato chattering once again echoed up and down the street.

The reserve troops behind the armored half-tracks opened covering fire on the door, but the bullets thudded uselessly into the thick wood.

As suddenly as it had opened, the door was closed, and once again a single file of advancing soldiers had been reduced to a pile of shattered flesh.

This time Luddeck did not bother to inspect the casualties. He motioned to his reserve troops beside the armored car, then climbed in beside the driver, pushing open the armored shield in front of his face so that he could watch the street. Three of the men from the second group were crawling slowly back to the safety of the other armored vehicle.

"Contact the lieutenant," he said to his driver and watched through the viewing slit as the officer at the other end of the street with the second vehicle moved inside it to answer his call.

Luddeck's voice was cold and menacing as he spoke into the radio. He left no room for questions. "Our vehicles will advance together, stopping five meters in front of the gates. The troops will follow, taking cover behind us. The heavy machine guns will blast anything that moves, while the men lob grenades through the windows and under covering fire place charges on the doors, then move inside. If the doors do not open, we will ram them with the vehicles. Do you understand?" He waited for the expected response. "Then move—now!"

He watched through the slit in the armor plate, and when the other half-track began to move forward, he gave the order for his men to proceed.

"They're getting smart," said Buhl from his post at the window. "Armored vehicles advancing, troops hidden behind them." He looked at Streetman. "It's only a matter of time now."

"I'd better tell Bishop to hurry it up," said Streetman and raced back to the rear of the warehouse. He followed a dim glow of light to a small room in the back and found Bishop and Swensen huddled over what looked like small blocks of a butter-colored material. He recognized the plastic explosives immediately and knew that they were preparing to booby-trap the escape route.

"Armored vehicles coming down the street," he said breathlessly.

Bishop looked up calmly. "Think you can hold them for a few more minutes, Chapman?" He was smiling.

"Yes," said Streetman.

"Good show. Three or four minutes and then both of you get back here."

Streetman left and moved back toward the front of the huge open warehouse. At the stairs he stopped and looked to see if Buhl had seen him return, but the Dane's eyes were riveted on the unfolding action in the street as the two armored vehicles slowly made their way toward him.

With a glance over his shoulder at Buhl, Streetman dashed up the stairs, down the hallway and into the office where he had seen Bishop and Swensen. He kicked aside the other boxes and pounced on the container he had seen Bishop use. Papers flying in every direction, he flung the contents aside, finally withdrawing the worn leather folder. He moved to the door and into the hallway where the light was adequate and removed the papers from the folder. Clearly written on the front page was the name, Niels Bohr, and the Copenhagen address of his Institute for Theoretical Physics.

Streetman leafed through the papers, seeing page after page of meticulously handwritten notes, diagrams, and formulas. Bohr's notes, he wondered, in amazement. But how? Why?

Still puzzled, he stuffed the papers back into the folder and hid everything under his arm inside his coat.

He ran down the stairs, then called to Buhl, who was still at the door. "Let's go! They're ready."

Buhl fired a short burst through the window, then ran to join Streetman at the stairs. "Back this way," said

Streetman and both raced to join Bishop and Swensen, who appeared in the doorway of the small back room.

"Everything all right?" asked Bishop.

"They're advancing cautiously," said Buhl with a quiet smile. "I think I gave them something to think about."

"Good lad," said Bishop. "Now let's get out of here."

"Major Bishop," said Streetman sharply, his voice hard and loud.

Bishop turned to face Streetman, his face puzzled then growing into a mask of total incomprehension as he saw the leather folder in Streetman's left hand, the Sten aimed at his belly in the other.

"Explain this, please," said Streetman quite calmly, pleased by the complete bewilderment on Bishop's face. It made him feel good to see the supremely confident British facade crumble before his eyes.

"My God," said Bishop, "what have you done?" He moved toward Streetman as if to snatch the folder from his hands, but Streetman took one step back and raised the weapon menacingly. "Don't be so foolish as to think that I won't use this."

Bishop stopped dead in his tracks, his face a tortured mask.

"Now," said Streetman, "we came to recover something, not to leave it." He held up the folder. "Explain this."

"There isn't time to explain. "If we don't get those papers back—you'll have ruined everything."

"This is not our mission."

"You don't know—or have to know—our mission," snapped Bishop. "Your job is merely to follow orders."

"I know more than you think I know," said Streetman. "I know that these notes are the work of the Danish professor of atomistics, Neils Bohr, and that if they fell into the hands of the Germans, it could be disastrous. I want to know why you're leaving them behind."

Bishop slapped his hands against his sides in exasperation. "They're phonies, you fool. The notes are fakes. Prepared by Dr. Bohr and British intelligence to fool the Germans."

"Why wasn't I told?"

Bishop's eyes were wild with anger, but the Sten gun aimed at his chest held him back. "If you were captured, you might have told. There was no need for you to know." Bishop's voice had a desperate edge to it.

"And what about the real notes? Where are they?"

Bishop looked around in dismay to Swensen and Buhl, who had started to move slowly away from Streetman and the aimed Sten gun. If there was to be shooting, he wouldn't get all three with one burst.

Machine gun fire shattered the windows outside and bullets whirred around the empty warehouse. The noise was deafening.

"The real notes?" screamed Streetman.

"They're gone. Madsen got here before us. He and Swensen picked them up yesterday. Our job was to lead the Germans here and let them think we had led them to the authentic documents. If they can be persuaded that these notes are genuine, it will throw their atomic research program into such chaos that the war will be over before they can ever recover."

Streetman's eyes twitched. "Madsen?" he said. Now it was his turn to be bewildered.

"Black parachute," said Bishop desperately. "So everyone including you and Iverson would think that he was dead. Bohr's notes are already back in Sweden."

Comprehension flooded Streetman's face as he realized what Bishop had done.

"Now that you understand," said Bishop furiously, "can we replace the documents and get the hell out of here?"

The thump-thump of grenades, and the high-pitched chatter of the machine guns started again.

"It may already be too late, you damned fool," said Bishop. "The Germans will be inside in moments." He stepped forward authoritatively. "Give me the folder."

Streetman swung the stubby barrel of the Sten gun, catching Bishop flush across the jaw and dropped him in a heap at his feet.

"I think not," said Streetman, training the weapon on the two Danes. Buhl was wide-eyed with disbelief. Swensen's eyes were cold as he calculated every possible move that he might make. His hand moved to the pistol in his belt.

A wicked smile raced across Streetman's face. "I wouldn't do it," he said to Swensen. He waved the Sten at Buhl. "You. Take off your shirt and wave it in the window. I want our friends outside to know that the fight is over."

Bishop stirred. He struggled to a sitting position. "You must be mad," he said. "Do you realize what you are doing?"

"Perfectly." His jaw was set, his teeth clenched.

Now it was Bishop's turn to understand. A horrified look of realization flashed across his face. "I can't believe it," he said. "You've been working for the Germans all along."

Streetman snarled a smile. "Finally, you understand," he said. He looked to Buhl, who had not moved. "I told you to get out there," he barked.

"I wouldn't get ten steps," said Buhl. "They'd cut me down as soon as I showed myself."

Streetman shrugged to show his lack of concern for Buhl's predicament.

Swensen spoke for the first time. "You might as well kill us now. We will not allow ourselves to be taken alive by these swine."

"Suit yourself," said Streetman, raising the Sten to shoulder height.

Swensen and Buhl pulled themselves erect and waited for the flash before the darkness.

"One moment," said a strange voice in the room, and a startled Streetman whirled to see Madsen, like an apparition from hell, rise up through the open manhole.

The surprise was momentary, and Streetman moved the submachine gun in that direction, but he was already too late. Madsen's machine pistol spat in rapid succession, sending three of its ten rounds crashing into Streetman's chest. Streetman was flung back against the wall next to the door, his body thumping hard against it, but he remained on his feet.

Still clutching the folder, he dropped his Sten gun and began to slide along the wall, leaving a wide swath of blood as he moved toward the door. Clutching the folder in front of him as if for protection he managed to stay on his feet.

At the door he turned his back to them, facing the warehouse, eyes wide open in disbelief, jaw hanging limply. His only thought was to deliver the folder to the Germans and explain to them what had happened. They, he was sure, would know what to do. They could somehow turn this disaster into a victory. His father had always told him that the Germans were invincible. Only traitors, politicians, communists, and Jews had prevented them from assuming their rightful position in the world. And the British! The same hated British who had killed his mother—or was it his grandmother—he wasn't sure anymore. His head was spinning, and his knees threatened to buckle and pitch him forward through the open door.

As the others watched, Madsen aimed carefully, then squeezed the trigger of his Mauser. The back of Streetman's skull exploded as the single projectile rammed home, and he was propelled forward, his legs moving as if he were running except that his brain could no longer control any such movement. His legs moved reflexively, carrying him ten yards into the warehouse, where finally he pitched forward, still clutching the folder to his chest, as he thudded face first onto the concrete floor.

The four men inside rushed to the door in time to see him twitch his last.

Outside, the Germans were raking the windows with machine gun fire, and bullets ricocheted everywhere around the empty warehouse. Luddeck gave a signal, and one of the half-tracks revved up and plunged against the double doors, which bulged and creaked against the pressure of the vehicle's great weight and powerful engine.

Buhl started forward for the folder, but Bishop grabbed him by the arm. "Forget it," he said, pointing to where the front gate was buckling under the pressure of the armored vehicle outside. "Let them find it on him," said Bishop. "That way we'll know they have it."

"Let's go," he said. "That door will cave in any minute."

They moved toward the manhole from which Madsen had emerged. As the two Danes scrambled down the steel ladder to the lower level Bishop slapped Madsen on the shoulder. "I must say it was a pleasant surprise to see you back here—you never did trust him, did you?"

Madsen shook his head. "Thank Iverson," he said. "He's the one who didn't break. London sent a message about Chapman."

Bishop looked puzzled.

"It's a long story," said Madsen as he slipped quickly into the sewer. "But don't worry. "I'll fill you in when we get out of here."

As Bishop disappeared into the sewer line behind his three men the door burst open under the relentless pressure of the armored vehicle, and the German soldiers rushed into the warehouse, splaying machine gun fire in every direction.

For ten seconds the sound in the cavernous room was overwhelming—machine guns chattering, engines revving, men yelling to contend with their fear. Then, except for a brief sporadic burst, silence took over. The men crouched in a circle around the half-track, weapons at the ready, peering fearfully around the smoke-filled room.

Nothing moved.

Ernst Luddeck climbed out of his armored vehicle and strode in. He held himself erect, looking to the right and left as he walked, Luger in hand. "I want at least one of them alive," he said, then made a quick motion with his gun hand, and his men scrambled off to search the warehouse.

As Luddeck, face grim, eyes colder than usual, waited for a response, he allowed himself to take in the scene. Huge empty space. Not the place he would have selected to hide valuable documents. But who could . . .

"Captain!" called a young private, racing towards

him, snapping him from his reverie. "We have found one of them."

"Alive?"

The soldier shook his head.

"The others?"

Again the soldier shook his head.

Luddeck strode past him toward the rear of the warehouse. In the back corner he saw the body of Karl Streetman lying face down where he had fallen. At that moment a sergeant emerged from the small back room, his face reflecting his fear of what he had to report.

"A sewer line, sir," he said, his eyes on the ground. "The others must have used it to escape."

Luddeck closed his eyes for one brief moment. "Escape!" The word had never entered his conscious thoughts. How could he have allowed this to happen? At that moment he knew that his career was over—knew that the war was lost. "Does anyone know where it leads?"

The men looked at each other anxiously.

No one said anything.

Luddeck, his face contorted in fury, his eyes mad, said to the sergeant. "Take a detachment of ten men and go down into the sewer."

The sergeant, happy to escape the expected rage of his commanding officer, seemed pleased to lead his men off into more battle.

The others, after completing their fruitless search of the building, had now gathered around the dead man. Luddeck placed his foot under Streetman and rolled him over. The dead man's eyes were wide open, his mouth caught in a snarl of amazement, frozen forever in the moment of his recognition of his own failure. His arms across his chest still clutched the folder.

Luddeck knelt beside him and not without some difficulty extricated the folder from Streetman's arms. He opened the leather flap and looked inside. He felt his heart begin to pump faster as he saw the contents and dared to hope what it might be. He looked up at his men who were gathered around him, each face young, curious, and eager.

Luddeck withdrew the pages, thinking that these

contents might save these eager faces from almost certain defeat.

He held his breath. When he saw the name, Niels Bohr, written on the cover, his heart leaped. He flipped through the pages of notes and formulas and calculations, his hopes growing in leaps and bounds. For the first time in years a genuine smile slashed across his stony features.

He stood up. "Who shot this man?"

The soldiers looked at each other. For a moment no one answered, then a corporal stepped forward. "I did, Captain. Through the smoke and confusion I saw him heading for that door when I rushed inside and cut him down before he could make it."

Luddeck beamed. "Corporal, you have just won yourself the Iron Cross—I will see to it personally." And I, he thought, have just won the everlasting gratitude of my Führer and the German nation. Visions of undreamed-of honors flooded his thoughts. Visions that were cut short by two sharp explosions that rumbled from the open sewer line.

Everyone rushed to the manhole.

"Grenades," someone said. "They must have caught up with them."

A figure appeared from the sewer—helmet missing, face bloody, uniform awry. It was the sergeant.

Two men pulled him up. "Explosion," he said, gasping. "they must have left timing devices behind in the sewers. We walked right into it."

Some others were climbing up the ladder now—four in all.

Someone asked about the rest, and the men shook their heads dejectedly.

Luddeck seemed uninterested. "Let's get out of here," he said. "We'll send a detail to pick up the dead later. I must get back to headquarters—I must be in Berlin by tonight."

As he marched out of the room the men who had just lost their friends and comrades looked at each other, the disgust evident on their faces.

The sergeant pulled himself erect. "All right," he said. "You heard the captain, let's go."

By the time the men filed out of the room, Luddeck had already crossed the warehouse floor and was sitting in the front seat of the armored car. His thoughts were already in Berlin and on the honors that awaited him. A calculating smile crossed his face when he remembered Schellenberg, who thought he would be satisfied with a post at the Abwehr. Luddeck's aims were higher than that!

The folder that contained the salvation of his nation and the answers to all his dreams was clutched securely next to his heart.

ABOUT THE AUTHOR

CHARLES ROBERTSON, who was born in Scotland, is a former high-school English teacher turned novelist. He lives with his wife and children in Stamford, Connecticut. *The Omega Deception* is his third novel.